"Marrying DAZZLING PROSE and sharp-eyed realism, *Althea & Oliver* is a gritty, sparkling triumph."

—**BENNETT MADISON**, author of *September Girls*

"Moracho's COMING-OF-AGE story carries rare insight and a keen understanding of those verging on adulthood."

—**BOOKLIST**, starred review

"URGENT and POETIC."

—**HELLOGIGGLES.COM**

"With BEAUTIFUL language and wrenching, complicated relationship dynamics, *Althea & Oliver* captures the painful state of longing that is adolescence perfectly."

—**COREY ANN HAYDU**, author of *OCD Love Story*

"A GORGEOUS, GLORIOUS, UNFORGETTABLE novel."

—**SARAH MCCARRY**, author of *About a Girl*

"Even if the book weren't ELOQUENT and HILARIOUS, it'd be a must-read for all children of the '90s. But thankfully, it is, and if you're smart, you'll run out and grab a copy."

—**BUSTLE.COM**

W9-BDE-567

Oliver

"Whatever happens, I won't see any of it." Leaning over, she tucks the blanket under his chin and he can smell cigarettes and lip balm and the sharp scent of her scrubs, and his stupid, stupid heart rends one more time with the memory of Althea, and if he weren't losing consciousness he would burst into an apocalyptic fit of tears, but instead his eyes close and the last thing Stella says finds his brain by way of some small miracle, right before his mind flickers like a candle and is snuffed out.

"But I will be here when you wake up."

Althea

"What are you doing back here?"

"I was looking for someone."

"Who?"

"Oliver," she whispers.

"You're here to see Oliver?" the nurse says softly.

Biting down hard on her lip, Althea gnaws away chapped, dry skin that stings when she tears it with her teeth, so as her eyes fill she can tell herself that's why she's crying. "I'm too late, aren't I?"

"For now. I'm sorry. It can wait, right? For a little while?" says the nurse. "It's not forever, just a couple of weeks. Whatever it is, it'll keep for that long, won't it?"

Althea wipes her face with the cuffs of her sweatshirt and heads for the door. "Yeah. It'll keep."

ALTHEA & OLIVER

CRISTINA MORACHO

speak

SPEAK
An imprint of Penguin Random House LLC
375 Hudson Street
New York, New York 10014

First published in the United States of America by Viking,
an imprint of Penguin Group (USA) LLC, 2014
Published by Speak, an imprint of Penguin Random House LLC, 2015

THE LIBRARY OF CONGRESS HAS CATALOGED THE VIKING EDITION AS FOLLOWS:
Moracho, Cristina.
Althea and Oliver / Cristina Moracho.
p. cm
Summary: "Althea and Oliver, who have been friends since age six and are now high
school juniors, find their friendship changing because he has contracted Kleine-Levin
Syndrome"—Provided by publisher.
ISBN 978-0-670-78539-1 (hardcover)
[1. Best friends—Fiction. 2. Friendship—Fiction. 3. Coming of age—Fiction.
4. Sleep disorders—Fiction. 5. High schools—Fiction. 6. Schools—Fiction.
7. Single-parent families—Fiction.] I. Title.
PZ7.M788192Alt 2014
[Fic]—dc23
2013041135

Speak ISBN 978-0-14-242476-6

Printed in the United States of America
Book design by Jim Hoover

1 3 5 7 9 10 8 6 4 2

AUTHOR'S NOTE: Kleine-Levin Syndrome is a real affliction. Incredibly rare,
it affects its victims, to some degree, in the way that I've described, and in reality, as
in the book, there is no cure. However, I've taken a great deal of artistic license
with KLS. Oliver's experiences—as well as those of the other boys—are in no way
meant to be an accurate portrayal of what it's like to live with it. For more information
on KLS, please visit the Kleine-Levin Syndrome Foundation: klsfoundation.org

For my parents

LOOK ME IN THE EYE

AND TELL ME THAT I'M SATISFIED.

WERE YOU SATISFIED?

—The Replacements

chapter one.

"WOULD YOU RATHER walk barefoot across a mile of Legos or get a tattoo on the inside of your eyelid?"

"That's fucked up." Oliver's words are blurry with fatigue.

"That's sort of the point. Pick one. Don't think about it for too long."

Althea is doing her best to keep Oliver awake until they get back to his house. The windows are rolled down and the car is whipped full of angry March air that beats her blonde hair around her face like a belligerent pair of wings. A screeching punk rock lament is on the radio. She shouts over the music as Oliver struggles to keep his eyes open, his head lolled back against the seat. Her voice and the chill of winter and the metallic thrum of electric guitars grow remote as he drifts off.

He thinks of the delicate skin on the soles of his feet and winces. A mile is too far. "Tattoo. I'd rather get the tattoo."

Althea's race to the house won't change what's about to happen, but she's driving like it means something, mouth cinched into a determined knot, speeding through a yellow light. "We're almost there," she says.

"Let me sleep," he says. "Shush."

"Don't shush me."

"You love it when I shush you."

It doesn't matter. He'll be asleep in minutes, wherever he is. Home in bed is his first choice, but he could do worse than the shotgun seat of his best friend's Camry. An hour ago he passed out in sixth period chem lab, dangerously close to a Bunsen burner.

"I'm so tired," he says.

"I know."

"What about you? Which would you rather?" asks Oliver, enunciating with effort, his tongue thick and uncooperative.

"The tattoo. Obviously." Althea punctuates her point by honking at the driver in front of them, who's creeping along College Road too slowly for her taste.

He unzips his jeans. Lifting his hips off the seat, he shimmies until his pants are around his ankles. He's wearing his favorite cherry-red boxers, and the sight of them is briefly cheering.

"What's wrong with your pants?" Althea asks.

"I'm trying to eliminate obstacles," he says.

"You should have done the shoes first."

"Fuck." Looking down at the hems of his jeans, caught on the heels of his tennis shoes, he finds the task at hand insurmountable. He kicks feebly, and his feet get tangled in denim. He makes a strangled, wordless sound of vexation.

"Just leave it," says Althea. "I'll fix it when we get there."

For her benefit, Oliver sits up straighter, resting an elbow on the open window and propping his head on one hand. "I got one."

"Let's hear it." She turns the volume down so he won't have to shout over Rocket from the Crypt.

"Would you rather . . ." His head slumps forward, but he rights himself quickly. "Would you rather . . ." Althea turns onto their block and his resolve weakens. He'll be upstairs in just a minute, under his down quilt, and he won't have to fight it anymore.

She smacks his arm. "Oliver!"

"Okay, okay." They're pulling into his driveway now. "Would you rather kill a puppy with your hands—"

"Like, strangle it?" says Althea, turning off the engine and unbuckling her seat belt.

"Whatever, or, like, drown it in a bucket." Oliver fumbles for the belt release button.

"I don't like this already."

She comes around to his side and crouches by the open door. Reaching beneath his crumpled jeans, she unlaces his shoes and eases them from his feet. The pants slip off without further opposition. "Okay," she says, patting his ankle.

Oliver emerges from the car in socks and underwear, his backpack still strapped over his black thermal hoodie. He falters, and Althea puts an arm around his waist for support.

"Let's remember this outfit," she says. "I think it's a winner. Maybe more of a spring look, though."

Climbing onto the porch, Oliver gropes for his keys. Across the street, their elderly neighbor Mrs. Parker is sweeping her sidewalk in a quilted navy housecoat and watching the pantsless Oliver with undisguised interest. His hand weaves in front of the lock; as his eyes lose focus, he can hear metal scraping against the door's peeling white paint. "Is she staring at me?"

"Don't you pay that nosy bitch no nevermind." Gently, Althea takes the keys and opens the door herself. "What's my other option? Besides the puppy?"

They ascend the stairs together, him leaning on her heavily now, and she leads him to his room. Pulling back the covers on his bed, Althea ushers him into it. The sheets are soft against his bare legs. When they were kids in flannel pajamas, they used to lie under the blankets in the dark and bicycle their knees against the fabric so they could see the green flash of static electricity. He nuzzles his head into a pillow.

"Or shoot a random person with a sniper rifle from a mile away?" he finishes.

"Those are my choices? Drown a puppy in a bucket or shoot a stranger I can't see?" He feels her weight on the bed next to him, her cool hand against his fevered face while she mulls his hypothetical question, her voice amused but already distant.

"Mmm-hmm. Which one would you . . ." It's impossible even to finish the sentence. When he wakes up, whenever he wakes up, it will feel like a shaky jump from this moment to that one. Then will come that panic of having slept through something important—a final exam, a birthday party, a soccer game in which he was the starting forward. Something is wrong with him, something must be, because it wasn't supposed to happen again and now it has, and he wonders if he should be fighting this harder than he is, but he's so tired and it's completely delicious right now to be in his bed. Sometimes nothing feels as good as giving up, that guilty relief coupled with a healthy dose of I-just-don't-give-a-fuck, and he wants to tell Althea not to worry, everyone needs a vice and this can be his.

"I'll tell you when you wake up. Hold that thought," she whispers, and he's gone.

Althea stays. Lying on her back, she watches the constellation of plastic stars on the ceiling slowly brighten as the remaining daylight drains away and the familiar features of Oliver's bedroom recede into the shadows. The diminutive television perches atop the scratched wooden dresser, its rabbit-ear antenna akimbo, the red standby light of the VCR luminous and eerie. His makeshift desk was her gift on his last birthday—a piece of plywood covered in a collage of his favorite album covers, supported by two sawhorses she'd pilfered from a construction site downtown. A collection of ticket stubs from movies and concerts, pages torn from Althea's sketchbook, and photographs of the two of them are all tacked to his enormous bulletin board. She's memorized the photo lineup: age six, under the Christmas tree at her house, a tiny Oliver wrapped in a string of lights; age nine, Oliver proudly brandishing a cast on his broken wrist while a jealous Althea pouts in a corner of the frame; age twelve, Althea with her hands swaddled in a pair of pink boxing gloves while Oliver cowers, covering his face; age fourteen, standing on Althea's porch the morning they started high school, Althea looking miserable and Oliver strangely enthusiastic; age sixteen, drunk at a Halloween party, dressed as Sid and Nancy, shouting something at the camera.

If he'd stayed awake for five seconds longer, she could have told him the answer to his question, although she suspects he already knows that she would save the puppy. They've been best friends for ten years, and it's not easy for them to surprise each other. The silent digital numbers of the clock radio reconfigure, moving ahead one minute. Althea counts to sixty as evenly as possible—*one banana, two banana*—but still arrives there first, and several more seconds creep by before the clock acknowledges another minute has passed. *How many more of those until he wakes up?* she wonders. Last time it was two weeks. A lot of goddamned bananas.

A day passes, and then another, and another. Every morning when Althea drives by Oliver's house on the way to school, she slows, not expecting to see him waiting for her, but hoping anyway. At night she can't sleep, and at school she can't stay awake, despite her ubiquitous thermos of coffee. A teacher teases her for nodding off in class, suggesting that maybe Althea has caught whatever it is Oliver has. The other students titter and she slouches in her seat, mortified to have called attention to herself. During lunch she eats in her car, stretched across the backseat, propped against the door like she's lying on the sofa in her basement, looking out the window instead of at the television. No one comes to find her. It's not that she doesn't have other friends, but they are more Oliver's than hers. She keeps to herself how unfair she thinks this is, that the one better equipped to go without the other is the one who never has to.

After school she goes home and makes lemon bars; baking

keeps her mind busy, requires the kind of multitasking that finally allows her to relax. At night she makes uninspired attempts at precalculus and chemistry, putting in the minimum amount of effort that will still achieve the desired result, then she shoves her work aside and takes out her sketchbook. Surrounded by music and the smell of freshly sharpened pencils, she turns off the part of her brain that's still picturing Oliver asleep. Eager to prove that she can, in fact, amuse herself, she sketches diligently until she's convinced she's lost track of time, filling pages with the dinosaurs she so often sees in her dreams.

They've been separated before, but this is different. It isn't like when she was periodically shipped off to spend forced time with her mother, in Philadelphia or Chicago or Denver or any of the other places Alice had lived since leaving Wilmington; she was steadily heading westward, like a slow-moving plague spreading across the country. Althea had missed Oliver then, fiercely, childishly, missed their routines and games and easy familiarity, especially in Alice's world of constant upheaval, where there was always a new boyfriend to meet, a new group of friends before whom Althea had to be trotted out, a new hobby or passion of Alice's that Althea was expected to indulge.

Something had changed in October, when her father, Garth, was out of town for a conference and she threw a keg party at Oliver's insistence, his misguided attempt to encourage her to socialize. He had spent the entire day bubble-wrapping Garth's trinkets and hiding them in the attic; they rolled up the Persian rugs and dragged them into the master bedroom. The trick, they decided, would be to devise an activity that would keep every-

one in the backyard rather than roaming around the house looking for things to steal or destroy. Which was how they ended up
filling a cheap vinyl kiddie pool with Jell-O and turning yet another keg party into a wrestling tournament. Plenty of girls were
more than eager to strip down to their underwear and flounder
around in the cherry-flavored mess. Althea was content to swill
her shitty beer on the sidelines and lament that they should have
charged money. No amount of alcohol or urging would get her
into the ring until Oliver asked if she was really so afraid of a
bunch of intoxicated debutantes. That did it. Removing only her
flip-flops, she climbed into the pool, macerated gelatin squish-
ing between her toes, and demanded to be challenged; an hour
later, she remained undefeated. When she was finished, Oliver
jumped in and tackled her, and they splashed around under a
starry southern sky. They tangled with each other, their clothes
soaked and clinging, their bodies dripping and sticky and smelling like too-sweet cough medicine.

The clouds came from nowhere. A flash of lightning; someone said "Oh, shi—" but his voice was cut off by the thunder.
Then it was pouring and everybody ran into the house, including
a dozen girls wearing nothing but bras and panties and Jell-O,
girls who would leave cherry footprints all over the floors, girls
who would sit on the furniture and dry themselves with Garth's
monogrammed towels and eventually leave the Carter residence
looking like the site of a mass homicide. Althea and Oliver stayed
in the pool, getting rained on and trembling with each roll of
thunder. She'd only had a couple of beers but was acting drunker
than she was, for camouflage, because as she watched pink rivu-

lets of rainwater stream down Oliver's temples and wrists, she'd realized something horrifying: She wanted him to kiss her.

He hadn't.

The following day, Oliver was reduced to a quivering mess, terrified of Garth's return; he prayed for a swift execution, while Althea insisted on playing a morbid game of Would You Rather—would you rather watch the other one die, or would you rather be killed first, knowing the other would have to watch you go? They cleaned frantically for hours. Finally, Althea sent him home because he was running a fever. He went to sleep that night and stayed that way for the better part of the next two weeks, and while he was gone she'd noticed there was something different about the way she missed him. It was colored with impatience and expectation, as if they had been in the middle of a conversation, interrupted just as he was about to tell her something important and she was forced to wait for the right moment to ask, "What were you going to say?" She was missing something that hadn't even happened yet and couldn't happen until Oliver was awake and accounted for and finally paying attention.

It had been her mother, of all people, who had intuited the shift, coming right out on the phone one day and asking if she and Oliver were having sex.

"I don't expect your father to talk to you about birth control," she'd begun, and Althea had cut her off at the pass, saying that her health class had covered the subject thoroughly. Nevertheless, Alice had barreled on. "Are you two still having sleepovers all the time? You're too old for that now, you know; you can't be sleeping in the same bed like you did when you were kids."

"Our raging hormones have yet to get the better of us."

"There are places where you can go to get the Pill. You don't even need to involve your father."

"I just told you I'm not having sex. Why would I need to go on the Pill?" Althea responded.

"You know, it can make your breasts bigger, too."

Althea had never told her mother of the shame her flat chest inspired, and she had marveled then at how, in their first conversation in months, Alice could identify the unbearably specific miseries Althea never shared with anyone. Althea had handed the phone to Garth out of sheer embarrassment, and he took the rest of the call in his study with the door closed. He had emerged red-faced and poured himself a scotch, and after that started leaving the basement door open when Oliver was over. Her parents' apparent confidence that she and Oliver either were or would soon be sleeping together only made her more disconsolate as she pitched and turned in her bed at night, wondering why Oliver remained willfully oblivious to what everyone around him appeared to consider a certainty.

"There's nothing happening with me and Oliver," Althea had protested into the phone, and in retrospect it was obvious that her vehemence had given her away.

"Oh, Thea," Alice had said. "Be patient."

Oliver wakes her up a week later. In the dark, she hears him padding down the basement stairs, recognizes those familiar footsteps. Garth is a heavy sleeper, and Oliver's been slipping into the Carter house with his own set of keys for years. According to the cable box, it's almost three a.m. Sitting on the edge of the couch, Oliver slides an arm around her waist.

"You're here," she mumbles, rolling over onto her back. The quilt slips away, and her T-shirt rides up. He joins her, biting lightly on her shoulder, his bared teeth pressed against her skin through the cotton. "When did you wake up?"

"I'm hungry," he says. "I want Waffle House."

"Waffle House is gross."

"I want Waffle House." Oliver's eyes are glassy and swollen, a slight purple sheen to the lids. His icy fingers loiter on her bare knee, and her leg breaks out in goose bumps, calling the blonde stubble to attention in a way that makes her follicles ache.

"But you hate Waffle House," she says.

"I don't care."

"Can't I just make you a sandwich?"

"It has to be Waffle House." Wrapping his arms around his knees, Oliver begins to rock back and forth, chanting "Waffles, waffles, waffles" in a little-boy voice she hasn't heard him use since there were still training wheels on their bicycles. She had known he would be upset when this second episode was over, but she wasn't expecting a peculiar, childlike regression.

"Did you just wake up? Does Nicky know?"

"Waffles, waffles, waffles." Already he has repeated this word so many times that it's in danger of falling apart and losing its meaning. Althea's goose bumps spread to her arms. The sofa shudders with the force of Oliver's insistent rocking. This is all totally unlike him, but she'll do whatever he wants if it means he'll stop this creepy chanting.

"All right," she says slowly. "Quit with that shit and we'll get you your fucking waffles." She slides off the couch and pulls on her jeans in a dark corner of the basement. "How is it outside?" she asks.

"Cold," he says, but when she reaches for her car keys, he stops her. "Let's walk."

On their way out the back door, she pulls her hair into a ponytail with a black rubber band. When she's done, he takes her hand and stuffs it into his own pocket. He won't answer any of her questions, but she has missed him so much that right now it's enough to be walking with him under the streetlights, see his breath bloom in the cold, and have their thumbs wrestling in the pocket of his black hoodie. The night is clear and smells like the ocean.

Oliver doesn't talk. He sings "Welcome to the Jungle" from start to finish twice, pausing occasionally to play air guitar for emphasis, the tendons in his neck straining with the effort.

"Are you feeling okay?" she asks when he finishes his encore. It's a stupidly pedestrian question, but she's compelled to say something.

"I'm hungry," Oliver says.

The Waffle House sign is made of letters like enormous Scrabble tiles. Inside it smells like syrup and cigarettes. The dozen other patrons are mostly truck drivers and college students, engrossed in their own nocturnal conversations. Althea and Oliver settle into a booth next to each other, Oliver against the window, and put their feet up on the other seat, tennis shoes squeaky against the vinyl. Their legs are the same length. Althea was taller through the first half of high school, but Oliver caught up over the last year. The jeans she's wearing actually belong to him.

The waitress approaches, a tiny redheaded woman with a gap between her front teeth, her arms and face covered in freckles. She takes their orders. "I'll be right back with your coffee," she says.

Oliver gives Althea a frantic look, tugging on her pant leg with canine urgency. "I'm starving."

"I understand."

Finally Oliver's food arrives and keeps arriving—pecan waffles, a cheese and bacon omelet, scattered and smothered hash browns, and grits. Althea drinks her coffee while he eats, his arm wrapped protectively around his plates, as though he is afraid at any moment she might try to take them from him. He eats noisily, without looking up or pausing to make conversation, chewing big, sloppy bites with his mouth open. A briefly masticated bit of waffle falls back to his plate, landing where the maple syrup and grits overlap. Althea stifles a gag and looks past him, out the window at the traffic rumbling by on the highway and her own ghostly reflection staring back at her.

When he's finished, the waitress clears and leaves the check on the table. Apparently sated, Oliver yawns, stretching his arms over his head. "Jesus. I'm so tired."

"You just slept for a week."

Even as she lodges her complaint, he rests his head on her shoulder. His breathing turns heavy, and Althea realizes too late, a mile from home, without her car, in the middle of the night, that she was wrong. It isn't over, and she doesn't have her Oliver back. He's come by in the midst of some strange intermission, and the lights are about to go down for the second act.

Althea snatches the check off the table. "Let's go."

"I'm fine right here." Lying down in the booth, he rests his head in her lap, tucking his fists under his chin.

"No way, come on. Get up."

"I said I'm fine here," he says, loud and peevish.

She can't get to her wallet with Oliver sprawled across her thighs, pinning her. "Get up," she says. Behind the counter, the waitress is beginning to stare.

He still won't move, so reaching down and taking hold of his collar, Althea yanks him upright, propping him against the window.

"I told you, I'm tired," he shouts, slapping her hands away.

The space between her shoulder blades tightens like a bolt is being wrenched into place. A mortified Althea watches the other patrons in the window's watery reflection, their chatter suddenly muted. The college students forget the cigarettes smoldering in their ashtrays, and older men in trucker hats with potbellies and thick wrists brace themselves against their tables as they contemplate intervention. Behind the counter, the grill is sizzling with home fries and bacon fat, but the cook has forgotten, holding his spatula in front of his grease-splattered apron as if he's wondering whether he might need to use it as a weapon. A harmless country song is playing on the jukebox.

Althea is shaky from too much coffee. Her body has lost

the ability to regulate its temperature—heat radiates under her armpits, dampening her sweatshirt, but her hands have gone icy—and her stomach feels like it's disappeared altogether. She fumbles for her canvas wallet, embroidered with a skull and crossbones and several unraveling red roses. The sound of uncoupling Velcro is impossibly loud inside the small, hushed restaurant. People are whispering as she counts out her limp dollar bills. Oliver's head lolls back onto the booth's cracked red vinyl.

"Don't do it," she says sharply, but his eyes flutter shut anyway. She kicks his shin, hard, and he starts awake, abruptly at attention.

"What the shit?" he yells. Flailing his arms, he knocks over the ketchup and the hot sauce; the maple syrup clatters to the floor, leaving a sugary ring on the faux-wood Formica. Althea hastily retrieves the pitcher from under the table, but before she can set it back in place, Oliver wrests it from her sticky hand and hurls it across the restaurant. She watches helplessly as it sails into the open kitchen, landing on the grill in a clatter of singed plastic and maple steam. The cook drops his spatula and leaps back, covering his face with his arm as a billow of purple-black smoke erupts, cloying and sweet and toxic. Althea mutters a profanity, her heart rabbiting wildly inside her chest. Leaving her pile of damp money on the table, she grabs Oliver by the wrist and together they bolt for the exit, past students she prays are not her father's. Inside their booths, the truckers shrink away.

She runs, and this time it's Oliver struggling to keep up with her long, desperate strides. The sky is getting light on the other side of the highway. Keeping a firm grip on his wrist, she tows him behind her in the wake of headlights and exhaust from passing cars. The sound of traffic fades behind them as they turn off the main road and wind through the narrow suburban streets, silent save for their sharp breaths and the rubbery smack of their shoes against the asphalt. Only when they get to their block does she let their pace slacken to a walk.

Althea bends double in his driveway, trying to catch her breath. Her ponytail has come unmoored and her mess of blonde hair falls over her face.

"Why did you do that?" says Oliver unkindly, panting hard.

From behind her veil of hair, Althea looks at him with disbelief. "Do what?"

"You got us into trouble. Why did you do that?" He's yelling and pouting.

"Keep your voice down." Straightening, she watches the houses around them, waiting to see bedroom lights flip on, neighbors peek out from behind their curtains.

"You shouldn't have done that," Oliver shouts.

"I didn't do anything. Just go inside. You're not making any sense." When she turns to walk away, he grabs her wrist and jerks her back to face him.

"Why did you do that?" he repeats, his voice softer and suddenly ominous. The motion sensor light ticks on in his driveway.

"Go inside, Oliver. I'm going home." He tightens his grip, bringing her closer. She tries to see him as the people in Waffle House must have seen him, as crazy or a freak or a threat.

"Where are you going?" he says. His hand slips inside the cuff of her sweatshirt, twisting at her skin, his fingers roughly edging toward her elbow.

"I just told you, McKinley. I'm going the fuck home."

"Come on, Carter. You know I hate to sleep alone."

The fine hairs on his cheeks and neck are illuminated by the harsh lamp above the garage, and it's his licentious smile that frightens her most of all. The leering expression looks grotesque on his face, and she is terribly embarrassed for *her* Oliver, not this impostor with his face and hands, one of which is still clutching her arm. But if this isn't Oliver, then who is it? Who's inside? The light in the driveway clicks off again, and again she turns to go. He clamps down harder, pulling so roughly that pain sparks in her shoulder.

"Let go of me!" she shouts, forgetting the neighbors, the hour, the sky lightening over her head. A garbage truck rolls down a neighboring street. Oliver releases her, but too suddenly. Stumbling backward as if she's been pushed, she catches herself before she falls. He reaches out, but she slaps his hand away, clumsily but hard enough to sting her palm.

"I'm so tired," he says, kneeling on the sidewalk. "I'm so tired."

"Get up," she whispers, trying to wrench him off the ground. He goes limp like a nonviolent protestor and slumps sideways, but he isn't being passive-aggressive. Oliver has fallen asleep. She lays him down gently until his cheek is pressed to the ground and he is drooling onto the mottled cement and she is sitting beside him, barely noticing as the chill of the sidewalk seeps through her pants.

The front door opens and Oliver's mom, Nicky, appears on

the porch, her long brown hair gloriously backlit by the foyer light.

"Why are you two screaming at each other like white trash in my driveway?" she asks, her voice a testy stage whisper. She observes Oliver's state of unconsciousness. "Did he just fall asleep?"

"Yeah."

Nicky comes down the steps like she's descending into the shallow end of a swimming pool—carefully, but with grace, one hand trailing lightly on the banister. "Help me get him inside. I can feel the neighbors' eyes on me."

"How should we carry him? Ankles and wrists?"

"We're not moving a dead body, Althea. Put his arm around your shoulder." They hoist him to his feet. "Come on, Ol, help us out a little."

Issuing a small grunt, he stumbles forward, nearly slipping out of their joint embrace.

"Unbelievable," Nicky mutters.

They coax a still-sleeping Oliver inside, depositing him on the couch. Though Nicky is wearing pajamas—cropped sweatpants and a long-sleeved thermal—Althea does not get the impression that she had been asleep. As Nicky drapes a chenille throw over her son, Althea waits for a reaction, some sign of dismissal or an invitation to stay.

"I'm sorry," Althea finally says. "He came into the basement and said he wanted Waffle House. I didn't realize he was still—still sick, I guess, so I took him there."

"He wakes up sometimes, but he acts weird. Not himself. I guess you saw. Why don't you come on into the kitchen? I'm going to make some tea."

The kitchen smells like Nicky, like jasmine and rosewater and tobacco. She uses her forearm to clear a space on the table, which is littered with old copies of *The New York Times* and the rubber balls she uses to exercise her hands. Oliver's art projects from elementary school, yellowed and curling at the edges, are still well represented on the fridge. Items that have been in one place for too long resemble artifacts from volcanic areas, covered in a thick layer of dust and ash. Potted plants and ceramic figures of geckos and bullfrogs line the windowsills under the sun-bleached strawberry curtains. The rusted watering can is perched on the edge of the kitchen sink, propped up against the tower of dirty dishes. The toaster oven, filled with crumbs, is notorious for periodically catching fire.

Nicky's cigarette smolders in a carved wooden ashtray. She's not even forty, and though it's been over ten years since Oliver's dad died, widowhood has not aged her. If anything, it seems to have trapped her in a severely extended postadolescence, full of cigarettes and mood swings and antisocial behavior—despite a steady stream of would-be suitors, Nicky hardly ever goes out. And though she complains about the neighbors' silent judgment, she does sometimes give the impression that she is daring them to come over and suggest she brush her hair, mow her lawn, or empty the ashtrays. Any fleeting thoughts Althea and Oliver had entertained as children of setting up their respective single parents had been quickly dismissed by an incompatibility so incontrovertible, it was obvious even to a pair of eight-year-olds. The only company Nicky ever entertains is Althea, who loves to hear tales of her long-ago life in Manhattan, when she lived in a place called Alphabet City, walked dogs for a living, and bought her clothing for a dollar a pound at a thrift shop way out in Brooklyn. There are also occasional visits from Sarah and Jimmy, her best friends from that life. In this one, she is a massage therapist at a fancy spa, spending her days opening the chakras of North Carolina's wealthiest denizens, and her evenings stationed on the front porch with the cordless phone between her ear and shoulder, talking to Sarah.

Althea sips her smoky tea. She can see the outline of Nicky's nipples through her thin cotton thermal, and looks away.

Nicky takes a deep drag of her cigarette and exhales with a shaky breath. "I'll take him back to the doctor tomorrow—later today, I mean. Not that I even know which doctor to see. But he's not going to show up at your house in the middle of the night again."

That doesn't sound like good news to Althea. Would she rather have this Oliver or no Oliver at all? It's so obvious, it doesn't even count as a question. "He would hate it. If he could see the way he was tonight, he would hate it. He'd be so embarrassed."

"If embarrassment turns out to be his biggest problem, I'll be thrilled. No one ever actually dies of humiliation. I swear."

A silence falls between them, and Althea is sure they are doing the same thing: enumerating all the invisible things that could, in fact, be fatal to a teenage boy, or at least fuck with his mind. After a moment, Nicky shakes her head and puts out her cigarette.

"Let's not get melodramatic," she says. "It's only happened twice. Now, don't you have to go get ready for school?"

That afternoon at track practice, Althea takes her place at the starting line, tightening her shoelaces and then her ponytail. Four of her teammates are staggered across the line beside her, and though she isn't willfully ignoring them, she makes no attempt at conversation, either. Oliver has always suggested that she try lacrosse or field hockey because she might enjoy a sport where she is given a stick and instructed to wield it against others, but she isn't interested in teamwork or strategy. Her tall, slim frame is built for speed, so she sticks to track. Althea has no desire to stand in a huddle.

Dirty gray rain clouds are blowing in off the Atlantic, and there's a clamminess to the air, the kind of wet cold that gets into your bones. Althea pinwheels her arms to get some blood flowing, lazily looking over the hurdles spaced out around the track. Hurdles and sprints are her best events, the ones that are hard and fast and turn off her brain with a nearly audible click.

The first time she'd ever hurdled had been on a walk downtown with Oliver late at night, when they came across an orange-and-white sawhorse abandoned on a side street where the construction was obviously long finished. There had been a dare, or a bet, or some prize had been offered, and within moments Althea was charging down the street. She saw herself leaping flawlessly over the sawhorse when she was still several strides away, the way you know a dart will find the board's center as soon as it flies from your hand. And then she did it, hair bannering out behind her, scarcely hearing Oliver's exclamation of delight.

Today is only practice—the season's inaugural meet is still two weeks away—but she looks to the bleachers anyway, where Oliver would normally be watching. He isn't there, of course, but Coach is raising the whistle to her lips, so Althea crouches into her starter's stance. Her stomach feels like it's being thrown down a flight of stairs over and over again.

Coach blows the whistle and Althea sprints forward, pumping her arms and legs as she heads for the first hurdle, but for the first time she can't see herself making the jump, and when she leaps she's stunned to feel her toe catch and the hurdle tip behind her. She's still processing her mistake when she reaches the next one, and though she doesn't falter going over, her timing is thrown off and she's trailing all but one other girl on the track. Instead of speeding up, she approaches each hurdle with more and more caution, trying to regain some sense of mastery or confidence, but she only succeeds in overthinking something that shouldn't require any thought at all, until finally she rolls up to the finish line in last place, her face hot with shame.

She is sweating hard, not from running but from nerves and barely stifled panic. None of the other girls offer encouraging smiles or rallying cries, and Althea realizes her lack of interest in the rest of her teammates may have sown an active dislike on their part. No one is openly laughing or even smirking unsubtly, but she knows enough to understand that on a purely mathematical level, the odds are good that at least one of the four new girls lining up is totally enjoying this public display of abrupt and relentless incompetence. Althea is so busy trying to divine which one it is—she is leaning toward Mary Beth, who has had a crush on Oliver for years—that when Coach calls her name, it takes a full beat to even register.

"Carter," Coach yells, and beckons her to the sidelines.

Althea jogs over dutifully. She likes Coach as much as she likes anyone who is not Garth, Oliver, or Nicky, and therefore relegated to the vast etcetera of humanity that constitutes "everyone else." A middle-aged woman with short, wiry gray hair and a clavicle so pronounced that Althea finds it slightly nauseating to look at directly, Coach preceded the era of teachers who cheerfully befriend their students. She has never revealed her first name or a single personal detail or indulged in a moment of locker room gossip with the girls on her team, nor does she regard them with the thinly veiled parental affection that seems to run rampant on other sports teams. Their mutual lack of interest in the more sentimental aspects of high school athletics has contributed to an easy, brusque rapport in which Althea takes a strange pride that, even from her coach, she requires so little.

"Yes, ma'am," says Althea.

"What's going on out there?"

"I can't see it."

"The hurdles?" Mystified, Coach looks out to the track, as if to confirm that an obscuring fog has not swept over the campus.

"No, ma'am. In my head—I can't see the jump in my head, the way I usually can."

Coach nods immediately. "You're choking. Overthinking it. Stop doing that."

"I can't focus."

"You're focusing too much."

"Yes, ma'am. How do I stop?"

On the track, the other hurdlers have circled around and are congregating at the starting line, chatting idly while awaiting further instructions. The rest of the team is spread out on the grass, stretching their hamstrings and inner thighs.

"You need to let your mind go soft. Like when you close your eyes to go to sleep at night. Like that, except standing up. And with your eyes open."

Miserably, Althea thinks of all the sleepless nights she has lain awake in her bed, held hostage by her inability to do exactly what Coach is describing. "Yes, ma'am."

Althea jogs back to her place on the line.

Crouched in position, she tries to unclench her brain. Staring down at her fingers splayed lightly over the clay-red ground, she lets her vision go fuzzy the way it does when she and Oliver have their staring contests, but her mind refuses to follow. Something is different. She can feel her vanished talent like a phantom limb, the empty ache of its subtraction from the short list of her assets, and she knows with spiteful certainty that it is gone for good.

Coach blows the whistle again, but this time Althea ignores the Pavlovian urge to lunge forward, fists pumping at her sides. Instead, she watches the other girls circling the track, then she turns, ignoring Coach's shouts, and walks off the field.

chapter two.

"THE BAD NEWS, Oliver, is that it happened again. The good news is that the doctors can't find anything wrong with you," Nicky says.

"You mean they still have no idea why I keep falling asleep?"

"According to them, you're perfectly healthy."

Sitting at the porch table, Oliver's mother is compulsively rolling her entire pouch of tobacco into slim, identical cigarettes and stacking them in a pyramid next to her half-empty bottle of pinot noir. The sun is well past its zenith, but still shines weakly through the branches of their street's namesake magnolia trees. Nicky's ashtray is already filled with a day's worth of tiny white cigarette ends—too delicate, Oliver has always thought, for a word as crass as *butts*. Her wineglass is resting on the front page of today's *New York Times*. She lifts it, revealing a series of overlapping red circles where the fibers have greedily sucked up the liquid. Bringing glass to mouth, Nicky does the same.

"What's with the alarm system?" He'd noticed it on his way out the front door, the pristine electronic keypad a disconcertingly

futuristic addition to their living room. "We didn't have that before. When did we get that?"

"A couple of weeks ago," Nicky admits. "Just to make sure you
don't wander off."

The phrase "wander off" makes Oliver think of six-year-olds
on leashes in shopping malls. "But I was asleep."

"Sometimes I have to wake you up so you can eat and go to
the bathroom. Sometimes you wake up on your own, and I find
you in the kitchen making sandwiches or eating ice cream until
there's nothing left. When you're done, you just go back to sleep."

"How did you get me to the doctor's office?"

"With great difficulty," says Nicky.

"How come I don't remember any of this?"

"I don't know. You didn't last time, either."

"What about work? Did you just not go to work for three
weeks?" Oliver asks.

"I set up a massage table in the spare room, saw a few clients
here."

The sunlight makes Oliver's mouth feel strangely metallic, like he's biting down on a piece of tinfoil. He's barely been
awake for an hour, but already he's anxious to the point of fatigue. Though this is his mother, his porch, his block, it all looks
the same but wrong, like an elaborate set constructed to trick
him into thinking he's in the right place. It's early April now,
officially spring, and though he understands that it's been three
weeks since he'd fallen asleep in chem lab, it's one thing to see
the date on Nicky's newspaper and another to truly accept that
he's misplaced twenty-one days as easily as a set of car keys. A

strong breeze rolls over them like a wave before dissipating, setting the bamboo wind chimes in motion. He hates their weird clicking sound, which Althea can imitate perfectly when she's in the mood to be irritating. Wind chimes are supposed to sound like church bells for your house, Oliver's always said, not this eerie clacking that makes him think of the articulated skeleton hanging in the biology classroom. His headache pulsates grotesquely right above his eyebrows.

The first time he got sick, it was more strange than scary. For two weeks he was ravished by sleep and fever—and then it was just gone. He had come to with the feeling that he had slept unsoundly. He knew he had had a long series of uninspired dreams that weren't worth trying to recall, but also had the sense that he had spent more time in bed than his mother would normally allow. The one fragmented memory that remained was the image of Nicky sitting on his bed with her back to him, then turning abruptly to say, "Are you on drugs? If you are on drugs I will fucking kill you," in the same exasperated tone of voice she used if he stood in front of the refrigerator for too long with the door open. And then he'd been subjected to spinal taps and MRIs and CAT scans, and after everything came back clean, the doctors had written it off as some kind of fluke. He'd missed midterms and the last two weeks of the soccer season, but catching up hadn't been unmanageable, and he did his best to go on like the whole thing had never happened.

The second time feels a little different. The idea of twice has some gravity, some weight to it, enough to frighten Nicky, he can tell. Having already been assured that it's not a brain tumor or an aneurysm or anything that involves a lot of his cells rapidly multiplying, he's not scared of the tests as much as what life will be like while they're waiting for the results. And the more time he spends at the hospital, the more they'll both start thinking of him as sick. He would be her sick child. She would be the mother of a sick child. It's too miserable even to contemplate.

Oliver's what everyone calls a "smart kid," the kind you show your math homework to so he can check the answers right before class starts. The grades come easily; even his extended absences can't jeopardize his scholarship to Cape Fear Academy. He loves science the most. What sounds like philosophy—chaos theory and string theory, the ceaseless searching for the unified field theory that would, at last, happily marry relativity and quantum physics, hyperspace and dark matter and the universe's fundamental grand design—is exhaustively underwritten by equations and formulas. It's all still science and math. Every proven scientific principle originated with some daunting mystery that had, against all odds, been solved. This knowledge, unfortunately, brings Oliver little comfort when another bewildered doctor pulls Nicky aside to ask her if she's sure Oliver's not on drugs, then writes him a prescription for Ritalin.

The phone rings. Oliver checks the caller ID. He hands it off to Nicky, saying, "It's alternate universe us"—his nickname for their mirror family who stayed in Manhattan, unburdened by children, when the McKinleys moved to Wilmington, North Carolina, and who remained intact when the McKinleys were fractured by the loss of Oliver's dad. Once, they had all been friends up north—Sarah, Nicky, Jimmy, Mack—and sometimes

Oliver wonders what would have happened if he'd been raised in a city of eight million, if Nicky had not left the place she so loved and then been widowed before she'd turned thirty. If he'd grown up riding subways and buses instead of bicycles and skateboards, how much of Oliver would he still be? And how much of Nicky had been subtracted the day his father died in that car accident?

"I'm going over to Althea's." Just descending the porch steps makes his calves ache, an unnecessary reminder that he'd been atrophying for three weeks. He turns to his mother, who is staring at him, ignoring the still-ringing phone in her hand. "Why do you look so worried? The doctors say I'm perfectly healthy."

Althea's house is filled with antiques and artifacts—crystal vases perched on mahogany end tables, casting their prisms of wintry light onto Persian rugs; clay pots and arrowheads and ancient terra cotta tiles propped carefully on glass bookshelves—items her father, Garth, has casually acquired during his many travels. Althea has never accompanied him. Oliver navigates the first floor with obsessive caution, still unsteady on his feet as he follows the scent of fresh popcorn toward the basement stairs.

Althea's on the couch with her sketchbook laid out across her lap, eyes comically widened and hand hovering over the cup of pencils on the coffee table, frozen in place at the sight of Oliver. "I don't care how hungry you are, we're not going to Waffle House." She indicates the red ceramic bowl of popcorn. "Eat that if you're hungry."

"Who said anything about Waffle House? Waffle House is disgusting," he says.

"Oh thank Christ, you're back to normal." She throws open her arms and he dives onto the couch, into her embrace, sending her pencils and sketchbook flying. "You're Real Oliver again, thank you, sweet merciful baby Jesus, thank you, thank you. How are you doing? Are you okay? Did you just wake up?"

He breathes deeply, savoring the moldy-sponge smell of their informal headquarters. Althea's basement is where furniture goes to die, where food can be spilled and the rug trodden upon with abandon. The couch cushions are dried out and cracked in places, their fake black leather flaking off into the gray shag, although that doesn't stop Althea from sleeping down here most nights. Battle-scarred side tables sit on either end of the couch, across from the television that takes a full minute to warm up while the tube shivers audibly inside it. There are cardboard boxes piled in the corners, mangled from surrendering their seasonal contents year after year—Christmas ornaments, Halloween costumes, camping gear. Even the duct tape holding the recliner's seat together is coming apart, unraveling on the sides in sticky silver threads that Oliver sometimes finds on his clothes long after he's gone home. Squeezing his eyes shut, he buries his face in Althea's neck, where he can best smell her coconut shampoo and the dull, clean scent of her soap. She strokes his hairline and murmurs a series of indistinct soothing noises.

"Why did you think I wanted Waffle House?" he asks.

"I guess Nicky didn't mention our excursion?"

"No, but apparently she installed an alarm system so we wouldn't have another one. What happened?"

"You woke me up in the middle of the night and you said you were hungry. You wanted Waffle House. I tried to pick the one with the fewest health code violations. And then it was like—Do you remember that obesity study we learned about in biology? The one with all the fat mice? It was like that."

In the study, scientists removed the gene that tells animals to stop eating when they're full. The control group, chromosomes intact, remained trim and lively, while the experimental mice grew in size until they resembled furry scoops of mashed potatoes. In the pictures, their feet didn't even show. There had been a close-up of a fat mouse's face, its eyes haunted and insatiable, as though it were pleading "Help me" and "Feed me" at once.

"That's what I was like?" Oliver asks. "A voracious rodent in distress?"

"If I were to list everything you ate that night, you would never stop throwing up. It wasn't just the eating, though. You were all id without the lid. Here," she says, picking up the sketchbook. "I drew it for you."

He snatches the book from her hands, paging past old drawings of the two of them driving in her car and lying on the beach and dancing in the pit at Lucky's, random moments she's chronicled from the previous year. She narrates the story as he absorbs her visuals of that night's events. Here he is, wandering into the basement; here they are, walking down the side of the highway under the streetlights; here is a mortified Althea, watching as he throws the syrup across the restaurant; here is his own face, unrecognizable. Althea has added a close-up of the fat mouse for comparison.

He thinks of the homeless people he sees downtown sometimes, a dozen garbage bags filled with cans and bottles strapped to their shopping carts, forming a hulking structure they coax along like a reluctant circus elephant while carrying on twitchy, one-sided conversations. No one comes out of the womb like that; it happens later, and Oliver wonders if it's starting to happen to him.

"So it was some sort of psychotic break, right? I'm crazy, I'm literally one hundred percent bona fide batshit crazy. I'll end up one of those sketchy guys who sits in the library all day, rocking in my chair and writing in my journal about my imaginary enemies until Nicky shows up begging me to take my medication."

"Don't start making your tinfoil helmet yet, please," Althea says. "I really don't think you're going crazy."

"How do you know?"

"Because you're lying here worrying about going crazy."

"That's it? That's all you have for me?" Oliver asks, annoyed.

"Look, I wish I knew more, I wish I had more answers, but I don't. I'm just as scared as you—"

"I seriously doubt that," he says, and regrets it immediately.

Sitting up, she pushes him away so roughly, he almost tumbles off the sofa. "The only thing that could possibly be scarier than not remembering the last three weeks is remembering them fucking perfectly."

"Okay, I get it, I'm sorry—"

"I watched you disassociate over hash browns," she shrieks. "It wasn't cool."

"Okay, okay, please, calm your jangled nerves. I'm sorry." He holds her tight until he feels the outburst gently halt, like a car pulling into a parking spot, and her rigid body relaxes as though she has just turned off the engine and engaged the parking brake. He knows she's right. There is not a single injury that has befallen him—his broken wrist when they were nine, the fiery case of chicken pox that confined him to his bedroom for ten days the following year, every disfiguring sunburn, bubbling runny nose, and strawberry-skinned knee—that she has not suffered with him, either in actuality or in her heart. "Nicky wants to take me to another doctor."

"But you're fine now."

"I'm fine *for* now," he corrects her.

Althea chews a piece of her hair, a nervous habit that replaced the illicit thumb-sucking of her childhood but abated, mostly, when she joined the track team freshman year. It flares up when she's sleep-deprived, overcaffeinated, or stuck in traffic. Watching her absently work the lock between her molars, he thinks—and not for the first time—that it's a small miracle she hasn't started smoking yet, and also a foregone conclusion that she will. She pulls her sketchbook back onto her lap.

"What are you working on now?"

She turns back to the present. "It's a dead frog," she says. "It's good, right?"

Her illustration of an ill-fated dissection frog is only half-finished, but rendered thus far in the eerie, Victorian style of old-fashioned anatomical drawings and vintage medical textbooks. She's even drawn the thin silver pins stuck through the webbed feet to keep the creature stretched out and firmly in place. The skin of the belly has been sliced down the middle and peeled back to reveal the internal organs, which she's labeled with Roman numerals. He studies the illustration for a long time.

Oliver doesn't see it coming, and the first thrown piece of popcorn catches him in the eye. Althea instigates as always, apparently too giddy with his return to allow his attention to stray from her for a moment. Things progress quickly until the contents of the bowl have been mashed equally into the carpet and her hair. From there they progress quicker still, until Oliver is facedown on the couch with a mouthful of damp upholstery, Althea's knee digging into his kidneys, his arm twisted and yanked up so that his hand waves like a pale flag over his head. Her weight bears down on him ruthlessly, and when he tries to move, bottle rockets of pain whistle and pop inside his shoulder. They are yelling so loudly—*"Say Uncle!"*—*"Fuck you!"*—neither hears the door open at the top of the stairs.

"Althea, let him go," her father says.

Panting and reluctant, Althea stands up, picking popcorn out of her hair. She blows her bangs out of her face but says nothing, glaring in her father's direction. Oliver knows this is one staring contest she isn't going to win. As Garth comes down the stairs, a tumbler of scotch in his hand, he stoops to avoid cracking his head on the beams.

Oliver's impression of his best friend's father was fully formed one summer night when Oliver and Althea were eight years old and Garth Carter taught them how to pitch a tent in the backyard. As they unrolled their sleeping bags, a skunk waddled out of the bushes and glanced absently in their direction. Petrified, the children collapsed to the ground, clutching each other, as if beset by a pack of feral dogs. Garth emerged from behind the tent, where he had been nailing the final stake into the ground, and restored himself to his full and considerable height. He clapped his hands together three times. The skunk turned and ran off into the night.

"Skunks hate noise," he had said. "You kids need to know things like that."

"Sorry about the yelling," Oliver says now, peeling his cheek from the sofa.

Garth waves his glasses, shrugging to indicate how little he actually cares. "I can hardly hear anything from my study. I just wanted to visit. Say hello to Oliver."

"Good to see you, sir."

"How are you feeling?"

"You know. Jazzed to be back on the show."

"Althea catching you up on everything you missed?"

"It really wasn't much," she says.

"Did you tell him about the track team?" says Garth.

"Dad, he's been here for, like, two minutes."

"What about the track team?" Oliver asks.

"Nothing," Althea says. "I quit."

"You quit?" Oliver looks at her askance.

"She quit," Garth confirms.

"I wish you hadn't said anything," Althea tells her father.

"I'm sure you were planning on telling him eventually."

"I'm sure how I might place in hurdles this year is the last thing on Oliver's mind right now."

Actually, Oliver would much rather be thinking about Althea's race times than what might be wrong with his brain, but standard best-friend-defense mode kicks into gear and he nods in agreement without meeting Garth's eyes. "I bet it got boring anyway, running around in all those circles. Give someone else a chance to win."

"Exactly," she says.

Ignoring her, Garth lowers himself into the recliner and turns to Oliver. "I think I've got one you're really going to like."

"I'm ready," Oliver says. Now he's sorry not to have the popcorn.

Garth teaches history at UNC Wilmington. A Southern gentleman from Savannah, where all of his family still resides, Garth quietly nurses—despite his outward trappings of erudite bookishness: reading glasses, ever-present glass of good scotch, and insistence on proper grammar—a fervent love of the lowbrow, particularly mass market paperbacks and poker. He organizes a weekly poker night among his department's faculty, and though his specialty is Latin American history, he uses these card games as an opportunity to collect a wide range of fucked-up historical anecdotes. This semester, one of Garth's colleagues is giving a seminar on ancient China, and Oliver loves the tales about brothers poisoning each other and eunuchs ruling through puppet emperors. A mildly contrite Althea massages Oliver's shoulder while Garth tells them the gruesome tale of an emperor from the Tang Dynasty; it begins with him falling in love with a concubine and ends with decapitated bodies lying in a ditch.

When he's finished with his story, Garth rattles the ice cubes in his glass with a dramatic flourish. Oliver is rapt. Althea is horrified. "Well. I've stunned you both into silence. It means my work here is done. I'm going out to dinner." He leans over and kisses Althea's forehead. She wrinkles her nose in faux protest. "You're not fooling anyone. You're all mush."

"Actually, I think I *am* fooling everyone. Who are you having dinner with?"

"Whom. Just this year's artist in residence. A writer, very distinguished. You'd like her."

"You say that about the artist in residence every year," Althea reminds him.

Popcorn shrapnel crunches under Garth's feet. He shakes his head at his daughter. "You could have just told Oliver that you missed him. Saved yourself an hour of vacuuming."

"Better not keep her waiting, Dad; it'll just give her time to think about your flaws."

Garth smiles wearily at Oliver. "Welcome back, Ol. She's all yours."

Once he's gone and safely out of earshot, Oliver turns to Althea. "So why did you quit track? What happened?"

She shrugs, avoiding his eyes. "I got tired of it. I just walked off the field one day."

"Just like that?"

She fiddles nervously with the pages of her sketchbook. "Just like that."

There's more she isn't saying, he's sure of it, and while he's sure he could coax it out of her given sufficient time, the idea is suddenly exhausting. If she wanted to tell him, she would—it's the fact that she doesn't that he finds unsettling.

Later, after Althea has finished catching him up on the last three weeks with her sketchbook, after she's made him turkey burgers and another batch of popcorn and they've watched a movie, Oliver stands up and announces he's going home.

"You could just sleep here," Althea says.

"I'll be okay." A fragment of popcorn has nestled in Althea's collarbone. He plucks it off her and pops it into his mouth, salt dissolving onto his tongue. Briefly, he reconsiders her offer to stay over, but in the last few months a new restlessness has made it harder for them to sleep in the same bed. He hears her weighted sighs in the middle of the night when she thinks he's asleep, feels her rolling over and over until she finally comes to rest with her nose buried in his neck, a shaky hand alighted on his hip. And he's afraid to spoon her now, or assume any of their chaste cuddling positions, for fear she'll brush against him and he'll be revealed in the most basic way a teenaged boy can betray himself. So instead, he zips his sweatshirt in a gesture of finality and pulls up his hood. "See you in the morning?"

She looks down at the spot where he touched her. "I was saving that for later," she says.

Back at his house, Nicky is asleep on the couch underneath one of her books, an aromatherapy candle flickering on the coffee table beside her—chamomile and peppermint, for rejuvenation. They cost something like thirty dollars at the spa, but Nicky gets them at a discount.

"Mom?"

She mumbles something and rolls over, the book slipping off her chest and onto the floor. He shuts off the lamp over her head and blows out the candle.

Nicky has changed his sheets, but still the idea of returning to bed, knowing he has spent the last three weeks there, is deeply unappealing. He sits at his desk, leaning back and staring up at the ceiling where those cheap plastic glow-in-the-dark stars form a random constellation. Althea put them there, one winter years ago. Standing on his bed, balanced on the toes of one foot in a rangy arabesque, she slapped them up one at a time, following his directions to create a haphazard version of Gemini, their star sign, before she lost patience and just pasted the rest on. He had been complaining about the weather, about how he missed camping and hiking, about how he was sick of being trapped in her basement playing board games.

"You can sleep under these stars until spring," she had said.

Inspired, he grabs his telescope—an old Christmas gift from Garth—and sleeping bag and slips out the back door into the yard. He trains the lens on the clearing of sky untouched by trees and the neighbors' satellite dish, and is reassured to see the stars are where they should be, Hydra still snaking its way across the heavens, Ursa Major and all its galaxies firmly in place. He tries to get a fix on the Owl Nebula, but it's not dark enough.

When they were ten, Oliver had somehow happened upon the unfortunate piece of information that in approximately five billion years the sun would run out of juice, ending life in the solar system. He'd been so pissed; it seemed so unfair. Althea assured him that by then space travel would be no big deal—everyone could just ship off to another solar system. When Oliver heard scientists claim that someday the entire *universe* would end, either tearing itself apart or collapsing in on itself—the theories varied—Althea had no answers, and Oliver was inconsolable. At night he lay in bed and tried to imagine it, the end of everything. Some scientist suggested it was possible that eventually, if humanity could last long enough, a wormhole could be found that would lead happily to a parallel universe that would go on after ours had come to its ignoble end. He had been casually dismissed, but Oliver found it deeply comforting, imagining people stepping through a portal in the sky as easily as boarding a plane, slipping into another dimension where soccer games and trips to the beach and arguments over whose turn it was to mow the lawn could all continue apace.

His enthusiasm for science in general and astronomy in particular has matured since then, and he loves the concomitant math and equations underlying these grandiose ideas about the universe, but in the back of his mind that original urgency remains, that there's more at stake than acing the SATs or getting into MIT—somewhere out there has to be a wormhole that is going to save us all.

Two months later, as their junior year is winding down, Oliver cajoles Althea into attending a house party thrown by someone they hardly know. When he arrives to pick her up, she is pacing around her bedroom in a short terrycloth bathrobe. The soles of her feet, pink-white like shells, are picking up dust from the floor. She is brushing her hair in long frantic strokes, anxiously trying to loosen the tangles.

"Could you please, for one second, just pretend you're a girl and help me pick something to wear?" she yells.

"To do that, first I would have to pretend that you're a girl." Even as he says it, he's studying the place below her neck, the dark crevice where the two sides of her robe meet.

That shuts her up. In truth, it's a decision that mostly comes down to which jeans and which T-shirt; her wardrobe doesn't consist of much else. But at the last minute she digs out a plaid pleated skirt and her steel-toed boots. She sits on the edge of the bed lacing them up while Oliver watches the muscles flex in her runner's legs. As her fingers nimbly work the frayed laces through the endless eyelets, he mentally removes the outfit she just put on while he was facing the other way.

"What?" she says. "You're staring."

He snaps back into himself. "The skirt and the boots. I don't know. Isn't it, like, a mixed message?"

"You're a fucking mixed message. You lost your vote ten minutes ago. Let's go."

The party is close, so they walk. Althea crosses her arms over her chest, occasionally smoothing her hair or running her fingers over her skirt, looking quietly alarmed that the hemline ends several inches above her knees. Oliver can see that she's already in a bad mood. If he doesn't take action, she's going to stand in a corner, sulk for forty-five minutes, and then demand to go home.

Reaching up, he swipes several leaves from an overhead branch, shredding them as they walk. The sap gets in between his fingers, sticking them together. "You know what I was think-ing? About tonight?" he says.

"Mmm?"

"Let's play a game. Make the party into a game."

"Like a drinking game?" says Althea.

"Not exactly. It's a new game; I just made it up. Let's try say-ing yes. To everything."

"I don't understand."

"Whenever someone proposes something, asks us if we want to do something, let's just say yes."

"This is your idea of a new game?" she asks skeptically.

"Yes. We will be receptive to all that the universe has to offer. And I shall call it: the Non-Stop Party Wagon." He tosses the leaf pieces into the air over their heads like confetti.

The first game Althea and Oliver ever played was Candy Land. One night, ten years ago, the babysitter canceled on a panicked Nicky, who in desperation took her son down the street to the house of a college professor who she knew had a little girl Oliver's age. Garth let them play in the basement, fed them red velvet cupcakes, and pulled out the only board game Althea owned, a gift from some relative. She won three times before Garth gently suggested they play something else. When Althea pointed out that she had no other games, her father produced a deck of cards and a pile of poker chips and explained the nuances of Texas Hold 'Em. When Nicky returned, Oliver and Althea were asleep on opposite ends of the couch in the basement, their cards pressed closely to their chests.

They never played Candy Land again, but in winter they

holed up in the basement after school, drinking hot apple cider around the space heater and honing their military strategies on the Risk board. In summer, when it was too hot to throw a Frisbee on Wrightsville Beach or float down the Cape Fear River on an inner tube, they played gin rummy and casino in the shade of Althea's porch, a pitcher of cranberry iced tea on the table between them, slices of Key lime pie going runny in the heat.

And then there were the games they made up themselves. Swaggering around downtown Wilmington wearing sunglasses, black clothes, and sullen expressions—that was called Playing New York. Whoever cracked a smile first lost. Sitting in the gazebo in August, complaining about the humidity, drinking limeade out of silver mint julep cups, and exaggerating their mild Southern accents—that was called Playing New Orleans. You won by keeping up your accent longest. Last spring, after catching *Deliverance* on cable late one night, they started passing the afternoons on the banks of the Cape Fear, stalking, chasing, and ambushing each other in the woods, although neither ever consented to squeal like a pig. That ended in a draw.

"Non-Stop Party Wagon doesn't sound like much of a game to me," she says, batting at the foliage in her hair.

"Then it will be easy to play," Oliver says.

"Come here." Standing close, she brushes leaf detritus from his shoulders. Her sweatshirt smells like the beach.

Often they are mistaken for twins, although their faces look nothing alike. Oliver doesn't have her high cheekbones, and she doesn't have his dimples. But they are both lean and narrow, and when she is dressed in his clothes, Althea's straight-up-and-down body doesn't look all that different. They have the same blond hair, pale skin, and blue eyes. She brushes her bangs out of those eyes now with one chapped, nail-bitten hand so she can scowl at him more effectively. She wrinkles her nose. "Okay. I'll play along."

When they arrive at the party, Oliver's own resolve wavers. It's as though someone rounded up every teenage misfit in New Hanover County and doused them with so much alcohol that if anyone lit a cigarette, the whole house would ignite. Taking hold of Althea's elbow, he shoulders his way through the crowd. The air is stifling, like breathing through a whiskey-soaked rag. His friend Valerie appears, wading through from the opposite direction, a plastic funnel and tube hung around her neck like a stethoscope. Another friend, Coby, shoves past them, precariously toting at least half a dozen cans of Natural Ice—tucked under his chin, wedged between his elbows and ribs, and stuffed in his pockets.

"Where the hell is he going?" Oliver asks.

"To hide them," Valerie says. "You've never seen him do that at a party?"

"We don't really go to parties," says Althea.

"All over the house. In the mailbox, in someone's underwear drawer. Toilet tanks are his favorite—they actually keep the beer cold. But he'll hide them anywhere that will guarantee him a beer later when everyone else is out."

"Christ," says Oliver. "He's like an alcoholic Easter Bunny." It fits Coby, though, the kind of guy who reads Bukowski and is building his own apartment over his parents' garage, presumably so he can continue to pilfer their bourbon long after he's limped across the finish line at Cape Fear Academy with the rest of the class of 1997; the kind of guy who has sex in your little sister's room at your house party and then steals the keg on his way out.

"Let's go downstairs," Valerie says. "The show's about to start."

Althea and Oliver exchange a glance.

"Yes," they say.

The basement is low-ceilinged and devoid of windows. A haze of beer-sweat stink and cigarette smoke hangs in the air, haloing the heads of all the miscreants. A table is set up for beer pong, red plastic cups stacked neatly on either side; in one corner a group Oliver vaguely recognizes from Hoddard, the local public high school, is playing a rousing game of Asshole.

There's no stage, just a misshapen rectangle of rust-colored shag carpet marked off with masking tape and filled with fourth-hand instruments and miles of uncoiling black cables. Oliver's friend Howard stands inside the box, nervously tuning his guitar. Oliver lifts his hand in a reassuring wave. Howard responds with a weak smile, gingerly testing the state of his blue Mohawk. His fine hair is too thin to stand erect on its own, so he thickens it daily with toothpaste and Elmer's Glue in order to spike it properly. The pervasive peppermint odor has earned him, of late, the unfortunate nickname "Minty Fresh."

"What are they called again?" Althea asks Oliver.

"I don't remember."

"He changed it," Valerie says. "They used to be the Great Expectations. Now they're the Freddy Knuckles."

They drink their beers and wait. The drummer picks anxiously at a fissure in his crash cymbal, and the bass player practices the same three notes over and over. Finally Howard gives Valerie one of those imperceptible best-friend signals—it could be a raised eyebrow or a subtle hand gesture. Oliver doesn't see it, but he knows it's happened because of the speed with which Valerie rushes to the back of the basement, turning off the stereo, dimming the lights, and hissing at the Asshole-playing contingent to shut the fuck up. When the basement is sufficiently hushed, Valerie returns to the area by the makeshift stage and cues Howard, and this time Oliver sees the signal, a small, decisive nod that visibly bolsters Howard's courage. Rubbing a guitar pick between his fingertips, he steps up to the mic and rushes through his introduction, then attacks his guitar with all the finesse of a raccoon pawing through the contents of a particularly redolent trash can. His bandmates are no better versed in their own instruments, but all three of them are unusually spirited performers, and there is at least a whiff of melody beneath the noise. Howard is also the lead vocalist, and there is something strange about his singing voice that Oliver can't identify until Althea leans over and screams in his ear, "Why the fuck is he singing with a British accent?"

Oliver shrugs. The music fills the basement as completely as air fills a balloon, and behind him the entire party is crushed into the space, a hundred teenagers thrashing about while watery beer spills over the sides of their Solo cups. Valerie is beaming proudly at Howard, her stumpy brown pigtails bouncing as she dances. Althea, despite her reluctance to leave the house ear-

lier, seems to be relishing this now, getting shoved by the crowd
and shoving back. He can't tell if it's actually the music she en-
joys or the volume or the shoving, but either way he's relieved.
She arches her long neck to finish her beer, her throat quivering
as she takes the last pull. Letting the can fall to the ground, Althea opens her eyes and catches Oliver motionless and staring,
just as he is nearly toppled by a swell in the throng. She grabs his
wrists, keeping him upright as a handful of eager kids jockeying
to get closer to the front move around them, until Althea and
Oliver are so thoroughly fenced in by the heaving sweaty mess of
drunk people that they can barely see the band. Overwhelmed,
he turns toward the stairs, but Althea tugs again on his arm,
more gently now.

"Stay and dance," she shouts over the music. "Your rules. You
can't say no."

She's right, as she is so infuriatingly often, so he stays and
lets himself get shoved around, pressed so closely against the
shoulder blades and shirts of his fellow partygoers that he can
smell their shampoo and the moist, musky scent of their perspi-
ration, and even, he's sure of it, the trace odor of toothpaste. Althea reaches out and nonchalantly plucks a full beer from some
stranger's grasp, quickly chugging half the contents before he
can protest, then passing the remains to Oliver. Howard empties
his own beer onto the kids closest to the mic and hurls the can
into the audience.

The end is anticlimactic. There's no stage for the band to
exit; they just finish their last song and start breaking down the
equipment before the tepid applause has even stopped. As soon

as it's over, it's as though they never played. Someone turns on the lights and the stereo and starts rearranging the cups on the beer pong table.

"Althea, come be my partner for beer pong," Valerie says, pulling on her sleeve. Althea looks at Oliver helplessly. He shrugs. He can't go back on his own rule now, although he knows beer pong is not her game. She'd be better off playing Asshole; no doubt she'd end up as president within a few rounds and have a great time spending the rest of the party telling people what to do. But Valerie's made her request; the proverbial die has been cast.

"Let's go make friends," Val says. "Expand the gene pool."

Coby reappears with a beer for Oliver.

"You didn't just pull this out of a toilet, did you?" Oliver asks, wiping the top of the can on his shirt.

"By the time it comes to that, you'll be too drunk to care." Coby gestures toward Althea with his beer. "What did you have to do to drag her out?"

"We go out," Oliver says.

"To parties? With other people?" Coby drinks. "Be real."

The cement floor is slick with spilled beer. From an unseen corner behind the laundry room comes the sound of muscular, robust vomiting. The president of Asshole is demanding that his secretary give him a lap dance while singing "I'm a Little Teapot" in a Russian accent.

"You're right," says Oliver. "We should do this more often."

Coby smirks. "Don't be such a prick. These are our peers."

They both snicker derisively.

As suspected, Althea is terrible at beer pong; hand-eye coordination has never been her strong suit. This is why they never go bowling or shoot pool. Coby cheers her on every time she plucks the Ping-Pong ball out of another red plastic cup and drinks its warm, flat contents.

"Got any plans for the summer?" he asks Oliver.

"I'm taking an astronomy class at UNC. Bulk up my college apps."

"You should go to Space Camp. That'll dazzle them."

"You got some big projects scheduled? You going to put up some drywall in that tree house you built above the garage? You should put up some of those Christmas lights—you know, the ones shaped like chili peppers? The ladies will come running."

"It's not the décor they come for," says Coby, resting a hand on his belt buckle and shrugging modestly. "It's the company."

"Come for the video games, stay for the syphilis."

"That was just a rumor."

Grimacing, Oliver finishes his beer. At the table, Althea is squatting to retrieve the ball, and as she gets up, she smacks her head on the underside of the flimsy table. Beer sloshes out of several cups on top. "You okay?" he yells.

"Only my pride, whatever," she replies.

"Dude, your girlfriend is drunk," Coby says to Oliver.

"You know she's not my girlfriend."

"You two aren't even hooking up?"

"No."

"Why not? You're together all the time." Coby shakes his head, seeming genuinely perplexed, as if proximity and opportunity should be enough.

"She's my best friend."

"So who *is* she hooking up with?"

"No one," Oliver says.

"Are you sure?"

He remembers the night of the Jell-O, the way Althea had looked at him in the too-small pool. "Yeah, I'm sure."

Althea misses another shot, and Coby applauds as she chugs. Valerie shakes her head, mourning her choice of partner.

"I knew Al shouldn't have played this game," Oliver says. "She's terrible at shit like this. Pool, bowling, anything with—"

"Balls?" Coby chortles.

"—spatial relations," Oliver finishes.

"Let me see if I can help her out." Coby is eager to be Althea's instructor, standing close behind her, demonstrating the gentle wrist flick necessary to arc the ball into an opponent's cup. She leans in to hear Coby's advice over the music, intent on improving her game, but even one-on-one coaching can't help her. When she misses her sixth shot in a row, Oliver turns his back. He can't watch anymore.

"Where are you going?" Althea yells across the table.

"To check the mail," he says.

Sure enough, there are two beers in the mailbox at the end of the driveway, nestled between the pages of the *Pennysaver*. He pops one open and puts the other in the pocket of his sweatshirt. Wandering back to the house, he's able to fully appreciate how many people are here tonight: kids running to greet one another, girls shrieking like harpies and falling off the porch while boys roll their eyes and feign disinterest. He vaguely recognizes

Jason, the host, who occasionally sells Coby pot, and they nod to each other across the lawn.

He goes inside to find Althea, but the girls have been replaced at the table. He steps out the back door. Howard and a girl wearing tight black jeans covered in useless straps and zippers are pawing at each other on a bench set back among the dogwood trees. His hand is clutching the back of her neck as if he's nervous she might sprint off into the shrubbery. The safety pin in her ear gleams in the moonlight. The screen door opens continuously to spill teenagers into the backyard or suck them back into the house. Howard whispers something and the girl giggles, pricking her hand gently on the spikes of his Mohawk. He slips a hand between her jacket and shirt, down to the small of her back, and pulls her close. Oliver finishes the beer in his hand, tosses it aside, and opens the spare.

The girls are in the kitchen, Valerie holding aloft a funnel full of beer while Althea, on her knees, eagerly waits for the foam to subside. The floor shudders with the drumbeats of "Lust for Life," which is cranked up on the speakers in the living room.

"Valerie's teaching me to funnel beers," Althea tells him. "She says I'm a natural because I seem to be lacking a gag reflex."

"Our girl here is going to make one lucky man very happy someday," Valerie says. "Go ahead, Althea. Don't forget to open your throat."

Althea wraps her mouth around the plastic tube, keeping it pinched shut until the last moment. She tilts her head back and releases, shooting all of the beer down her throat in one impossibly long swallow. When she's drained it she stands, wipes her mouth with the inside of her wrist, and hands the beer funnel back to Valerie. "Oliver's next," she says.

Coby approaches. "Anyone seen Minty Fresh? I need a partner for beer pong."

"He's out back, expanding the gene pool," Oliver says.

"Fuck yourself," Coby says.

"I swear on my eyes," Oliver says. "Some girl with zippers."

"Unbelievable. He looks like a clown, he smells like toothpaste, and he's still getting more action than either of us. It's a sad fucking state of affairs."

"Jealousy is not a good look for you," Valerie says.

"Please, like you wouldn't switch places with him in a second," Coby says.

"Fair's fair. He saw her first. Oliver, come here."

"I'll hold it for him," Althea says, taking the loaded funnel from Valerie. "Oliver, get down on your knees."

"Whatever we're doing," Coby says, "I want to be next."

Oliver can't figure out how to open his throat. His lungs fill with liquid, and he tears the tube from his mouth, spilling the rest of its contents across the floor in a thin foamy puddle. He wheezes but can't draw in any air; for a few panicked seconds, he's suffocating. Finally, some of the beer comes out his nose and he coughs up the rest, spraying it across Althea's bare legs while everyone hoots with laughter. She bends over to dry her knees with a dish towel, and Oliver, still on the floor, gets a quick look up her skirt, a harrowing glimpse of the space between the tops of her thighs, a flash of blue panties and taut cotton. It's so quick it's over before it's begun, but it's just long enough to make him regret his earlier comment. *First, I would have to pretend that you're a girl.* She's a girl, all right.

Coby asks Oliver to be his partner for beer pong instead, and Oliver can't say no. Every time he tries to leave the table, Coby asks him to stay for just one more game. By the time he makes it back upstairs, there's no sign of Althea anywhere. He wanders around in a gentle haze. Things seem to be operating on a three- or four-second delay. That's fine with him. Pretty much everything is fine with him. Eventually he finds his way into the master bedroom. A sliver of light shines under the door of the attached bathroom. As he raises his hand to knock, there's a crash and the spectacular, decadent sound of heavy glass shattering into a thousand pieces.

"Hey," he says, knocking on the door. The occupant gasps. He recognizes that sharp intake of air. "Althea, is that you in there making all that beautiful music?"

"Ollie?" she whispers, regressing to his childhood nickname. She opens the door a crack and looks around frantically. Satisfied there are no witnesses, she grabs him by the wrist, pulling him inside the bathroom and locking the door. "I did a bad thing."

The bathroom is large and opulent. There's a glass-enclosed shower in one corner, an enormous Jacuzzi in another, and a bathmat between them as thick and soft as the carpet in Althea's living room. Dried flowers hang from the walls and lavender clay pots of potpourri are lined up in a row on the toilet tank. A series of vanity bulbs frame a large blank square on the wall above the sink, and below them, twinkling like a galaxy of fallen stars, the mirror lies shattered and dazzling across the porcelain.

"Did you do that?" he asks.

"I thought it was the medicine cabinet, so I tried to open it, and it came off the wall instead," she says.

"Why were you trying to get into the medicine cabinet?"

"It's sort of great-looking, isn't it?"

The light from all the vanity bulbs reflecting off the fragments piled in the sink is a gorgeous, arresting sight. He's never seen anything like it. It makes him think of all the antiques in Althea's house, all the glass figurines that make him so nervous, all the things people buy with abandon because they think they're so lovely, and none of them compares to the beauty of this disaster. There's no doubt that this, this is the mirror's finest moment.

Althea covers her face with her hands, peeks at him from a crack between her fingers, and catches him staring at the sink. "See?" she says softly.

"Shush."

"Don't shush me."

"You love it when I shush you."

Someone knocks on the door. "Who's in there?"

Althea chooses this moment to begin laughing uncontrollably.

"Hello? Okay, seriously, you aren't supposed to be in there." It sounds like Jason.

Althea can't stop herself, clutching the windowsill, holding her stomach, and shaking from head to toe. Jason pounds on the door.

"Coby? Is that you? I swear, if I find you fucking in my parents' bathtub again, I'm gonna mess you up like a goddamn car crash."

This new piece of information incites a fresh fit of hysteria. Jason keeps banging on the door, and Althea turns on the faucet in the bathtub.

"Coby, you motherfucker! I'm serious!" Jason shouts.

It sounds like he's ramming the door with his shoulder. A voice speaks up from somewhere behind Jason. "Coby's not in there, he's at the beer pong table. He just kicked my ass."

"Then who the hell is fucking in my parents' bathtub?" Jason hollers, slamming the door with his fist for emphasis.

A siren wails in front of the house. At once, it seems, the entire party erupts with a cry of "Cops!" and everyone starts running. The bedroom instantly clears. Screen doors slam shut. The music cuts off abruptly, leaving the house feeling hollow as its occupants flee. All the noise is coming from outside now, and it seems like Althea and Oliver might be the only two people left when they hear heavy footsteps on the stairs. A dispatcher's voice crackles on a radio. Althea gives a nervous titter, and Oliver claps a hand over her mouth.

The bathroom window opens onto the slanted roof of the back porch. "It would seem," he whispers, "that we are out of options."

"I'm not going out that window," says Althea. The radio sputters again, closer, in the hallway this time.

"Non-Stop Party Wagon. You can't say no." He climbs out. Reluctantly, Althea follows.

In the backyard, kids are stashing their drugs under potted plants so they can return and find them later. The red and blue lights in the driveway sweep rhythmically over the scene. Cops burst out the back door telling everyone to stay where they are. Hand in hand, Oliver and Althea scoot toward the edge of the roof until their feet are dangling below the gutter. They ease themselves off, falling briefly through space until they land, crouched, in the wet grass. They run through the dogwoods and the shallow creek that borders the property, then across the neighboring backyards, climbing fences and setting off motion sensor lights. With the sirens behind them, the sense of urgency fades. Slowing to a walk, they catch their breath.

This late hour has always been like their living room, the temporal equivalent of Althea's basement, whether they were reading to each other in a pup tent in his backyard, building a fort of blankets and cardboard boxes in her basement, or whispering to each other via two-way radios while they lay in their respective beds, sending schemes for future mischief across the airwaves between their houses.

The sky is still dark, the moon like a curved piece of broken glass, and a bird sings above them in a young sugar maple. They look at each other with gauzy surprise. Althea sidles up to the tree, peering into its branches, but the bird is hidden in the early summer leaves. It waits a beat and then begins again, a different tune but the same somehow, like the next verse in a torch song. Enraptured, they squint through the mess of buds and leaves as the bird trills on.

After who knows how long, Althea wraps her hands around the tree trunk, no thicker than her waist, and gives it a gentle shake. The bird does not emerge.

"I want to see her," she whispers.

"I don't think she wants you to."

She jostles the tree again, harder, the muscles in her wrist flexing under her pale skin. Leaves rustle and branches sway, but the bird stays put, giving no hint of her location, continuing her song.

Althea tenses, jaw clenched with frustration, tightening her grip, getting ready to give it another go. Oliver knows this look, the wicked determination that is both the best and the worst of her. She's forgotten the party, the shattered mirror, even Oliver's presence at her side; this one bird has her full attention. He figures he has about thirty seconds before she starts shouting obscenities and tries to climb the tree. He puts a hand on her slender wrist; her bones feel avian and small.

"Leave it alone," he whispers.

Casting up a final, reluctant glance, she relents; the taut muscles go loose again. She releases the tree trunk, but Oliver clings to her, mysteriously unwilling to let her arm drop back to her side. Her expression changes as her interest turns from what's happening in the tree above them to what's suddenly happening underneath it.

Pulling her toward him, Oliver traces her blade of a cheekbone with his fingers, letting his other hand rest on her hip while hers find his waist. Through the cotton of her skirt, her hipbone fits perfectly into his palm. The salty air is warm, and except for the bird's blithe singing, the street is muffled under its canopy of blooming trees. This is the summer they wanted. The ocean is much too far away for him to hear, but he almost believes that's what's pounding in his ears. There's not a single light on in any of the houses, no random car catching them in its headlights as it passes. Their town is asleep around them in the long hours before morning. He can feel Althea's blood pulsing faintly in her veins. She smiles at him shyly, biting her lip to suppress a nervous giggle.

He closes his eyes, making it impossible to tell who moves in and closes the final inches. All he knows is their lips finally meet in their first kiss. She tastes like beer and peppermint; he catches a whiff of smoke from her long hair. Her bare knees brush against his jeans. Her lips and tongue tentatively mimic the motions of his. Leaning into her, Oliver staggers, and she stumbles backward into the tree, pulling him along. Bark scrapes his knuckles. Drunk and giddy, they punctuate their giggles with more kisses. He nibbles her neck. Althea, infamously ticklish, shakes with silent laughter, her head thrown back against the tree. Her skin is warm and saline against his lips. He kisses his way back up her neck, her throat vibrating against his mouth as her laughter trails off.

"I think we finally scared that bird away," he whispers, and kisses her again.

Oliver is learning to kiss as he goes, guided by some unknown instinct. He strokes her hair back, out of her eyes and off her forehead. Their kisses are tender and earnest at first, mindful of their own newness. Her hand finds his; their fingers interlace. Cupping his cheek sweetly in her palm, she gently squeezes his bottom lip between her teeth and then releases it.

Pressing her against the tree, he clutches at her hipbone, her neck. Their hesitation vanishes along with their nervous laughter; their kisses grow strident and insistent. Althea's fingers dig into his shoulders; they climb his chest, tugging at his shirt. He's almost sad they're not on their own Magnolia Street; what a show this would make for Mrs. Parker.

Althea breathes faster. He traces the muscles that run the length of her bare thighs. The fantasy he had earlier in her room returns. Running his hands up her sides, he grazes her breasts and she gasps softly, a brand-new Althea sound he's never heard before. Now he's panting, too, their legs intertwined against the tree, their identical heights putting them exactly at eye level.

"Oliver," she whispers in a raspy voice. "Maybe we should go back to my house." Her cheeks are flushed, eyes glassy.

He nods.

They untangle themselves, Althea smoothing her ruffled hair and skirt. Taking her hand, he breaks into an easy jog, which she, of course, turns into a race. She slows down to let him keep pace, then pulls away again, laughing while he chases her with no chance of ever catching up.

The charge home is quick, too quick, and suddenly they are standing in front of her house. The haze is lifting from his vision. Though his usual lucidity has not yet returned, he is abruptly aware of what they are about to do, what Althea is offering him as she starts up the path to her door.

"Wait," he says.

"What? Oh, you're right. We should probably go in the back."

"No, just—just wait."

"What?" she asks, irritated.

Oliver can only shake his head.

"What's wrong?" Her words slur together like ice cubes melting in a glass. "Come on."

It's her impatience that betrays her. Sensing his reluctance, she's realizing that the moment under the tree has passed. She's trying to seize what's left of her chance to get this thing done, because once it's done they can't undo it. To her this is some kind of first step, a necessary catalyst that will set off a series of reactions and completely transform their relationship. To him it's just an experiment, the test of a curious hypothesis. That's exactly the reason he is glued to the sidewalk, refusing to follow her down to the basement and at last make proper use of that old couch. If he goes inside with her, then what? Is he going to wake up as her boyfriend just because he got drunk and made out with her under a tree? Isn't it better to disappoint her now, before, than to do it in the morning?

"I'm not—" He pauses. "I'm not ready."

She tucks her fingers inside the sleeves of her sweatshirt, thumbs poking through the holes in the cuffs. Her shoulders come up around her neck as if she's trying to retract her head, turtle-like. "That doesn't even mean anything, you know. What are you, cupcakes in the oven, waiting for the timer to go off? Are we sitting at a red light, waiting for it to turn green?"

"Al, I'm sorry—"

"Why did you even let it start, then?" She raises her voice, heralding the return of the irascible Althea.

"I was drunk," he says.

"Are you fucking serious?"

"That came out wrong."

"You know what? Go ahead. Stick your head a little further up your ass. If you have trouble, I can help." Turning to enter her house, she laughs abruptly. "Oh my God."

Oliver is wary of her sudden change in mood. "Now what?"

"We left the bathtub running at Jason's."

chapter three.

ON HER WAY to school Monday morning, Althea brings her car to a perfunctory halt in front of Oliver's house. He isn't waiting for her outside, so she taps the horn, just long enough to elicit a loud, squawking honk. The customary next step is to ring the doorbell continually until he emerges, breathless and annoyed. Reaching for the release button on her seat belt, she hesitates, stifling a yawn. She had barely slept the last two nights, thrashing around on the couch, alternately cringing at the memory of Oliver's hand up her skirt and wondering if he might come over and do it again. She lay awake for a very long time imagining him slipping into the basement to apologize for his unbelievably stupid comment about only kissing her because he had been drunk. He would explain that he had been afraid or not ready or whatever—she played out every possible semantic variation on this sentiment, and in the end decided all that mattered was that when he finished his brief speech he would lay his palms delicately upon her cheekbones and pull her face to his.

But Oliver hadn't materialized the rest of the weekend, and

now she's exhausted, with a whole day of school in front of her and the kind of headache that makes her eyes feel full of grit. If he couldn't be bothered to sneak into her house and say he was sorry, she decides, then fuck him. He can take the bus to school.

By lunchtime she's edgy. What if he wasn't running late this morning but purposely avoiding her? What if he is actually angry with her for some reason? She checks the cafeteria, then the back field, and even the library, but she can't find him. She's making her third pass by his locker when she runs into Valerie, drinking a Dr Pepper, a book tucked under her arm, wearing a shirt that looks like she screen-printed it herself, a skull with a knife and fork where the crossbones should be. It reads BON VIVANT in curvy letters.

"If you're looking for Oliver, I don't think he's here today," says Valerie. "At least, he wasn't in English."

They meander the halls together while Valerie drinks her soda.

"What are you reading?" Althea asks.

Valerie flashes the cover of the book, which gleams under the fluorescent lights. "Minty Fresh told me to read it. It's about the diamond trade. That industry is so totally fucked. The diamonds are all in a vault at De Beers, and they're not even worth anything. But people buy them because they see some ad that tells them to. Their value is completely invented."

She spends some time elaborating about the wars that erupted among diamond sellers a hundred years ago, how De

Beers emerged victorious and ran a monopoly so unapologetic, they had to keep their offices overseas in London, where they declared their goods "conflict free" even though their origins usually couldn't be traced, and doled out gems to distributors in small amounts. Althea pictures the vault, underground and elusive, metal drawers lined with imperial blue velvet, opening soundlessly to reveal their treasures. She imagines the tall diamond baron with a pocket watch who slips into his vault on lonely nights to caress and count his jewels. As Valerie goes on about the misallocation of the world's resources, the flaw in the system that allows that place to exist, Althea nods but thinks if such a thing were hers, she would never give it up, either.

"Someone figured out a way to make diamonds in a machine," says Valerie. "Can you imagine? The technology's still rough, but maybe in another twenty or thirty years they can put De Beers out of business."

"I like your shirt," Althea says.

"I can make you one sometime. I still have the screen."

"Yeah?"

"Come over one day next week, when school's out." Valerie pauses in the middle of the hallway, tossing her empty soda bottle into a trash can several yards away. "Is Oliver the only person who calls you Al?"

"My dad, sometimes. His mom, sometimes. I try not to encourage the Al thing. People already think I'm a tomboy because I'm best friends with a guy. Having a boy's name doesn't help."

"You think there's something wrong with being a tomboy?" Valerie says.

Althea realizes she's made a misstep here, Valerie being something of a tomboy herself. "It's just not true. If I were a tomboy I'd probably be cutting school right now to go build a tree fort by the river. Which would be great."

"Mmm," says Valerie in a noncommittal tone.

Althea redirects. "So you're calling him Minty Fresh now, too?"

"He asked me to. Says he likes it better than Howard. He even changed the name of the band to Tartar Control," Valerie says. "Do you think Oliver's sick again?"

"I don't know. I haven't talked to him since the party."

"I'm sure he's fine. You're not worried, are you?"

Althea considers telling Valerie everything that happened on the walk home. Isn't that what most girls would do? Unfortunately, Althea is not well versed in sharing anything personal, and Valerie's the one person even less equipped to give advice about boys. "Not really," Althea says at last. "Maybe a little."

It's Nicky, not Oliver, who's waiting on the porch the next day, confirming what Althea has already surmised, that Oliver is asleep again, Oliver isn't coming. He misses those cherished last few days when the rigid structure of forty-minute periods erodes into polite anarchy, seniors visiting favorite teachers to say goodbye, other students emptying their lockers into garbage cans and returning overdue books to the library.

Without Oliver, Althea inhabits an awkward place. Too familiar now with his other friends to remain anonymous in her solitude, she watches from the outskirts of their circle as junior year comes to an end, listening to Minty Fresh and Valerie speak in their own best-friend pidgin while Coby observes her in this freshly vulnerable state. Plans are hatched to drink beer and attend Minty Fresh's band practice, but when they walk outside, Althea silently heads in the direction of her own car.

"Carter, aren't you coming?" Coby shouts after her.

She hates the way he calls her by her surname, that forced intimacy. "I can't," she says. Offering no explanation, she turns away.

It's Valerie who stops her. "Come on, Althea. It's the last day of school. You can't just go home." Leaning in, she lowers her voice so the others can't hear. "You know he won't be there. You might as well come with us."

Althea frantically calculates the ramifications of Valerie's invite. Where is this band practice? How long will this band practice last? To how many hours is she committing if she says yes? What is she supposed to do when she gets there, just sit and watch the band? If so, that might be okay, she could do that, but if not? Then what? Two, three, maybe four hours of beer and conversation—would it be so bad? Absolutely. It sounds profoundly awkward. She wants to go home, return to her sketchbook and her vigil.

On the other hand, when Oliver wakes up, she could have an actual story to tell him. He'd be so impressed that she'd willingly taken a solo ride on the Non-Stop Party Wagon. She could dazzle him with her newfound social skills; she could be new and improved for him. She thinks of her empty basement and all the time to kill before Oliver returns. Chewing a piece of hair, she watches Coby watching her, waiting for an answer.

Reaching into his shirt pocket, she pulls out his cigarettes. "Sure. Can I have one of these?"

Althea brings two generous slices of Key lime pie out to the gazebo, where Garth is making his way through a pitcher of sweet tea and a mass market paperback, its title spelled out in embossed red letters. A spy novel, not a mystery novel—she can tell by the submarine and the Soviet flag on the cover. He wears a white T-shirt and khakis, his long legs stretched out and crossed at the ankles. His left forearm is significantly more tanned than his right from resting on the open window of his car while he drives. His biceps are so white, they gleam.

"Guilty pleasure reading?" she asks.

"I don't believe in guilty pleasures. If you enjoy something, you just enjoy it. No sense feeling guilty about it. What's this?" he asks as she hands him a plate.

"It's pie. You know. For eating." She demonstrates by taking a bite.

Garth follows her example and makes a noise of delighted surprise. "Delicious."

"It better be. I think I gave myself carpal tunnel squeezing all those Key limes."

"Where did you even find Key limes?"

"I know a guy."

They eat. The gazebo falls quiet, except for their forks chiming against their plates, but elsewhere the neighborhood is full of summer's rich sounds: mourning doves and the humming of insects, the rubbery echo of a basketball bouncing in someone's driveway down the street. When the last bits of graham cracker crust have been pressed against their thumbs and licked away, Althea moves the plates to the floor and lies down with her head on her father's thigh, her leg dangling over the low wall of the gazebo, heel kicking against the wood.

"What happened to the visiting artist?" Althea asks.

"She was just visiting, remember?"

"There'll be another one next year."

"That there will." Garth sounds confident about his prospects.

"You're rich, right?" she says.

"Pardon?"

"I mean, we have money."

"Technically, I have the money, and you have the benefit of my continued good will. And we're not rich. We're comfortable."

A patch of clouds parts and sunlight streams through the slatted roof of the gazebo. Althea shades her eyes with her wrist. "How come you never take me anywhere?"

"Like to get ice cream?"

"Like someplace not in Wilmington. We always have the summers off together, but we never go away. Well, *you* go away, but you never take me with you. You just leave me here and tell Nicky to keep an eye on me."

"Did you see a commercial for Disney World and now you're feeling deprived because you've never been?" Garth shifts uncomfortably under her weight.

She sits up and gives him an accusatory look. "You're a history professor. Haven't you ever had the urge to show me Pompeii? Make me climb the steps of some Aztec temple so you could translate a bunch of pictographs and explain the details of their human sacrifices?"

Garth glances longingly at his paperback. "Althea, as appealing as all this father-daughter globe-trotting sounds, you never showed any interest in doing anything over the summer besides going to the beach with Oliver or camping out with him in the backyard."

"We could have taken him with us somewhere."

"He's not like a stuffed animal you could have packed into your suitcase. Nicky couldn't afford a big trip like that, and she never would have let us pay his way. She would have seen it as charity. You remember what happened when I gave him that telescope for Christmas? Can you imagine if we tried to take him to Europe?"

Glumly, Althea does remember. After his freakout over the inevitable end of the universe, Oliver had become fascinated by the night sky and started camping in the backyard with his star chart and listening to Garth's stories about the constellations— Cassiopeia, hanging upside down in her throne, heroic Orion, and of course their favorite, the twins, Castor and Pollux, the brightest stars of Gemini. He'd even joined the Cape Fear Astronomical Society, going to meetings at the Unitarian Universalist Church one Sunday a month to listen to guest speakers talk about the Hubble Telescope and the Magellan probe, and traveling to dark sky sites outside the city where the view of the stars was less obscured by light pollution. That Christmas morning, Althea and Oliver had both been awed by the telescope—even her brand-new skateboard had been momentarily forgotten when Oliver tore open the wrapping paper to reveal a present that must have cost Garth hundreds of dollars. Nicky had held up bravely in the moment, thanking Garth graciously and smiling when Althea opened her mosaicked picture frame. But in the months that followed, Nicky was more reluctant to accept Garth's invitations to take the four of them out to dinner, and quicker to reach for the check when she did, even though she was in the middle of working her way through massage school. Fortunately, Althea and Oliver were fast approaching the age where they were loath to be seen in public with their parents anyway, and the dinners became a thing of the past.

The following Christmas, Nicky allowed her parents to come down from New Jersey, and the stress of trying to cook a ham for them had nearly given her a breakdown. Oliver had escaped to Althea's in a panic after he overheard them trying to convince Nicky to move home, and Nicky's response that if she left the house where she had lived with Mack, it would be like he had never existed. Althea promised Oliver that they would run away before she ever let him be shipped off to New Jersey, a place for which Nicky felt such derision, it contorted her face just to speak of it. Later that night, after her parents had gone to bed, Nicky came over, too, exhausted from the battle with her parents and the ham, and the four of them had watched *Die Hard* in the basement and eaten an undercooked lasagna Althea had made herself. Their Christmas tradition reasserted itself after that, sans gifts from the adults.

"And you won't go anywhere without him," Garth concludes. "You stay here because that's what you always say you want."

"Well, now he's gone somewhere without me. And I'm stuck here without him. Can't you send me to Europe for the summer or something?"

Garth seems to soften, sipping his iced tea and watching her pick a piece of dead skin from her heel. "Where would you go?" he asks.

"I don't know. Which part do you think I would like?"

He stares out into the backyard, thinking for a moment. "Greece. One of the islands, maybe, so you could be near the beach and go swimming every day. A place where you could go exploring and there aren't too many people. I think you'd find all the history and mythology inspiring. You'd fill your sketchbook in no time."

"Great. Let's go right now."

"Girl, I'm not going to book two tickets to Crete knowing that if Oliver woke up tomorrow they'd go to waste." Althea doesn't contest this, instead admitting to its truth by staring at her feet. "Until you can stand to be separated from him, you'll have to amuse yourself here in Wilmington," he says.

"There're only so many times I can drive through the car wash."

"If you really want to go away, you could always go visit your mother. I'm sure she'd love to have you for a visit."

Althea cringes at the suggestion. "I'm not visiting her until she moves to a coast. I couldn't handle being landlocked with that woman."

Garth says nothing, unmoved either to defend or further

criticize his ex-wife. Althea wonders at his restraint. There is a moment of silence.

"What do you think it is? With Oliver. What do you think is wrong with him?" she asks.

"I don't know. It's like a fairy tale, or something mythological."

"It's too shitty to be a fairy tale."

"Come on now, you've read the Brothers Grimm. Fairy tales are unbelievably shitty. You know there's a version of 'Sleeping Beauty' where she's raped in her sleep? Al, you have to have a little more grit than this."

"I feel like a sucker," she says. "I feel like he's making a sucker out of me."

"He's not doing anything. He's just sleeping."

The sting of Oliver's rejection is just as fresh as it was the night of the party. "He's done plenty, believe me."

Althea doesn't really mean to pay Valerie a visit; she's just biking around town, and when she passes Val's house, there she is on the front lawn with Minty Fresh, washing a collection of enormous pots and pans with a garden hose. They wave at Althea and call her name, so she has no choice but to stop and dismount, carefully laying down her bike on the soggy grass. An old tape deck is balanced on the porch railing, blasting a punk rock anthem replete with bagpipes and electric guitars. Valerie dries the pots and pans with a large pink beach towel, stacking them in a rusty shopping cart.

"What's with the dishwashing?" Althea asks.

"We just finished our shift with Bread and Roses," Minty Fresh says. His jeans are astonishingly tight, like denim leggings cuffed over his combat boots.

"Since when do you guys care about feeding the homeless?"

"We thought it would be a good way to meet girls," Valerie says. "But now we like it."

"We get the food out of Dumpsters, bring it back here to cook, and then serve it in the park for free," says Minty. "You should come with us sometime. Oliver's always saying that you're kick-ass in the kitchen."

"Nicky's cooking has just lowered his standards," Althea replies. "You feed the homeless garbage?"

"It's not garbage!" Valerie protests vehemently. "You have no idea how much good food gets thrown away just because it stops looking perfect on the shelf in the supermarket. It's beyond all reason."

Coby emerges from inside the house. Standing on the porch, he lights a cigarette, then uses his Bic to pop the cap off his bottle of Fat Tire, oblivious as it clatters to the floor. When he sees Althea, he smiles, taking a long pull from his beer as he comes down the steps to greet her.

"Hey, Carter," he says.

She's not expecting a hug, but here it is, Coby's skinny arms around her, and honestly, it doesn't feel all bad. He smells like smoke and sweat and freshly shorn grass—like summer, a normal summer—but she takes a step back anyway.

"Hey," she says. "Don't tell me you've taken an interest in community service."

"Fuck a bunch of that. I came to have at the leftovers."

"Goddamnit, Coby," shouts Valerie. "I told you not to drink my dad's beer."

"He won't miss one beer," says Coby.

"Don't leave that bottle lying around for him to find; you'll get me in trouble."

"Am I allowed to put it in the recycling, or should I bury it out back?"

"How about you just shove it up your ass?"

"God, I really hate it when Mom and Dad fight," Minty says.

Althea reaches for her bike. "Well, I'm glad I stopped by."

Coby grabs her by a belt loop. "Hold up, you just got here."

Disarmed by his urgency, she ignores the way his fingertips graze the gap between her shirt and the waist of her jeans.

Minty finishes rinsing the last pot, watered-down split-pea soup sinking into the grass. He hands it off to Valerie, then wipes his hands on his pants and tenderly checks the vertical status of his Mohawk. "We have to go, anyway. Dumpster diving at the Food Lion."

Coby turns to Althea. "What do you say, Carter, you wanna go do something? I can toss your bike in the back of my truck."

"Go do what?" Althea asks suspiciously.

He pauses for a minute. He looks like he's thinking, like he's digging deep, like he knows it has to be good, that if he suggests video games or something equally pedestrian she'll snort and go home and that will be the end of the story. Then his eyes brighten.

"What?" she says.

"You know what? I'm going to make it a surprise."

Reluctantly, Althea allows herself to be led down the driveway to Coby's truck, an aged white Ford F-150 pockmarked with rust, and winces as he tosses her bicycle into the bed behind the toolbox. She settles herself in the passenger seat, which is covered in a fine layer of what appears to be silt; the cab reeks of stale cigarettes and pot. There's an empty can of Pabst in one of the cup holders. The radio is, naturally, tuned to the classic rock station, and REO Speedwagon sings "Take It on the Run" while Coby drives them farther away from the relatively civilized college town of Wilmington and deeper into what is just North Carolina. Althea snorts as they pass a pawn shop with a shiny orange banner out front that reads WE HAVE GUNS adjacent to a liquor store in a strip mall.

"Jesus Christ," she says. "Look at where we live." The more distance there is between her and the water, the more anxious she begins to feel.

They park at the end of a long dirt road. Coby reaches across the front seat and grabs a fifth of Old Crow from the glove compartment. He takes a slug and passes it to Althea, who follows suit and hands it back; then he slips it into the waistband of his pants. Together they hike silently up the road, shaded by a canopy of old elm trees. When they finally emerge, they're confronted by a hulking, skeletal structure four stories tall, with gaping holes in the brick walls where the windows used to be. Even in the middle of a sunny afternoon it's a disquieting sight, made more eerie by the silence. Althea has never seen this place before, but she recognizes it immediately from stories and pictures and the occasional newspaper article wondering when the decrepit death trap will be torn down at last.

"Is this the old meat-packing plant?" she asks.

"Yeah."

They have to climb up to get in through the first floor. Coby weaves his fingers together and boosts her up. Althea is staggered by the inside of the gutted building. It's as vast and silent as a cathedral. The floor is covered in crumbling bricks and cement rubble, and everywhere is the detritus of decades' worth of teenage exploration—spent cans of spray paint, empty beer bottles and broken glass, cigarette butts and used condoms. The walls are covered in layers of graffiti, an explosion of neon, illegible tags, proclamations of love, the occasional pentagram. Someone has drawn a wicked mouth with yellow teeth around a gaping hole in one wall. A flight of stark cement stairs stands in the middle of the room, leading dizzily upward, M. C. Escher on mushrooms.

"Pretty cool, right?" Coby says.

Althea nods.

"I know a guy who did some serious Satanic shit out here."

"Nobody actually worships Satan," says Althea.

They explore the first level, rooms beyond rooms, huge portions of the floor missing so they can look directly into the chambers of the basement. Althea wonders what they were for when the plant still operated.

"Want to go upstairs?" she asks finally, eager to see more.

"Let me go first," Coby says. "You have to be careful; there're all kinds of holes in the floor and shit."

She follows him up, trying to keep her eyes on her feet as they navigate the precarious staircase, her tennis shoes further pulverizing the little bits of cement that are everywhere. Coby reaches back, and after a moment's hesitation she takes his hand, just to be safe.

"This place has been here for ages," he says. "My dad's drug dealer—"

"Wait, your dad has a drug dealer?"

"He's like a family friend who happens to sell my dad pot. His name is Zorro. Anyway, he used to party here when he was in high school. Says he even knew a couple of kids who died here. The place is supposed to be haunted."

"Minty Fresh would say it's haunted by the spirits of all the animals that were slaughtered here," Althea says.

"Minty Fresh needs to get laid."

There are almost no walls left on the top floor at all, just the studs holding up the roof. Coby stands at the edge, looking out over the woods and drinking Old Crow. Althea takes another drink herself, then wanders off until she finds herself standing at the top of the old elevator shaft, staring all the way down into the basement.

When they were nine years old, Oliver broke his wrist. It was a rainy day and Althea was bored, so he suggested they build an obstacle course on the basement stairs, piling up soup cans and pots and stacks of magazines until the steps were covered in debris. They were going to take turns slaloming down on a flattened cardboard box. Seeing Althea's anxiety, Oliver volunteered to go first. After delicately navigating his way to the top, he waved fearlessly down at her, then took his position on the box and pushed off. A third of the way down, the cardboard snagged on an old shoe tree they had found in Garth's closet. Althea watched from the foot of the stairs as he tumbled toward her too quickly, end over end like a dislocated Slinky, coming to rest in a whimpering Oliver-ball at her feet.

After his wrist was set and Nicky and Garth gave them their respective lectures, Althea set out to break her own wrist. She tried smacking it repeatedly with a variety of household objects—a silver candlestick, a bottle of bourbon, a heavy glass ashtray—but it remained intact, albeit bruised. Eventually she found herself at the top of the stairs, screwing up her courage.

You can watch your best friend fall down the stairs, but you won't have any idea how it feels. Then suddenly you're the one going headlong into the basement and you realize, *So this is what falling down the stairs feels like*, and it couldn't feel any other way. She didn't break her wrist, but Garth found her in a similar heap at the bottom, with a gash under her hairline that required stitches.

There's nothing she can do now, no comparably stupid thing, that will help her understand what's happened to Oliver. She misses him, but if he were awake she wouldn't be here, wouldn't be seeing this incredible and terrifying place, so does that mean she has to be sorry for any good thing that happens while he's sick?

"Don't stand so close," Coby says, and only then does Althea realize her toes are gripping the uneven edge.

Coby is holding a brick, and for one wild second Althea imagines he intends to brain her with it, that maybe people worship Satan after all and she is meant to be his sacrifice today. Instead, Coby lofts it into the space above the empty elevator shaft, where it seems to hover in the air briefly before plummeting down to the bottom with a wickedly satisfying thud Althea can feel in her guts.

"There's more," he says, pointing to a pile in the corner.

They throw bricks into the shaft for a while, then climb up onto the roof and sit, legs dangling over the side, surrounded by the muted lushness of the trees, warmed by the summer sun. Coby produces the whiskey and a pack of cigarettes, and they both partake.

"I wish I'd brought my camera," Althea says.

"We can come back another day." He wipes the sweat from his forehead with the inside of his wrist and pulls up the sleeves of his T-shirt so they rest on his shoulders. "You're not as uptight as you seem, you know."

"I seem uptight?" Althea says, annoyed. Preppies are uptight; Althea is just angry.

He shrugs. "You used to. When I heard about how you quit the track team, just walking off the field, I was pretty impressed."

"How do you know about that?"

"Word got around. Why'd you do it, anyway?"

Althea doesn't know if it's the whiskey, but the idea of lying seems too exhausting. "I just couldn't do it anymore. I mean, literally. I could feel it. Whatever thing I used to have, it's gone. Like that." She snaps her fingers. "So I quit the team right there. Before anyone else could figure it out."

"You know there's a name for that."

Althea takes a long drag of her cigarette. "Losing?"

"Steve Blass disease," Coby says. "He was a pitcher for the Pirates. Out of nowhere he lost his ability to throw a baseball accurately. He went from the majors to the minors, then he retired."

"Steve Blass disease?"

"Sometimes they call it Steve Sax syndrome. He was a second baseman for the Dodgers when he started fucking up every throw to first. He got it back eventually."

"You know an awful lot about baseball," Althea says.

"I collected baseball cards when I was a kid."

"How wholesome."

"I don't know where people get the idea that baseball is wholesome," Coby says, flicking his cigarette butt off the roof. "Ever heard of Dock Ellis? He threw a no-hitter on acid once."

"They put that on his baseball card?"

"That's a series I'd like to see. Instead of runs and innings, list felonies and stints in rehab."

"It doesn't seem fair," Althea says. "That there can be a name for what's wrong with me, but not for him. For Oliver."

"There's nothing wrong with you," Coby says, reaching for the Old Crow again. "Things are just changing."

"I really don't mind," Althea reassures Nicky for the third time, watching from the couch as she flits around the living room locating her car keys and wallet, shoving everything into a fringed brown handbag that hangs down almost to her knees.

"I'll only be gone a couple of hours," Nicky says, crumpling a shopping list—Althea can make out *wine, gas, pasta sauce,* and *asparagus* crudely written in red Sharpie—and stuffing it in the back pocket of her jeans. "I've just never left him when he's like this. It makes me nervous, even with the alarm."

"Are you sure you don't want me to go instead?"

"Thanks, sweetie, but that's okay. It shouldn't take long."

Anxious as Nicky may be, Althea suspects she's also eager for a brief sojourn outside the house, an iced coffee, and low-impact chitchat with a perky cashier at the liquor store. All the windows are open and the curtains billow in the breeze, but the steady influx of fresh air can't outmatch the damage done by Nicky's chain-smoking and the wastebasket in the kitchen, overflowing with moldy coffee filters and the rotted husks of avocados. The most committed agoraphobe would be eager to run errands, too.

"There's not much left to eat, but go ahead and make yourself tea or lemonade or whatever else you can find," Nicky says. "I don't expect him to get up anytime soon; I woke him this morning to have some cereal and—well, you don't need the details. He should just sleep. Otherwise, I'll be back as soon as I can."

Taking off her shoes, Althea plants herself Indian-style on the sofa, fumbling for a nearby magazine—*Spirit of Change,* a holistic quarterly—as if to demonstrate how comfortable and settled she is and that Nicky is free to go. "It'll be cool. Don't worry."

Nicky hovers over the couch on her way out the door, worrying the frayed leather purse strap between her fingers. "Thanks for doing this."

"Not a bother."

Althea is surprised by how empty the house feels after Nicky leaves. Though she has never babysat, this is a lot like how she imagines it would be: a mother reluctant to part with her child; the sleeping charge; the place to herself and the time her own. In the movies, this is when the babysitter makes the clandestine call to her boyfriend, inviting him over for some hushed petting on the couch, but the only boy Althea has ever kissed is the one for whom she is temporarily responsible.

When Nicky called and asked for a favor, she didn't specify what that favor might be, and so now Althea is marooned at the McKinleys' without her sketchbook or pencils or any of the things she would normally need for entertainment. While the average babysitter might be content to search the master bedroom for clues to the inner life of its inhabitant, Althea already knows enough about Nicky, and the rest of the house is territory that's been well covered over the past decade. Every square foot is as familiar as Althea's own home: the spot on the carpet still slightly matted from an unfortunate Silly Putty incident; the tear across the framed thrift store seascape, where Oliver had thrown an unripe orange at Althea's head and missed; the pale brown stain on the underside of the very couch cushion where Althea now sits, the first casualty of her menstrual cycle.

She had been mortified nearly into shock that day, unable to answer when Oliver asked why she wouldn't come outside to ride her skateboard with him; why she, in fact, refused to move from the couch. When she finally revealed the source of her shame, he blanched—she saw it, the flicker of disgust on his face—but recovered quickly, leading her to the bathroom and the cabinet where Nicky kept her "you know, stuff," hiding Althea's soiled clothes in the bottom of the trash and lending her a pair of shorts. By the time she finished cleaning herself up, he had flipped the cushion over, hiding the last bit of evidence. "Can we go outside now?" he had asked. It was only later, when Oliver was in his room poring over the periodic table, that Althea had attacked the stain with dish soap, cold water, and paper towels, until at last it only looked as though someone had spilled a weak cup of tea.

This house holds only one mystery that interests her, and she's alone for barely fifteen minutes before she's drawn to it. Oliver's bedroom reeks; she can smell it from the hallway before she even opens the door. The window is cracked but the room is close, the hamper's odor barely stifled with rosewater and scented candles. And Oliver himself, pungent and jaundiced, sleeps in gray boxers and a dingy white T-shirt, arms around a drool-ringed pillow. His right leg is kicked behind him, his bare foot hanging off the bed, but his left knee is practically at his chin: a freeze-frame of a runner in motion, a single cell of animation out of context.

Despite his lack of social skills when he comes alive in these episodes, however strangely he inhabits his body, he at least can walk and talk. But asleep like this, breathing shallowly into his fetid pillow, unaware Althea is in the room, he does look—if not sick, if not ill, then at the very least unwell. Even though he's in here, a living, breathing person with dirt under his nails, sighing in his sleep and rolling over onto his back, the bedroom feels forlorn and desolate. The lamp shade is covered in dust pills and the tape on his *Freaked* and *They Live* and Weezer posters is coming undone, losing its stickiness in the summer humidity.

She squeezes her eyes shut and wills the alarm clock to go off, for Oliver to reach out and slap the snooze button and mumble about setting traps for the muskrats. And she would say, *Wake up, Ol, you're dreaming.* And he would say, *That's okay,* but he'd open his eyes anyway and say, *I had the weirdest dream,* and she would say, *Yeah, tell me about it.* He would be back in his body again.

Wresting the pillow from his grasp, she removes the filthy pillowcase and replaces it with a fresh one from his closet. As she slides it back under his head, he nuzzles her hand, smiling. She sits on the edge of his bed and strokes his greasy yellow hair.

She leans closer, moving her hand to his cheek. When she closes her eyes, she can see his face as clearly as if she were still watching him sleep. Every day, she sees him everywhere.

Like a fairy tale.

It had come out of nowhere, this unsettling, inexplicable thing, and every time Oliver went to a new doctor and told the story all over again, Althea thought guiltily of the part he didn't know—that it was when she realized she wanted him that he had first gotten sick, that as they were wrestling in the rain and she was imagining for the first time what it would be like to be pinned underneath him naked, his sickness was set in motion. And though she knew it was ridiculous to believe the two things were connected, they had arrived simultaneously—her desire, his exhaustion—both as mysterious and unshakable as any evil witch's curse.

She brings her lips to his, gently, and just for a moment.

There's no magic in it. He's not there. Feeling ridiculous, she pulls back, but stays where she is. If she went into the living room and tried to read *Spirit of Change* or go through Nicky's records, it would be only minutes before she found herself returning to this same spot. Even with Oliver unconscious, there's still no place she'd rather be.

Oliver opens his eyes. There's no warning, no twitching lids or soft murmurs to warn her. It's like the supposedly dead killer at the end of a horror movie abruptly coming to and giving the audience one final scare. Althea gasps.

"Jesus Christ." It worked. Did it work?

"I'm hungry," he says.

Not really. She had not succeeded in bringing back the real Oliver, only his fat-mouse doppelgänger.

"Your mom went to get you something to eat. She'll be back soon."

"But I'm hungry," he says.

"Soon."

"You look nice."

"You look like shit," she says.

His eyes are ringed with red, his face creased from the pillow, his white T-shirt pitted and ripe from the heat. It's not the real Oliver, but he feels real enough, and suddenly her joy is palpable at the sight of his dimples and his blue eyes, the patch of downy hair in the hollow of his throat, that divot of skin and bone she loves so much she would huddle up inside it, she would live there if she could. Stretching out next to him, she rests a finger in that spot and tries to pretend that everything is normal.

He lies there, staring at her. She flushes under his gaze, her hand rising instinctively to fumble with her hair. This is unexpected, to suddenly have his full attention this way, the intensity of his look unabated by their usual jokes and banter. The silence is so complete, it seems to encompass the entire block; she can't hear any of the summer noises that should be filtering in through the window.

He pulls her onto him so she is sitting up, straddling his waist. Working his hand underneath the hem of her shirt, Oliver meticulously traces one cold finger up her spine, slick with sweat. She feels him harden beneath her. He loiters over each vertebra, doodling around her bones with the tip of his finger, his chest rising and falling inside his soiled shirt. Althea is holding her own breath, unsure of what will happen when he reaches the base of her neck and finishes his game. She shivers but doesn't look away.

Cassandra-like, she can see what's about to happen before it does, but she's powerless to stop it. Althea's whole body is waiting for Oliver, and has been, and when he finally pulls her down her eagerness devours her guilt, leaving nothing but the crumbs.

It's a vicious kiss that meets her there, none of the hesitation or tenderness that was under the tree that night. It's greedy instead; they both are. In the past Althea has wondered: If she had never seen people kissing, would she have thought of it herself? She has never understood the instinct that makes a person want to take hold of someone else's head and try to get as far inside as possible; but here she is, whimpering for more of his sour, filmy tongue in her mouth, his hands skating up beneath her tank top, climbing her rib cage like a ladder to her breasts.

She thought she knew his body. Their wrestling matches and their naps—none of it prepared her for this, for discovering all the other parts of him she can finally, finally access. And she's always been stronger, but now under his weight, she understands how his boyness trumps her girlness, that he doesn't have to be stronger, he just has to be what he is now—hard-driven fingers and shoulder blades winging furiously inside his skin—and he would best her every time. He has a fistful of her hair and a mouthful of skin and she can't focus, can't think. Althea names his bones to herself as she runs her hands over them—scapula, clavicle, hyoid. Humerus and sacrum and mandible. This is no wrestling match, this isn't even really Oliver, she thinks, only his cranium, his femur, his radius. It's not Oliver pulling off her black cotton underwear, not Oliver inside her up to his knuckles as the medical terms all fall away.

She gets to work taking off his boxers, but he flips her over onto her stomach and pulls them off himself. Wedging his arm between her waist and the mattress, he grabs her hip bone and uses it to draw her closer, jostling her legs apart with his knees, and she lifts herself to meet him.

When it's finished, he strips the pillow and uses the fresh case to wipe the mess from the small of her back. This time it's up to her to hide the evidence.

She isn't bleeding. For some reason she always thought she would.

Oliver rolls over onto his back and she curls up beside him, head resting on his shoulder, her palm idly drifting across his stomach. She hopes he'll say something but he doesn't, so she closes her eyes and tries to ignore the way his breathing slows and deepens. He is already falling back to sleep.

"Ollie?" she whispers.

"Mmm?"

"Can't you wait? Just a little longer?" But she knows she's only talking to herself.

Later that week, Althea is dangling her feet off a dock above the river while Minty Fresh and Valerie swim in the water below. Coby sits beside her; she ignores him as best she can. Shirtless, he looks even skinnier. There's a slight concavity to his chest, a permanent slouch to his narrow shoulders, a fragility about his wrists and ankles.

"Get in here," Valerie yells up.

"I'm busy," she says, and she is, tending to a bottle of Fighting Cock and a cigarette, observing the others with the same casual, removed interest she might afford a group of strangers at a party while deciding whether to approach and introduce herself. The night is hazy but the moon is out, illuminating the water like a lightbulb through a sheet. Earlier that day, after watching *Rollerball* on cable, Valerie found two pairs of skates in her garage and decided she wanted to reenact her favorite scenes. She and Althea spent the afternoon wiping out and knocking each other down, skinning their knees and elbows, while the boys, shirtless, sipped sweet tea and sprawled out in lawn chairs, cheering them on.

"How you feeling?" Coby asks.

"Like I took a real beating," says Althea.

"What are you doing tomorrow?"

"Probably drive over to Val's and do it again." She dips her hand into the river and uses two wet fingers to snuff out the cherry of her cigarette. Water runs blue down Coby's legs, the hair straightened and pasted to his skin. For a second she's tempted to reach over and squeeze his thigh, just to watch him get hard inside his shorts, to drag him off into the woods or straddle him awkwardly in the backseat of her car or send Minty and Valerie away and do it right here on the dock. And then for the rest of her life, in dorm rooms, at dinner parties, she could lie and say that was her first time, something proper and suburban—the bottle of brown liquor, the boy who had wanted her for ages, the summer before her senior year of high school, losing her virginity under the stars with someone who would remember it later. *Why can't I have a do-over?* she wonders. *Why can't I have a stupid story like that one?* Slapping away a mosquito, Althea watches Val and Minty play together in the water.

"I know," says Coby out of nowhere. "They seem so virtuous sometimes."

"Minty Fresh has been leaving Bread and Roses pamphlets on my windshield when I'm not looking. Trying to get me to join up, spend the rest of my summer digging in Dumpsters and feeding the homeless. Whatever, I probably should."

Coby groans. "Don't. Why would you do something like that?"

"I don't know. Penance, maybe?"

"For what?"

Not wanting to share the extent of her sins with him, she searches for an answer that will satisfy. "For not being virtuous, like they are."

"Virtue is for pussies. I hope you're not losing sleep over this."

"What about you? Do you ever lose sleep over anything?"

"You know. The usual. Politics. I worry about global warming. The rain forests. Baby dolphins strangling in the plastic thing from one of my six-packs. Guilt over my support of the tobacco industry. That shit takes a big toll on me." He snickers.

"Come here. We're going to play a game."

"What game?" he asks, scooting over. "How do we play?"

She presses her left forearm against his right, sealing up any space in the middle. His skin is rough against hers, swathed in dark, bristly hairs.

"If you move first, you lose." She strikes a match. Dangling the flame for a second, she meets his eyes, daring him to beg off. There's no hesitation in his stare, just a greedy acceptance of the challenge. "Ready?"

"Go."

She drops the match into the shadowy crack where their arms meet. Instinct takes over and they both jerk away as soon as the fire hits.

"That was totally pathetic," Althea says.

"I'm embarrassed."

They wrinkle their noses at the smell of singed hair.

"Let's try that again," she says, lighting another one. He nods resolutely and extends his arm.

This time she is prepared for it—the white-hot sting of the initial landing, the flare of pain that follows as the match sears her skin. She inhales sharply, whispering a profanity and balling her other hand into a fist, pounding her thigh, ragged fingernails pressing into her palms as she squeezes her eyes closed, clenching every muscle in her body so tight she's afraid they could crack the very bones wrapped inside them. And then it's over—Coby has pulled his arm away, examining the spot where the flame erased his hair and a smart red welt has flowered.

She rests her forehead on her knees, laughing into her thighs. The pain in her arm worsens as the nerves realize what happened, but with the discomfort localized to one spot, the rest of her body feels loosened, stretched out, as if it's suddenly roomier. The relief is even more intense than the burning was. Adrenaline and alcohol mingle in her blood, singing a strident fight song. Her nose runs; she swipes at it absently with the back of her hand.

Breathing heavily, Coby puts a hand on her shoulder in an almost brotherly gesture. "Do you feel better now?"

"Let's do the other arm," she says.

Minty Fresh swims over, treading water right beneath the dock. "Get down in here," he says. "We'll baptize you. Cleanse you of your sins."

"I was baptized once," Coby says. "It didn't stick."

"What," Althea says, "you don't believe in God?"

"I believe in God. But I don't think he believes in me."

"That's about the saddest fucking thing I ever heard," Valerie yells, laughing, sweeping her arm across the surface of the river to splash the two of them on the dock, soaking the matches and rendering them useless. Setting the bottle aside, Coby dives in after her, leaving Althea alone to watch the others cavort. Minty Fresh glances back at her, something sad and knowing in his look. She wishes he did have the power to absolve her.

Coby's alcohol has failed to smother her senses. The woods are exceptionally loud, not just with her friends' shouting, but the vibrations of the crickets and cicadas, the resonating belches of the frogs, the whispers of the leaves overhead. The water shimmers beneath her feet, and across the river is a hinterland of blackness so dark it pulsates. Woozily lying back, she throws her burned forearm over her eyes.

"Are you okay?" Valerie asks, placing a hand gently on Althea's ankle.

Althea leaps up, sprinting off the dock and into the woods. They call for her—"What happened?" "Is she sick?" "Where did she go?"—shouting her name, pleading with her to come back.

The wind stings the raw, bloody skin on her knees and elbows and the fresh burn on her arm. The too-vivid world abruptly retreats, leaving her alone in the woods, claustrophobic with the understanding that she is going to be stuck in her own head forever.

She peels off her shirt and wriggles out of her shorts. The yelling has almost tapered off when she dashes out of the trees and down the dock like it's a runway and she's been cleared for takeoff, feet pounding the wooden planks, flying off the end and hanging in the air just long enough to hear them cheer before she plummets into the water, almost losing her panties on impact, river weeds tangling around her legs. The Cape Fear wraps around her. Underwater, everything is muffled and remote, and she wishes, she wishes she knew how to keep it that way. Althea sends this new wish out into the universe—that the peaceful emptiness she feels down here might last, that when she surfaces, when she climbs out of the river and back into the world, she'll still feel gone.

chapter four.

OLIVER CAN'T FIND his aviator sunglasses. The street looks blown out, overexposed, the hubcaps and fenders of parked cars shimmering maliciously. It's not just the bright light that pains him, but having his eyes open at all, having to see. He clenches one hand into a weak fist several times, trying to get used to being in his body again after so long—two months this time. Is he hungry? When was the last time he ate? In his rush to leave the house and get away from Nicky and her questions—she wanted to know how he was feeling before he had been awake long enough to divine the answer himself—he had neglected to shower or even brush his teeth, and now he's embarrassed by his sour smell, intensely aware of the rancid film in his mouth. His hair, normally so neat, has grown into a shaggy mess. He runs a hand over his cheek, where the blond stubble is verging on full beard; his nails, at least, seem recently clipped, but the thought of Nicky performing this chore while he slept is beyond mortifying. Slipping into Althea's backyard, he squints in the sun. There's movement in the gazebo, ice against crystal, the rustle of pages.

"Oliver? That you?" Garth looks up, surprised.

"It's me."

It looks like Garth's been planning on making a day of it. There's a stack of books about the Aztecs on the bench beside him, an errant mystery novel wedged into the middle, a pitcher of honey-colored sweet tea filled with lemon slices, and a plate of red velvet cupcakes within reach.

"You've got some setup out here," Oliver says.

"Welcome." Garth plucks a cupcake from the plate, arranges the rest in a neat circle, and offers them to Oliver.

"What are you working on?" Oliver indicates the books. "Is that for a class?"

"My next book, actually."

"What's it about?"

Garth slips effortlessly into professor mode. "Two Spaniards, Gerónimo de Aguilar and Gonzalo Guerrero. They were survivors of a shipwreck that landed them in what's now Mexico in the early 1500s. They were captured by the Maya and came very close to being sacrificed, but they were enslaved instead. Guerrero married, and he fathered some of the first mestizo children. When Cortés heard there were two Spaniards living among the natives, he sent for them. Aguilar came on as his translator, working in tandem with La Malinche, but Guerrero wouldn't leave his family. Of course, neither of them fully understood Cortés's intentions, at least not at first, but it didn't take long to realize what they were."

"So what happened?" Oliver asks.

Garth laughs. "It's Mexico now, isn't it?"

"I mean to the two Spaniards."

"You'll have to read the book to find out."

Oliver contemplates human sacrifice, trying to imagine it as something normal, like setting off fireworks on the Fourth of July. It's August now. He missed Independence Day this year. He wonders who won the hot dog eating contest.

"Where's Althea?" he asks finally, in a scratchy voice that doesn't sound like his.

"I think she's over at Coby's, hanging out."

Oliver bites angrily into his cupcake. How does Garth even know Coby's name? How did Coby come to exist in the universe of the Carter household? The cupcakes are Althea's work—rich and moist, minimal frosting, not too sweet, not too red. She hates to use food coloring, and for years she's been searching for a good recipe without it.

"You don't like him either," Garth says.

"Is it that obvious?"

"Your poker face hasn't improved much since you were six."

"So you've met him?" Oliver asks, surprised.

"Just once, briefly."

"And? What? Was he rude?"

Garth shakes his head. "He was oversolicitous. He seems— How to put this? I've seen it occasionally in my students. He seems not to understand how to strike the right tone with people, like he's either trying too hard or not hard enough. It makes one very aware that he isn't showing anything really of himself, which of course raises the question 'Why not?'"

"Because he's creeptastic."

"I thought he was a friend of yours?"

"Not really. He's the kind of guy who just keeps showing up until no one remembers who was friends with him first, so when you figure out that you don't like him, you don't want to say anything, because you're afraid you might offend whoever brought him along."

Garth sips his tea. "Well, Althea's going to be thrilled to see you. She gets lonely without you. I think this time it lowered her standard for company."

A deepening disquiet settles in Oliver's gut. Something's gone wrong. Everything looks the same—the azalea bushes, the tear in the back door screen, the loosely coiled garden hose tossed carelessly to the side of the driveway. Another late summer day has reached that imperceptible pivot, when the gasoline hum of lawn mowers and the delighted cries of children give way to the nuances of cicadas and the rhythmic hiss of sprinklers fanning lawns with manufactured rain. But there's something ominous about this placid afternoon. Oliver imagines he's woken up in a different world, a stranger, darker place than the one he left in June, and even as he tells himself this is ludicrous, he's already convinced it's true.

"Is everything cool?" he asks.

Their eyes meet. Garth pauses, a frosting-covered finger en route to his lips. A mourning dove calls from the highest branches of a nearby tree. For the first time Oliver can remember, Garth blinks first, and looks away.

They don't see him arrive, so Oliver is able to watch them from the ground, just the two of them, drinking a beer on the roof of the garage. Coby is wearing his I ♥ SOCCER MOMS T-shirt, a greasy lock of dark hair falling into his eyes. Althea's pant legs are pulled up above her knees, her long toes wrapped monkey-like around the edge of a shingle, black bra straps electric against her white wifebeater (could it be Coby's?) and her tan, tan skin. Oliver's sunglasses sit smugly on her face. She's dyed her hair black. She's too skinny. She's smiling at something Coby said.

Althea opens a book of matches. Pressing her arm against Coby's, she strikes one and lets it fall, clenching her fists, biting down on one knuckle. Oliver opens his mouth but can't speak. Coby shouts wordlessly, a string of vowels rigid with pain, pulling his arm away and letting the spent match fall to the roof. Althea draws in a ragged gasp, like someone who's been underwater for too long desperately breaking the surface.

"You win again," Coby says, picking up his beer.

Again?

Coby sees Oliver first; his shoulders slump even as he struggles not to let his disappointment show. Oliver wants to throw Coby off the roof of his garage. He wants to shatter the beer bottle in Coby's hand and use the shards of glass to slice him into pieces.

Following Coby's gaze, Althea turns her head. She lifts the sunglasses, blinking stupidly in Oliver's direction. He forces a smile, and she recovers, as if she's realizing that she's happy to see him, rising to her feet with such enthusiasm that Coby grabs the back of her pants to keep her steady on the pitched roof.

When she reaches the ground, she does exactly what Oliver had hoped she would do, which is wrap one hand around the back of his neck and pull him close. He presses his forehead against her shoulder. Even as he relaxes against her, she goes taut like piano wire in his arms. Coby gets blurry in the background. She smells like ChapStick and sulfur and burned hair.

"I've been waiting for you," she says.

He closes his eyes and Coby goes away altogether. "I got here as soon as I could."

When they finish their embrace, he's shocked to find himself looking down at her for the first time ever, her eyes no longer perfectly level with his, but a firm inch below them. Behind her new mess of black hair, she blinks, confused, then checks to confirm he's wearing his usual tennis shoes.

"The fuck?" she blurts out. "Am I shrinking?"

She grabs her messenger bag from inside the apartment and bids Coby a cursory good-bye, leaving him sulking on the roof. Oliver throws his bicycle in the back of the Camry while she gets behind the wheel.

"Punch it," he says, and she does.

Down by the water, they drink their coffee. Shoes abandoned, feet dangling off the dock. Althea lies back. Summer's not over yet, they haven't even started senior year, but she's already full of plans for Halloween, her favorite holiday.

"I was thinking Jack and Sally this year," she says. "I'll do some fake stitches around my neck, make myself a patchwork dress, and we'll get you a pinstripe suit at Goodwill. Or a topcoat."

"I don't want to wear all that whiteface. I hate makeup. If we do Jackie O and JFK, I just have to paint a bullet hole on my forehead."

"Yeah, but then I'm the one covered in blood. And I have to wear a wig."

"You have to wear a wig to be Sally, also," Oliver says.

"I can just dye my hair orange." She tugs absently on his belt loop and he grabs her skinny wrist. He runs his thumb along her fresh burn, blistering and slick. There are other burns that have faded, bruises old and new. It's Coby he suspects is at fault somehow, Coby he imagines as the cartoonish red devil that spent the summer on her shoulder, poking her with a pitchfork, growling in her ear, egging her on while Oliver slept, wrapped in his white sheets.

Althea removes the plastic lid from her cup so she can chew on it. Sometimes hanging out with her is like playing Whac-A-Mole; even as one tic is suppressed, another rises to take its place.

"Go ahead. Have a cigarette," Oliver says fatalistically. She pulls out a pack of Marlboros, takes her time with the chosen smoke, making sure the paper isn't torn and tapping the filter a few times on her book of matches. Oliver is sad to see how expertly she shields the flame from the wind, how she inhales and exhales with ease, like he always knew she would. "Since when do you hang out at Coby's?" he finally asks.

She shrugs. It's getting dark, but his sunglasses are still atop her head, the same glasses he searched for only to find that she had had them the whole time, wearing them while she was at the beach and drinking beers on Coby's roof. It infuriates him that his stupid sunglasses saw the summer he slept through. He imagines her lifting them from his dresser, thinking he didn't need them anyway. He snatches them off her head, as if by doing so he could get this tiny piece of summer back. A flyaway lock of her hair catches in the hinge.

"What the shit?" she says.

"These are mine, you know."

"I know they're yours. I was going to give them back."

"What happened to your arms?" Althea flicks the rest of her cigarette into the river. Pulling her knees to her chest, she wraps her arms around her legs, lowering her head. The fear he felt in the gazebo runs through him again, stronger this time. "Why won't anyone tell me what's going on? You're being all cagey, Garth was acting weird—"

Althea's head snaps up. "You saw my dad?"

"—and I don't understand why I woke up in the fucking Twilight Zone and no one will tell me what the hell happened!" Oliver yells.

"Ol, I know you're upset—"

"Don't do that. Don't act like I'm making it up," he says wearily. "Don't do that to me."

"You've been asleep for *two months*!" she shouts. "Of course everything seems all fucked up! It's not surprising that when you go to sleep in June and you wake up in August, it's not a seamless transition. It doesn't mean there's a Wilmington-wide cover-up with you at the center."

"Humor me. For once," he says harshly.

"I promise, okay? In a couple of days you'll feel better and everything will go back to the way it was before and it'll be like it never happened." Reaching into her back pocket again, she pulls out her cigarettes and flings them into the river. "See?"

They sit, both curled into angry balls, listening to the water lapping against the dock. Edging closer, she puts her arms tentatively around his neck. "It must be awful," she says.

Relenting, he returns her embrace, and they huddle together in the dwindling purple light. "I missed my birthday."

"I'll make you a cake," she says.

"I missed your birthday."

"It rained."

"It's like a joke," he says. "A total fucking joke."

Holding her, he remembers the walk home from the party; so recent those memories are to him—her laughter in his ear, her eyelashes against his cheek. And the stupid thing he'd said after, that he'd done it because he was drunk. It's here again today, that same tugging want, making everything just a little more goddamn confusing.

"So is Coby, like, your boyfriend now?" he asks her.

Althea laughs. "Christ, no. You haven't been asleep *that* long."

Oliver knows it's not normal that he's never had a girlfriend, that she's never had a boyfriend, that they never even talk about what it would be like. To talk about sex would have inevitably drawn attention to the possibility that they might someday have it with each other, or that they would someday belong to other people. The territory was just too dangerous. Still, Althea's answer fills him with enormous relief.

"I hate your hair," he says.

"You need a shower."

"I just want everything to go back to normal."

"I know."

Nicky cooks for him that night, or tries to, coating chicken breasts in flour and capers and lemon juice, singeing the kale around the edges and scraping burnt jasmine rice out of the bottom of the pot. Typically, when she ties on an apron, Althea is around to avert these minor disasters, readjusting the burners on the stove while Nicky is waist-deep in the fridge hunting for the chardonnay, or adding black pepper and paprika to whatever pan needs it when Nicky turns her back to put on another album by the Replacements, but Althea has bowed out of this meal, perhaps wisely. As Nicky moves around the kitchen she speaks wistfully of New York: her old stack of takeout menus, scallion pancakes and shrimp dumplings delivered in the middle of the night, floppy slices of pizza so cheap you could pay for them with the change in your pocket.

"People talk about how expensive New York is," she says as they carry their plates to the front porch. "But you can still get two slices and a root beer for five bucks. It's about all you can get for five bucks, but, you know."

This is when he normally inquires about her former life in the city, listens to her wax nostalgic about Alphabet City and the early days of rock and roll. She's told these stories many times, about dinner parties thrown in cramped walk-up apartments and stifling summers spent on the beach at Coney Island, and he can imagine it all perfectly—Nicky in some red gingham sundress with her hair pulled back in a bandanna serving red wine in plastic cups, or napping on a towel with a Corona in her hand and a copy of *Pride and Prejudice* open across her face. And always in the background of these stories his father hovers, a blue-eyed phantom sharing cigarettes with Nicky on the fire escape, drinking her lemonade on the beach. He imagines their laughter as a breathing, perpetual thing. Oliver looks down at his plate. His father must have done all the cooking.

"The soccer team started practices already," Nicky says, "but I can call Coach if you want."

Oliver shakes his head. "Don't bother."

"Are you sure?"

"I'm in no shape for sports. No point in spending the fall on the bench."

"Did you find Althea this afternoon?" Nicky asks, cutting her chicken into tinier and tinier pieces.

"She was at Coby's," he says with distaste.

"Why didn't she come over for dinner?"

"She said she didn't want food poisoning." He digs at his plate for a decent bite of rice.

"What did you think of her hair?"

"You've seen it?" Oliver moves on to the capers, trying to spear them with his fork.

"I see everything."

"Have you seen her around much?" he asks.

"Here and there." Nicky turns her attention from her food to her wine.

"Does she seem different to you?"

"I'm not sure the black hair suits her."

"If you know something, could you please tell me? Because I've had this really bad feeling since I woke up today, and no one is giving me any straight answers, and Garth was acting funny when I went looking for her, and I just want to make sure that she's okay."

Nicky doesn't answer right away. "Why are you so worried about her?"

Oliver thinks of the burns on her arms. And of Coby. "I didn't say I was worried."

"Are you jealous?" she asks delicately.

This gives him pause. "Is that what that is?"

"Could be." She smirks into the mouth of her wineglass.

"Was I an accident?"

Nicky almost drops the glass. "Are you serious?"

"You were what, like, twenty-one when you had me?"

"I was twenty-two, and no, Ol, you were not an accident. You were—you were a very pleasant surprise." She smiles.

"Do you ever wonder—"

"No. I never wonder. About anything. Except why I can't cook. Sometimes I wonder why I can't make my son a decent meal. But that's it."

"Why didn't you have me in New York?" he asks.

"Why are you suddenly so interested?"

"I just am."

Nicky stares out at the lawn, watching the intermittent spark of fireflies. "We could have stayed in New York. I've heard a lot of stories about couples in small apartments turning dresser drawers into makeshift bassinets and stuff like that. All our friends were there. Sarah was there. Jimmy, too—he was already on the scene then. He really didn't want us to go. But we didn't want to stay and be the novelty act, the super-young married couple with the baby still living on Avenue B and trying to be cool. Our life was parties and shows and friends, going out all night and then watching the sunrise from our fire escape. We knew if we tried to shoehorn a baby into that, we'd be setting ourselves up for a lot of disappointment. I wanted to focus on you and Mack, and not be thinking about all the things we couldn't do anymore. So we left. We got to be pioneers. We struck out for new territory." She waves away a mosquito.

"Why Wilmington?" Borrowing her orange Bic, he lights the citronella candle on the table.

"When you live in New York City, you think every other place is the same, this big, generic landmass of Not-New-York. We'd been here once, just for a weekend, to visit some friend of his at UNC, and we liked it here. It seemed as good a place as any."

"Did everyone think you were crazy?"

"They thought we were totally fucking insane. I would have, too, if Sarah had told me they were moving down south to have a baby. Mack came home one night after drinking with Jimmy, and he had all these little notes scribbled on a cocktail napkin, and he was like, 'Okay, check it out. I did the math. We have this kid now, and by the time he's eighteen and out of the house, we'll barely be forty. We'll still be cool. And we'll have gotten the kid thing out of the way. It's really more practical, when you think about it.' It was the Californian in him, so laid-back about shit. You definitely get that from him. In some ways he was totally right. We got our shit together way before any of our friends, had a kid and bought a house and did all those grown-up things when everyone else was still sleeping around and spending their rent money on records and acid and tequila. And we had a good time doing it, you know, until he died. We were lucky for years, and then we weren't."

It had been a clever plan, and most of it had come to pass. Nicky was still cool and not even forty. Child-raising and home ownership had been checked off her list of life goals, and those years Mack had promised they would find on the other side now stretched out before her. There was just one thing missing.

Oliver squeezes another lemon slice over his kale, trying to cover the flavor of burnt wok.

"You don't have to bother. I know it's inedible," she says.

Relieved, he sets down his fork. He wishes he had another red velvet cupcake.

Nicky hands him a stack of mail. College brochures. "These came for you over the summer."

Oliver flips through the catalogs, replete with images of glorious foliage and students in repose on vast, meticulously manicured lawns. "Where are the ones from UNC?"

"Come on, Oliver, you can do better than a state school."

"We can't afford any of these."

"Let me worry about that. We can figure something out."

He looks with longing at the pictures of MIT and RPI, the well-appointed laboratories, formulas written on dusty green chalkboards. Mack's parents have been pushing for Caltech, hoping to get him out on their coast so they can finally spend some serious time together, but he's transfixed by the idea of New England, crisp autumn breezes and snowy afternoons in the library. He sighs and pushes the pile back across the table toward his mother.

"It's not happening," he says.

"You can't give up, Ol—"

"How am I supposed to go away to college like this? We spend all that money and then, what, just hope I don't sleep through the semester? If I go to school at all, it'll be here. I'll have to live at home and go to Wilmington. Go Seahawks."

"Wilmington doesn't even have an astronomy program."

He shrugs.

"How would you like to go to New York?" Nicky asks.

"What for?"

"I got a call this week from a doctor there."

"I don't want to go back to the doctor. It never does any good."

"This is different. He says he knows what you have."

The front door is open; they can hear the Zombies album on Nicky's stereo. Across the street, Mrs. Parker's television flickers like blue candlelight behind her tightly closed curtains. "What does he say I have?" he asks.

"Kleine-Levin Syndrome."

He wants Valerie to silk-screen those words onto a shirt that he can wear every day, or engrave them onto a pair of dog tags, or print them on a button he can pin to his backpack. He wants an artifact, something tangible, something he can point to the next time his temperature rises and his joints start aching and that sinister fatigue becomes the focal point of his entire being. And then he can say, *I'm not making this up. I'm not on drugs, I'm not crazy, I'm not pretending. This is real. I'm just along for the ride on the Non-Stop Sleeping Wagon, and the only rule is I can't say no.*

"Do you think he's right?" Oliver asks. "Do you think that's what it is?"

"I'll show you," Nicky says, and ushers him inside to the living room, where she pops a tape into the VCR. "There was a piece on CNN a few years ago. They sent me a copy of it."

She puts her arms around him, kissing the top of his head. Then she points the remote at the television and hits play.

A teenage boy wrestles with his dog in a backyard while the reporter's voice-over sets the scene with the usual cheesy intro—just an ordinary kid, everything was fine, until one day, it all changed forever.

"I just got so tired," the boy says, describing how his first episode began with an urgent nap on the linoleum beneath his locker at school.

"His teachers thought he was on drugs," says his tearful mother, seated next to the sympathetic father. "But we knew that wasn't our son, he wouldn't do that. We knew it had to be something else."

"She's lying," Nicky says, lighting a cigarette. "Of course they thought it was drugs."

"Should I get you some popcorn?" Oliver asks.

"Can you believe they let her wear those jeans on television?"

"Shush."

The parents elaborate on the strange behavior that occurred during their son's ten days of near-constant unconsciousness, the eating and confusion and childlike regression. Oliver feels a sharp stab of recognition, like the excitement of discovering another person who loves your same obscure favorite band. This is him, without a doubt, this is what he has, and he's not the only one after all.

The family gives a litany of the misdiagnoses and describes the despair of watching the episodes return every few weeks.

"*Every few weeks?*" Oliver shouts.

They had filmed their son while he slept, hoping it would help the doctors better understand. There's a lot of time-lapse footage of the boy in bed, occasionally rolling over in his sleep. During one of those strange waking hours he wouldn't recall later, they filmed him sitting on the floor of their living room, rocking back and forth and babbling a series of incoherent syllables, blank eyes unseeing while his parents ask him a series of innocuous questions—*Where do you go to school? What's the dog's name?*—that he obviously has no hope of answering. Later, when he's back in bed, his mother tries to wake him up to eat some dinner and he slaps her across the face. Oliver, who had been mortified by the Waffle House debacle, where only a dozen other patrons witnessed his tantrum, is enraged on behalf of his fellow sufferer, whose fat mouse has been broadcast on national television. Still, he can't stop watching. So this is what he's like.

"This is him," Nicky says as the video cuts to a young Latino doctor with curly, exhaustively gelled black hair and a warm smile. "That's the guy in New York."

"No wonder you want to go up there and meet him."

"Give me a break."

The doctor, identified on-screen as Dr. Crespo, describes what is known about Kleine-Levin Syndrome, which, it turns out, is almost nothing. It affects mostly teenagers, and among those, mostly boys. He reiterates the symptoms, addresses the debate of whether it's a sleep disorder or a neurological condition, and then casually mentions that while there is no cure, most patients "either outgrow the episodes or experience a marked reduction in their occurrence once they've reached adulthood."

"Wait a second," Oliver says, pausing the tape. "He can't stop it?"

"Don't you want to watch the rest?"

"Your boyfriend Dr. Curls just gave away the ending. There's no cure? Nothing he can do?"

"He says he's putting together a study in the fall with other kids that have the same thing. At a hospital in the city, St. Victor's. He thinks you'd be a good candidate. He can't stop it altogether, but they might be able to find a treatment, something that would shorten the episodes, lengthen the amount of time between them. I'd have to talk to the insurance company and fill out some paperwork, but I think I can get you in."

"How long would I be there?"

"A couple of months, maybe."

"Two months in the hospital?" he asks. "No way."

"If we can't get you some help, before this time next year

you'll lose another two months anyway. Dr. Curls there"—she points to the TV—"is your best shot."

"I don't care." Oliver shakes his head.

"You say you don't care, until it happens again."

"Maybe it won't happen again."

"You believe that?"

"I have to. Otherwise I'm just waiting for the next time."

Nicky stands abruptly, storming back out to the porch to collect their dishes. She scrapes his uneaten food onto her plate. What's left is enough for a full meal. He hates when she gets like this, her patience suddenly evaporating without warning.

"What?" he says, following her into the kitchen.

She dumps the dishes in the sink. "I'm glad you can be such a little Zen master about this. I'm glad you can still worry about things like Althea's hair color and who she might be sleeping with. I myself am a bit preoccupied these days. I am wired to think about nothing other than what's wrong with you. I am incapable of doing anything besides waiting for the next time you go off the air and I have to sit here for weeks, incapable of doing anything besides waiting for it to be over. So I don't care, Oliver, if you want to see more doctors or not. You'll see all the fucking doctors I want you to and yes, you'll go to a hospital in New York so that eventually we can both have the luxury of thinking about other things."

"Yeah, I know, I'm supposed to be out of the way by next year so you can get on with your life. I apologize for the inconvenience. I don't want to mess up the schedule," he says.

"Don't be spiteful," she says.

"We have to make sure you get your chance to have all that

fun you missed. I hope Sarah still knows where to get acid."

All of Nicky's facial muscles freeze, but when she speaks, her voice is trembling. "I thought this was good news. I thought you'd be excited."

"Because a doctor I've never met says I have a disease he can't cure? What's so exciting about that? How do you even know he's a doctor? He looks like a starting forward for Real Madrid," Oliver shouts on his way out the door. "All he did was give it a name."

Althea doesn't look surprised to see Oliver knocking on the basement window. She gestures for him to come in and he gestures for her to come out.

Bring your car keys, he mouths, overenunciating so she'll understand.

She doesn't argue, doesn't ask why, just meets him in the driveway five minutes later and hands him a sweatshirt.

"What's this for?"

"In case you get cold. Where are we going?"

"We're running away."

"Cool."

If Oliver had to pick one spot as something approximating his proper place in the world, it would be the shotgun seat of Althea's car. As she threads their way out of the neighborhood and onto the highway, he feels he is right where he belongs. He hates driving, but he loves being a passenger, the whisking sound of the road beneath the tires and the blurry, intangible scenery that fades before it can even register. Like the rest of the world, the Camry is subject to the whims of their imaginations—it can be a pirate ship or a roller coaster or a subway train hurtling toward Coney Island—but tonight Althea makes it exactly what he needs it to be: a white noise machine. She says nothing as she drives, and there's nothing charged about her silence, nothing that implies she is waiting for him to start doing the talking. At night, with no traffic, her impatience behind the wheel vanishes, and it seems to him that she could drive like this forever as long as he were sitting to her right.

Althea pulls over at a rest stop, a stout brick building filled with restrooms and vending machines, with a few picnic tables on the side of the road. It's deserted except for them.

"How's this?" she says, as if it had been their destination all along.

"Perfect."

He expects her just to turn the car around and go back, but instead she kills the engine and gets out, gesturing for him to follow. They lie on their backs on one of the tables. The sky has clouded over and there's nothing to see in the way of stars, but the air is fresh against his face and even the wooden planks of the table feel good, like they're straightening out a kink in his spine. They can't be more than thirty miles from home, but he can't remember the last time he's even been that far. It's still out here, the world beyond Wilmington. It hasn't vanished due to lack of interest on their part. He reaches across the table and takes her hand.

"Why did you dye your hair?" he asks.

"So people would finally be able to tell us apart."

He laughs until she joins in. It's the exact right answer. They both know he isn't ready for a real one.

chapter five.

ALTHEA HAS AN IDEA.

"Hey, Ol, do you have more of those pills?" she asks.

"Which ones?"

"The round ones. Sort of linen-colored."

Valerie and Minty Fresh prick up their ears like terriers.

"Pills? Yes, please." Coby looks at Oliver expectantly.

Oliver shrugs and digs dutifully through his backpack to retrieve the small orange bottle. Their inability to provide Oliver with a proper treatment for KLS has not stopped the good doctors of North Carolina from prescribing him a plethora of amphetamines and stimulants. In high school, pills are a currency better than money, and Oliver generously shares his bounty, holding out a handful like candy, watching the others eagerly devour them as such. Althea washes hers down with the Southern Comfort Coby is toting around in an iced tea bottle.

Down at Lucky's, Minty Fresh and Valerie have put together a Halloween punk show to raise money for Bread and Roses. The flyer Althea designed has been taped to every telephone pole in Wilmington. Althea and Oliver have decided on post-assassination Jackie O and JFK, figuring there will be plenty of Goth kids who love wearing makeup dressed as Jack and Sally. At Goodwill, they picked out a pink suit for Althea and the perfect tie for Ol, promptly dousing both in fake blood. Her hair is tucked under a brown flip wig, and there is a bullet hole painted on his forehead. Val and Minty are dressed as the farmers from *American Gothic*, although his Mohawk is razor-thin, six inches high, and formidable. The parking lot is filled with kids masquerading as the obvious—zombies, skeletons—and yes, as suspected, the cast of *The Nightmare Before Christmas* is out in force. For a lot of the girls, it is the first year they've realized that Halloween costumes are a clever excuse to show up to a party half-naked. There are lots of Wonder Women in metallic tube tops and Betty Boops tottering around the parking lot in red minidresses and stiletto heels.

"Look at that shit," Althea says, as a French maid in Doc Martens bends over to tie her shoelace, giving everyone a good look at her underwear. "She's flashing her fancy stuff all over the place. My father would have a heart attack."

"You look positively upstanding in comparison," says Valerie.

"I don't know about that," Althea says, smoothing her blood-soaked skirt. "But at least my business is covered."

It's another clear, warm night; stars are coming out in the navy blue sky, and a breeze blows through the parking lot. Bands are loading in their gear, and kids are handing out homemade stickers and flyers for upcoming shows; plans for after-parties out by Seagate and Silver Lake are passed between groups of friends along with flasks and packs of cigarettes. Leaning against Althea's car, they take turns drinking from Coby's bottle until it's empty, and he tosses it into the woods.

"What do y'all feel like doing after the show?" Minty asks.

"I don't know about you guys," Oliver says, "but I feel like solving a mystery or something."

Inside Lucky's, someone hits a chord on an electric guitar. The sound draws the parking lot dwellers inside. It's really Minty Fresh's show, and as they follow him in, people wave and call out his nickname. He gets onstage to introduce the first band, dragging Valerie up with him so the crowd can fully appreciate their costumes. He holds up a broom instead of a pitchfork, and the kids all cheer as he thanks them for supporting Bread and Roses.

"Holy shit," Oliver shouts at Althea. "Do you realize that Minty Fresh has become, like, their leader?"

"Right?"

The first band is terrible but spirited. They call themselves the King Dorks. Every member is adorned with a pocket protector and a crown from Burger King, and they play for about twenty minutes. Each subsequent band is slightly more adept at their instruments, although for the most part the songs all sound the same—short, fast, deafeningly loud. There's no emcee or announcer between bands, just hurried chaos as one band rushes offstage while the next is setting up, nervously tuning their instruments while someone tries to uncoil a cable from around their legs.

When Minty's own band, Tartar Control, comes onstage, he doesn't rush through his mic check or sneak worried glances at the audience. A girl at the back of the club—definitely not Valerie, the voice is too shrill—yells "Minty Fresh!" with a buoyant whoop. He chuckles quietly without looking up from the set list he is toeing into place with his Converse, as if random girls scream out his ridiculous nickname all the time. The electric-blue Mohawk that looks so outsized bobbing down the hallways of their high school is perfectly at home onstage. The members of Tartar Control have not mastered their instruments, but their leader's new confidence gives their raw sound just enough polish to elevate them, slightly, above the rest of the mediocre musicians onstage tonight.

Minty doesn't play so much as he performs—wisely, he no longer employs a British accent, but he still has a hard time looking up from his guitar, so sometimes he just lets it hang around his neck like an afterthought, grabbing the mic stand and leaning toward the audience, or pointing a finger accusingly in their direction, or gesticulating the way he does when he's standing in front of his locker telling a story. The crowd surges toward the stage, reaching for him the way he's reaching for them.

It doesn't take long for the pill and the liquor to dovetail inside Althea, unbuttoning her diffidence like a blouse and casting it aside. She dances, wig shaking, arms held over her head, ricocheting off her friends, who form a tight circle around her. Toes crushed inside her thrift store heels, her calves ache as one song bleeds into the next, and for a while, seventeen years of the cringeworthy moments that plague her incessantly—a wrong answer she gave in math freshman year, the solution so obvious the whole class snickered; a school-yard retort falling flat by the handball courts; an unduly loud laugh brayed out a second too late; the doomed kiss under the sugar maple tree; and, of course, that afternoon in Oliver's bedroom, the awful secret she can't quite bring herself to regret—are silenced. Pressed against him now, dressed like his wife, she knows that tonight they look not like twins but like a couple, and if any night is for pretending, it's this one, so for a little while at least that's what she'll do, pretend that it's real and that she did no wrong, and so all these miserable snippets that repeat and repeat and repeat are blessedly, briefly silenced by the throbbing of the crowd and Althea's frenetic movements within it as Tartar Control arranges and rearranges the same three chords with a stalwart driving momentum.

And then it's over. Minty thanks the audience and the band starts packing up their equipment, coiling cables and breaking down the drum kit, the rattle of the cymbals a weak echo of the previous moment's din. The throng of people loosens around Althea, making her abruptly unsteady on her feet, her forearms goose-pimpling from the sudden drop in temperature. The house lights brighten and Lucky's starts to clear out, and some-how she has lost Oliver. Valerie brushes past, fighting against the flow of traffic, followed by a tiny girl with bleach-blonde hair and a septum ring, wearing a dress made from a faded Rainbow Brite pillowcase.

"Come on," Val says as she passes. "We're going to find Minty in the back."

Walking away, she holds one arm out behind her, its wrist covered in black rubber bracelets. Only when the pillowcase girl reaches for Val's hand does Althea realize it wasn't meant for her.

The girls' fingers intertwine, tipped with matching glittery nail polish. They stay close as they maneuver through the remains of the crowd.

"Have you seen Oliver?" she shouts after Valerie, but she's already gone.

Coby taps her shoulder. Holding two fingers to his lips, he nods toward the door. Hesitating, she looks around the club one more time, trying to spot the only boy here who is wearing a tie.

As they walk toward her car, Coby lights two cigarettes and hands her one. Sweat runs in tendrils at the top of his forehead. He's not discernibly in costume, although he is unusually spiffy, dark hair freshly washed and parted down the middle, wearing a black button-down shirt and khakis. "What are you supposed to be?" she asks. "A date rapist?"

"I'm not supposed to be anything," he says.

"Shouldn't you be chatting up one of these half-naked girls?"

He shrugs. "I've already slept with half of them."

Althea watches the entrance, hoping to see their other friends getting ready to leave. Jason, ill-fated host, is sitting on the open tailgate of his pickup drinking a beer, surrounded by a group she vaguely recognizes from the party at his house. When Oliver finally emerges, she instinctively drops what's left of her cigarette, coughing out a last lungful of smoke. Just as he spots Althea and Coby over by her car, the French maid grabs his arm and starts talking.

"Who the fuck is that?" Althea says.

Coby tsks. "She's a pigeon."

"A pigeon?"

"She's an extra," he says. "Etcetera."

"If she's etcetera, why is Ol talking to her?" she asks.

"Althea, you're the First Lady. She's the help. I wouldn't sweat it. I'd be more worried about Jason, if I were you."

"What about Jason? That was ages ago. He doesn't know who was in that bathroom."

"That's not what I heard."

She can't look away from Oliver and the maid, noting with some satisfaction that he is eyeing the corner of the parking lot where they are waiting. Maybe she's deluding herself, but it seems like he's trying to edge his way out of the conversation. "What did you hear?"

"That it's hard to be discreet when you're jumping out a window. How do you think I know about it? It's not like you ever told me."

"If Jason knows, he knows," she says. "I don't see what he can do about it now."

Finally Oliver breaks away and heads toward Althea's car.

Coby shakes his head and lights another cigarette. "It wears me out sometimes, watching you watching him. What's going to happen if this doesn't go your way?"

Her entire body can feel Oliver's approach, like he's a magnet and she's a collection of iron fillings that needs him to hold her together. Or maybe that's just the pills. What she doesn't tell Coby is that she suspects she has already lost. It's been months since that night under the tree, months since he's woken up, and still Althea and Oliver have never spoken of it, and—outwardly, at least—his wish for normalcy has more or less come true. They go to school. They take the SATs. They go to shows. They watch movies in her basement on rainy nights and listen to Garth's stories. They eat pizza in Oliver's living room with Nicky, drinking cream soda from old salsa jars and playing her records. Althea isn't stupid. She knows about Occam's razor. If Oliver wanted to kiss her again, he would do it. But here she is, dressed as Jackie O to his JFK, laying it all on the outside chance that he might sleep with her again, for real—just once would be enough—so that she might finally stop feeling like she had stolen something from him she could never give back.

Coby is still waiting for an answer.

"Anarchy," she says.

He tucks his pack of cigarettes into the pocket of her suit jacket. "Maybe you'd better hang on to these," he says, just as Oliver arrives.

"I think we should get going," Oliver says. "I don't like the look Jason was giving me over there."

"What about Minty and Val?" asks Althea.

Jason separates from his friends and begins crossing the asphalt toward them.

"Let's just go," Oliver says. "We can catch up with them later."

"I don't know what you think he's going to do in front of all these people," she says, searching for her keys.

Coby glances at Jason, walking unhurriedly in their direction. "I heard he was pissed. His dad really nailed his ass to the wall."

"How Dickensian." Jabbing her key at the handle of the door, she sways on her feet.

"Forget it, Carter. I'm driving." Oliver relieves her of the keys.

"But I hate the way you drive."

"So do I." Reaching down to open the door, he stops. "The fuck? Al, did you see this?"

As Jason finishes his languid stroll across the parking lot, Althea sees the key scratches down the length of her car, deep, intentional gashes in the silver paint, beginning above the front wheel well and running across both doors, trailing off under the trunk. Tracing one of the scratches with her finger, she follows the gouge to its conclusion, reeling at this deliberate act of retribution, looking up to find herself faced with the boy who doled it out.

"Jesus. That's so fucked up. Who would do something like that?" Jason's hands are stuffed in the pockets of his jeans, his curly blond hair sticking out from under his John Deere trucker's hat. He has a face as round and broad as a dinner plate.

Clearly Jason has come to taunt her, but he's erred in doing so. If he's already exacted his revenge, then there's nothing more to fear. Instead of finding Althea contrite, as he clearly hoped, he's just made her angry. An engine revs inside her.

"Who would come out here while you were dancing and willfully destroy your property?" Jason continues. Under his arms, sweat rings brighten an otherwise faded orange shirt. His friends are watching from the bed of his truck.

"It's an excellent question," she says, taking a step toward him.

"Althea, get in the car," Oliver says.

The warning is meant for Jason, but it sails over his head. She takes another step.

Jason dangles his car keys from one finger and smiles. "Why would anybody want to key your fucking car?"

Stepping between them, Oliver tries to keep Jason and Althea apart. Coby is standing off to the side with a weirdly focused expression on his face. Inside Althea the engine revs again, and she is so, so ready to hit the gas.

"You already keyed her car," Oliver says to Jason. "You're even, so back off, okay? Don't make it worse."

"What about you?" Jason counters, batting away Oliver's outstretched hand. "I didn't key *your* car."

"I don't have a car, so I guess you're shit out of luck."

"What, you think I'm scared of you because you're a fucking head case?" Jason says. "You think you go psycho in one Waffle House and I'm not going to kick your ass? You were in that bathroom, too, you crazy—"

Before Jason can finish, Althea tucks her chin and drives her head into his chest, grabbing his shoulders and hanging on as the world tilts crazily and the ground rushes up to meet them. Jason hits the asphalt and lies stunned beneath her. His keys go flying, but his hat remains atop his head, albeit at a skewed, jaunty angle. Holding his arms, Althea presses her knee into his stomach while he looks up, winded, his blue eyes circled by long, girlish blond lashes. Saliva bubbles in one corner of his mouth. "Get the fuck off me!" Jason gasps.

"You motherfucker," she shouts, lowering her face so it's inches from his.

"Fuck you, bitch."

Althea pulls back her arm like the sprung handle of a pinball machine, poised to set its hapless metal sphere into motion. Oliver grabs her by the wrist and pulls her up.

"Stop it," he whispers.

A crowd has gathered, and Minty Fresh and Valerie are closing in from its fringes. Althea shoves Oliver aside. While Jason staggers to his feet, she finds his car keys by her back tire and dangles them in his reddened face. He reaches for them and she snatches them away. She winds up her arm again and he flinches—"like a bitch," she'll say when she tells the story later—but instead she pivots, hurling his keys into the same scraggly patch of woods where Coby had ditched the empty bottle. She is going for distance and she gets it, the keys arcing beautifully, their parabola disappearing amid the darkness and the trees, everyone watching so breathlessly, there is a barely audible clink when they land. It's the only clue Jason will have in their retrieval. She flashes him a winsome smile as a parting shot and gets into her car.

Oliver dives into the driver's seat and peels out, leaving Coby in the lot with the rest of the onlookers, but she can see him smirking as the crowd disperses in the taillights. The inside of her chest is warm. The muscles in her legs are cramped and twitchy, like she just ran down thirty flights of stairs. She lights one of Coby's cigarettes and exhales out her open window. Her hand trembles as she raises it to her mouth.

"Can we, like, skip to the part where this is a hilarious anecdote?" she asks.

"No more speed for you," Oliver shouts. "Were you absent on the day in kindergarten when we talked about why we don't hit?"

"Did we also cover what to do when someone keys your car?"

"In all fairness, you did destroy an expensive mirror and flood his bathroom."

"Fuck a bunch of that. Remember the Jell-O massacre at my house? I didn't go out looking for vengeance after that, did I?" she says.

"You didn't have to make it worse," he says. "I don't want to be looking over my shoulder for that asshat every time we go to a party."

"Why are you defending him? Did you not hear what he said to you? I can't wait to run into him again. I hope I'm this drunk when we do. And if I were you, I'd want as many sucker punches as I could get."

"I don't want sucker punches!" he says.

"Then what *do* you want? If you don't want me to dispatch our enemies, then tell me what you do want. Tell me and I will procure it."

He pauses.

"Tell me!" she shouts.

"I told you months ago. I want things to be normal."

After a thoughtful moment, she tosses her cigarette out the window and rolls the window up. Without the sounds of traffic, the car is too quiet and the silence is full of tension. Althea rests her forehead against the cool glass. She can still feel herself tackling Jason, the certainty of his weight, their joint fall to the ground, and the unexpected intimacy in the moment when she was straddling him and he was looking at her, defiant but afraid, seeing into the darkness of her anger and intentions.

"I don't want to pretend like everything is the same."

"That's not helpful," Oliver replies.

"I think you had better set a more realistic goal. You're talking about normal and not normal, but what you really mean is then and now. You didn't wake up in a parallel universe. It's more like you got into a time machine and it took you into the future and you don't like it here."

"Because things are fucked up and I don't know how they got that way."

"Don't do that!" she shrieks. "Don't use it as an excuse! You're sick and that sucks, but don't use it as an excuse to point a finger at me for everything."

Oliver pauses, long enough for her to wonder if he's going to pretend he doesn't know what she's talking about. He turns onto their street and pulls into her driveway, and only after he's killed the engine does he answer.

"I'm sorry. I know you're pissed. But I want things back. The way they were. I know it wasn't fair, the way it happened. The first time we ever—you know—and for me to disappear like that after. That must have really sucked."

Althea pauses, choosing her next words carefully. "What exactly do you think I'm so upset about?"

"That night," he says. "After the party. Things ended really abruptly. I know you were disappointed. I thought you wouldn't want to talk about it, but if it will make you feel better, we can."

"Make me feel better," she repeats. The measured tone of his response infuriates her. The immediate, electrified feeling she had in the parking lot is gone, and with it the potential for infinite and lawless possibilities. The night reached its zenith when they sped away from Lucky's, and now she is trapped in the car riding out the downward trajectory. Or it could, she realizes, just be the pills wearing off. "Did you really think I was all devastated because you denied me the honor of, like, thirteen seconds of drunken intercourse?"

"That's not exactly what I meant," he says, hands still clutching the steering wheel at ten and two.

It seems so ridiculous to be harping on the night when they didn't have sex when all she can think about is the day that they did. "I'm not upset because of that."

"Then what is the fucking problem?" he shouts.

Althea can't have this conversation with the parking brake between them. Jumping out of the car, she runs around to the driver's side, flings the door open, and pulls Oliver out. He stands there with his arms crossed, waiting for her answer, while she searches his face for any vestige of that boy who had been ravenous for her. "Tell me you're faking," she says. "Tell me you remember but you're just embarrassed. I won't care. Just tell me it registered."

"You're speaking in riddles and I don't understand."

"I'm not upset because we *didn't* have sex, I'm upset because we *did*. And you don't remember, and it's like it never happened, but it *did* happen, and you keep complaining because things are different except that nothing's different."

He stares at her. "Wait, what? What do you mean, we had sex?"

"What else could I possibly mean?"

"When? Althea, *when*?" he yells.

"When you were sick."

"I was asleep?" he cries. He covers his face with his hands.

"Christ, I'm not a fucking rapist. You were awake, but, you know. Like the fat mouse."

"I feel nauseous. I told you, I said I wasn't ready—"

"You wanted to," Althea says stridently.

He pushes her, grabbing her arms and pinning her against the car, screaming into her face. Rage contorts his features and gives her a glimpse of something she recognizes, reassurance that there's another side to him she didn't make up. "You stupid bitch, *it wasn't me!* You knew it wasn't me, you knew I wouldn't remember, how could you let it happen? I didn't want to, I told you—"

"Oh no? You didn't *want* to? What did you think happened, then? Do you think I forced you? Do you think I held you down and made you do it?"

It's their proximity that gives him away. Betrayed by his own body before he can protest again, he responds to her closeness, to their tension. She holds his gaze, feeling him waver as his body seems to remember what he can't. As they stare each other down, the flicker of desire on his face is driven away by disgust, disdain for her and maybe for himself as well.

"You knew it was a big deal to me," he says. "You knew I never would have wanted it to happen like that. How could you not tell me? You've been lying to me for months."

"You said you wanted things to go back to normal."

He shoves her against the car again. She winces, but she doesn't seem to notice. "You said I was imagining things. I asked you on the dock why everything seemed so fucked up, and you pretended that nothing happened. How could you keep it a secret? When did you turn into such a creepy fucking scumbag?"

"It wasn't exactly how I pictured it, either," Althea shouts back. Her legs are shaking. "How the fuck do you think I feel, that it didn't even make an impression on you? It's like I'm the only one it happened to. Do you think that's what I wanted?"

"I think you wanted what you always want. To win, to get your way."

"Have I been acting like a winner? Do I seem triumphant to you?" she asks.

"Then why did you do it?"

Althea stares at him, knowing if he even has to ask, it's already over, she's already lost. "I don't think I could have stopped it. And if you could remember, you would know what I mean, and you would know that I'm right."

Releasing her, he takes a step back, shaking his head. There's gravel in his voice, a roughness she's never heard before. "I'll tell you what I know. This, you and me, this is all just geography. If it had been some other little girl who grew up down the block from me, I would have been her best friend for ten years, too, until I realized one day that I wasn't sure I even liked her very much. You're like an incumbent president that no one can stand but you get reelected anyway; you have the advantage because you're already in, and when someone's in it's so much fucking harder to get them out. It should be you, you know," he says flatly. "It should be you that has this fucking thing. If you threw a pitcher of syrup across a Waffle House and started screaming for no reason, it would just seem typical."

Again Oliver shakes his head ruefully, like he's not even that surprised, like he should have known better, like what else could he expect, then he breaks away and runs for home.

Coby hears her coming up the stairs and waits for her in the doorway.

The apartment above the garage is as fixed up as it's ever likely to be—a few posters tacked to the walls and a brown velveteen couch he bought at a yard sale, opposite a small television. It hasn't changed at all since the summer, when she spent plenty of evenings drinking on the roof, listening to the classic rock wafting up from the garage where Coby's dad worked on his Mustang and smoked joint after joint of Zorro's product. It smells of cigarette butts floating in the last half inch of beer at the bottom of a bottle. A few Bukowski poems, hammered out on an old typewriter, are nailed to the walls. Something about the reproductions is comforting; she dreads the day Coby starts writing his own offensive missives. Through the doorway off the main room, Althea can see his bed, a mattress thrown down on the bare floor next to a milk crate full of books. A Mexican rap album is playing on the stereo.

"Got anything to drink?"

Coby pulls a six-pack out of the mini-fridge and sets it on the aged black trunk that serves as a coffee table. She tugs two beers free from their plastic nooses and throws one to him.

"I thought I'd seen the last of you for tonight."

"I was bored. You got a deck of cards?" she says.

He produces one from somewhere in the bedroom and squeezes into a spot on the floor between the couch and the trunk. Splitting the deck in two, he riffles the cards together, then begins to deal.

"Seven times," Althea says. "You have to shuffle seven times."

"Is that a superstition or something?" he asks, collecting the cards and cutting the deck again.

"It's mathematics," she replies. "What are we playing?"

"Egyptian Ratscrew?"

"Sure."

As the six-pack dwindles and the pile of cards in Althea's hand grows, her anxiety slowly abates. The game gives her focus at the same time the beer throws a layer of gauze over everything, making it easier to sit across from Coby and laugh at his unfunny jokes while she trounces him again and again. Even as the pace of their game increases, she's filled with a steely calm. A wave of apathy gently washes over her, lapping pleasantly at the edge of her consciousness.

Coby produces two glasses, surprisingly heavy and clean, like Garth's crystal highballs, and pours a little tequila into each. He tips his glass toward hers and says something she doesn't understand.

"What was that?" she asks as she touches her glass to his.

"It's a Polish toast. It means 'a thousand more.'"

As she brings it to her lips she has a glimmer, a mental sneak preview of the rest of the night, beginning with this small sip and culminating with her doubled over in agony somewhere, most likely the floor of Coby's bathroom, and nothing but trouble in between. Oliver was right. It should have been her with the disease. And she should have grown up on this block, with Coby as her perpetual playmate. She's nothing like Oliver. He was the good twin and she was the bad; she had even dyed her hair black to prove it.

"I'm sorry I haven't come around," she says.

"I get it. You've been busy." Coby turns on the TV and grabs a video game controller from the floor.

She couldn't see herself in Oliver, except when he was sick. Those were the only times he collapsed to her level. But Coby has been down here all along. Nobody would ever look at Coby and wonder what he's doing with someone like Althea, just as Coby would never look at Althea and ask her why she is the way she is. If she hadn't been blinded by history and circumstance, she might have seen it sooner, but here on the couch, alcohol clarifies everything. Despite the many ways in which she finds him wanting, there is something endearing about Coby, something reassuringly *boy* about the way the cuffs of his jeans hit the tops of his shoes, and the tendons that flex in his thumbs when he plays video games.

They toast again—*a thousand more*—and this time Althea takes it literally, imagining her future in this stifling apartment, playing Mortal Kombat and stealing liquor from Coby's parents, who would eventually evict them for wrapping his father's Mustang around the inevitable telephone pole. Renting another apartment somewhere, filling it with drunken arguments and cigarette smoke instead of furniture until they set it on fire during a match game tournament and end up sleeping in her car, a fifth of whiskey in the glove compartment amid Minty's vegan propaganda and maps of places they would never visit. Someday, there would be a mobile home and a trailer park and eighteen identical white wifebeaters flailing on a clothesline.

Soon Althea's apathy returns, a warm blanket she wraps around herself, pulling it tight as she joylessly plays Duke Nukem until the bottle is empty and Coby takes the controller and tosses it to the floor. Placing one hand unceremoniously on her breast and winding the other through her hair, suddenly he mashes his face to hers, and she is clinging tenuously to her indifference. His lips are oddly cold, and the Mexican rap album is on repeat for what must be the third or fourth time. Moving her tongue mechanically inside Coby's mouth, she tries to translate the lyrics in her head; all she can pick out are random words, something about a flavor, a butterfly. She raises her arms impassively as he slips off the bloodstained suit jacket of her Halloween costume and removes her tank top. He fumbles with the clasp on her bra; a full twenty seconds pass without success. She brushes him away and unhooks it herself. The sooner this is finished—well, then the sooner it will be finished. So she pulls his T-shirt up over his head, and when he reemerges from underneath it, he kisses her with even more enthusiasm; he's mistaking her impatience for lust, for excitement. Desire, even. He takes her hand and leads her into the bedroom. They flop onto the mattress, unbuttoning, unzipping. Coby kicks off his pants and Althea wriggles out of her skirt and then they are naked, and the look in Coby's eyes terrifies her because it's victorious. Althea has never been more grateful for the anesthetic properties of alcohol; maybe tomorrow she won't even remember this. *People black out all the time from drinking,* she thinks. *Maybe I'm blacked out right now and I just don't know it yet.*

She thinks of Oliver crushing himself into her. All the parts of him that were so familiar, and still, so much was new. The look on his face when he pulled her down to him. Not victory, but need.

Coby fumbles with a condom and sits up when he's ready.

"Turn over," he says abruptly. "Get on your knees."

With every one of Coby's grunts she's sobering unwillingly, like a diver headed for the surface before she's ready. When it's over, the panic goes away and is replaced with something worse when Coby pulls out and looks down with disdain and says:

"By the way, you're bleeding."

"Excuse me?" she says.

"You're bleeding."

"I'm bleeding?" she says, her voice ringing shrilly in her ears. "The fuck did you do to me?" Althea rolls over and wipes herself with her hand; sure enough, her fingers come away red.

"Lots of girls bleed their first time," he says. "It gets better, you know. It hurts less."

It seems impossible that anything could ever hurt more.

"That *was* your first time, right?" he says.

She grabs her underwear and pulls it on impatiently. The rest of her clothes are in the living room. Coby follows her there, smugly watching her dress. She stalks out the door, not feeling the gravel under her bare feet, not stopping or looking back. She gets herself to the car and steadies herself on the bumper. Bending over, she sticks a finger down her throat, evacuating as much of the tequila and beer as she can. Doubled over in pain. The night has wound up pretty much where she predicted it would.

Althea is tired of being right all the time.

There's a rumbling in her chest like a train pulling into the station, and then she is crying. Althea can't remember the last time she cried that wasn't at a movie, but here she is, the final shreds of dignity dispersing, her breath still sour with tequila vomit, her pubic hair itching because it is matted with her own blood. Suddenly the last four months seem like nothing but a series of tactical errors made in quick succession. *If ever there was a time to let the tears rip,* she thinks, *this would probably be it,* so she sits on the ground and lets them.

Oliver knows her schedule so well he can avoid her easily; by lunchtime on Monday, she's convinced that's what he's doing. When the last bell rings, she races from her class to his, waiting eagerly by the door as the other students file out, but Oliver does not emerge. She looks inside the classroom, but he isn't there.

"Hey, Al." It's Coby, sallow and thin, wearing a black pro-vegan shirt Valerie and Minty Fresh have been selling to support Bread and Roses. It says MILK IS FOR BABIES in white ink, and Althea remembers the day she helped Valerie make the screen for it, spreading some of Nicky's old newspapers on the floor of Oliver's kitchen while Minty Fresh played his guitar at the table and Oliver searched an old cookbook for new recipes to make for BAR on the Internet. Coby's shirt is stained, his pants are too long, and the torn cuffs have wrapped around the soles of his tennis shoes. He's smiling that awful smile at her, and even though he has her attention now, his hand lingers on her shoulder. "If you're looking for Oliver, I don't think he's here today."

Althea just stares at him, saying nothing.

"You feeling better?" he asks.

Later, when she tries to tell the story, the best Althea will be able to say is, "And then my head exploded." But it is so much more than that. It's like that dream everyone has when you're trying to run away from something or run toward something, but your legs won't work right and you can't get any traction. When Althea throws the first punch and it connects squarely with Coby's jaw, it's how that dream would feel if everything came together, and instead of having to convince your body to do what you want, it's your mind that can't process how fast your body is suddenly able to go.

Coby doesn't see it coming. It lands beautifully, snapping his head to the side. The pain shoots up her hand and wrist, quick and electric. He turns to look at her, mouth agape, and he must think she was just making a point, because he doesn't see the second one coming, either. This one catches him in the nose, and something gives inside his face; blood leaks matter-of-factly from his nostrils.

"What the fuck—" he starts, wiping the blood and looking at his hand in disbelief.

The third punch is a left, aimed at his cheekbone, and this time it blows his head back and his feet go out from under him. On the third punch, Coby goes down.

Around her all motion has ceased, everyone is staring, and

Althea doesn't understand why no one has tried to stop her, and she hopes it's because Oliver is standing right behind her and everyone is waiting for him to do it. She waits for his familiar tackle but it doesn't come, and she has the thought, tender but fleeting, that Oliver doesn't want to stop her, Oliver wants to see Coby torn to pieces also, and before Coby can get up, Althea drops to her knees and straddles him, switching back to her right hand as she hits him again and again, remembering the future she imagined for them, how a picture of the two of them eking out their pathetic life together came to her so easily, had been so real she could smell his dirty socks poisoning their trailer. Blood is oozing from a cut above his eye, from his split upper lip, and there is a stir in the crowd as they realize she isn't going to stop until somebody stops her, and that's when the arms wrap around her, dragging her to her feet, but it's not Oliver, it's someone else, a hostile grown-up, probably Principal Nelson, whose stubble scrapes against her cheek as Minty Fresh and Valerie rush to get Coby out of harm's way. He pushes himself backward with his feet and hands, crab-walking, as he looks up at her, bewildered. Minty and Val help him to his feet while eyeing Althea with what she supposes is justified trepidation.

Even though she's not struggling, Nelson keeps his arms locked around her while Coby disappears around the corner of the hallway, and her face aches from her first smile in days.

chapter six.

OLIVER'S JACKET IS ZIPPED, his duffel bag over his shoulder; he's watching Nicky sift through the mess on the kitchen table when the doorbell rings. "That's probably the taxi," he says.

Fanning out a pile of medical journals, she discovers a thick paperback, the title in raised red lettering. "What the hell is this? Is this yours?"

"It must be Garth's."

"What's it doing in our kitchen?" she asks.

"I don't know how half this crap gets in here."

"Should we take it back?" There's a bookmark two-thirds of the way through. "He wasn't even finished with it. Maybe we should drop it off before—"

"No. Give it to me." Oliver snatches it. "We have to go."

"Althea should be home from school by now; don't you want to say good-bye?"

"We already said our good-byes. Hurry up."

"I'm almost ready," Nicky insists.

"You need to be really ready. Ready like Freddy."

The doorbell rings again.

"Just tell him to wait a minute. I'll be right there." She compiles a haphazard stack of random sections from the newspaper.

"Mom, you're never going to read the business section."

She threatens him with the offending material. "Get the fucking door!"

Oliver expects to find an irate cab driver standing on the porch, but Valerie and Minty Fresh greet him there instead. They're strangely lacking in their typical enthusiasm, nervously pacing the rotting wood boards in their combat boots, hands identically stuffed in their back pockets. Had they been worried by his unexplained absence at school? Had they somehow gotten wind that he was leaving for New York and wanted to say good-bye? Instead of being heartened by the possibility of their concern, Oliver's irritated. He'd been so close to a clean getaway.

"What's going on?" he asks.

"Something's happened," Minty Fresh says. He hesitates and looks at Valerie, one of those best-friend glances loaded with meaning, in this case probably something like *Do you want to tell him or should I?*

"I'm actually on my way out, so maybe we could make this kinda quick?" says Oliver.

"It's Althea," Valerie says. "Something happened at school today. She was still in Nelson's office when we left; I think they were trying to find her dad, but we're pretty sure she's going to get expelled."

Oliver puts up his arms like he's fending off an attack. "Stop right there."

"Did you hear what I just said?"

"Not another word. Whatever it is, whatever she did, I don't want to know."

"You're going to have to hear about this sooner or later," Valerie says.

"I don't think so."

"Are you and Althea in a fight or something?"

"Something," says Oliver.

"Does it have anything to do with Coby?" Minty asks.

"What does Coby have to do with anything?"

Valerie and Minty Fresh have another of their silent exchanges. Without his permission, Oliver's brain starts sorting and compiling information—Althea, expulsion, Coby—and presenting him with possible scenarios involving these three elements. The results sound like the titles of dysfunctional children's stories: *Althea and Coby and the Aborted Arson Attempt. Althea and Coby and the Locker Full of Pills. Althea and Coby and the Inevitable Felony Charges.* "Never mind. I said I don't want to know, and I mean it."

"We're really worried about her," Valerie says. "Can't you at least talk to her, make sure that she's okay?"

"Fuck her if she's overwhelmed by the trappings of her totally normal adolescence," he yells, dodging Valerie's outstretched, sympathetic hand. "And just shut the fuck up about Althea and Coby. As far as I'm concerned they can have each other." His eyes have filled.

"Oh, Oliver," Valerie says, putting her arms around him. "I'm sorry."

"Fuck off," he says, sniffling. "You and your pigtails."

"What's with the luggage?" Minty asks, noticing Oliver's duffel.

"I'm going away." Grasping the strap of his bag, Oliver reminds himself of his own story, *The Mysterious Case of Oliver's Medical Problems*. This is the only one that interests him now.

"Where?" Valerie presses.

Here's what Oliver had imagined: slipping away undetected. His absence gradually dawning on everyone, who would initially assume, with reason, that he was just home sick with another episode. Eventually someone—Althea, of course—would come by the house and find it empty. No Oliver, no Nicky. The school knew where he was going, had instructions to send him his assignments, but none of his teachers would volunteer the information, and it might be weeks before anybody thought to ask. And in the meantime, they—Althea, really—would have no idea where he was, and yes, as juvenile as it was, he hoped this uncertain time would be spent reflecting on her mistreatment and underappreciation of Oliver McKinley.

It hadn't started that way. He hadn't mentioned the study in New York to anyone because it would have undermined all his efforts to act like everything was normal. Then, after the show at Lucky's, when he was finally trying to screw up his courage to tell Althea he was leaving in two days, she had dropped the sleep-fucking bomb and made it clear that the Normal ship had sailed months ago. After all his anxiety about telling her, knowing it would send her into a rage that he hadn't mentioned it sooner, he ended up screaming at her for a change and was surprised to find the act intensely cathartic. This bit of insight, however, had been eclipsed by his disgust at her. And now, as he's about to make his quietly melodramatic exit from Wilmington, she's apparently one-upped him again.

"There's a doctor in New York. He wants to check me in to the hospital for a while."

"Oh," Valerie says.

"When will you be back?" asks Minty Fresh.

The taxi pulls into the driveway and honks.

"I don't know. Don't tell Althea, okay?"

"Are you sure you don't want to know what happened today?" Valerie asks.

"Of course I want to know. That doesn't mean I want you to tell me."

LaGuardia Airport doesn't seem like the kind of place that would send a person on a visceral nostalgia trip, but Oliver is still surprised to see Nicky emerge from the terminal into the chilly November evening without so much as a sentimental glance in either direction. He's in a daze himself, head still aching from the plane's dry recycled air. The last time he was on an airplane—the first time, really—he went to visit Mack's parents in California, but that was a long flight, and there had been time to make the mental transition from east coast to west. This trip was only a couple of hours, not nearly long enough to prepare himself.

Nicky, on the other hand, is all business, waiting in line at the taxi stand, hustling Oliver into a cab, and giving the driver directions as if she disembarks from planes here all the time. The inside of the taxi smells like vinyl and sweat; there's a miniature ear of Indian corn hanging from the rearview mirror in anticipation of Thanksgiving.

Settling back into his seat, Oliver tries to mask his excitement and mirror Nicky's indifference instead. But as they hurtle toward Manhattan, the skyline growing larger above them until they disappear into a tunnel underneath it, he's heedlessly optimistic. Wilmington had seemed big until Althea got her car and they realized they could traverse the entire city in fifteen or twenty minutes. New York fills Oliver with a sharp, euphoric hope. Looking at this city now, grasping its size and scope—someone here is going to be able to help him. He indulges that thought as their cab sits in traffic, the buildings rising around them like cliffs. He thinks about being able to make promises, saying "Yes, I'll be there" without having to add the "unless."

The cab driver leans on the horn, with no discernible effect. Nicky reaches across the backseat to rest a hand on Oliver's neck, keeping her eyes on the meter.

After they check in to the hotel near the hospital, Nicky insists they go out to dinner. At home they hardly ever eat in restaurants. Even if they could afford to, Nicky prefers the womblike environs of Magnolia Street, where she can drink her wine and her tea and smoke at leisure. But the hotel has that sterile feeling that makes her insane—the air freshener smell, the printed strips around the toilet seat, the pillows that crinkle like they're filled with newspapers. She asks him if he would like to have sushi, real sushi, not the boxed kind they buy sometimes in the supermarket. He almost asks for pizza instead. She's gone on about New York pizza for his entire life, slices so floppy and enormous you have to fold them in half and wolf them down while the oil runs up your wrist. But they passed enough pizzerias in the taxi for Oliver to realize it's the kind of meal you eat in five minutes perched on a plastic stool. Nicky's looking like, for once, she could do with a little more ceremony.

At the restaurant, Nicky acts like he's never even seen a California roll. She shows him how to break apart his wooden chopsticks and rub them together to smooth out the splinters. She explains that he's supposed to eat the pickled ginger by itself to cleanse his palate, not drape it over each piece of fish like that idiot at the next table. When she starts to explain what the wasabi is and how much of it he should eat with each bite—"Do not rub it around in your dish of soy sauce, you will embarrass us both"—he loses his patience.

"Mom, I understand wasabi. I've seen it, I've ingested it. We're old friends, wasabi and me. Relax."

There's a candle on their table, flickering inside its smoky votive, and a shallow waterfall built into the wall behind Nicky, whispering a steady cascade from the ceiling to the floor. The combination has a hypnotic effect. She fiddles with her chopsticks. In her favorite red sweater with her hair loose around her shoulders, the candlelight soft on her face, she is still sort of beautiful, Oliver has to admit, and he wishes there were more waiting for her in North Carolina than a sink full of dirty dishes and a roster of clients who want their chakras opened through the healing power of massage.

"How long are you going to stick around?" he asks her.

"A few days. I'll spend some time with Sarah and Jimmy. It's been too long since I've seen them. I guess I'll have to go out to New Jersey to see my parents." She sighs, clearly unenthused by the prospect. "Anyway, I'll wait until you're all settled in and then I'll head back to Wilmington."

"You and Sarah got big plans?"

"We're not going to take acid, if that's what you're implying."

"Why don't you move back here?" he asks.

"To New York?"

"Yeah."

"And where will you live?"

"I mean, after." He wants to say *after I go off to college*, but that's a big question mark for now. "Once I move out, eventually."

She blows into her teacup and stares at the ripples. "I don't know."

"I think you need to spend some time around people your own age."

"You're not in a position to be giving advice, my son."

"Don't you think Dad would say the same thing?"

Nicky sets her tea aside and pours a cup of hot sake from the carafe. "It's not so easy to consult your father on these matters, considering he's been dead for ten years."

"That's what I mean. He's been dead for ten years."

Nicky smiles. "Are you worried about me? Is that it? You think I'm lonely?"

"Never mind." He rattles the ice in his water glass, the sound reminding him instantly of Garth.

"Of course I'm lonely sometimes. But you know what?" She gestures around the restaurant with her chopsticks, singling out a couple her age eating their sushi in silence. The husband drops his piece into the dish of soy sauce and it splatters all over his blue button-down shirt. His wife shakes her head while he dabs at the stain with a wet napkin. "They don't look particularly happy, do they?"

Oliver follows his mother's utensils as she points out other people—another couple, younger, is holding hands under their table, but across from them their friend is compulsively tucking the same piece of hair behind her ear and watching the door, bowing her head slightly when the waiter comes by and clears the fourth, unused place setting.

"What about her?" Oliver asks. In the corner, a girl in her twenties is sitting alone, holding a book open with one hand and deftly maneuvering a glass of wine toward her mouth without looking. Setting the wine down, she turns a page, then eats a single piece of sushi, chewing it slowly, resting her chopsticks on her plate. After a moment she takes another sip of wine, smiling at something she just read.

Nicky refills her cup. "When she goes to bed tonight, she's not going to lie there wondering if she said the right thing. And at the end of the day, there's not a lot of people who can say that."

"You think that will be enough for you? For the next forty years?" His voice is abruptly unkind.

"Why are you harping on this tonight? You think after you

move out I'm going to start taking in stray cats just to have some-one to talk to? I'm going to start spying on the neighbors and stealing their recyclables just to keep myself busy?"

"I guess I've assumed that going crazy was always part of your plan."

"And you're the only thing standing between me and insanity? I'm touched, Ol, thank you for keeping the darkness at bay all these years." She throws back the rest of her drink.

"Maybe you should take it easy on the rice wine," he says.

"Maybe you should take it easy on your mother." She plays with a lock of her hair. "I'm not saying I don't see your point. The other day, Sarah asked me what I thought the rest would be like. I didn't know what she was talking about. She said, 'The rest of our lives. What do you think it will be like?' And I honestly didn't know. Another forty years is a long time to spend in Wilmington. But the idea of living here again, but alone this time . . . I don't know."

Oliver's memories of his father—Mack, she had called him, short for McKinley, even though his first name was Charles—have faded to a corduroy jacket that smelled like tobacco, being pushed high on a playground swing, onions and garlic sizzling in a pan on the stove. There was a dog then, too, an enormous mountain dog named Jeremiah that loved to knock Oliver over and lick his face to pieces. Mack and that dog went everywhere together.

Mack is still real to Nicky. Even after ten years, her memories of him are vivid enough to haunt or amuse her, depending on her mood. And Oliver feels guilty sometimes. With so little to remember, there is not much to miss, and Nicky grieves alone for the husband and father Oliver wouldn't know if he saw him now. And sometimes he's angry that she hoards her memories, that she hasn't kept Mack alive more for Oliver, the last tiny piece of him that's left. In the end, the guilt and anger are always fleeting, because it's pointless. Nicky is Nicky and Mack is gone; the dog ran away after he died; Oliver grew up without a father and doesn't know life any other way.

"Am I anything like him?" he asks.

"You're everything like him," Nicky says softly, tipping the carafe over her cup and finding it empty.

He stares at the waterfall behind her. Right after Mack died and the McKinleys were halved, down the street Althea's mother was packing her bags, cleaving her own family. At six years old, a pair of twins was born. The other day at the coffee shop, the cashier looked past Oliver before taking his order, waiting for Althea to appear. She'd never seen them apart. There's no picture of Althea in his duffel bag, none of her sketches pressed between the pages of his notebooks. No one in New York will even know that she exists.

"I just don't want you to end up like Mrs. Parker, sweeping the sidewalk in some ugly housecoat," he says.

"What if it's a vintage housecoat?" she says, flagging down the waiter and holding up the empty carafe, indicating she's ready for another. "What if it's something really kicky?"

The doctor is wearing too much hair product. He's too tall, too young, and too handsome, and immediately Oliver is distrustful. Oliver likes a doctor with a robust head of white hair and tortoiseshell glasses, the easy, comfortable trappings of seniority. This guy looks less like a doctor than like an actor hired to play one. Nicky waits outside while Dr. Curls gives Oliver a thorough physical.

"So, you came all the way from North Carolina?"

"That's right," Oliver says.

"How do you like it down there?"

"It's fine. I guess I don't really have much to compare it to." He squints as the doctor shines a light in his eyes.

"First time in New York?"

"For me, yeah."

"Your mom's been here before?"

"My mom used to live here. In Alphabet City." It's a new low, leaning on his mother's past for credibility.

Dr. Curls makes a brief, Muppet-like noise to indicate that he's impressed. "So you're, what, a senior in high school?"

"Yeah."

Blowing on his stethoscope, the doctor reaches under Oliver's paper gown to listen to his heartbeat, then moves the stethoscope to Oliver's back. "Take a deep breath."

When he's finished with the exam, the doctor sits on the rolling stool and looks up at Oliver, perched on the table with his bare legs dangling. "So, how many of these sleep episodes have you had so far?"

"Three."

"And what do you remember about the events leading up to the first one?"

"I'm not sure I understand what you mean."

"Most KLS patients experience some sort of incident before their first episode. It could be an injury, maybe a head trauma or just a night of heavy drinking. Anything like that happen?"

"I guess you could say there was an incident," he tells Dr. Curls, recalling the night of the Jell-O wrestling party. "Beer. Stress. Sleep deprivation."

"All right," says the doctor. "What do you say you go change and then we have a seat in my office and talk to your mom about what happens now?"

Oliver's given his own hospital room, modified to accommodate the length of his stay. There's a twin bed, a nightstand with a gooseneck reading lamp, a small wooden dresser missing several of its drawer pulls, a plain desk with various profanities etched into its surface, and a chair. The desk reminds Oliver of his first days at elementary school, being assigned his seat and seeing the work of the previous occupants, how shocking the expletives seemed at first but how staring at them day after day took away their power to unnerve him. He has his own bathroom with a shower, no tub, a plastic shower curtain instead of a glass door. There are various pieces of medical equipment next to the bed. Every night before he goes to sleep, a nurse comes in to tether him to these monitors and machines; in the morning, a different nurse comes in and unhooks him, followed by the doctors.

During the day he's free to hang out with the other KLS patients in a common room not unlike that of a mental ward—cigarette-scarred couches, a TV, clipboard-wielding nurses on the periphery. The study is composed solely of teenage boys, the most common sufferers of Kleine-Levin Syndrome. A tutor comes in the afternoons to help them with their schoolwork, but beyond that their days are devoid of any structure. As a result, the lounge has taken on the atmosphere of a fraternity house, a keg party without the beer. For months or years these boys have been the only ones in their towns or cities—"or even states," boasts the boy from Alaska with the shiny black hair—who could lay claim to this disease. Now there are more than a dozen of them, comrades thrown together, constantly sprawled out in the lounge, legs flung over the arms of their chairs or holding one another's feet for sit-ups, bonding hastily in a semi-simian manner. Having spent his formative years primarily in the company of Nicky and Althea, Oliver is ill at ease in such a heavily male environment. The public ball-scratching, the incessant discussion of bodily functions, the flippant assessments of the female nurses—he is poorly versed in these fraternal machinations. Most of the time, he stays in his room, breezing through the AP physics assignments from school, reading graphic novels and *A Brief History of Time* and listening to *Parklife* on his Discman.

But every couple of days an orderly comes in to change the paper-thin sheets and wipe down the walls of the shower, and Oliver slips out to let him work. Then he has no choice but to join the others in their makeshift living room, unless he wants to mill around the nurses' station, which they've made clear they don't particularly like, or sit on the floor outside his room waiting for the orderly to finish, which makes Oliver feel like he's rushing the guy unfairly.

So when the knock on the door comes one afternoon as Oliver is about to start a history assignment, he gathers his books and pencils and walks down the luminous white hallway toward the sound of adolescent boys competing to be heard over the television.

Oliver sinks into an institutional blue chair by the dirt-streaked window with a decent view of the busy avenue below. The other guys are draped across the furniture in flip-flops and track pants, jeans and heather-gray sweatshirts with the names of their high school football teams or concert shirts from stadium tours, major American cities listed on the back. As he always does, Oliver looks around for a Minty Fresh or even a Coby, someone with a Mohawk or a homemade shirt or too many zippers on his pants, someone with bloodshot eyes, generally looking not entirely aboveboard. The lounge has the unpleasant feel of a locker room before gym class. Oliver opens his book across his lap and tries to concentrate. A dozen stories down he can see two women huddled together against the wind, one with bright pink hair, the other holding her IV stand close to keep it from rolling away. Oliver wonders if this is standard practice at hospitals in New York City, to let the patients outside for regular cigarette breaks.

"Anybody seen CT?" one kid asks. In the manner of a traveling carnival that has picked up misfits across the country as employees, the boys in the study refer to one another by their state names and abbreviations. This works out better for some than others. The boy from Alaska is known affectionately as AK-47; poor Kentucky is mocked ruthlessly for carrying the name of a popular lubricant.

"Where the hell have you been? CT went down yesterday morning." AK-47 seems to have prevailed as the unexpected alpha male. He has the best seat on the couch as well as control of the remote.

Surreptitiously surveying the group, Oliver confirms their ranks have dwindled. There are only about eight boys left; the rest have succumbed to KLS sleep episodes. Confined to their rooms, they are under constant surveillance by the cameras mounted everywhere, and rumors circulate constantly about who did what in the semipsychotic state familiar to them all. The only boy actually from New York fell out practically as soon as they first took his blood pressure; for this he was dubbed a "pussy" by the rest of the crew. The remaining eight have proved to be hardier than anticipated.

"He was going to lend me his Sega," the first boy says.

"Go in there and take it," AK-47 says, shrugging. "He can't use it now."

Whoever organized the study had the foresight to ensure the television would get ESPN. The Winston Cup Series is airing live from Atlanta. Garth has a secret love of NASCAR; Althea and Oliver had sometimes found him standing at the end of a neighbor's driveway, having an animated conversation with someone he barely knew about the Bodine Brothers or the controversial finish at the 1991 Banquet Frozen Foods 300. Althea speculated that Garth couldn't find other professors willing to proclaim their allegiance to this proud Southern tradition, so he resorted to pacing up and down Magnolia Street waiting for his male neighbors to come outside and check their mail, and then he would pounce.

"What is this shit?" NJ asks. "I want to watch football."

"It's the NAPA 500," Oliver says. "It's the final competition of the NASCAR season."

"Like the Super Bowl?"

"Sure."

"You from NC, right?" Kentucky asks hopefully, perhaps seeking a kindred spirit in a fellow Southerner. He's wearing a Browning baseball cap; if they were to team up, Oliver gives it about two hours until New Jersey starts cracking jokes about KY and NC polishing their rifles together.

"Wilmington," Oliver says, going back to his history book.

A willowy nurse walks into the lounge. She has curly blonde hair and slim hands, and Oliver loves her simply because she is the only nurse, male or female, who isn't wearing orthopedic shoes. Pointing her digital thermometer at the boys like a weapon, she orders them to line up against the wall.

"Again?" New Jersey says.

"Just do it," says the nurse.

No one's temperature has spiked enough to indicate he might be getting close to having a KLS episode. The nurse's eyebrows furrow slightly with poorly hidden consternation.

"Maybe we're just not trying hard enough," AK-47 says. "Maybe we should all go back to our rooms and count sheep."

Oliver smiles at the nurse when she inserts the plastic tip into his ear. He does not envy her this job; over her shoulder, he can see the rest of the boys ogling her admittedly perfect ass. "You should really be handing out poisoned apples. I hear they work every time."

"Sooner or later," she says, not without some glee. "Sooner or later."

Predictably, she has barely left the room when the others begin talking about what they would like to do to her, given ten minutes and access to the broom closet.

"I'm telling you," says another boy—Minnesota, perhaps, based on the accent—"if she comes into my room after I go down, I can't be held responsible for my actions."

"Dude, you told us you came on to your sister once when you were sick. Do you want to be held responsible for that action?" AK-47 says.

Minnesota pouts. "Whatever."

"I wandered into my neighbor's house and ate everything in their fridge," Kentucky says.

"Oh, who *hasn't*?" says New Jersey dismissively.

"Yeah, except on Thunder Road or wherever the fuck you live, people probably don't sleep with their shotguns and get hard-ons at the prospect of killing an intruder," Kentucky says. That gets a snicker, and he sits back, temporarily secure in his beta male status.

"At least here no one will freak out if I take a shit on my bed," another guy says. "It's been known to happen."

This revelation prompts AK-47 to launch into a protracted tale that combines elements of all the others—a neighbor's house, fecal matter, and an unwanted sexual advance directed at a wildly inappropriate recipient.

The orderly who was cleaning Oliver's room earlier appears in the hallway, diligently circling the floor with a filthy mop and water. Gathering his books, Oliver retreats from the common room.

"NC, where you going?" Kentucky calls after him.

Oliver mumbles something about needing to study.

That night, Oliver gets into bed and waits, reading *The Big Fat Kill* by the light of the gooseneck lamp. There's a quick rap on the door and a nurse enters. It's not the blonde nurse, but an older woman with extremely thin eyebrows and graying brown hair pinned into a wispy bun.

"You ready?" she says. He may not like her shoes, but he appreciates her businesslike approach.

"Bring it on," he says. It comes out more serious-sounding than he intended.

She straps a blue band around his chest and another around his abdomen; these are supposed to monitor his breathing while he sleeps. When she bends over him to glue the electrodes to his temples, he can smell Twizzlers on her breath. From here, he can tell she has no eyebrows at all, that she's just drawn on these slender lines where her eyebrows should be. The adhesive from the electrodes is cold and sticky in his hair. She wraps an oximeter around his index finger, a strip that looks like a Band-Aid but actually monitors the oxygen levels in his blood.

He tries to remember if Nicky had a ritual for tucking him in at night when he was small. Did he have a favorite bedtime story? Was there a song he made her sing? Mostly his childhood memories involve Althea and their two-way radios, her high lilting voice whispering, "Over and out, Ollie." He always countered with the more reassuring, "Back on the air tomorrow, Al." Sometimes he's amazed at things they knew when they were kids that have since been forgotten—Morse code, Esperanto, the ingredients for a good stink bomb. With what has all this useful knowledge been replaced? Precalculus? Althea probably retained the stink bomb recipe; Christ, by now she's probably obtained a copy of *The Anarchist Cookbook*, which she's using to lay siege to all her perceived enemies, whomever she blames for the unfortunate turn her life has taken—Coby, Cape Fear Academy, maybe even her own father.

"You're all set," the nurse says.

In the morning, Oliver is still getting dressed—he refuses to sit around in sweats or pajamas all day; it makes it harder to pretend he isn't sick and in the hospital—when there's a quick rapping at the door. At first he doesn't respond. He's become accustomed to hospital etiquette, where a knock isn't a request for permission to enter but rather a heads-up that the door is about to open. After a moment, the knock comes again, louder.

"Yeah?" he says, hastily zipping up his jeans.

The willowy blonde walks in. "Hey there. Good morning."

"Morning."

"You got a few minutes? The doctor would like to see you."

Oliver looks around, confused by the intimation he might have conflicting plans. "I think I'm free."

"Great. Follow me, handsome."

She called me handsome.

She leads him back to the office where he and Nicky had their consultation with the doctor. He's there, filling out paperwork, stethoscope slung jauntily around the collar of his white lab coat, his thick black hair finger-styled to perfection. Oliver takes a seat in the slippery leather chair on the other side of the desk, perching cautiously on the edge. The nurse leaves, gently closing the door behind her. Oliver pretends she is leaving reluctantly. The doctor looks up, pushing his papers aside.

"How are you doing, Oliver? You settling in all right? Making yourself comfortable?"

"I haven't redecorated my room or anything, but yeah, I'm comfortable."

"You know, if you need anything, you can just tell Stella. We do our best to be accommodating."

"Stella?" Oliver nods toward the door. "Was that Stella?"

"Yes. She's very good."

Oliver doesn't like the familiar tone Dr. Curls uses here, as if he knows all sorts of things at which Stella is very good. "I'll do that."

"Great. It must be something, finally being around other people who have this condition. Maybe makes you feel less alone, less isolated?"

"All due respect, sir, but being in the hospital instead of high school is pretty isolating."

The doctor laughs. "Now, Oliver, I know you're from the South, and I appreciate your manners, but you don't need to call me 'sir.' Manuel will be just fine."

In their sockets, Oliver's eyes roll of their own volition. "Sure thing."

"I understand that being in the hospital can be an alienating experience, but at least these boys are your peers."

Hardly, Oliver thinks.

"And they can appreciate what you've been through in a way no one else ever will."

"I have no doubt."

"You've been extremely cooperative over the last week, and we appreciate that. But as we explained, it's very uncertain that we'll be able to provide you with any real medical assistance. There's so much about KLS that we don't know, and part of this study's purpose is to learn more. If we can translate some of that new information into an experimental treatment, great. But there's no guarantee we'll be able to send you back home in any different condition than you came to us. You need to manage your expectations."

Oliver shifts uncomfortably in his chair, already irritated with this conversation. "I'm aware of that, Manuel."

"There are symptoms of KLS that have nothing to do with the sleep episodes. You must be aware of that, aren't you?"

"Could you be more specific?"

"Depression, of course. Anger and hopelessness. Have you ever felt anything like that?"

Oliver laughs bitterly. "Hopelessness? Is that what that is?"

Manuel looks at him sympathetically. "Yes. That's what that is. We're hoping that the chance to meet some other boys with KLS, spend some time with people who can really understand you, might help you feel better. Maybe feel a little normal for a while. Do you understand what I'm saying?"

"I'm not sure."

"Oliver, you've been keeping yourself somewhat isolated so far. There's nothing wrong with that; I know this isn't a resort, it's a hospital. Socializing isn't what you came here for, and it's not at the forefront of your mind. But I want to ask you to consider opening up a little. You don't have to spill your guts to a bunch of strangers, of course. But think about sharing more of yourself than you have been. I'm pretty sure you'd be surprised how cathartic it can be."

The heat register below the window kicks on, exhaling a warm breath of dry, recycled air that instantly sucks the moisture from Oliver's sinuses. "I'm not much of a bonder."

"I realize that. That's exactly why I'm suggesting you challenge yourself here—"

"I'm here. That's the challenge. For both of us."

Dr. Curls can't seem to sigh loud enough. "Oliver, we're bringing in a counselor to start holding group therapy sessions with all the patients. I'll expect you to at least attend."

Oliver shrugs. "If you want. If it'll make you feel better."

"You don't think it might make *you* feel better?"

"There's only one thing that could do that," he says.

"I'm sorry to say, I'm surprised by your attitude."

Oliver thinks of Althea and her bony, beautiful knuckles. "It's not an attitude."

"Then what is it?" For the first time, the doctor sounds annoyed.

Standing, Oliver makes for the door. "You nailed it. Anger. And hopelessness."

chapter seven.

ALTHEA STAYS IN the basement.

Pajama-clad, expelled from Cape Fear Academy, she finds the subterranean appealing. Under the old quilt she's had since childhood, the one Alice made her, she watches the same movies over and over, movies about genetically engineered monsters and apocalyptic weather that threatens the whole world. These movies are soothing, especially the moments before the storm breaks or power is restored to the compound, when rescue seems impossible, complete destruction inevitable. Her interest flags when the helicopter lands and the survivors are ushered to safety, or when the newly sworn-in president makes an optimistic statement about the future. *Fuck that shit,* she thinks, going back to the beginning, when all signs of impending chaos were there and everyone but the hero chose to ignore them.

She needs time to figure out what happened that afternoon in the hallway, when she was straddling Coby and doling out punch after punch. Just like something gave in Coby's face beneath her fist, something had given inside her as well, like the pop and flare of a spent lightbulb. Now there's just a tiny filament left, rattling around in the muddy glass. She doesn't mind feeling like a blown fuse. It's what she wanted all this time. She hopes it lasts.

The door opens at the top of the stairs and she pulls the quilt over her head. There's a wooden creak, and then another, and soon she can feel Garth standing over the couch. She smells garlic and noodles and tomato sauce; he's brought dinner. With Althea refusing to leave the basement, cooking duties have reverted to Garth. She chews the collar of her shirt, the cotton spongy against her tongue. A sliver of light invades her cocoon as Garth turns down a corner of the quilt. When she doesn't protest, he peels back a little more, exposing her whole head and shoulders. He holds out a plate.

"Sit up and eat this."

She takes the plate and twirls a fork listlessly through the spaghetti. Garth sits in the recliner.

"I made some phone calls today to other schools. If you take this semester's finals, and you pass, you can start at Laney after winter break."

Althea shrugs. Under the sauce, she can see the impressions of his fingers in the meatballs.

"You don't have to like it there. You just have to graduate from high school."

"Can't you homeschool me?"

"Wouldn't that be fun for us," he says, widening his eyes with sarcastic enthusiasm.

"Then Laney it is."

Garth sighs. "You realize UNC is not the sure thing it was

before. You're going to have to try harder. Act like you actually care about going to college."

"What if I don't care about going to college?"

"Then start looking at art schools. Lord knows you've got the time on your hands."

"You'd send me to art school?"

"We're rich, remember?"

"I thought we were comfortable."

"I'd be a lot more comfortable if I could get you out of the house. If art school will do it, I'll happily throw some of the family's old lucre at the problem. There's also the matter of what you're going to do between now and the start of next semester."

She makes a sweeping gesture that encompasses the basement.

Garth gets up from the recliner and sits next to Althea on the couch, slipping underneath the blanket with her. "Isn't this cozy? It smells like wet sponges down here."

"I expect that's the mold."

"It doesn't bother you?"

"I don't really notice it anymore."

Althea nibbles a few strands of spaghetti. Piercing a meatball with her fork, she splits it into two pieces, then halves those pieces, then halves them again, until there's nothing left but mush. There was a math theory they learned last year, that you can divide something in half and divide it in half again and go on and on, reducing it to smaller and smaller pieces, but it would never disappear completely. It's one of Zeno's paradoxes.

Garth lays a wide, tangled swath of Althea's hair, rife with split ends, across the flat landscape of his palm and shakes his head. "I still don't understand why you had to dye it black."

Annoyed, she pulls away. "Did you come down here for a reason?"

"For someone who says she doesn't care about getting expelled from high school, you seem to be taking it pretty hard."

"It's so humiliating. Everyone knowing my business. God, it was so public." She has to cover her face with her hands just thinking about it, the hallway filled with people watching her pummel Coby. Why couldn't she have at least waited until they were outside in the parking lot?

"Mortification fades. I promise."

"How do you know?"

"After your mother left."

Althea looks at her father's legs, stuffed into the small space between the sofa and the coffee table. He must have been a great dancer once; she's seen the wedding photos, knows he wore the hell out of a three-piece suit. He must have been a lot of things before he was married, before he was divorced, before he was a single father to a spoiled, petulant teenager.

"Have you talked to her?" Althea asks.

"I thought I'd let you have the pleasure of filling her in on your latest debacle."

"You seem to be taking it in stride."

Garth grows serious, always a disturbing turn of events. "You know, after talking to the school and everything, I've noticed that no one seemed particularly surprised that Coby was on the receiving end of your anger. He's not very well liked, is he? Even Oliver doesn't like him, and Oliver likes everyone."

Not everyone, Althea thinks. *Not me, not anymore.* "I think

Coby's going for that lovable asshole thing. He's got the asshole part down, for sure," Althea says, trying to keep the mood light, but Garth isn't biting.

"Al, listen. Obviously, I'm upset you got expelled. I'm disturbed that you lost control and hurt someone so badly. It's scary. I'd even guess that you scared yourself. And everyone who was there that day said that you and Coby were just talking and then . . . well. But if something happened, if Coby did something to you, maybe not right then, but if he—"

"Dad, are you asking me if he deserved it?"

Garth leans his head back against the sofa. "I don't know what I'm asking. I guess I'm asking why you did it. I'm clinging, here, to the hope that you at least had a reason. Although the idea that he hurt you in some way—"

Althea snaps to attention. "Oh God, Dad, no, he didn't—it wasn't—no. He's a creep, but not like that."

"So he didn't deserve it."

"I didn't say that, either."

"I don't understand."

Althea shakes her head. "I'm still working it out myself."

"Just do me a favor. Call your mother tomorrow," Garth says.

She squishes part of the meatball between the tines of her fork. "Why?"

"It's a bit much to keep it to ourselves. Just call her." He pulls a few strands of spaghetti off her plate and dangles them into his mouth, licking the sauce from his fingers. "Did I use too much sugar?"

"Not quite."

"Do you want something else? Ice cream or popcorn?"

"I don't want anything. I don't think anything's going to help."

Garth settles in, finding the remote control under his thigh and pointing it at the television. "What is it tonight? Monsters or weather?"

"Dinosaurs."

"Perfect."

In the morning she wakes rolled in her quilt like a burrito. Face pressed into a cushion, she notices for the first time how much the couch smells like a waiting room.

Upstairs, next to the coffeemaker, Garth has left his address book. It's an ancient thing, a miniature three-ring binder filled with tiny gnarled pages, held together by a rubber band. Althea finds the most recent phone number they have for her mother, listed under *A* for *Alice*. A dozen others are crossed out.

At the table with her coffee and the cordless, she punches in the numbers, holding each one down so that it makes a loud, satisfying beep. Then she waits, listening to the static of the long-distance connection, imagining the pigeons perched on the wires that are transmitting this call to New Mexico.

Alice answers on the second ring. "To what do I owe this honor?"

"I guess you have caller ID now," says Althea.

"You're not pregnant, are you?"

They haven't spoken in six months.

"Why would I call you if I—never mind. I'm not pregnant." Already restless, she paces the kitchen.

"Are you in trouble?" Alice asks.

This gives Althea pause. Retreating to the basement, she finds her messenger bag, rifles through it for her cigarettes. "Why don't you define 'trouble' and we'll go from there."

"Did you get expelled?"

"How did you know that? Have you talked to Dad?" Fishing for her lighter, a pack of matches, anything.

"Of course you got expelled. I knew your father should have sent you to public school. It's practically impossible to get expelled from a public school. You just about have to stab a teacher. You didn't stab a teacher, did you?"

"Is it still called stabbing if I used a shiv? Or is that shivving someone? Or shanking? I can't remember. I'll have to look it up." The only book of matches she can find, at the bottom of her bag with a handful of pennies and crumbs, is empty.

"It's only shanking if you use something you carved from the heel of your shoe. A shiv you can make out of anything." There's music in the background, playing somewhere in Alice's house, a sincere voice and an electric guitar.

"How do you know that?" Althea asks.

"I know things. I have cable."

"Are you listening to Bruce Springsteen?" Althea climbs back upstairs. In a kitchen drawer she finds the orange barbecue lighter.

"Thea, seriously. What's going on?"

Taking her cigarettes and coffee out onto the gazebo, Althea lies down on the bench, staring up at the wooden frame her father built himself. "I got expelled."

"But for what?"

"At the time I thought it was an act of retribution."

"And now?"

"And now I'm not so sure."

Althea imagines Alice in her house in Taos, wearing turquoise jewelry she made herself, surrounded by homespun clay pots filled with handpicked flowers. When she married Garth, she loved the idea that he was a professor, picturing a series of teaching positions that would allow them to move every two years, being set up in a different university apartment each time, a constant parade of new people to entertain. Instead, Garth got tenure, bought a house, and Alice kept moving, choosing to pursue what Althea envisions as a life of basket- and blanket-weaving, cruise vacations for singles over forty, a medley of eight-week workshops and book clubs packed with women who incessantly discuss self-actualization and holistic methods for treating perimenopause. Althea finally lights her cigarette, not bothering to cover the phone's mouthpiece.

"You're smoking now, too?" Alice asks.

"I guess things aren't going very well."

"Someday you're going to end up in therapy, paying someone a lot of money to tell you this is all my fault."

"I can get someone to tell me that for free."

"I'm sure your father says it all the time."

This isn't actually true, but Althea doesn't say so. The opposite of those kids who yearn for their divorced parents to reunite, she's often disappointed by how little enmity Garth shows toward Alice. "How are things with you?"

"Getting ready for the winter. I bought a new pair of snowshoes. Thea, you don't sound okay." There are breakfast sounds on Alice's end, maybe a pan scraping against the stove, or a fork whisking egg yolks in a dish until they're frothy. "Where's Oliver?"

"He expelled me, too."

"That won't last," Alice says quickly.

"I don't know, Mom. He seems pretty for sure about it." Althea stubs out her cigarette on the heel of her shoe, wondering if it would, in fact, be possible to fashion a shank out of the hard rubber.

"Did things finally, you know, progress? Romantically?"

"No comment."

"Honey, it was bound to get complicated. He's a teenage boy. Give him a few minutes; he'll get distracted by something shiny and forget whatever you did to make him so mad."

"How can you tell the difference?" Althea asks. "When someone calls 'game over,' how are you supposed to know if it's for real or not?"

"If it's only the first time they're saying it, then they don't really mean it. The fourth time, maybe the third, that's when you start taking them seriously." Alice chews in Althea's ear.

"How many times did you have to tell Dad?"

"Your father did not give chase, Thea. In the end, I only had to tell him once."

I was only five, Althea thinks. *Was I supposed to give chase, too?* "You got any boyfriends out there?" she asks, sipping away at her coffee.

"A couple. Garth seeing anyone?"

"A steady procession of nubile undergraduates." Surveying

their backyard, Althea tries to picture Garth in a smoking jacket, holding court for a seraglio of coeds in tight jeans and bikini tops while he secretly wonders when he can return to his study and finish reading his latest mystery novel. "So if Dad had chased after you, you'd still be married?"

"Who the hell knows? Maybe the guy upstairs. Maybe not even him." Another big sigh. "Look, you know if you wanted to, you could come out here for a while. I've got a spare bedroom. Some extra snowshoes."

Alice might be a perfectly good mother, if Althea would only give her a chance. But Althea sees dream catchers, unfinished wooden rocking chairs, Native American–themed bedspreads. Some kind of weird healing tea that tastes like the ground; too many paintings of wolves and coyotes. Ten minutes on the phone with Alice is one thing; ten days in her adobe house would be quite another, and if there's an Alice-shaped hole in her life somewhere, it's safely in Althea's blind spot. Still, as often happens during these rare conversations with her mother, Althea feels herself softening unwillingly.

"Just so you know, Dad never blames anything on you," she says. "He doesn't talk about you like that."

"I suppose that's nice to hear. Look, Oliver loves you. Have you tried apologizing?"

"I don't think he'll listen. I did a really bad thing. If I were him, I wouldn't talk to me."

"You make him listen," Alice says, like she really believes it's that simple. "Just trust me. Talk to him."

Mrs. Parker has her work cut out for her today, sweeping autumn leaves into the gutter even as they continue to jump ship from tree branches above her. As she stands in front of Oliver's house, Althea can hear the chiding sound of bristles against concrete, *tsk tsk tsk*.

The house looks different. The curtains are drawn and the driveway empty. The latest Sunday *Times* is wedged between the screen and front doors, still wrapped in wet, filmy plastic. Althea can't imagine a clearer sign that something is not right. Looking over her shoulder, she can see Mrs. Parker shuffling a small pile of leaves from one end of the sidewalk to the other, her lips pressed into a thin, mirthless line. If she knows where the McKinleys have gone, she certainly isn't telling. Althea will have to find her answers elsewhere.

Valerie opens her front door, not looking too surprised to find her there.

"Hey," Althea says, hovering awkwardly. On the other side of the threshold, the house smells warm and spicy, like ginger.

"Hey."

"How's it going?"

"Okay, I guess." Valerie glances back inside. "Look, I'd invite you in, but—"

"Is that Althea?" Minty Fresh shouts from the kitchen.

"Yeah," Valerie says.

Minty comes down the hallway, wiping his hands on his apron and nodding hello. "Figured you'd be by sooner or later. Don't know what took you so long."

They're not cold, exactly. Whatever uneasiness they'd shown at school, in those moments when they were helping Coby to his feet and she felt weirdly euphoric, is gone. Disinterest, more than anything, has replaced it. No one is better equipped than Althea to understand how superfluous other people can seem when you are convinced you already have the only ones you need. Still, it stings to be on the other side.

"I went by Oliver's house today, and there's nobody there, and it looks like there hasn't been for a while. I thought you might know where he is. I just wanted to know if he's okay."

"He's okay," Valerie says.

Althea tries on a friendly smile. "Good, that's good. So where is he?"

Valerie and Minty Fresh exchange one of their impenetrable looks. Finally Minty speaks. "We're not supposed to tell."

Her smile falters. "What do you mean?"

"We promised," says Valerie. "I'm sorry."

"You promised? Who did you promise?" Althea asks.

"Oliver."

"He left town and made you promise not to tell anyone where he went?"

Minty shoves his hands into the pockets of his apron and stares at the floor, scuffing his boot along the doorframe. It reminds Althea of how he used to be, just another awkward, too-skinny guy who was trying to teach himself three guitar chords and thinking about starting a band, sometime, maybe. She glares at him. *I knew you when, you little shit,* she thinks. *I remember when you were Howard and nobody thought you were cool.*

"Not exactly," says Valerie. "Look, we know you and Oliver are in some kind of fight, and he asked this one thing of us before he left, and we don't want to get in the middle."

"So just me, then. I'm the only one who isn't allowed to know where he is?" Althea is incredulous, and so ashamed. Standing here, begging these acquaintances for information about her only friend in the world, who had apparently denounced her to them before he left. Somewhere inside the house, a toilet flushes, and a few moments later Coby appears. His black eyes have faded to yellow patches; his split upper lip is fused together with a mealy scab. A new bump rises in the middle of his already-broken nose, which has been pushed over to one side of his face. "Careful," he says to Val and Minty. "She might try to beat it out of you."

"Jesus Christ," Althea says.

"That's why I didn't want to invite you in," Valerie explains.

"Thanks?" She can't take her eyes off Coby's face. He smiles at her. As always, he seems to be enjoying the discomfort of the people around him.

"She's freaking out," he says to Valerie and Minty. "You're really not going to tell her?"

"We promised," they say.

"Well, I didn't promise him shit," Coby says. "Come on, Carter, let's go have a smoke." He steps outside, brushing past her in the doorway.

She follows him to his truck, stopping when he gets in the driver's seat, not quite believing he would willingly share an enclosed space with her. He reaches across and opens the passenger door. "Come on."

"You're really going to tell me where he is?"

"Carter, don't be a pain in the ass. Get in the truck and I'll tell you."

Althea listens to Coby talk. He relays what he knows about the sleep study in New York, that Oliver will be gone for months and no one knows when he'll be back, that it hadn't been an emergency but had probably been in the works for some time.

"What do you mean?" she asks.

"After he left, Valerie and Minty Fresh asked Nelson whether they should be passing on their assignments, but the tutor from St. Victor's had already arranged everything with his teachers. Even before you two had it out, he was already planning to leave."

"Did he tell anybody what our fight was about?"

"Althea, news flash: Nobody gives a shit what your stupid fucking fight was about." He puts the truck into drive and starts to pull away from the curb.

"Stop," Althea says. "I didn't say we could go anywhere."

He brakes. "Why can't you even try?"

Inside his oversize sweatshirt, Coby looks insubstantial. It's so obvious it was never a fair fight. It was never even a fight at all. Still, she can't quite bring herself to be sorry. He had drawn the first blood, after all.

"Because it worked out so well last time?"

"We could have fun, and you know it."

"Fun? Seriously? I beat the shit out of you in front of the entire school. That's the most fun we're ever going to have." There's a peculiar freedom in sitting here, talking to Coby. He's impossible to alienate, but Althea is careful not to mistake this for loyalty or love. How unfair that Coby is the one ready to pick up where they left off, while Oliver continues to shun her, even from another part of the country.

"You can sit in your basement and wait for him, but he's not coming. He's gone," Coby says. "And I'm the one who had to tell you where he went, so what do you make of that?"

"That you're trying really hard to make a case for what a good guy you are."

"I wouldn't bother. You never liked me because I'm a good guy, and I'm not pretending to be one. I'm just like you."

The cozy numbness that's enveloped her for the last two weeks is wearing off like anesthesia, and here she is, back in her own head, the most dangerous place for her to be. What will happen when she wakes up tomorrow and has to face another long, angry day, every hour marked by the worst kind of claustrophobia? Coby's unspoken invitation—*Stick with me, kid, and we can give each other what we both know we deserve*—is looking less like a worst-case scenario and more like her only option.

"What you are," says Althea, opening her door, "is a hate crime waiting to happen, and I never liked you at all."

Later, Althea ventures upstairs to her bedroom to ferret out some clean clothes. She sits on her bed and studies the photographs and sketches on the wall. As a child, when she imagined the transition into adulthood, she saw an older version of herself emerging from the toy chest at the foot of her bed to take over the task of actually *being* Althea. Young Althea would retire to a combination heaven/surveillance station to live the rest of her life vicariously through Adult Althea, who would conveniently arrive fully equipped with good judgment, a high school diploma, and large breasts. Now she looks down at her small chest and sighs. It's clear that Adult Althea isn't coming, she's not in stasis somewhere, shimmering in a golden chrysalis while her curvy adult figure is perfectly crafted by a series of hardworking angels, preparing to unleash a sharp-witted Amazon into the world. This is it. Flat-chested and prickly and sad, smart enough to know when she's being stupid but too stupid to act any smarter—this is what she's got to work with. She stares at her pictures and thinks of her parents and wonders whether some histrionics from Garth could have made the difference.

That night, Garth serves dinner in the kitchen and they perch on stools at the counter. Beyond the doorway, the mahogany table in the dining room gleams, vast and empty.

"I saw you moved your car. Did you go for a drive today?" he asks.

"It killed an hour." She spears a pearl onion with her fork. *Now eat it*, she thinks. Staring at her hand, she tries to will it to obey, but she can't bring the tines to her lips. Instead, she ducks her head, bringing her mouth to the small, boiled vegetable. *Now chew.*

Garth swiftly dissects his entire steak, slicing the meat into evenly sized pieces, extracting the bits of fatty gristle and setting them on the rim of his china plate. Only when the labor of his meal is completed does he take his first bite and set about enjoying it. "I think I like this marinade."

She waits until he's finished. "Tell me that story again, about Castor and Pollux."

Of all the ancient myths, this is her favorite. Castor had a gift for taming horses; Pollux was an able boxer. Twin brothers, inseparable. Lord Macaulay had written about them in *Lays of Ancient Rome*: "So like they were, no mortal might one from other know." Famed adventurers, they fought with Jason and the Argonauts. "Back comes the Chief in triumph, who, in the hour of the fight, hath seen the Great Twin Brethren in harness on his right." Eventually Castor was slain in battle, and the heartsick Pollux begged to give his own immortality in exchange. He struck a compromise with Zeus. The brothers would alternate—one day in the underworld, the next with the gods. As Garth finishes his story, he fetches his bottle of scotch from the cabinet above the sink.

"It's like the ultimate Would You Rather," says Althea, watching as he pours his ritual two fingers over the same number of ice cubes.

"I suppose now we know which twin you'd be," he says with a faint smile.

"I was thinking about what you said, about going to visit Mom," she says.

Silently, Garth corks the bottle and replaces it, then stands on the other side of the counter with his drink. "Suddenly we're a long way from the Greeks. What made you change your mind?"

"When I go outside, I feel like I'm in one of those science fiction movies where something's wiped out all the people and I'm the last person on earth." Althea is surprised by her honesty, but her father's expression doesn't change; he just looks at her like they're in his office having a student-teacher conference.

He takes a sip of scotch. "And how long are you planning to visit?"

"Just a few days. I was thinking I could spend Thanksgiving with her."

"Have you talked to her about this idea yet?"

"I wanted to talk to you first."

"You were the one who didn't want to be landlocked in the desert with your mother. If a change of scenery sounds appealing, I'm not sure I can blame you." He carries their plates to the sink, rinsing them off with his back to her.

Althea hates lying to him, hates making him believe that she actually needs her mother, but it's the only way. "I just don't see how it could be any worse than staying here."

Drying his hands on a dish towel, Garth holds her gaze, his poker face flawlessly intact. "Althea, you're almost eighteen. You can decide for yourself. It's up to you."

She has months' worth of solid evidence to the contrary. She wants to tell him about the toy chest, about the version of herself with good judgment who has yet to arrive. Instead, she slides off the stool, surprised that her legs still support her. "I guess I'll go start packing."

"Wait," he says. She pauses in the doorway. "I'm thinking about going to Mexico over winter break to do some research. You're always saying I never take you anywhere. Maybe this time you'd like to go with me?"

"Seriously?"

"I think you'll find the rituals of human sacrifice quite fascinating. We can work out the details after you get back."

Althea blinks at him, confused. She got herself expelled from high school and is apparently being rewarded with a trip to Mexico—although in truth she suspects that Garth doesn't trust her alone anymore. "Okay. Human sacrifice. It's on."

chapter eight.

OLIVER IS HAVING a hard time.

Studying in his room is proving difficult. He pushes aside his books to trace the marred desk with his fingertips, searching for the words of a vandal who had something other than bodily functions and sex acts on his mind. There's not one initial-filled heart scratched into the wood, not one misspelled declaration of affection. Just a fully illustrated series of *Fuck yous* and *Suck my cocks* and other statements in the same unimaginative vein. He misses his desk at home, the collage of album covers Althea had shellacked onto an old plank of wood, the sawhorse she had stolen for a base.

Kentucky sticks his head in the door. "It's therapy o'clock," he says.

Abandoning his work, Oliver returns to the lounge, where the regular furniture has been pushed aside and a bunch of plastic chairs are arranged in a circle.

The therapist is late. The guys fidget in their chairs. Two more have gone down. Minnesota and the boy known to shit on his bed are among the missing; Oliver fears for the orderlies. There are about six of them left, sitting impatiently, staring at the clock on the wall, shooting one another irritated glances, all except for Kentucky, who had the foresight to bring a book to read.

"It seems like all we ever do here is sit and fucking wait," AK-47 grumbles. "I'm sick of waiting to go to sleep so they can hook me up to the machines and figure out what the fuck is wrong with me. What they should really do is give us booze. That's what did it for me the first time." He looks for someone to encourage him to tell the story.

It's New Jersey who obliges. "Oh yeah?"

"First time I ever got wasted—I mean, really wasted. Not just beer wasted. Wild Turkey wasted. My parents found me in the bathroom, wrapped around the toilet. They couldn't wake me up. Thought it was alcohol poisoning. They took me to the hospital, I got my stomach pumped and everything. That's what they told me, anyway; I don't fucking remember. But after, I still wouldn't wake up."

"How long did it take them to figure out it wasn't alcohol poisoning?" Kentucky asks.

"I actually did have alcohol poisoning. It just confused things. And then I woke up, except I wasn't really awake"—here the others nod, understanding implicitly—"and I started freaking out, throwing shit, tearing out my IV, cursing at the doctors." AK-47 chews a thumbnail. "My little sister was there. I pissed on the floor and went back to sleep. So anyway, they should bring in a few bottles of Wild Turkey, we'll have a real good time, and that'll be the end of the story."

The room is silent. No doubt everyone is imagining a small girl watching her older brother urinate on the floor of his hospital room. No doubt the image is different in everyone's mind— maybe she's seven in one, eleven in another, hair in braids or straight down her back—but the effect is the same. Even though AK-47 has black hair, Oliver pictures his little sister delicate and blonde, hugging a nubbly stuffed dog and squeezing her eyes shut as her brother unzips his pants, their father too distracted to usher her out of the room.

"That happens a lot, you know," says Kentucky. "A lot of initial KLS episodes are triggered by alcohol."

"So what, it's, like, our fault?" AK-47 says. "You're saying if I hadn't gotten shit-faced, I never would have gotten sick?"

"That's bullshit," says another guy. "I didn't do anything and it happened to me anyway. I just thought I was coming down with the flu."

"Look, I've never been drunk in my life and I'm still here. I jerked off in front of my mom once," Kentucky says.

"Seriously?" Oliver says.

"Not to, like, completion or anything. But I whipped it out, apparently."

"How do you know?" AK-47 asks. "She didn't tell you, did she?"

"The doctors told her to keep a log. Of all my behavior and shit. I read it one day when she was at work."

"Are you fucking crazy?" NJ shouts. "You *never* read the log! My mom has one, too. You *never* read that shit!"

"Don't you think I know that now?" Kentucky yells back. "I

can't even look her in the eye anymore. But I picked it up and I couldn't stop reading."

"You read the whole thing?" Oliver asks. He has no idea if Nicky had kept a log. In any case, the house is such a mess that he wouldn't even be able to find it.

"I read the whole fucking thing," Kentucky says mournfully. "God, it was so cringeworthy."

"Was the jerking off the worst of it?" AK-47 asks.

"I don't know, it depends on your point of view. Would you rather jerk off in front of your mom or call her a fat cunt?"

"Fat cunt" is the unanimous response.

"I wandered into my neighbors' house because I ate the gallon of ice cream in our freezer and I was still hungry, and I almost got shot. After that my folks kept closer tabs. And every time I was in the hospital—every fucking time—I got in trouble for grabbing the nurses." Kentucky shakes his head. "Fucking humiliating."

The group therapy session hasn't even started yet, and already for Oliver it's taking on the flavor of a hostage situation.

"My girlfriend dumped me," NJ says, picking up the thread. "She came over one day when I was sick, and when I woke up she wouldn't even talk to me. I still don't know what I did. Also, I tried to fuck the Venetian blinds in our living room. My brother told me about that one."

Oliver is sweating, his heart beating enthusiastically. His foot jerks, and he pulls it onto the chair, stilling it with both hands. "Id without the lid," he mutters.

"What's that, NC?" Kentucky asks.

"Just something a friend of mine used to say. About what I'm like. When I'm sick. 'Id without the lid.'"

"What's that mean?" NJ asks.

Kentucky answers for him. "It means no internal censor. It means no impulse control. I mean, that's the question, right? If all teenaged boys want to do is eat, sleep, and jerk off, then maybe when we're sick we're just ourselves times a million."

AK-47 looks closely at Oliver. "What about you, NC? You ever wander into your neighbors' house in the middle of the night and raid the fridge?"

A boy who has embraced the nickname AK-47 is not someone to whom Oliver wishes to confess feelings of violation and lost innocence. "Not exactly," he says.

"Come on, I bet *something* fucked-up happened. I can tell just by looking at you."

Oliver squirms in his chair. "There was an incident at Waffle House. I'd rather not get into the particulars." He thinks back to his earlier conversation with Dr. Curls. "Do you guys ever feel, I don't know, hopeless?"

"I stopped looking forward to things." Another guy speaks up. "Because I didn't know if I would be around when they happened. Holidays, parties. I'd hear about a movie coming out that I wanted to see and then I'd tell myself not to get too excited, because if I got sick I'd miss it. It's like everything is just a big question mark now. None of it's up to me."

"My best friend tells me to look on the bright side. Like I'm being forced to live in the moment," says AK-47. "That I should just accept it."

"I don't see how that helps me go to college," Oliver says.

"Nope," NJ says. "I'm not accepting shit."

"Seriously," Kentucky adds. "This isn't an AA meeting. I'm not here to recite the Serenity Prayer. I'm here to make it stop."

The therapist finally arrives, a balding man in black jeans and cowboy boots. He takes his seat in the circle, puts his hands on his knees, and looks around at the group.

"So, how's everyone doing?" He's greeted with silence. "Who'd like to start?"

The guys look at one another, wordlessly closing ranks.

"Oliver? How about you?"

Irritated at being singled out, Oliver crosses his arms and shrugs. "I got nothing."

The session ends after an exceedingly uncomfortable hour. As the therapist leaves, Stella enters in his wake, clipboard in hand, wearing a long-sleeved thermal under black scrubs covered with dozens of tiny pink guitars. Instead of lining her charges up against a wall, she comes around to each one, popping a fresh plastic cap onto the digital thermometer with admirable expertise. She visits Oliver last. One particularly springy curl dangles in front of her eye, and he resists the urge to pull it taut and watch it bounce back into place.

"Hey, handsome," she whispers. "What's doing?"

"I'm okay."

"Missing home yet?"

"Not really."

Stella slips in the thermometer. "I'll bet you miss your girl-friend."

"I don't have a girlfriend." With a foreign object inside his ear canal, his voice sounds hollow and distant. The thermometer beeps and she removes it, her smile turning distracted as she checks the readout. "What is it?"

"Ninety-nine. Point nine."

He never imagined he'd feel relief at the thought of an episode, but he does now. Althea had referred to his sickness as a time machine that would only take him into the future, and that idea has never appealed to him more. Let the KLS catapult him forward three weeks, a month this time. If it's his ticket out of this awful room, well, then, he won't complain. "I guess I'm on my way, then."

"You gonna check out, leave me with all these guys?"

"Sorry, Stella. It's what I came for."

"I guess I'll have to pick a new favorite once you're gone."

He wonders if this is what Althea's done. "I think you'll find me difficult to replace."

"I'm sure I will. Let me ask you something: Do they make all the boys this sweet where you come from?"

"Nope. Just me." He's sure his smile has turned goofy and ridiculous now.

"Well, hang in there another day or two if you can."

"I'll do my best," he says, and for her, he will.

chapter nine.

ALTHEA WAS RIGHT. She really is fooling everyone.

The plan was simple: Tell Garth she was driving to New Mexico for Thanksgiving, then shoot up the coast to New York instead. Find Oliver, beg his pardon, maybe go to the museum to check out the dinosaurs. Then she'd go back to Wilmington, take her finals from home, avoid Coby at all costs, spend a week or two following Garth around some ancient temples, and when Oliver returned from the hospital things would go back, more or less, to normal.

She fills an old camping backpack with her sketchbook, clothes, toiletries, the tapes Minty Fresh and Valerie made for her over the summer—riot grrrl mixes from Val, a badly dubbed copy of Tartar Control from Minty—her own worn-out copies of the Gits' *Enter: The Conquering Chicken* and Concrete Blonde's *Still in Hollywood* and Sugar's *Copper Blue*, and the *Doolittle* cassette she had borrowed from Oliver and never given back; she rolls up the old quilt and straps it to the pack like a bedroll. She uses half a loaf of bread to turn the entire contents of the fridge into sandwiches—cream cheese and marmalade; roasted chicken, Craisins, and arugula; even the garlic mashed potatoes get slathered between slices of seven-grain and wrapped in tinfoil. And from the very bottom of her sock drawer, she takes the stack of old birthday cards from her mother and finally removes the cash that until now has remained spitefully unspent over the last dozen years, thankful, for once, for her ability to hold a grudge. She shoves the cash, about two hundred dollars, in her unraveling canvas wallet, along with the calling card and the money Garth left her on the kitchen table; she takes the Toyota through the car wash one last time and hits the road.

It's another beautiful autumn day in North Carolina, cloudless and only a little cool. Once Althea's on I-40 she is soothed by the rush of the asphalt beneath her car, the trees and telephone poles a blur outside her window. She turns up the music and sings along to the Gits, trying to fill the inside of the car with her voice and the shriek of electric guitars, buoyed by the remainder of Oliver's pills. An hour passes, and another and another. She pulls over at a rest stop somewhere in Virginia and sits on a picnic table, eating a black bean and sour cream sandwich and drinking a warm soda. The mouth of the can tastes like the inside of her car. There's a metal trash bin a few feet away from the picnic table, and she underhands the can in its direction and misses. It falls to the ground and rolls back toward her, the rest of its contents emptying into the grass with a carbonated sizzle.

If the great thing about driving is that—like drinking, like a punk rock show—it turns off Althea's brain, then the problem she doesn't anticipate is that this hypnotic effect will wear off after the first six hours and she'll just be bored as hell. She goes through the sandwiches, crumpling each one's tinfoil into a flower she tosses on the seat beside her; *Oliver's seat* is how she thinks of it, and now she's slowly filling it with garbage. She wasn't expecting this, to be bored, because whenever she imagined being on a road trip she pictured Oliver beside her, providing the entertainment. And, as always happens when she's bored, her mind begins to work, a Ferris wheel of distressing memories and unwanted thoughts that takes on more unpleasantness even as she manages to unload what's already there. Stuck on I-95, she gives up trying to halt the rotation and lets the memories pass before her one by one, to the sound track of "100 Games of Solitaire" in a car fogged by cigarette smoke.

The winter morning she saw her mother's vintage luggage— someone who moved as much as Alice did might have had a more practical set, with rolling suitcases and garment bags, but no, she held fast to her trunks and train cases—stacked on the front porch. The week that followed was the only time she ever saw Garth go without shaving or polishing his shoes. It wasn't long after that when Oliver showed up on the same front porch, apple-cheeked and clad in overalls, Nicky sheepishly asking Garth, whom she barely knew, to keep an eye on him for a few hours.

The Althea-and-Oliver vignettes that come up, one after the other, are not the happy ones. The time she locked him in a closet while he keened his protestations, or tricked him into giving up his Halloween candy, or tormented him into writing a paper for her. And that summer afternoon with Fat Mouse Oliver, the fight with him in the driveway after the show at Lucky's. And then Coby shows up—the disastrous night of tequila, Egyptian Ratscrew, and getting screwed; and the climactic scene in the hallway, when she gave everyone—*everyone*—irrefutable proof that she did not belong among them. If she wanted, she could invert it all, look at it like a solarized picture, like her mother's absence had warped something inside her, and Garth's indifference had not helped, and Coby had wrought his own well-deserved thrashing with the five words she would never stop hearing: *By the way, you're bleeding.* But she can't, she can't look at it that way.

She thinks of what to say to Oliver when she gets there, tries planning a big speech but knows it's pointless. There's really only one thing to say. *I'm sorry.*

"Have I ever called you anything, you know, really awful when I was sick?" Oliver asks Nicky on the phone that night.

She exhales smoke loudly into his ear. "Like what?"

"Just—anything really upsetting. Anything I would have been ashamed to call you under normal circumstances."

"If it would make you ashamed, I wouldn't tell you. Why are you worrying about this, anyway?" He hears a car driving by; she must be sitting on the porch.

"I was just wondering." A lone orderly wheels his bucket down the empty hallway, salsa music blasting from his headphones.

"Let me guess," Nicky says. "You were sitting around with the Spur Posse and they started trading horror stories and now you can't stop speculating about what you may or may not have done."

"Pretty much."

"Ol, I don't want to sound like I'm summing up a fucking parable or something, but when are you going to stop worrying about the things you can't control and start worrying about the things you can?"

Talk about the Serenity Prayer. He hits the receiver against his head a few times and wonders: *What if I could just knock loose the part that's broken and shake it out my ear?* "How are you doing? Is Mrs. Parker your new best friend yet or what?"

"I have a date this weekend."

"With Mrs. Parker?"

"No, you little asshole. With a guy I know from the spa."

"Did you tell him you have a teenager? I bet it'll blow his mind to smithereens."

Now she waxes philosophical. "I think it's so weird when people say 'I have a teenager.' It's like saying 'I have a Ferrari' or 'I have a first edition of *The Great Gatsby*.' I don't have you, Ol, I made you, and all I can do is hope you'll take care of me in my old age."

"It's the nursing home for you, first chance I get."

"That's sweet."

"Look, things are starting to happen up here. My temperature is over a hundred and my knees are killing me. I just wanted to let you know I don't think we'll be having these little chats for much longer."

"Are you going to lose your mind if you wake up and I have a boyfriend?"

"Only if he's a fucking yoga instructor. Or one of those Reiki freaks."

"He's not a colleague, he's a client."

"I hate it when you call them clients. It makes you sound like an escort." Oliver can't imagine Nicky out with any man who would frequent a spa on a regular basis. She accepts dates so rarely, it's difficult to imagine her with anyone at all. Maybe he's an athlete, an aging minor-league pitcher who needs his shoulders tended to by a talented massage therapist, or a fireman with back problems from years of carrying people out of burning houses. *Please, let him be a hero,* Oliver thinks. *Please let him be someone who loves what he does. Please let this guy not be a fucking joker. Let him not be someone with a standing appointment for colonic irrigations.*

"You didn't answer my question, you know. When are you going to—"

"When I learn how to tell the difference," he says.

It's after midnight when Althea finally crosses the George Washington Bridge. She cranes her neck for a view of the city she's come so far to visit, and there it is, lit up like a landing strip. The skyline familiar from movies and photographs is now right outside her window, its buildings almost close enough to touch. This is the city Nicky spoke of, the place where all her stories started. The brake lights of all the cars ahead brighten into a jeweled thread weaving its way down the west side of Manhattan. Opening the window, she lets a brittle November wind lash the inside of the car, and finally the hypnosis brought on by driving starts to dissipate, and she's overcome with a euphoric optimism. This is going to work, because it has to. She'll say she's sorry, Oliver will say he didn't mean it. They'll call a do-over, and everything will go back to the way it was, because it has to, because it can't stay like this.

In the morning there's a tap on the door as Oliver is working the electrode adhesive out of his hair.

"Yeah?"

It's Kentucky, forlorn in his Browning cap and camouflage pajama pants. "Hey."

"Hey," Oliver says.

"I thought you went down, but one of the nurses told me you were still awake."

Oliver's arms are heavy. "I don't know for how much longer."

Kentucky looks disappointed. "Really?"

"Yeah."

"Then I hope I'm next. I'm sick of those fucking gorillas, talking shit and making fun of our accents."

"They're the ones with the accents."

Kentucky smiles. "New Jersey's out. I heard he sings a song from *The Little Mermaid* whenever he gets up to take a piss."

When Oliver laughs, he can still feel the place around his chest where the band was tightened the night before. "You're kidding."

"I'm serious."

"Which song?"

"Stella didn't say."

"That's what we should be doing for entertainment. Fuck the TV. We should be staking out New Jersey's room, waiting to hear the chorus of 'Under the Sea,'" Oliver says.

"My money's on 'Part of Your World.'" Kentucky edges farther inside and sits at the desk.

Maybe this is what college is going to be like—guys wandering in and out of one another's rooms in flip-flops and pajamas, sussing out the few tolerable companions among a veritable sea of morons.

"You picked up that 'Id without the lid' thing really quick the other day. You read a lot of Freud?"

"I guess when you find out you beat off in front of your mom, you get a little curious about Freud." Kentucky spins himself around in the chair.

Oliver peels another chunk of glue from his temple. This is what Minty Fresh should have been using, not toothpaste. "Why did you want to come here?"

"I was bored. And I wanted to tell you about *The Little Mermaid*. I wish you had darts in here or something."

"I mean New York. I mean the study."

Kentucky tears a piece of paper from Oliver's spiral notebook. He folds the rough edge and deepens the crease with a fingernail, then lays the page flat and tears the uneven bit away. "They say we're sick, right? Sick people go to the hospital." He makes more folds in the paper. "And I'm pretty sure I scared the shit out of my parents. That night in the neighbors' kitchen—that put my mother over the top. What about you? Did you figure you'd come up here and they'd fix you, turn you into a normal kid?"

"I guess," says Oliver.

"That never really occurred to me. I'm a fifteen-year-old boy. There's a fucked-up version of me and then a less fucked-up version. Believe me, if they walked in here tomorrow and said you were cured, it wouldn't solve all your problems."

"What you said the other day, about it being like ourselves times a million. Do you really think that?" Oliver asks.

Looking down at the carvings on the desk, Kentucky mulls this over, adjusting the brim of his cap. "Freud would probably say yes. Me? I'm not so sure. But sometimes I do think that the reason we don't remember? It's our fucked-up brains showing us mercy. Even if the show is still on the air, we stop recording. So we'll be spared the memory. We can never play it back." Kentucky sets an origami frog on the desk. He presses on its back legs, then releases it and sends it flying. "You know any alcoholics?"

Immediately Coby comes to mind. "Not yet."

"They say getting sober is the easy part."

"You know a lot of alcoholics?" Oliver asks.

"I live in a dry county, but yes."

"Do they say that before or after they get sober?"

"Usually it's right before they fall off the wagon again." Kentucky says this wearily, as if it's a complaint he's heard firsthand, and more than once.

Oliver bends the neck of the lamp this way, then that. "What if something happens that you want to remember? And it happens while you're not recording?"

"Like what?" Kentucky asks.

"Like—something that only happens once."

"I don't understand."

"Never mind." Oliver stands up. "Let's go reclaim the lounge."

"Something that only happens once? What, like chicken pox?" Kentucky presses.

"Never mind," Oliver mumbles, avoiding his new friend's eyes.

Kentucky's face reddens with burgeoning comprehension. "No shit?"

"No shit," says Oliver, sinking back down onto the bed.

"You lost your—"

"Yeah."

"How?"

Oliver bites the insides of his cheeks. "I have this friend back home. My best friend, since we were kids. She grew up down the block." He hesitates. "I don't really know how it happened."

"You didn't—" Kentucky can't even finish the thought. "Did you?"

Oliver shakes his head. "No, no, it was nothing like that. She wanted to, she'd been wanting to forever. But I told her I didn't want to, that I wasn't ready, and she did it anyway. And when I woke up, she didn't tell me. Not for months. So isn't that kind of like the same thing?"

"So you're saying she— Is that what you're saying?"

Oliver winces. "I don't even know what I'm saying." He remembers Althea screaming at him in the driveway: *Christ, I'm not a fucking rapist.* He didn't argue with her, not on that point. Something about that word doesn't feel right. It's too broad, not specific enough to describe what Althea did to him. Kentucky can't even say it out loud. "No, that's not what I'm saying. Not exactly."

Kentucky looks baffled. "I don't get it."

"What don't you get?"

"Is she ugly or something?"

"Fuck you, she's beautiful."

"Listen, I pulled out my dick in front of my mother. AK-47's little sister is going to need years of psychotherapy. New Jersey got dumped for some infraction he'll never even know about. That shit is all irreparable. You just told me you got laid."

"But it's like I wasn't even there."

Irate, Kentucky leaps to his feet and points to the door. "New Jersey tried to fuck a window treatment! You fucked your beautiful best friend! What the hell are you doing here, man? Go find this girl and screw her brains out! And this time you will remember!" He shakes his head. "Christ on a cross, NC, you should have told that story the first day you got here. You would have been holding the remote this whole time."

"I don't want to have stories to tell!" Oliver shouts. "I want my fucking life back! I got laid, sure, and I have no idea what it was like. I have no idea what I was like."

"What, you're worried you weren't any good?"

"That's not what I mean. I mean— Why is this so hard to grasp? When it happens, it's supposed to change your life, divide everything into 'before' and 'after.' And instead I'm in some weird limbo. It used to be I was a step behind all my friends. I get sick, time stops for me, they keep going. Now I've even fallen behind *myself*. And how can I ever catch up? It'll never be my first time again. Not with anyone. Not with her." Even as the story has galvanized Kentucky, Oliver is wiped out by the telling. Lying back on the hospital bed, he throws a forearm over his face. "We get to stop recording, but we don't get to hit pause, and we don't get to rewind."

Kentucky launches his frog across the desk again. "What does your girl say about all this?"

"She's not my girl. I was so pissed when I found out, I stopped speaking to her." Exhaustion falls over Oliver like a billowy sheet; it lands on his face and knees first, and then settles over the rest of his body.

"Look, I hear you. It would bother the hell out of me if I couldn't remember my first time. Not that I've *had* a first time. You know what I mean. But listen, you've heard everyone else's stories. Doesn't it seem possible that you were the aggressor? If she'd been wanting to for ages, and you finally made a move, maybe she just, I don't know, couldn't help herself."

"I can blame KLS for my bad decisions. She's got no excuse for her lack of impulse control."

"What's her name?"

"Althea."

Kentucky shakes his head. "You got some beautiful girl named Althea in love with you, and you're stuck here talking to me. I'd be pissed, too."

Stella walks in, brandishing her thermometer. When she leans over to check Oliver's glands, he can smell the nicotine on her lips and in her hair.

"How are you feeling?"

"I think it's time."

"Let's get you set up." She turns to Kentucky. "Would you mind excusing us?"

"Can I ask you something first?"

"Sure."

Kentucky looks solemnly at the nurse, and as she looks back, Oliver is aware of the gulf in years between them. This woman weathered her own uncertain adolescence and made it out on the other side. Oliver realizes if he could fast-forward ten years, he'd see that he, too, had done the same, that the unknown territory between now and then would be navigated much as the past had been—inelegantly, and with great confusion, in a clumsy but dogged fashion. KLS might force him to skip ahead here and there, but he's going to have to do all the hard parts himself. The thought exhausts him further.

"Do they assign you what color scrubs you have to wear?" asks Kentucky. "Or do you get to choose?"

Althea stands outside the hospital, smoking and planning what she'll say. Her neck aches from sleeping in her car overnight; she craves a cigarette even though she's in the middle of one, and she knows she could stand out here all day and never be ready to go in. He's up there, an elevator ride away. All she has to do is push through the revolving doors and traverse that marble lobby, find his room in this enormous building, and open with some whimsical remark about the weather in New York. That should do it. Some whimsy, the weather, a big smile. Right. Or maybe he'll just be so impressed by her devotion, that she's driven all this way to offer one of her rare apologies, that he'll forgive her on the spot.

Two women spill out of the revolving doors, giggling and looking over their shoulders, one of them wheeling an IV stand behind her, a hospital bracelet around her wrist. Her friend places a hand on her elbow, steering her away from the entrance. The patient looks a few years older than her friend, the friend a few years older than Althea. The two are full of mischief, mirth, giddy over their brief escape. The friend has pink hair and a nose ring; the patient sports the kind of slick bob that can only be achieved with various efforts and appliances.

Pink pulls out a pack of cigarettes and offers one to her friend.

"You light it," the patient says. "They always taste better when you light them."

Pink obliges, and soon the two are enveloped in their cloud, taking intensely grateful drags.

"We need to ditch my mother," the patient says, gesturing with her free hand. "She's got to be shined on."

"She's scaring the bejesus out of all the doctors," says Pink. "Yet I find her presence oddly soothing."

"Soothing like a car alarm. You've got to do something. She's got to go."

"She needs an activity. A way to be useful. Useful somewhere else."

"Should we tell her the dogs need to be walked? Give her the keys to my apartment?"

Pink shivers. "Your mother is wearing a Donna Karan suit and I'm standing here dressed like a street urchin. Which of us is the more likely candidate to pick up dog shit in the East Village?"

The patient's eyes widen. "That's it! We'll send her back to my apartment to pick up clothes. Get her to go pack a bag for me."

Pink nods enthusiastically, pointing at her friend with the lit end of her cigarette. "Yes. But. You need to fixate on an item that she won't be able to find. To make sure she's there for a while. Something you absolutely need. Something that's in *my* apartment."

Althea listens, envious, as the two work out their scheme. They seem unlikely cohorts. She wonders how two such women found each other in this city. Nicky only told the story of meeting Oliver's dad once—a party, a friend of a friend, it had not been interesting—but Althea loves the tale of her friendship with Sarah, how they lived on the same floor of their apartment building and eyed each other for weeks, first smiling, then saying hello, daily pleasantries at the mailboxes extending into longer conversations, Nicky gathering the nerve to invite Sarah over for dinner. "A shot in the dark," she called it. They spent a long night on the fire escape with a bottle of wine, listening to cats howl in the courtyard below and their upstairs neighbors singing a pornographic duet of sighs and moans. By the time the sun rose, Nicky said, she knew that was it. She knew she was in it with Sarah for life.

"Are you sure?" asks Pink. "You're sure you don't want your mother here? She really, really wants to be here."

Her friend holds up the hand with the IV. "This right here? This trumps your conscience. As long as I'm schlepping one of these things around, you have to do what I want."

"And what you want is to trick your mother into going back to your apartment?"

"For hours. Yes. That is what I want."

"Your wish is my etcetera," Pink says.

Their strategy fully formed, she wheels her friend's IV back toward the entrance, the two women firmly leashed together. Althea watches them go.

"That girl looked so sad, don't you think?" A gust of wind carries Pink's whisper back to its subject.

Her friend shrugs, the plastic bracelet slipping down her wrist. "It's a hospital. What do you expect?"

They forge a path through the revolving doors and the lobby Althea has been trying to cross for two hours. Imagining herself drawn along in their wake, she pushes through the doors before they can stop spinning, letting the duo's momentum tug her forward.

If Oliver had ever fantasized about going to bed with Stella, this would not quite be what he'd imagined. She waits outside while he changes into his pajamas—an old pair of sweats that he's cut into shorts and his favorite Johnny Cash T-shirt. Everything aches now, his ankles and wrists and even the base of his neck, and his head is warm and heavy. As he gets into bed, he expects to feel grateful, but his exhaustion is unexpectedly mingled with anxiety. For the first time since he arrived, he realizes that the outside world has not ground to a halt simply because he's quarantined here. Nicky joked that she could have a boyfriend by the time Oliver wakes, but it's actually possible, isn't it? And what else could be going on out there?

Stella knocks on the door. "You ready?"

"I guess."

She enters, standing over his bed. "Don't look so worried."

"I hope this wasn't a terrible idea."

"Shush."

"Don't shush me," he says automatically, but she doesn't know the rest of her lines. He tries to cue her. "You're supposed to say . . ." But the rest comes out an incoherent, sleepy mumble. In his head he can hear it perfectly. *You love it when I shush you.* "Fuck."

"I'm supposed to say 'fuck'?" asks Stella.

Abruptly, Oliver sits up, panicked. "This was a bad idea. Why did I come here?"

"So we could help you. Relax, okay? I'm here to help you."

"I don't know why I'm so nervous." His voice trembles.

"Here." Reaching behind him, Stella fluffs his pillows, then punches them to make an indentation for his head. "Lie down."

If he says one more word, he's going to cry. He obeys.

As his reward, Stella starts to sing. Her voice is cracked and raspy but warm, filled with honey, and it fits the slow, mournful song she's chosen. He closes his eyes and listens as she presses the sticky electrodes to his temples again and hooks him up to all the equipment, sadness filling his chest until it's tight against the rubber strap.

Even half-asleep, Oliver can sense Stella's graceful movements around the room. But it's Althea's image that swims onto the stage of his eyelids, blissed out and covered in cherry Jell-O, then driving her car down the highway, one elbow resting on the open window, the other hand masterfully piloting the wheel. He remembers when that was enough for her, just a ride in the car or a day at the beach, and he wishes he could have given her another ten years of days like that, when all it took to make her happy was him in the shotgun seat and twelve hours when they had nowhere to be.

Suddenly the idea that Stella might see him in the midst of this coming episode, that he might unwittingly grope her or say something profane or relieve himself on the floor while she watches, seems inexpressibly horrible. He would rather go back to Wilmington right now than risk sacrificing her kindness and ruining one more person's good opinion of him. When she's finished her song, he opens his eyes with tremendous effort.

"Will you look after Kentucky while I'm out?" he says. "Make sure the gorillas aren't giving him a hard time."

"They're not gorillas," she says. "They're just a bunch of boys, all as scared as you."

"Still."

"Okay."

"You won't be here, right?"

"Here where?"

It's getting harder to string words together in a coherent fashion. "You won't see . . . me," he manages.

She smiles, understanding. "Whatever happens, I won't see any of it." Leaning over, she tucks the blanket under his chin and he can smell cigarettes and lip balm and the sharp scent of her scrubs, and his stupid, stupid heart rends one more time with the memory of Althea, and if he weren't losing consciousness he would burst into an apocalyptic fit of tears, but instead his eyes close and the last thing Stella says finds his brain by way of some small miracle, right before his mind flickers like a candle and is snuffed out.

"But I will be here when you wake up."

Althea steps out of the elevator, fists thrust into the pockets of her jeans, shoulders hunched in her down vest, hood hanging over her face. A long, shiny hallway stretches out before her, then makes a sharp right turn. Somewhere a television is broadcasting sports; an announcer's voice drones faintly over the cheer of a stadium crowd. Two boys come careening into sight, sliding down the slick floor in socked feet, almost crashing into the wall at the end of the hallway. They run back in the other direction, vanishing behind the corner again. There is an audible thud and the squeak of skin against linoleum as one of them wipes out, then braying laughter.

Althea tries to parse the ruckus for Oliver's voice, but she can't make it out. Still, her breath quickens at the very thought of his nearness, that she might get to bury her face in his neck and smell that familiar Oliver scent. Fabric softener and honey pomade, and apples, faintly, always. Here, will he still smell the same? Her body aches, not just from the long drive and sleeping in her car, but from the memory of Oliver wrapped around her, or idly holding the loop on her carpenter's pants, Oliver's lips pressed against her throat, Oliver smoothing out all her nerves and tics.

But that is not all she misses. The Oliver-faced imposter who fisted his hands in her snarled hair and yanked—she wonders if she'll ever see him again and is saddened by the thought that she might not. If they fix Oliver here, like he wants, that other Oliver will be gone, the Id will have a lid, and everyone will celebrate the death of the fat mouse; Althea will be the only one to mourn the insatiable boy who had been famished for her.

Edging forward, she pauses with one hand on the curved reception desk. Emboldened, she keeps going, hugging the wall until she can finally peek around the corner and see the cluster of boys in a common room at the end of the hall, sprawled on broken-down couches and institutional chairs, watching football and doing push-ups. She recognizes one of the boys who was skidding around in his socks; he's limping back to his seat. Two other boys are having a hushed conversation on a sticky-looking sofa.

There's still no sign of Oliver. She thought being here would galvanize her, but instead she's unexpectedly, unrelentingly weary. The environment is so alien, enough to make her realize how small their home galaxy of Wilmington is. There, they orbited the same swimming hole, the same coffee shop, the same houses of their three same friends. Here, in this hospital, is one infinitesimal chunk of the rest of the universe—these boys, whose own dramas have led them to the study; the dizzying city baying against the windows; the pink girl from downstairs and her more polished friend. Althea is reeling suddenly from the scope of it all, as if an invisible thread tethering her all the way back to Magnolia Street has suddenly snapped, leaving her adrift and violently conscious of the distance between herself and all that she's known.

The two boys on the couch fall silent. One remains clearly preoccupied, fastening and unfastening the wristband of his watch. The kid next to him reaches over and slaps his back heartily in an awkward, earnest gesture of comfort. Recognizing Oliver's pain on another boy's face makes the desperation in the room suddenly palpable, despite the air of faux indifference—she can recognize it anywhere, feigned apathy, having honed her own brand for years. The thing for which they all came here, this endlessly evasive cure, they all want it so, so badly.

A door down the hallway opens and Althea leaps back, startled, pressing herself closer to the wall. In the lounge a boy in camouflage pajama pants looks up from his magazine, staring at her from underneath the brim of his baseball cap as a blonde nurse emerges from the room, quickly closing the door and sliding a medical chart into the mounted plastic box. Before Althea even sees the name on the binder she knows that it's Oliver's, that he's behind that door.

"Who are you?" the nurse asks sharply. She has long fingers and narrow green eyes, and Althea is speechless with jealousy. "What are you doing back here?"

"I was looking for someone."

"Who?"

Althea struggles to form the one word she's spoken more than any other. "Oliver," she whispers.

The anger evaporates from the nurse's face. "You're here to see Oliver?" she says softly.

Biting down hard on her lip, Althea gnaws away chapped, dry skin that stings when she tears it with her teeth, so as her eyes fill she can tell herself that's why she's crying. "I'm too late, aren't I?"

"For now. I'm sorry. It can wait, right? For a little while?" says the nurse. "It's not forever, just a couple of weeks. Whatever it is, it'll keep for that long, won't it?"

Althea wipes her face with the cuffs of her sweatshirt and heads for the door. "Yeah. It'll keep."

chapter ten.

ALTHEA BUYS A FORTY of King Cobra.

She takes the bottle of malt liquor, neatly tucked inside a paper bag, and walks down to the pier. Staring out at the river, she drinks her King Cobra and smokes. A party boat drives by, blasting dance music over the shrill laughter of its passengers. After it passes, the only sound is water, lapping noisily against the gravel.

Instinct brought her to the water. Unable to complete her mission, but unwilling to turn around and drive home, she left Manhattan for Brooklyn, keeping Oliver close but putting a river between them. She found a place Nicky never mentioned, a tiny crook on the map called Red Hook, a postindustrial maritime neighborhood full of unobtrusive places where she could sleep in her car, where it smelled like the water and she could see the Statue of Liberty from a small gravel beach near the pier.

New York is fucking cold. The sun has long since set. Althea's empty belly piggishly soaks up the contents of the bottle. The pier, the park, the surrounding docks and warehouses are deserted. In Wilmington she's used to trespassing in the dark, stealing around the riverbanks at night or taking an unlit shortcut home on foot. But the woods are never quiet; there are crickets and foxes, skunks, of course, and the perpetual rustling of the creatures that go unseen. Here there's nothing, not a car passing with a gentle swish nor a mistaken songbird trilling invisibly from the highest branches of its tree. Just the rhythm of the water, so hypnotic it might carry Althea off to sleep on her bench, if the wind weren't so damn cold. She feels numb yet oddly sated; for so long Oliver had been her sole preoccupation, and without the prospect of touching him or talking to him, she's rendered inert, wiped clean of all will and desire. Shivering violently in her vest, she fills herself up with booze and waits for King Cobra to tell her what to do; he doesn't seem to have a lot to say.

When she's finally drunk enough for the shivering to subside, she gathers her cigarettes and car keys and stands, swaying a little. She chugs the last three inches of flat malt liquor and drops the empty bottle into a trash can, woozily saluting Lady Liberty before she turns to go. But those last three inches are three inches too many, and suddenly all forty ounces are backing up on her, and she's clutching the mouth of the garbage can on either side, doubled over and retching. Her nose fills with the smell of industrial plastic trash bag and rotten banana and acrid bile as sour liquid spills out of her, unprompted, and her gagging drowns out the sound of the river. When it's finished she stays there, catching her breath; her eyes have filled and her nose is leaking. She spits a few times and stands up, shaking it off, wiping at her face with the cuff of her sweatshirt. *Okay, that wasn't so bad*, she thinks. But then she realizes her hands—previously holding her car keys and Marlboros—are empty, and there's only one place these items could be.

"Motherfucker," she whispers, and rolls up her sleeves.

It's too dark to actually see into the trash, so she keeps her eyes on the Statue of Liberty while she gingerly delves into the slick refuse and feels around. Her fingers graze the banana peel she smelled, the cold glass of her empty bottle, the soggy pages of a magazine. The smell is ungodly, vomit and vinegar and sour milk, and everything she touches is soaked with her puke. It's the cigarettes she finds first, that unmistakable flip-top box; removing the cellophane wrapper, she tucks the pack safely into her pocket. Holding her breath, she makes another foray, digging deeper until she's up to her shoulder and gagging from the stench, dry-heaving, eyes burning as her fingertips troll the bottom of the plastic bag through the forty ounces of regurgitated malt liquor that's collected there. Out on the river, a lone duck paddles toward the rocky beach.

Finally, almost accidentally, the metal loop of her key ring slips around the tip of her index finger. Securing the keys in her fist, she jerks her arm out of the trash so quickly, she barely notices her forearm catch on something sharp and jagged. It only feels like a pinch at first, then a hot sting, then warm and wet.

Drops of blood form a neat line in a slit up the side of her wrist, slowly at first, then gathering momentum as they run down her arm, sticky and warm. Clamping down on the wound with her other hand, she staggers backward and drops to her knees on the pier. The sting spreads, becoming deeper, searing through the rest of her that is still so cold. She wipes ineffectually at the blood pooling in the crook of her arm, whimpering, face pressed to her knees, the overripe denim rough against her cheek as she smells the iron of her blood, the stale smoke in her hair, and her beery puke.

Rising unsteadily to her feet, she stumbles off the pier and finds her car. Tearing a T-shirt into small strips, she douses one with water from her bottle and dabs at the wound, then uses another as a makeshift bandage. She digs the beach blankets out of the trunk. Hunkered down on the floor of the backseat, holding her arm above her head, swaddled in her quilt and the sandy relics that still smell like Wilmington, she tries to think of this as camping, imagines herself in a tent with her father, listening to one of his ancient mythological stories, trying to remember a single one that had a happy ending.

That night Althea dreams of dinosaurs. The theme is familiar; for years she's dreamed dozens of variations. Sometimes she's alone in a prehistoric forest watching a herd of triceratops from behind a cluster of iridescent jade ferns, or being chased through the streets of downtown Wilmington by a clumsy T. rex she can easily outrun, or she's crouched on the sawdust-covered floor of a warehouse the size of a football field, hiding, stifling the sneeze that will inevitably give her away to the trio of feathered velociraptors seeking her out. These dreams have never frightened her. She was always at least vaguely aware she was asleep, but at the same time they seemed real enough to be exciting. They were certainly more interesting than Oliver's pre-KLS dreams, thinly veiled anxiety metaphors about history exams or being left behind in the woods after a camping trip. When she pointed that out, he had groaned and asked her if she had to be competitive about even their REM cycles.

Tonight the dream is different. In it, she sleeps in her car underneath her blankets. Her icy hands are clutched between her thighs. Two deinonychus watch her through the window, smoking cigarettes and speaking in low voices. One taps on the glass with a curved onyx talon, chuckling. Gone is the fantastic element of wonder as well as the certainty that she isn't actually in danger. She may be able to take Coby or Oliver easily in a fight, but she'll be no match against two theropods with crested heads and spiny fishbone teeth. She can't hear what they're saying, but she feels them watching her, discussing. Beer bottles clink together. Her car keys are in her vest pocket, digging into her side. Is there any chance she could lunge into the driver's seat, start the ignition, and drive away before they could smash her windshield and devour her? Probably not. *Garth is going to be so pissed,* she thinks.

The clouds are still pink when she wakes, agitated by her first nightmare in years, uncertain what brought it on. Rifling through the glove compartment, she hopes for a rogue granola bar or stale bag of candy, but there's nothing to eat, only a broken pair of sunglasses, Minty Fresh's pamphlets, and a stack of old lottery tickets that have been there since she inherited the car from her grandmother. It's been too long since she showered; the car smells like vomit and garbage, but it's too cold to roll down the windows and air it out. She ties up her greasy hair and wipes at a stain on her pants with a spit-dampened thumb. Her arm still aches.

Last night she parallel-parked on a residential side street, hoping the apartment buildings would serve as a windbreak. It took her twenty minutes to maneuver into the minuscule spot, and she had felt a tiny rush of excitement at doing it without Oliver guiding her in with a series of hand gestures from the sidewalk. She gets out of the car to stretch and cases the block to determine if it's still early enough for her to squat down and relieve herself by her bumper; she decides it is. Hunkering down between the Camry and the adjacent SUV, she makes a noise of satisfaction. Some small pleasures are the same anywhere. Eye-level with her fender, she watches the sidewalk to make sure no one's coming and sees something so chilling that if she weren't in the process of emptying her bladder, she might have lost control of it altogether.

There's a pile of cigarette butts, half a dozen, not two feet from where she's crouched. White-filtered. Not her brand. And two sea-green Rolling Rock bottles lolling on the ground beside them.

She's barely finished but she stands anyway, hastily pulling up her pants and fastening her zipper with shaky hands, piss soaking warmly through the crotch of her jeans. The side-street hush that seemed so peaceful minutes before is malevolent now, a trap she didn't spot soon enough. Flinging herself into the car, whispering *"Go, go, go!"* under her breath, terrified and rib-crackingly lonely, she peels out of the parking spot she'd been so proud to find last night.

One of Minty's pamphlets lists the locations of all the East

Coast chapters of Bread and Roses, where they cook and where they serve. She still has some money left, but she doesn't know how long she'll need to make it last. The addresses for the Brooklyn chapter don't mean anything to her; she locates them on her map, tracing her finger from Red Hook along the Belt Parkway and Leif Ericson Drive to the tiny park in Coney Island where this afternoon the Minty Freshes and Valeries of Brooklyn will be giving away free food.

Winding through increasingly narrow and deserted streets, she emerges on Surf Avenue, low and empty, a shabby discount furniture store facing the shuttered arcades and beach shops on the opposite side of the wide thoroughfare. Only Nathan's looks as she had imagined it, the restaurant itself dwarfed under the signs that proclaim it as THE ORIGINAL, WORLD FAMOUS FRANKFURTERS SINCE 1916. Beneath the bombast of the newer billboards, the humbler yellow signs remain, advertising the clam bar and the seafood as well as the hot dogs, referring to Nathan's as a delicatessen.

She parks by Nathan's, home of the annual hot dog eating contest. Every Fourth of July Nicky comes over to watch it on ESPN, reciting the stats of each competitor before game time and then screaming ferociously at the television until it's over, Garth blanching slightly and a mortified Oliver shrinking into his side of the couch. Afterward, they barbecue in the backyard and Althea and Oliver stage their own competition, eating until they're sick, lying in the gazebo to recover while Nicky and Garth drink mint juleps and eat Althea's apple pie directly from the pan. But Oliver slept through this July, so Althea had spent Independence Day with Coby, setting off bottle rockets and drinking Southern Comfort.

The smell of the ocean is wildly comforting, and she follows it to the shore across a splintered boardwalk that rattles under her feet. It isn't like her beach at home. The gray sand is punctuated with broken Corona bottles and cigarette butts, and there's a deserted amusement park to her back, but that's the same ocean rolling in against the shore. Closing her eyes, she lets the salty wind whip her hair around her face and she listens to the seagulls screeching at one another and the waves crashing over and over, an endless feedback loop of God's own soothing white noise. She might fall asleep standing up right here if it weren't time to go collect a free meal.

It's easy to spot the small group in the park, huddled around a folding table draped with a banner that reads FREE FOOD. Behind the table are a guy and a girl a few years older than Althea, doling out hot food from large aluminum containers on stands warmed from underneath by little burners that remind her of chemistry class. About half a dozen people wait in line. Dead, frosty grass crunches under Althea's tennis shoes as she crosses the park, hood up, sunglasses on, to join them. It could almost be a backyard barbecue except all the guests are homeless, mostly older men with patchy beards wearing torn cargo pants and coats over jackets over sweatshirts. She tightens her grip on her bag.

It's the food that has her real attention—spinach and mashed potatoes and something that looks like meatloaf but is probably made from lentils, if this chapter is as fervent as Minty Fresh about sticking to its vegan credo. He pestered her and Oliver mercilessly about going vegan, snorting with derision every time they said they wouldn't give up cheese. "If I put cheese on shit, you two would eat it," Nicky used to complain, but she would have done anything to make her cooking edible. As Althea takes her plate from the petite blonde girl, whose hair spills from under her black knit cap and pools in the hood of her jacket, she averts her eyes—from the girl, from the boy with her, from the cluster of people eating on the benches. Originally she intended to go back to the beach and eat there, but now that she's holding the plate she can see the diced garlic in the spinach and the traces of red skins in the potatoes and it's all she can do to wait until she's sitting on a bench to dig in. Some of the others go back for seconds or even thirds, but she can barely finish the helping she's been given. Satisfied, she lights a cigarette—the best kind of cigarette there is, the kind you smoke after a good meal.

She's barely closed the pack before she's approached by a man with lentils worked into his beard. "Excuse me, miss," he says. "Do you have another one of those?" She ends up passing around her pack and lighter to everyone in the park.

As the sun begins to dip in the sky, the occupants of the other benches drift away to their unknown destinations. The blonde girl and her partner, a thin boy with glasses and red hair, speak quietly behind the table. They're not what Althea was expecting, but she's not sure what she was expecting— more Minty Freshes, she supposes, severe hairstyles and militant zipper pants. She thought, if anything, the Brooklyn versions would be more extreme.

It seems like they're bickering. The boy's face has tightened, and the girl's hands are on her hips. He begins covering the food, continuing their argument with disinterest. Whatever it is can't be very serious. It might be moments like this Althea misses most, about Oliver, about everyone back home. The fleeting disagreements that seem so charged—which record to play, whether to stop and ask for directions—and then pass so quickly, tapering off with no real resolution necessary. This one looks like it's concluding, the guy bundling up plastic forks and knives, the girl refastening her ponytail, turning away from the table and bounding across the grass toward Althea, yelling something in her direction.

"Sorry?" Althea says, shrinking, cinching her hood around her face.

The girl waits until she's reached Althea's bench to speak again. "To eat," she asks. "Did you have enough to eat? I wanted to make sure, before we pack up the food and take it home."

"I did. Thanks. It was good."

"I made the fake meatloaf myself," she says proudly. "You should come back tomorrow; we do a big spread for Thanksgiving." The girl puts her hands in her back pockets and looks up at the weighty clouds sweeping in off the Atlantic. "It might snow."

Althea removes her sunglasses. Even without them, the sky is darkening quickly. "You think so?"

The boy is struggling to fold the banner as the wind unfurls it comically. "Matilda!" he yells. "Get over here."

Matilda takes another look at the leaden clouds sinking toward them every second. "It's gonna do *something*." She lowers her gaze to Althea, grinning. "You don't talk much, do you?"

Althea looks at the ground helplessly. "Sorry."

"Don't be sorry. It's just an observation. You from California?"

"California?" says Althea, perplexed.

Matilda tugs on the disintegrating sleeve of Althea's sweatshirt. "You're underdressed for New York."

"I didn't think I was going to be here long enough to need a new wardrobe."

"Fucking hell," says Matilda, seeing the bandage on Althea's arm. "What happened here?"

"I cut myself, it's fine—"

"That looks filthy. Let me see it." She reaches for Althea's sleeve again.

"Don't!" Althea pulls back. "If I just look at it wrong it starts bleeding again. Please. Don't touch it."

Relenting, Matilda lights a cigarette.

"North Carolina," Althea says finally. "I came from Wilmington, North Carolina."

"Really?" Recognition lifts Matilda's eyebrows. "I just talked to a couple of kids from there. A few weeks ago. They got my name from someone, called and asked for advice, some recipes. Shit, what were their names?"

"Valerie and Minty Fresh?"

"You know them?" Matilda says, surprised.

"We were friends, yeah."

"They seemed nice. Minty Fresh seemed a little on the overzealous side."

"You have no idea," Althea says.

She's about to explain about all the pamphlets he left under her windshield, how she found them in the glove compartment and they led her to Coney Island, when the wind sends a green beer bottle rolling down the sidewalk behind them with a hollow, desolate momentum. It freezes her in place, their pleasant conversation forgotten.

"Are you okay?"

"I just—It was that beer bottle. It reminded me about this nightmare I had last night."

Matilda nods, wide-eyed. "Must have been some bad dream."

"It wasn't actually a dream. Part of it was. I mean, I don't think it was actually dinosaurs watching me sleep in my car." She rubs her eyes, trying to focus.

"Someone was watching you sleep in your car?"

"I think so." She explains about the dream and finding the cigarette butts and beer bottles on the curb in the morning. Matilda listens attentively, her shoulders tightening under her coat when Althea describes the moment when the deinonychus had tapped on the window. "I don't know, maybe it *was* just a dream."

"You're really lucky," says Matilda seriously.

Althea nods.

"You don't have any place to stay?"

Althea shakes her head.

"What are you going to do about tonight?"

Althea shrugs.

"Okay, so we're back to the not talking." The boy is signaling Matilda, beckoning her back across the park. She raises her gloved hand, fingers splayed, mouthing, *Five more minutes.* "Look, we live around here. Why don't you come back with us, stay at our house for the night?"

The boy has his hands cupped around his mouth, yelling Matilda's name.

"I should go, your friend needs you." Althea hastily puts on her sunglasses, yokes her bag around her neck.

"Are you sure?" The concern in Matilda's voice is sincere enough to bewilder Althea.

"I'm sure. I'll be okay. I'll sleep someplace safe." She rushes toward the exit of the park.

"Come back tomorrow, okay?" Matilda hollers.

Nodding once, Althea secures her hood and keeps going.

Althea buys a cup of coffee and goes back to the boardwalk. Digging the calling card out of her wallet, she finds a pay phone. She was supposed to let Garth know when she arrived safely at her mother's house in Taos; it's time to make a preemptive strike, lest he grow concerned and dial Alice first. Fortunately, Garth has yet to succumb to the allure of fancy technologies like call waiting and caller ID.

"Hello?"

"Hi, Dad," she says.

"Althea?"

"Yeah."

"Are you there already?"

"I just got here," she says, staring out over the Atlantic Ocean. "I made good time."

"You did. Is everything okay? You getting settled?"

"What are you doing?" She wants to be able to picture him, perfectly, wherever he is in the house.

"Just making some notes for the book."

"So, napping?"

"Don't be smart."

"I can't help it." She presses the mouthpiece of the phone to her vest while taking a heavy drag of her cigarette. And then: "Maybe this wasn't such a good idea."

"Althea." She can hear him sitting up on the couch in his study, and the whole image snaps immediately into place—his books spread around him, the sleep lines on his cheek, a half-eaten sandwich forgotten somewhere on the floor. Removing his glasses, then rubbing one eye with the heel of his hand, then pinching the bridge of his nose between his fingers. His voice is an outline; the rest she can fill in easily herself. She wonders if he's doing the same thing, envisioning her safely ensconced in Alice's guest room, surrounded by crystals and mediocre Southwestern art. Instead here she is, standing by the aquarium, hoping the distant sounds of the sea lion show aren't leaking into the pay phone.

"Maybe I shouldn't have come here," she repeats.

"You just got there," Garth says. "Do you really want to turn all the way around and come back?"

"I don't know."

"Just give her a chance. I know you don't know her that well, but you're already there. You might as well let her try to be your mother for a couple of days. Maybe you'll like her."

Even though she knows he's talking about Alice, it's Matilda who comes to Althea's mind. "What if she doesn't like me?"

Garth's teasing smile makes its way into his voice. "Now, girl, why on earth wouldn't she like you?"

"Don't be smart."

"I can't help it. I've got a PhD and everything."

Althea changes the subject. "How's the book going?"

"Did you know that Cortés was supposed to leave Spain for the New World a year before he actually did? He was injured fleeing the bedroom of a married woman from Medellín and had to postpone his departure."

"Sounds like a real class act."

Garth warms to his subject. It sounds like he's reading an excerpt from his book-in-progress. "Fifteen years later, when he was living in Cuba, he almost missed his chance again. The man who assigned Cortés to the expedition was rethinking his decision because he was afraid that Cortés was too headstrong to remain loyal. When Cortés got wind of that, he cut his preparations short and left Cuba with his crew. And after they arrived on the mainland, he destroyed the ships so his men would have no choice but to follow him."

"Jesus."

"Try to enjoy yourself. And don't let your mother overcook the turkey. Okay?"

"Okay."

No *I miss you*, no *I love you*, just a click and the hiss of the empty line. She tries not to hold it against him; he thinks she's safe in Taos, New Mexico, wrapped warm and tight inside one of her mother's Navajo blankets. For just one second, she wishes that she were.

It was Minty Fresh who started drinking coffee first—not because he liked it, but because he found a vintage Popeye thermos at Goodwill and wanted an excuse to show it off. Later, they filled the thermos with gin or whiskey, whatever they could quietly loot from their parents or convince someone to buy them at the liquor store. But in the beginning it was always coffee, some fair trade dark roast Minty Fresh learned to enjoy, and eventually Althea learned, too. She never gave him enough credit for that aspect of his personality. The thermos came first, and he found a way to fill it; he gave himself an enormous blue Mohawk and then reinvented himself as a boy worthy of one; they'd given him the most ludicrous nickname they could think of, and he'd owned it.

If Minty Fresh were set loose alone in New York City, he wouldn't be sitting around wondering what to do. Already he would have concocted half a dozen missions that had to be completed before nightfall; already he would have made half a dozen new friends. Picture him sitting on this bench, tightening the laces of his combat boots. Picture Valerie chugging a Dr Pepper and fooling with her hair. Picture two people who actually seem to know what they're doing. And then ask yourself what they would do if they were here.

The second Brooklyn address on the pamphlet isn't far, just a few streets away from the park and the water. The houses are large, some almost Victorian, not unlike her own back on Magnolia Street. Several are abandoned, the windows and doors boarded up with plywood spray-painted with graffiti. Others are decorated for Thanksgiving, jointed cardboard turkeys hanging off porch railings above neatly trimmed hedges. The block is at a strange impasse, somewhere between the suburban and the postapocalyptic.

She parks a few houses down. Slouched in her seat, she watches the front door. Then she pulls out her sketchbook and draws the two deinonychus from last night's dream, giving one a cigarette and the other a bottle of beer. It gets dark. It gets colder. She cracks a window and chain-smokes, wrapped in her childhood quilt.

Matilda comes out of the house, a sack of garbage over one shoulder. She heaves the bag into an overflowing trash can almost as big as she is and drags it to the curb, with that recognizable sound of heavy plastic scraping against concrete. After she wrangles the can into place she pauses, hands on her hips, her breath turning to vapor in the late November chill. Althea rubs her hands; she's not sure she won't freeze to death in her car overnight or be murdered. Matilda sits on the steps and pulls out a pouch of tobacco, and Althea thinks of Nicky.

Althea is so stiff, she almost falls over getting out of the car. Her sweatshirt cuffs are down over her icy fisted hands. Even in her dinosaur nightmare she hadn't been this afraid. Putting one numb foot in front of the other, she closes the distance between herself and this stranger, taking a shot in the dark.

"Hi," Althea says, sitting on the step next to her.

Matilda grins widely. "Good. You're here. I can stop worrying." She flicks open a Zippo, holds the flame to her cigarette, and snaps the lighter shut in a single well-practiced motion.

There's a quarter on the sidewalk, and Althea reaches for it.

"Don't," Matilda says. "I'm superstitious. That quarter showed up there last week and I've been having good luck ever since. Now I'm terrified to move it. I keep meaning to come out here with a glue gun. Fucking shellac it into place if I have to."

Althea looks at the quarter with a new reverence. Abruptly, she realizes how pathetic she must appear—unshowered and shivering, her blood-crusted bandage peeking out from under the cuff of her sweatshirt, her need completely transparent. A siren wails somewhere closer to the ocean. Althea discreetly massages her aching calves. The front door opens above them, and a girl with curly dark hair and deep olive skin sticks her head out.

"Hey, Management, Kaleb says it's your turn tonight."

Matilda waves her away. "Tell your shiftless boyfriend not to worry." The curly haired girl retreats inside.

"'Management'?" Althea asks.

"It's what they call me sometimes."

"Was that your roommate?"

"One of them. It looks like I was wrong about the weather," Matilda says, nodding up toward the clouds parting in the night sky to reveal the waning moon. "It's weird. I'm never wrong about that shit."

"Maybe it was your lucky quarter, kept the snow away."

"Snow I don't mind. I'd rather save my luck for other things. You probably don't get a lot of snow in Wilmington, I guess."

Althea shakes her head. "We don't really have cold like this."

"How long have you been here?"

"Just a couple of days."

The door opens again, and this time it's the guy with glasses from the park. He glares at both of them, but when he yells, it's at Matilda. "Are you going to—"

"Can't I have five fucking minutes to myself?" she shouts, her warm, friendly demeanor falling away. "Jesus H. Christ bleeding and suffering on a motherfucking cross. And close that goddamn door, you're letting all the heat out." She waits until he's back inside. "Sorry about that. They make me crazy out of my jonzo sometimes."

Matilda and this guy must be close if she can yell at him like that. It's comforting to be witness to that sort of intimacy again. "How long have you been doing Bread and Roses?" Althea asks, just to keep the conversation going.

"A couple of years. It's— it's good. It's sort of— I guess it's sort of simple. Hungry people are easy to help. You just show up with food and they eat it. Most people really hate to ask for anything. But when they're hungry, they're a lot less likely to let pride get in the way."

"I guess if there's anything worth sacrificing your dignity for, it's something to eat. "

"You know what the great thing is about dignity?" Matilda asks, turning to Althea. Her cigarette smolders between her fingers, dangerously close to her hair. Smoke halos her head, and Althea watches her small mouth carefully. "Dignity regenerates. It's like a starfish. You can tear it apart, and it grows all its little arms back."

"I think I'd prefer sea-monkey dignity," says Althea. "Just add a little water and watch my dignity grow."

Matilda chuckles. "You could set it on a coffee table next to your Chia Pet pride." Standing, she brushes tobacco crumbs from her pants and tucks the pouch away in the inner pocket of her jacket. "I have to get going. It's my turn."

"Turn to what?"

"Scavenge for food."

"You want a ride?"

"Thanks."

Embarrassed by the condition of her car, Althea scrambles to eliminate the evidence of her trip and predicament, tossing the tinfoil flowers into the back with her ragged quilt and empty coffee cups, plucking at the air freshener strung from the rearview in an effort to enhance its odor-masking capabilities.

"Your gas light is on," Matilda says as they pull away from the curb.

"That's okay. You can get about another forty miles after it comes on."

Matilda is strangely at ease riding shotgun with a stranger, telling Althea when to turn and where to pull over. She pulls the seat up a good six inches, erasing the space normally filled by Oliver's legs. At a shuttered corner bakery, Matilda hops out and rings a bell at the side door; she's greeted by a tall black man wiping his hands on an apron, his face smudged with flour. Even with the windows rolled up, the yeasty smell of fresh bread seeps into the car, engaging the scent of stale cigarette butts in a spirited competition. The baker gives Matilda a trash bag filled with bread that's still good, just too old to sell. Matilda reaches up to kiss his cheek, wiping away the stray flour.

They make several stops like that one, Matilda running into the alley entrance of a restaurant and emerging with another bag of food. "I'm not a princess or anything," she says as they drive, "but I'd rather get the goods before they're thrown in the Dumpster instead of fishing them out. Standing waist-deep in refuse does nothing for me, but I guess some people like Dumpster diving as a point of pride."

"Like Chia Pet pride?"

Matilda grins. "Exactly. So what are you doing in New York, anyway?" She leans into the back, opening one of the bags and taking out a Kaiser roll. "You want one?"

"I came on a reconnaissance mission."

"You a government agent?" Matilda asks through a mouthful of bread.

"I'm a fucking prize joker, is what I am." Althea bangs her fist against her dashboard and groans. She pulls up her sleeve and watches fresh blood soak through the shirt-bandage. "Oh, fuck everything."

Matilda says nothing, but after a moment starts to give her directions.

Back on Matilda's street, Althea parks the car and lets out a very deep sigh. Matilda hands her a roll. Althea considers it, but instead rests her head on the steering wheel, exhausted by the idea of having to accept somebody's help.

"Do you need a place to stay tonight?"

The temperature in the car is already dropping. Althea doesn't care if she has to sleep underneath the sofa with the dust mites, as long as it's warm. "For serious?"

"I'm a big fucking sucker, what can I say? I also find riding around in your car very handy."

"I will drive you to every bakery in Brooklyn if you want."

"Tremendous. Get your shit and help me with our loot."

They stagger onto the porch under the weight of the night's bounty. Matilda drops her bags and turns to her, suddenly dead serious. "Just one thing."

Althea braces herself for some terrifying revelation about the house's residents, although at this point there's very little, be it sexual proclivities or criminal activities, that could stop her from following Matilda inside and passing out on the first flat surface she can find. "Sure."

"If you turn out to be a liar, a thief, or a junkie, you and I will tangle. There's only one rule in this house, and that's because it's a given that standard human decency applies."

"What's the rule?"

Matilda looks affectionately at her home. There are a few ears of Indian corn on the door in anticipation of tomorrow's holiday. "Don't burn it down. Please."

"I can abide by that," Althea says.

The house smells like a Bloody Mary full of cigarette butts. Paint is peeling off the walls, dusting the carpet in the front hallway, and the banister of the stairway to the second floor is covered with scratches and scorch marks. There is a waist-high stack of newspapers—not the *Times*, but the *New York Post*. Althea glances at the top of the pile. The headline reads, simply, AWESOME, over a picture of the Yankees celebrating their World Series win from atop a parade float. The entryway is filled with literally dozens of pairs of shoes—mostly tattered Chuck Taylors and Vans and combat boots so shabby the leather has worn away at the tips, exposing the steel toes. Matilda kicks off her green tennis shoes and Althea follows, tossing her shoes on the pile, wondering briefly if she'll ever be able to find them again.

"Warriors, we have company," Matilda yells.

"Warriors?" Althea asks.

"Like the movie *The Warriors*? About the gang from Coney Island? Can you dig it?"

Althea shrugs. "You lost me."

Matilda starts to hang a left around the staircase, toward what Althea assumes is the living room from the sounds of video games and the grunts and profanities typical of their players. When was the last time she walked into a room full of people she didn't already know without Oliver at her side cracking wise or singing a song he made up on the spot or putting an arm around her and telling her to stay close? If he were transported into this house just long enough to whisper one thing in her ear before he disappeared again, what would it be? She imagines him, in his JFK suit for some reason, his hair slicked back, leaning against the staircase. Oliver, taking it all in, mouthing something at her as she turns the corner, trailing behind Matilda.

Non. Stop. Party. Wagon.

Althea can't believe that's the best she can do.

Glasses Boy is curled up on a Papasan chair in a corner by the window, reading a graphic novel Althea recognizes. The curly-haired girl from before is sitting on the couch next to a black guy who wears only gym shorts, presumably the aforementioned dilettante boyfriend, and they're each leaning forward and clutching a controller. Yet another boy is sprawled out on a teal velour recliner, earnestly following the game while cradling a skinny gray cat in his arms. The girl is the only one who notices Althea and Matilda enter; everyone else looks up just to see why she hit pause. Glasses peers at Althea over the top of his book, throwing it to the floor as he recognizes her. He groans, exasperated, and turns to Matilda.

"What the hell is wrong with you?" he says.

She points at him, stabbing the smoke-filled air with her finger as her earlier ferocity returns. "You belay that shit right now! I mean it."

Matilda makes the introductions—Leala and Kaleb on the couch, Glasses is Ethan, and Gregory is the one whispering to the cat. He holds it above his head.

"This is Mr. Business," Gregory says.

Mr. Business yowls. Althea murmurs hello to the cat, to everyone.

"She's going to crash here," Matilda tells them.

"How do you do that, Management?" says Kaleb. "How do you take out the garbage and come back with some girl who needs a place to stay?"

"It's my special gift."

The living room might be large, but it's hard to tell with so many people and so much stuff. There are comic books and old VHS tapes littering the rug between the couch and the television; the cables for the video games and the stereo lie there in a tangle. Bunches of dried flowers hang upside down over the window. An enormous potted ficus towers over Ethan, nested in his chair. There's a full ashtray the size of a dinner plate on the coffee table, and everyone has a can of Natural Ice at their feet. A lone snare drum sits in the corner, an acoustic guitar propped against it. A sewing table is set up next to the TV, with a quilted box spilling thread and buttons and scraps of fabric around an old Singer. Above the couch hangs a tapestry, a portrait of some saint. Althea's eyes linger there.

"That's Saint Cajetan," Matilda says. "He's the patron saint of the unemployed."

"I never realized there was a patron saint for the unemployed."

"There's a patron saint for everything," Leala says. "Did you know that Saint George is the patron saint for people with syphilis?"

"Yeah," adds Gregory, "that's why Ethan lights a candle to him every night."

Kaleb shakes his head. "Please, you gotta get laid to catch the syph. Ethan will never need to pray to Saint George."

"And when you had crabs," Ethan says, "who did *you* pray to?"

Gregory whoops with laughter while Leala looks at her boyfriend with angry, slivered eyes.

"I got that shit from a toilet seat," Kaleb protests. "Baby, it was before I even knew you."

"Don't talk to me. Unpause the game so I can hand you your ass."

"That wasn't right, Ethan," says Kaleb. "That was not correct."

Ethan snickers without remorse. "You know what you can do if you don't like it."

Leala and Kaleb resume play, Gregory continues his conversation with Mr. Business—"Are you my business kitty? Yes, you're my business kitty"—and Ethan retrieves his book. Other than his irritation, her presence has barely registered with Matilda's housemates. Is it that commonplace? Does Matilda do this all the time?

"Let's get your stuff upstairs," Matilda says. "You're probably exhausted. You can meet everyone else tomorrow."

"Everyone else?" Althea asks, trying to imagine even more people packed into the cramped, filthy house.

"It's sort of an ensemble cast type of thing around here. We need as many housemates as possible so we can make rent. Ethan and Gregory actually share a room; they sleep in shifts a lot of the time. Kaleb and Leala share a room, too. There are a couple of people who crash in the living room, or wherever they can. People come and go a lot. Do you have a big family?"

"I'm an only child."

"You get used to it. The chaos, I mean. You can sleep in my room for now."

Althea doesn't even bother to turn on the light. Pitching facedown onto the bed, she wraps her arms around a pillow that smells like spent matches. Her quilt is still in the backseat of the car, but she falls asleep anyway, too tired to care.

In Wilmington, it was easy to forget where she was waking up. She slept at Oliver's so much, and he at her house, that she often had to rely on the sound of the alarm clock to clue her in. Oliver preferred a shrill ringing bell, Althea the dulcet tones of NPR. But when she wakes up in Matilda's house for the first time, there's no disorientation. There are loud voices downstairs; Althea can already tell some of them apart. Leala's and Kaleb's rise above the others, engaged in a fiery debate about whether they should serve mashed potatoes or a yam casserole in the park for Thanksgiving.

Compared to the mess downstairs, Matilda's bedroom is minimalist. No piles of clothes or books, no towering stack of CDs threatening to topple. But the walls—the walls are a different story. All four have been painted with green chalkboard paint and covered with names and telephone numbers, a clumsy calendar with days marked for cooking, collecting rent, and serving food; notes about whose turn it is to buy toilet paper and when Mr. Business last got his shots. There is a series of lists: *Bands That Might Play at a Fund-raiser, People I Owe Phone Calls, People I Owe Money,* with a great deal of overlap between the last two. Around all of this are song lyrics and movie quotes, only some of which Althea recognizes. A few of the notes are in different colors and handwritings, cryptic messages: *Tell Steve not to give up on me; Non excidet; Where is a dumpling?*

Althea is still trying to decipher these when there's a soft knock on the door and then Matilda slips in, holding two mugs of coffee. She gives one to Althea. There's a Shakespeare quote on it: THERE IS NOTHING EITHER GOOD OR BAD, BUT THINKING MAKES IT SO. Part of the handle is broken off. She takes a solid slug of the coffee and flinches.

"I know," says Matilda. "It's got legs. Come smoke with me."

She leads Althea to the bathroom, where she turns on the shower and sits on the floor with her back against the tub. "It's a neat trick. You fill the room with steam and let it open up your lungs, then you smoke a cigarette. It's like mainlining the nicotine." She quickly crafts a roll-up and seals it with a pointy pink tongue. Then, pulling today's issue of the *Post* from a rack next to the toilet, she flips until she finds the horoscopes. "What's your sign?"

"Gemini." Althea lights a Marlboro.

Matilda's feet are tiny, the toes perfectly proportioned, like a doll's. The temperature in the bathroom rises, and the mirror begins to fog. "Let's see. How about this? 'You've come a long way, baby, so take a load off and relax. With your moon in Saturn, your financial position is not looking good, but fortunately you will encounter a bunch of slackers who never pay for food. Ask someone to explain how alternate side of the street parking works.'"

"That's not really what it says."

"It's more fun to make it up."

"How does alternate side of—"

"I have no fucking idea. Ask Kaleb." Matilda taps the slim cigarette over the toilet.

"How long have you lived here?"

"In the house? A couple of years. Ever since I dropped out of college. It's Ethan's—his mom cosigned the lease, God bless her. We get a lot of dirty looks from the neighbors, but we pay the rent on time and try to make most of the noise on the weekends. The security deposit's probably a loss, though."

"Why'd you drop out of college?"

"College is bullshit," she says. "Most of us didn't graduate from college. Hell, most of us don't even have real jobs and we're doing okay."

From her vantage point Althea can see the black mold growing underneath the lip of the toilet seat.

There's a knock on the door. "What the hell are you doing in there?" It sounds like Ethan.

"Fuck off, man, we're busy," Matilda shouts.

"Hurry up, we've got cooking to do. It's fucking Thanksgiving, remember?" Even muffled, he sounds irritated.

"Just go ahead and ignore Mr. No Fun out there," she whispers to Althea.

Ethan pounds on the door again, harder. "I'm not going to piss in the kitchen sink just because you ladies are having a heart-to-heart in there. And this food isn't—"

"Yeah, yeah, I know. Jesus H.!" Matilda stands up. Reaching down, she extends a hand and helps Althea to her feet. "You going on that recon mission today?"

Ethan bangs on the door once more, for emphasis.

"Why don't you put me to work instead?" says Althea.

"Why don't you do me a favor first," Matilda says, wrinkling her nose, "and take a shower."

Stationed in the living room, Althea peels potatoes over a bucket. Mr. Business stalks into the room and meows at her, his tail quirked in the air like a question mark. Jumping onto the couch, he kneads her thigh with his claws.

"So where do you sleep, Business? Do you get a corner of the bathtub or something?" Althea asks him.

"He sleeps with Gregory," Ethan says as he walks in, a peeler in his hand. He's taller than he looked last night when he was curled in a ball on his chair; he has freckles under the downy hair on his arms and Oliver-fingers, widest at the joint. Batting Mr. Business off the couch, he sits next to Althea and grabs a potato.

"I thought this would go faster with two people," he says. The tendons in his hands stand out when he peels, so distinct Althea imagines she could reach out and pluck them like the strings of a guitar.

"Just about everything does."

They work in silence for a while. The sunlight coming through the curtains reveals that someone has written *Fuck You* in the quarter-inch of dust on the television screen. Their reflections are warped across the curve of the gray glass. From the kitchen on the other side of the house there's music, laughter, the occasional shriek when someone burns himself on a hot pan, and then the run of the faucet over the wound. But Althea is in the living room, paired off as always. Ethan reaches over her to grab another potato. He smells like lemons.

"You're in high school, right?" He starts peeling at warp speed; clearly, he does this a lot. Althea tries to imitate his style.

"I was."

"You're not now?"

"I got expelled," she says.

A long ribbon of skin falls into the bucket. He looks at her. "How old are you?"

"Seventeen. How old are you?"

"Shouldn't you be finishing school?" He drops the naked potato into the bowl and grabs another.

"Shouldn't you have a job?"

He pauses. "I'm twenty."

"Did you graduate from high school?" Althea asks, hacking away with her peeler now.

"Of course."

"Well, you're twenty and I'm seventeen and you graduated from high school and I didn't, but we're both sitting here peeling fucking potatoes, aren't we?"

"Yeah," Ethan says. "I guess we are."

Dust dances in the sunlight. Althea's wrist aches. Just holding the clammy potato makes her nauseated. Matilda's leggy coffee has got her racing.

"I walk dogs," Ethan says.

"Pardon?"

"I walk dogs. Sometimes for money, for the neighbors. And sometimes I volunteer at the animal shelter, walk the dogs that are in the kennels all day."

"You can do that? Just go walk a dog?"

"Most of the dogs that come in are pit mixes, street dogs, or old fighting dogs, whatever. They're beat-up and skittish and underfed. They bite and nobody wants them, and most of the time they end up euthanized. But once in a while one shows up that you can tell isn't a stray. Even if he doesn't have any tags, you can tell someone's looking for him. He's too friendly, he looks too good. And you know someone out there is going crazy, they're putting up flyers, they're going around their neighborhood to all his favorite places, calling and calling his name." Ethan lofts his second potato into the bowl. Rolling the handle of the peeler between his palms, he looks at Althea.

"You comparing me to a dog?" she says.

He points at the bucket with the blade. "We see it all the time, when we're out serving. 'Platinum card homeless,' we call them. Kids come down from Westchester during the summertime, live on the streets spare-changing for forties, and when the weather turns cold they go home to their parents—"

"I get it. Platinum card homeless, that's really clever. Thanks for your insight and your charming stray dog analogy." She grabs the bucket and bowl and heads for the kitchen.

"I hear you have a car," he says.

"So?" She turns, standing in the doorway.

"Who pays the insurance?"

A potato to the head would probably hurt like hell, and she'd love to nail Ethan right across the bridge of the nose, snapping his glasses and blackening at least one of his eyes. It's Thanksgiving; at some point she'll have to call her father and lie to him again, tell him that she's helping Alice cook cornbread stuffing and making sure the turkey doesn't dry out. She remembers the popcorn fight with Oliver and how it ended with Garth coming downstairs to break it up. Garth, with his boundless stockpile of historical tales and his perfectly polished shoes; Garth, standing over the barbecue holding an enormous metal fork, trying to rescue a burger fallen among the coals; Garth, who can effortlessly lecture an auditorium of snickering undergraduates on the sexual practices of ancient Greece, yet cannot speak to his own daughter about similar, more pertinent matters. Who was this beak-nosed boy to talk to her about her beloved and imperfect father, who did, in fact, pay her car insurance, but was so detached he would probably be hard-pressed to name the make and model?

Mr. Business reaches up, sinks his claws into her jeans, and stretches. "Your fucking mom pays my insurance," says Althea.

"You're quite the charmer." Ethan takes his graphic novel from the coffee table and folds himself into his chair. "Make sure you ask Kaleb about alternate side of the street parking."

In the kitchen, Gregory is dancing Matilda around, crooning in a not-bad impression of Tom Waits, while Kaleb chops zucchini and Leala washes carrots in the sink.

"Waltzing Matilda, wa-altzing Matilda, you go waltzing Matilda with me," sings Gregory, leading her across the kitchen.

There are several enormous steel stockpots going. The walls are covered in vinyl contact paper with a rocket ship motif; row after row of Polaroid pictures of their friends are aligned on the refrigerator door, labeled with names and dates. A sagging flowered couch is pushed against the back wall. On a stand-alone cabinet in the corner, a coffeemaker and a rice cooker sit side by side, their red lights aglow, mugs, bowls, and chopsticks nestled together on a shelf below.

Gregory spins Matilda around on her bare feet. The song slows and takes a beat, leading into the final chorus.

"Fuck!" Kaleb yells, throwing his knife onto the cutting board and examining his thumb.

"Are you okay? Let me see." Leala pulls up the window shade so she can get a better look in the sunlight.

"You didn't bleed on the zucchini, did you?" Matilda disentangles herself from her dance partner. She takes the bowl of potatoes, leaving Althea's hands empty and nervous, instantly searching for something to do.

"Your fucking zucchini is fine, I'm the one—"

"Don't be a baby," Leala says. "All you need is a Band-Aid. Christ."

Kaleb holds his hand above his head as he follows her out of the kitchen. The zucchini lies unattended. Althea steps up to the cutting board and rinses off the knife.

"I'll finish these," she says.

A couple of days later, on the way to Nathan's, Althea finds a flaming orange parking ticket tucked under her windshield wiper. "What the shit is this?"

"I told you to find out about the parking," Matilda says. "What happened here?" She runs her finger along the crooked path Jason keyed into the paint.

"It's a long story."

They get their food to go, eating on the boardwalk despite the cold. "I thought you were a vegetarian," Althea says.

"The best part about being a vegetarian is eating meat every once in a while."

"I can't imagine that's a very popular view back at the house," Althea says.

"Don't mention this little excursion to anyone. I'll get a lecture from Ethan about factory farming and then Leala will go on and on about how this hot dog is going to be lodged in my colon until I'm thirty or I pay someone two hundred bones to flush it out with a hose." Matilda sips her soda. "It's exhausting to care about something that much, to put in all that effort. Whenever I quit smoking it's so much work, and every time I slip up there's this thrill, because I just stop caring. Sometimes it's a relief not to give a shit." She takes another bite of her hot dog. "Remember when you were a kid and you used to try so hard to climb up a slide, just so you could turn around at the top and go back down? I don't know if that makes any sense."

"It makes sense."

Matilda finishes eating and skillfully rolls a cigarette. With everything shut down for the season, Coney Island feels more like a movie set than a real place, all potential energy and no kinetic. The sky above them is heavy and gray, the parachute jump propping up its share of the clouds. Althea can't believe the Atlantic Ocean just steps away is the same one she swam in back home, in the before time, the long long ago.

"It's funny," Matilda is saying now. "The cat just followed Gregory home a few months ago, all the way from the subway. He didn't want to let him in, you know; he was a stray cat, we didn't know where he'd been. But the cat just sat on the porch and cried and scratched at the door, he kept jumping up onto the windowsill to look inside, and finally Gregory said, 'Well, I guess he means business.' So that's how we got the cat, and that's how the cat got his name."

Althea indicates the pouch of tobacco in Matilda's shirt pocket. "Do you mind if I give that a try?"

Matilda hands it over. "Have at it."

Slipping a paper from the thin cardboard packet, Althea holds it between thumb and forefinger and fills it with a fat pinch of tobacco.

"No, that's too much," Matilda says.

Althea puts some back, spreading the rest evenly down the fold in the paper. Grasping the ends between her fingers, she rolls the contents tighter, then uses her thumbnails to create an even crease.

"I talked to Valerie," says Matilda.

"Oh." Ducking her head, Althea draws her tongue across the thin line of adhesive, sealing her makeshift cigarette. She surveys the mess and shakes her head.

"Sometimes it works better if you use two papers at first. Gives you something a little more solid to work with."

Althea pulls two more from the packet, tears open her first failed attempt, and starts again. "What did she say?"

"How about you tell me what happened instead?"

"You want to see if our stories match up?"

"Yeah."

To tell her version, Althea goes all the way back to the night the babysitter canceled on Nicky. In truth she doesn't even really remember, but she knows the story from her father. How Nicky had stood there in a denim jacket covered with patches of obscure hardcore bands, her black nail polish mostly chipped away, asking a neighbor she barely knew to watch her son so she could go to work. Althea had hidden behind one of Garth's corduroy-clad legs, while Oliver, all dimples, shook Garth's hand and introduced himself like a miniature adult. Althea doesn't dwell too much on the next decade, quickly skipping ahead to Oliver's sickness and how it dovetailed with her burgeoning, inconvenient feelings, and the series of debacles those two things wrought. She doesn't gloss over the part about Coby, either, although she finds it strangely difficult to remember the details of what happened in the hallway; it's hazy, like something she had done while drunk. The best she can say is, "And then my head exploded." She's sure Valerie was able to relay it better anyway, having borne witness. By the time Althea's finished, she's finally put together something resembling a cigarette, which she lights with a great deal of relief. "I think that's pretty much the gist of it. I'm guessing I went into a little more detail than Val."

"They say context is everything," Matilda says.

"It is at that."

"It was Ethan's idea. I didn't want to at first, but he was right."

"He doesn't like me," says Althea.

"He will. That's why he wanted to do it now. Before we forgot that you hadn't always been here. We like spontaneity, not surprises. I have to be sure whatever happened in North Carolina isn't going to follow you up here."

"There are no outstanding warrants against me. I know that getting expelled for beating up a classmate isn't real savory, but I wasn't leading a life of crime. It was more like I knew I was ruining everything, and I couldn't stop." She points with her cigarette at the yellow paper carton cradling the remains of Matilda's hot dog. "Imagine that feeling you get when you're a vegetarian eating a hot dog. Imagine that feeling times a million.

Climbing up the slide to turn around at the top and go back down. That's what I am, I guess. A backslider."

Matilda shivers and tucks her knees under her chin. "Valerie said Coby had it coming. She said you must have had a good reason, and it sounds like you did. That's why your things aren't waiting for you on my porch. But I'll tell you right now, if you ever raise a hand against anybody in this house—"

"I won't, I promise—"

"—you'll be out faster than you can say 'vegan curry.' And what about your parents? The last thing I need is some hostile adult showing up at my door."

"You don't have to worry about that. I'll take care of it."

"Do you like it here?"

"I do," Althea says.

Before Matilda has even moved, Althea understands she is about to be hugged. She braces herself for physical contact, allowing Matilda's arms to encircle her shoulders. Althea returns the embrace, swallowing up the tiny blonde girl.

"What do you think?" Matilda asks. "Do you mean business?"

chapter eleven.

OLIVER CAN'T MOVE.

His eyes are open. Or he thinks they are. But it's strange; even though he's lying on his belly with his arms around the pillow, its thin, papery case rustling in his embrace, his view is of the hospital room—the thrift store desk, the low, spinny chair, and the white door, which comes ajar as he stares at it. No, something's not right. He tries to roll over and can't.

Oh, come on.

Scaling back his efforts, he focuses on one arm, his left arm. Trying to slide it out from under the pillow, all the while watching the door, though he knows his face is buried in the mattress. His arm doesn't budge, but the door edges open another couple of inches. *What the fuck?* He concentrates on his leg next—*What is the big deal, I used to do this all the time*—and still there's nothing.

Help! he shouts, except he doesn't shout at all. *Stella, are you there?*

Logic would dictate that he's dreaming, but he knows he isn't.

He can't move or speak, but he is most definitely awake in his hospital room, the oximeter Stella wrapped around his finger still in place, the rubber strap tight around his chest, and the electrodes pasted onto his temples. The door has swung a little farther into the room, and though he can't see beyond it, he can hear the terse, economical exchanges of the doctors and nurses in the hallway and their footsteps as they pass him by, oblivious to his distress.

He downshifts to a low, guttural groan. It's not a dream, but he knows the rules the way he would if he were dreaming, and if he can just coax his vocal cords into producing one small sound, it will break the spell and he'll have his body back. So he reaches into his throat and tries to make something happen—any noise will suffice. And even though he's doing everything right, there's no result, and that's when he starts to panic, thinking that maybe he's paralyzed for good, or that he's gone into some kind of coma—don't they say that it's never been proven that people in comas are unaware of their surroundings, that maybe when you're comatose you can still hear what's going on around you, didn't he read that somewhere? His silent moan intensifies, and he tries again to thrash his arms and legs, and now he's really freaking out, because how will the doctors and nurses know he's awake if he can't tell them, how long will he have to lie here trapped inside his brain without any access to his nervous system, like the Metallica video about the soldier who loses all his limbs and his nose and ears and—

And then it's over. His fear escapes his mouth as a single staccato shout, and suddenly he's sitting up, panting, his heart pounding so hard, he can see the cotton of his shirt quiver. The door to his room is as firmly shut as when Stella tucked him in, however long ago that happened. It's no longer clear if he was dreaming. Not that it matters—the panic was real enough. He tears off the electrodes and the oximeter, strips off his shirt, and wriggles out of the enormous rubber band. He's sure they can see him on the camera and that one of the nurses or doctors will be arriving shortly to debrief him, but he can't stand the thought of staying in here one second longer. Dressing in a fever, he stumbles out of his room, heading for the lounge.

There are holiday decorations everywhere—shabby red tinsel taped to the walls, an electric menorah on the windowsill, paper snowflakes hanging from the ceiling. The television is off, a first as far as Oliver can recall. The reason is obvious, and it makes him smile. The room is empty, save for Kentucky, who is fully stretched out on the couch reading a book, so absorbed he doesn't see Oliver until he leans over and whispers, "Hey."

"Go Seahawks," says Kentucky, resting his open book across his chest.

"Yeah, whatever."

"Welcome back."

"How long was I—"

"About four and a half weeks," Kentucky says.

Oliver sighs. "So Thanksgiving and Christmas are—"

"Over."

"What about New Year's?"

"It was close, but you woke up in time. A few days to spare, even."

"Where is everyone?" Oliver asks.

"Some of the guys are still down; the rest are off with the tutor somewhere."

"Why aren't you?"

Kentucky holds up his book, Howard Zinn's *A People's History of the United States*. "Independent reading."

Oliver takes his favorite chair in the corner, by the window. It's only late afternoon, but already the sun is sliding down behind the New Jersey skyline, casting its incendiary orange brilliance on the Hudson. "When did you wake up?"

"I never went down at all," Kentucky says. "Can you believe that? I've been awake this whole time. For a couple of days I was the only one. Had Stella all to myself. They don't know what to do with me. They can't make it happen, but I don't know how long I'm supposed to wait around. And you know if I did leave, I'd be out before my plane even landed in Louisville. That's just the way the universe works."

"Maybe it's done. Maybe it's never coming back."

Kentucky shakes his head ruefully. "It isn't done. I can tell. It's fucking with me—just long enough to make this whole thing a gigantic waste of time. My parents told me to stick it out, stay awhile longer, see what happens. I think it's easier for them. To have me be someone else's problem for a while."

Something in his voice reminds Oliver of his conversation with the doctor and the warnings about the other side effects of KLS, the ones that happen in between the episodes—the anger, the depression. Hopelessness, Dr. Curls had called it. Oliver can see it in his new friend now.

Before he can reply, Stella appears in the doorway, holding his chart. She's wearing a pair of checkered Vans. A delicate gold chain circles her long, perfect neck. It's not the kind of thing he can picture her buying for herself, and possible narratives begin to unfurl: She inherited the necklace from a beloved grandmother, who on her deathbed pressed it into Stella's hand when they had a rare moment alone, so her sisters wouldn't be jealous, and she has kept it like a secret for many years, wearing it only to work where no one will understand its importance; it was a gift from an old boyfriend, who gave it to her right before they went away to different colleges, and then he died of a sudden and unexpected illness, and though it probably wouldn't have worked out anyway, Stella idealizes this boy who remains eighteen and perfect in her heart forever and she can't love anyone else, and he's the reason she became a nurse in the first place—

"Hey, Oliver," she says, and he forgets the rest of her stories before he can invent them. "Welcome back. How're you feeling?"

"Okay, I guess. Did you miss me?"

She smiles. "The doctor would like to see you."

"Sure." He looks at Kentucky, already returning to his book. "Don't go anywhere."

"Not likely."

On his way out of the lounge, he pauses by the couch, whispering so only Kentucky can hear him: "I didn't do anything bad while I was down, did I?"

"If you relieved yourself in anyone's presence, I didn't hear a thing about it."

———————————————————

Something about the way the doctor sits behind his desk reminds Oliver of a pilot in a cockpit surveying the world, like he can see beyond the walls of his office into the rest of the hospital and, beyond that, the city. He makes a show of opening Oliver's chart and reviewing several of the most recent pages, but this strikes Oliver as being strangely perfunctory. Of course he already knows what he needs to know in order to have this conversation.

"So, Oliver. How are you feeling?"

"A little stiff."

"Do you know how long it's been since we talked?"

"About a month. Right? Not counting anything I might have said, during—you know."

"You wouldn't count any of that?"

"No. And I'd rather not know how much of 'that' there was, if you don't mind."

"Of course not. That's also completely up to you. Is there anything you'd like to report? Anything you noticed, anything unusual? I know that you don't remember much, if anything, but think of us like the detectives you always see on those television shows. The tiniest detail can be incredibly important, even if it seems like nothing to you."

"I can't think of anything," Oliver answers, suddenly wanting nothing more than to be back in the lounge with Kentucky.

"You're sure? Nothing at all?"

"Sorry, Doctor. Nothing at all."

"Is there anything you'd like to know? Do you have any questions for me?"

"All I really want to know is what happens now. I did what you needed so you could get your data or whatever. So now what do I do?"

"Whatever you want," the doctor says.

"What if I want to go home?"

"Of course you can go home, Oliver. You can go home anytime you want. This is all completely voluntary. You're here because you want to be. When you stop wanting to be, we'll call your mother, she'll come get you, and you can go."

"Really?"

The doctor laughs, loud and genuine. "We're not holding you against your will."

Instantly, Oliver feels foolish. It's not that he thought they could keep him here if he wanted to leave. Now that he's thinking about it, he realizes he doesn't know what he believed. Or if he even does want to leave.

Dr. Curls continues, "But I will say that it could be very helpful if you decided to stay awhile longer."

"Helpful for who?" Oliver asks sharply.

"I'm not sure what you mean by that."

"I'm just saying, I've been here for almost two months. I've done everything you've asked me to do. I even had a very conveniently timed KLS episode. But you keep saying there isn't anything you can do for me. And, all due respect, I appreciate that a lot of what you're doing here is research, but I came here to help myself. Not the medical journals."

The doctor struggles to maintain his compassionate demeanor, losing for a moment before his mask of empathy reasserts itself.

"I know you're frustrated, Oliver. I get it; I really do. But you have to understand, just by being here and letting us study you and do our research, you're helping yourself enormously. We're still a long way off from understanding KLS. Any treatment we might try would be extremely experimental."

"Like what?"

The doctor wearily massages the bridge of his nose. "There is some evidence that treating KLS patients with lithium can sometimes reduce the frequency of the episodes and make them shorter when they do happen."

Oliver leans forward in his seat. "So there is something. Why didn't you say so? Why haven't we tried it yet?"

The doctor sighs. Closing Oliver's medical chart, he sets it aside so there is nothing on the table between them. All of his solicitous pretense falls away, and what's left is not unkind, but a countenance as weary and dissatisfied as Oliver himself. Dr. Curls, Oliver realizes, is on the verge of speaking to him like an adult, like a person instead of a patient, and Oliver senses a rare opportunity that will likely not present itself again.

"Please," he says. "Please. No bullshit."

"In order for the lithium to be effective, you would need to be on it all the time. Some of the side effects can be . . ." He pauses.

"No bullshit," Oliver repeats.

The doctor nods, smiling faintly. "Weight gain. Hand tremors. Eye twitches. Constant thirst. Vertigo. Slurred speech. Psoriasis. Hair loss. Lethargy. That's just a handful, randomly chosen from a very long list. And once you start taking it, once the levels of lithium build up in your blood, you would not be able to stop, not without weaning yourself off over a period of several months. It's not a sure thing or a simple fix. You should discuss it with your mother if you want to pursue it.

"I know what you really want from me, Oliver, maybe even more than a cure. You want me to be able to look inside your brain and understand why this is happening to you. But I don't know. I'm trying, I'm really trying. But I still don't know." The doctor who had been so confident and charming during his CNN interview now looks as defeated as the boy he's failed to help.

A reckless, heady rage starts in Oliver's guts and spreads until he can feel it buzzing in his head. "I came all the way here. I left my mother and my friends and my senior year of high school because I was sick of being the freak with this disease, and now you're telling me the only choice is to let you make me a bigger one?"

"Oliver, I know you just want to be like other kids your age—"

"I don't want to be like other kids! Other kids are assholes! But I'm done pretending this is all just a minor inconvenience when it's ruining my fucking life."

"We could try the lithium. The possible side effects are exactly that—possible."

"Why did you tell me I shouldn't feel hopeless when you knew there was no hope?" Oliver shouts, and charges out of the office.

chapter twelve.

ALTHEA SLEEPS IN the kitchen now.

Though the floral fabric is faded and stained, the cushions threadbare and flattened, the couch in the kitchen has become her favorite spot in the house. Throughout the night, people wander in and out to fix themselves bowls of rice or get beer from the fridge, but the abiding noise from the living room is muffled in here, making sleep actually possible. The hum of the appliances, the lingering smells of whatever meal has been cooked last, the luminous numbers of the digital clock on the stove—she finds these things all comforting.

She knew she couldn't stay in Matilda's room indefinitely, but had hesitated staking out a place elsewhere. Then, after Althea tried a couple of nights waking up to the gasping sounds of coffee brewing and sunlight illuminating the rocket ships on the makeshift wallpaper, the two girls came to a tacit agreement. Matilda moved back into her room and Althea took her place, putting her clothes on a shelf in the pantry, below the boxes of cereal and cans of vegetarian baked beans. She drew a friendly looking pterodactyl on Matilda's wall as a thank-you.

She'd called Garth a few days after Thanksgiving and told him that being landlocked on the mesa was not as unbearable as she had feared, that she had discovered red chiles and was on a mission to perfect her recipe for huevos rancheros, and that Alice was annoying but well-intentioned and fortunately occupied much of the time with her various endeavors. She made sure to work in a few comments about the long drive and how it seemed like she had just arrived and already it was time to leave, and then it was Garth himself who suggested she stay longer if she wanted to, and if it was all right with Alice. Althea assured him that it was, and they agreed she would stay through New Year's, and then go to Mexico with Garth. She knew Alice would never call North Carolina, that as long as she kept checking in with Garth she could keep the ruse going at least through the holidays. She's not the one who thinks ahead—that's Oliver's department—so she's asked herself every day what he would do, how he would pull off a scheme like this. She'd phoned a few times after that to report on her increasingly deft snowshoeing skills and the glory of New Mexican sunsets, tapering off her updates as Garth got wrapped up in the end of the semester and planning the upcoming trip to Mexico. At first she'd congratulated herself on these clever machinations, but as Christmas grew closer and her phone calls to the hospital continued to prove fruitless, she had to consider the possibility that she might run out of time.

But time is working in other ways. For a long time after the Coby incident, it was the first thing she thought about every morning—the eyes of all her classmates, Coby's stunned face, the ache in her hand. Not guilt so much as surprise that it happened at all, and humiliation that it had been so public. For so long, she'd woken up wincing, mortified. But this morning the wincing doesn't come, only the desire for coffee.

Stretching out, she kicks someone; weight shifts on the other end of the couch.

"Sorry," Althea says, sitting up.

Ethan's copper hair sticks out from under a blanket. He mumbles something. One freckled arm emerges, then another, then his face, printed with sleep. "My glasses. Do you see my glasses anywhere?"

Still wrapped in Alice's quilt, she retrieves them from the kitchen counter. "What are you doing in here?"

"Sorry. Gregory's in the bed and Kaleb's asleep in my chair. He had some stupid fight with Leala about a game of Risk. I got up to brush my teeth, and by the time I came back he was passed out. Sorry to sort of barge in, but it was the only spot left in the house." Ethan cleans his lenses meticulously with a corner of his striped brown comforter.

Althea pours coffee for them both. "I didn't even notice."

"Sooner or later you learn to be a heavy sleeper around here," he says, blowing on the surface of the coffee and taking a tentative sip. Althea downs hers in a few scalding gulps. "Christ," he says. "I didn't realize it was possible to drink coffee that fast."

"You have to be really committed to inducing a heart attack," she says, fishing for clean clothes inside the pantry.

Upstairs, Mr. Business is leaving the bathroom, tracking bits of kitty litter that stick to the soles of Althea's feet and make them itch. She keeps her eyes closed in the shower so she doesn't have to see the blackened lines of grout between the tiles or the gritty scum along the bottom of the tub. While she gropes blindly for the shampoo and soap lined up on the windowsill, the moldy curtain liner brushes against her leg and she bats it away, shuddering. She quickly lathers the thigh that made contact, down to her calf, the delicate ankle, her calloused foot. Abruptly, she realizes that because it's hers, this foot is her responsibility; she's the only one looking after these knobby knees and quick-bitten fingers, and it makes them seem suddenly, relentlessly fragile.

"Althea? Is that you? Can I come in and pee?" Matilda shouts from the hallway, rapping on the door. Before Althea can even respond, she comes in and sits on the toilet with a sigh of relief.

Shutting off the water, Althea sticks her hand beyond the dreaded foul curtain.

"Towel me, please," she says.

That night, Gregory, an aspiring stand-up comic, insists on practicing his routine for a tepid audience. Ethan reads in his chair, Leala and Kaleb are struggling to get to the next level of Chrono Trigger, and Matilda is at her sewing machine, altering an oversize Metallica T-shirt into a fitted halter top. The assorted cast that Althea is learning to recognize—the diminutive drummer who waits tables at a nearby restaurant and is always chewing on a cinnamon stick, the Columbia dropout with nothing to his name but a MetroCard and a backpack full of socks, the effusive tattoo artist with the pierced tongue and chipped teeth—are elsewhere in the house, scouring magazines and newspapers pilfered from the neighbors' recycling bin for free activities taking place anywhere in the five boroughs.

On the floor by the couch, Althea eats a bowl of brown rice doused with sesame oil and soy sauce. The cat is at her side, his little motor running, trying to nose his way into her dish. An avid reader of fantasy novels, Gregory's routine is laced with jokes about griffins and lycanthropy. As he's going for a punch line, Leala's avatar dies and she throws her controller to the ground, narrowly missing Mr. Business's head. "Let's go out. Let's go do something," she says.

"Wanna make out?" suggests Kaleb.

Gregory is annoyed. "I was in the middle of a fucking joke."

"Everybody up. Come on. You, too, Ethan." Leala leans over him and gently pries the book from his fingers. "Is it not Friday night?"

"I don't want to," Ethan says.

"You heard her," Kaleb says. "Up. We're going out."

"To do what? We don't have any money."

"Money? Money?" Leala shouts. She and Kaleb have Ethan cornered in his chair. "Money is for people with money! Since when do we need money to have a good time? All you need is a commitment to fun. Where's your commitment to fun, Ethan?"

"It's cold outside—"

"What a fucking joke you are." Kaleb shakes his head. "'It's cold outside'? Seriously?"

"What are we doing?" Matilda asks, tearing open the shirt with a seam ripper.

"I haven't gotten that far yet," Leala says.

The drummer, the dropout, and the tattoo artist stand in the doorway. "We going out?" the tattoo artist asks.

Half the room says yes, half the room says no. Kaleb starts to undress.

"Oh, come on," Ethan says. "Why do you always have to get naked for no reason?"

Kaleb unbuckles his belt. "Right now I'm getting naked so I can slap you in the face with my dick."

Gathering the final grains of rice with her chopsticks, Althea speaks. "Y'all ever thought of having a scavenger hunt?"

Everyone turns to stare at her. "Goddamn," says Kaleb, down to his boxers. "She can talk."

"A scavenger hunt?" Leala asks. She and Kaleb exchange a lustful glance. "Someone get me a piece of paper."

Hours later, a tipsy Althea straddles an enormous bronze bull in the desolate Financial District, clutching one of his horns to avoid falling off, while Matilda snaps a Polaroid. Temporarily blinded by the flash, Althea blinks furiously, her eyes tearing in the harsh winter wind. Her ass is freezing from sitting on the bull for five minutes while Matilda searched for the camera in the messenger bag filled with their night's acquisitions. Steam rises from several manhole covers, and there's no one on these streets except for her teammates, hooting and hollering, drinking forties of St. Ides out of paper bags—"wino sacks," Gregory calls them.

"It really does feel like Gotham City down here, doesn't it?" Ethan helps her down off the sculpture.

Matilda's hands, like her feet, are delicate and undersized. She needs both to hold a forty properly. Bringing it to her mouth, she looks like an unhinged toddler sipping from her bottle. "Good work, Gemini. Let's check it off the list."

"What's next?" Gregory asks.

"We're right by the 4 train," says Dennis, the tattoo guy. "We can go up to Astor Place and spin the cube."

"Yes," Matilda cries. "Let's go, go, go!" She sprints toward the green globe above the subway station. Everyone follows. The cobblestones are unforgiving under Althea's sneakered feet.

All the enthusiasm in the world can't make the subway come. Underground in a train station as deserted as the streets above them, there's nothing they can do but wait, compulsively check the time, and drink. Matilda, Gregory, and Dennis confer over the remaining items on the list while Althea paces the platform and Ethan leans out over the tracks, looking down the tunnel for any sign of an arriving train.

"Could you not do that?" Althea says. "You're too close to the edge. It's making me nervous."

Setting down his bottle, Ethan jumps onto the tracks. "There's nothing coming. It's not a big deal." He waves his arms for emphasis, a conductor in an unlikely orchestra pit.

"Get back up here!"

"It's fine, I'm telling you." A gigantic rat carrying half a bagel runs across the tracks not far from Ethan's foot. "I think I've made my point."

Briefly overwhelmed by vertigo, Althea sits on a bench while he hoists himself back onto the platform. She's pretending to show great interest in a discarded issue of that day's *Daily News* when he joins her. Althea turns over the paper. Though baseball season is long over, the Yankees are still on the cover of the sports page, aglow from their World Series victory. Farther down the platform, Matilda is getting hysterical about the minutes slipping by. Gregory has her by the shoulders, trying to calm her down.

"I don't want to lose! I fucking hate losing!" she's saying, her voice enormous in the empty station.

"I'm sorry I was a dick when you first moved in," Ethan tells Althea.

"Did Management tell you to say that?" she asks, nodding in the direction of the errant blonde girl shouting a soliloquy on the merits of being a winner.

"She doesn't control my every move, you know."

Althea considers this. "Have you known her a long time?"

"As long as I've known anyone, I guess." He takes a long pull from his bottle, then offers it to her. Althea drinks several swallows of flat malt liquor, wiping away a trickle that escapes down her chin. It tastes like the gas station where they bought it. "It was me who started the Brooklyn chapter of Bread and Roses. I bet you didn't know that. I bet you just assumed that it was her." Althea doesn't say anything. "It wasn't her. It was me. I found the house. I started the chapter. Then she dropped out of Vassar and moved in."

"Are you saying she took over?"

"No," says Ethan sharply. "I needed the help. And she's good at it. Probably better than me. But she gets—you know that day when you first came to the park? I knew it. I fucking knew it the second you walked up to that table, that you were going to end up staying in our house. And it was a stupid thing for her to do."

"Thanks a lot," Althea says, draining the rest of his forty.

"People aren't cats. You can't just take in the strays. We're only supposed to serve meals. It's not fair. You're a young, cute white girl, so you get to come home with us. Everyone else gets a meal and we send them on their way." He fills his cheeks with air and lets it out thoughtfully. The ink from the newspaper has blighted her fingers; she wipes them on her jeans, almost worn through at the knees. Ethan cleans his glasses on his shirt, and she watches his blue eyes unfocus without them, his face hollow and incomplete. "And I know," he says, replacing his glasses, sharpening his gaze on her face, "that you are not a stray."

An approaching train rumbles unseen down the tunnel, a hint of thunder gaining momentum. Althea starts to get up, but Ethan catches her elbow. "It's coming from the other direction."

It sounds like the noise is coming from everywhere. "How can you tell?" she shouts as the subway bursts into the station across the tracks. The brakes engage with a metallic shriek; she plugs her fingers in her ears, but again Ethan touches her arm.

"Don't do that," he shouts. "It makes you look like a tourist."

The nearly empty train sputters to a halt and performs in a perfunctory opening and closing of doors. No one gets on or off. When it pulls away, she suffers through the tumult.

"How did you know?" she asks when the station is quiet again. "Which way the train was going?"

"I can just tell."

Althea scrapes away the St. Ides label with a fingernail. "Why did Matilda take me in?"

"When we were in high school, Matilda made a real point of not getting stuck in any one clique. She had punk friends, she had square friends, she had friends who did theater and friends who skipped class to do acid in Washington Square Park. I don't know, she just likes collecting people. She'd make a great politician. But, you know, she's great. She wouldn't take you in if she didn't like you." He glances at the newspaper again. "You know why I hate the Yankees so much? Because even in December, they're on the cover of the sports page. It's like their fucking season is never over."

"You sound like a bitter Mets fan."

"There isn't any other kind."

"I hate it when Mets fans complain about the Yankees," she says. "You've got two teams in this city. You could have chosen the team that always wins. But you didn't. So sack up and quit whining. It's the price you pay, rooting for the underdog."

"I'm from Queens; I didn't choose to be a Mets fan."

"So if you could have chosen, you would have chosen the Yankees?"

"Of course not."

"Then shush."

A stale wind blows through the tunnel, ruffling the pages of the *News*. Matilda whoops.

"Now our train's coming," says Ethan. "Let's go."

After turning the cube at Astor Place and making a crayon rubbing of the plaque outside the Eleventh Street baths—"A bathhouse as a historical landmark?" Althea asked, prompting a brief treatise from Ethan on its significance—and completing a number of other tasks, all documented by a hell-bent Matilda, the exhausted crew returns to the Warrior house. They arrive as the sky is lightening, but before the sun has risen over Coney Island.

The other team—Kaleb, Leala, the drummer and the dropout—has not yet arrived. Only Mr. Business greets them, nibbling at the cuff of Gregory's jeans as Matilda dumps the contents of her messenger bag in the center of the living room.

"Fuck!" she shouts. "This means they're still out there scoring points while we're sitting around here waiting!"

"Actually," Ethan says, "it probably just means they're stuck on the D train."

"Is there anything else we can do before sunrise?" Dennis asks. "Isn't there something on the list we can do here?"

Matilda skims the remaining items. "What do you think constitutes a 'radical change in appearance'?"

"A new tattoo?" Dennis says eagerly.

"We don't have time for that," she says, looking at Althea. "Listen, Gemini. We're going to have to cut off all your hair."

"Excuse me?" Althea says, clutching the black tangles with both hands.

"We'll get a lot of points," Matilda says. "It'll put us over the top. It'll secure our victory."

"You've got to take one for the team, dude," Dennis tells Althea.

"It's my fucking hair!" she yells, backing away.

"Your roots are coming in anyway! You've got a hairdo like a skunk. Look, sometimes you have to cut off a finger to save the hand." Matilda rummages in her sewing box for a pair of scissors.

"Or the hair, in this case. You've got to cut off your hair to save the hand!" shouts Gregory.

"Your roots do look pretty terrible," Ethan admits.

"With your cheekbones and that long neck, a nice pixie cut will be a good look for you," Matilda says, changing her tactics. "Now come upstairs! The sun will be up any minute. We don't have much time."

"Skunk hair," Dennis says.

The four of them circle around Althea, Matilda making snipping motions with the scissors, everyone hissing skunk noises—*"Psssssss"*—and shouting that winners have to pay the price, that champions have to be willing to make sacrifices. She's only known these people for a month, and now they're edging toward her, Matilda brandishing the scissors in a vaguely threatening manner, demanding to scalp her so they can win a scavenger hunt, and Althea asks herself if she should be afraid. She imagines the headline on the cover of the *Post*—WAYWARD TEEN SLAIN BY BROOKLYN SLACKERS—and the accompanying sidebar, listing statistics about runaways and the trouble they find in New York City. Matilda reaches for a lock of Althea's hair.

"Get away from me with those goddamn scissors," Althea shrieks, her clammy hands clenching into fists at her sides, that familiar racing feeling returning as they surround her, hemming her in.

"The whole scavenger hunt was your idea in the first place!"

Gregory shouts. "You can't let us down when we're in the home stretch!"

Dennis, who looked so menacing at first with the three black birds tattooed around the base of his throat and the fat plastic plugs in his ears, is doubled over with laughter, and Gregory's skunk imitation is so ludicrous, and even Ethan is snickering with a hand over his mouth, and Matilda's determination isn't grim but joyful. In their secondhand clothes and their slipshod living room, presided over by Saint Cajetan, it's clear they're not a throng of would-be wrongdoers or a company of aspiring mavericks, but just another pack of kids looking to make their own fun. Still, Althea feels her nostrils flaring, gets a bitter, metallic mouthful of what she used to think was adrenaline, but knows now is the flavor of an impending bad decision. She grinds her teeth. A brief, unearned hatred flares in her for all of them, as bright and hot and soothing as a match against her skin.

"Don't fight us," says Matilda. "It's easier if you don't fight us."

"You're only making this harder," Ethan says.

Imagine Minty Fresh, she thinks, imagine Valerie, imagine their jealousy if they could see her here, with the exact people they were trying so hard to be; and those people are begging Althea to help them win their game. Imagine even Oliver, inventor of the Non-Stop Party Wagon, urging her to stop fighting everyone and just say yes. And if he were here, she would ask him, the person who knows her best: *Do you think so, Ol? Do you really think it'll help?* But he isn't here, and never will be, so instead Althea takes her best guess.

"Fine!" she yells. "Fine! Cut off my fucking hair!"

Picturing Oliver, taking his imaginary advice, Althea realizes it's the first time she's thought about him for hours. At least since the start of the scavenger hunt. What about before that? She must have thought about him at some point today.

But then Matilda is dragging her upstairs, sitting her on the closed toilet, and wrapping a towel around her neck. Gregory stands in the tub snapping Polaroids while Matilda hacks away. Ethan brings a can of Natural Ice to anesthetize the patient. She accepts this act of kindness with what she hopes is grace.

"I'm sorry about what I said when I first moved in," she says, chunks of hair falling into her lap. "That thing about your mother."

"Just shotgun it," he counsels, and she does.

chapter thirteen.

OLIVER'S NOT INTERESTED.

"Your mom's on the phone," Kentucky says from the doorway.

"Tell her I'm busy."

"What could you possibly be doing?"

"I don't know, make something up," Oliver says.

Kentucky returns a minute later. "She says if you don't take her call, she's going to get on a plane and come up here."

"For Christ's sake." He lurches into the hallway and picks up the pay phone's receiver, dangling from its serpentine silver cord. "What?"

"You've been ignoring my calls."

"I haven't really been in a talking mood." He's been awake for a day and he's spent most of that time rereading the same chapter of *Hyperspace*, staring at the ceiling of his room, and trying to remain curmudgeonly in the face of Kentucky's relentless overtures.

"Manuel says you've barely come out of your room since you woke up," Nicky says.

"Did he tell you the rest of it? Did he tell you about the lithium?"

"He mentioned you two had a heated discussion. Oliver, this is exactly what I warned you about. I didn't want you to be disappointed. These people never promised they'd be able to help you right away."

"Oh, they can help me, all right. They can dope me up until I'm a shuffling zombie who can't put together a sentence. I'm just not sure it sounds like a real improvement to me."

"If you're that unhappy, you can come home, you know. He can write you a prescription and recommend a doctor in Wilmington to monitor you when you start to take it."

"I haven't decided if I want to do it or not." The receiver smells harshly of the all-natural cleanser the custodial staff uses on everything. Purportedly made from a top-secret blend of herbs, the concentrated liquid resembles Jägermeister in odor and appearance—only the cleanser's claim to be nontoxic sets the two apart. Oliver gags into the phone.

"You could just try it, you know," Nicky says. "It might be fine. You might not have any side effects at all."

"This was supposed to be it, right? Coming here was the last resort, the Hail Mary. And what do I get? Another shitty Would You Rather. I don't want to have to decide between the lesser of two evils. Haven't I lost enough already?"

When he hangs up the phone, he heads straight for Kentucky's room. He's sitting up in bed, reading Noam Chomsky.

"Let me ask you something else," says Oliver.

Reluctantly, Kentucky closes *World Orders Old and New.* "Yeah?"

"What's your real name?"

"Will."

"Will, what do you say we make a break for it and get the fuck out of here?"

It's snowing outside. Oliver is taken aback, although it is not the first time he has slept through a change in seasons and been caught unawares upon waking. The flimsy jacket he wore in early November is woefully inadequate for late December in New York, this deviously cheerful, almost-New-Year's weather that has filled the streets with hordes of tourists and tired children and forbiddingly beautiful women in knee-high boots with impossibly high heels and cheekbones that remind him of Althea's. It's full-on evening now, but weirdly bright, streetlights and brake lights and lights from the windows of bars and restaurants and department stores turning the soft patter of snow into a kaleidoscope of shimmering, metallic colors.

For two boys who have been locked up in an almost exclusively beige hospital for nearly two months, it's all a little much. Oliver leads Will down the street in an earnest imitation of someone who knows where he's going. Broadway is laid out before them like an exercise in perspective, terminating in a luminous explosion of colored light so intense that the sky above it looks like daytime. Oliver assumes this must be Times Square and says so to his traveling companion.

"I don't want to go there," Will says. "That could melt our brains."

"Fair enough," Oliver says, taking them what he hopes is east.

His knowledge of New York geography is extremely limited and almost entirely based on his mother's stories and the subway map shower curtain they'd had for a while before it had grown gray with mold and been replaced with a leopard print monstrosity he finds profoundly embarrassing.

"I'm starving," Will says, pointing to a hot dog cart. "I want one of those. Do you have any money?"

"Could we have two hot dogs, please?" Oliver asks the vendor.

"You want mustard? Relish?"

"Make it however you would eat it," says Will.

The vendor makes a face. "I don't eat these."

"How do we walk to Alphabet City from here?" Oliver asks.

"That's a long walk."

"We've got the time."

A bus rumbles by, an ad for *Beavis and Butt-Head Do America* across its side. Will points to the cartoon duo as he's wrapped in a hot blanket of exhaust. "So, which one do you want to be?"

The snow evaporates as it makes contact with the streets and sidewalks, but leaves a dusting on the plump black trash bags lined up on the curbs.

"I wonder if they've realized we're gone yet," Will says. "I hope we didn't get Stella in trouble."

"You know what's weird?" Oliver says. "I don't even care."

"Think they'll call our parents?"

"Of course they'll call our parents."

"You don't seem real worried," Will observes.

"My mom's a shouter. It's annoying, but the consequences are minimal."

"What about your dad?"

Oliver shakes his head. "It's just me and my mom."

"Oh."

"He died when I was little. He didn't walk out or anything."

"You don't have to explain," Will says, turning up the collar on his jacket.

The subway passes under their feet, sending a rush of air up through a grate in the sidewalk. "People usually assume he left us. My mom hates that. They were really happy. She doesn't want people to pity her. They do anyway, but I guess it's different."

"I'm really sorry."

"It's funny; Althea's mom split around the same time, but people always think she died."

"No one likes to think that moms can leave. Too unnerving."

"Al loves to make people uncomfortable, so she usually makes a joke like, 'My mom's not dead, she's just defunct.'" Oliver reflects on this briefly, thinking of the many times Althea had used that line or one of its variants to alienate any new adult who showed interest in her, how he had repeatedly watched her reach for her trusty defense mechanism as automatically as Will's neighbors would grab the shotgun under the bed at the first sound of an intruder.

"I'm sure this friend of yours has a lot of good qualities, but she sounds fucked up."

"She is at that," Oliver admits.

"What about you?" Will asks.

"What about me?"

"Your dad. Did it fuck you up?"

Oliver laughs. "Something sure did." He presses his temples with his fingertips. "Something's not working in there."

As they get farther downtown and evening evolves into night, there are more and more bars and drunk people. If they were overwhelmed by Midtown, they are woefully unprepared for the insanity that is the East Village at night. Will stays close, and together they hug the inside of the sidewalk, trying not to get knocked down by foot traffic.

The snow is coming down harder now, and the weather has given the night just enough sense of occasion to send the city's revelers into overdrive. There is an electricity crackling among all the people, like when a famous musician dies or a new president is elected or a beloved underdog baseball team clinches the pennant, like some exciting piece of news is traveling down Avenue A toward Oliver and Will in a palpable ripple of energy, and overwhelming as it is, Oliver has the feeling that, at any moment, this urgent and unimagined revelation is going to reach them and tether him with some invisible thread to all of these strangers pulsing in the streets.

Of course, he knows that's wrong. There is no revelation circulating, only massive amounts of alcohol, consumed with gusto by the ten thousand people all hoping to get laid tonight in the same twelve-block radius. It's like Jason's party times a million, all the hooting and hollering and sweaty jostling, so much of it in the hope that at some point in the night you'll rub up against the right person and that'll be, as Nicky likes to say, the end of the story. But inflated or not he feels it anyway, that sense of possibility, the anticipation, like it's already New Year's Eve and the clock is poised at five minutes to midnight and everyone is waiting breathlessly for the moment that will elevate the ordinary into something singular and amazing.

Oliver doesn't even realize they have stopped walking until the door to a karaoke bar opens, unleashing five addled patrons onto the same small square of sidewalk where he and Will are now frozen, as well as the chorus of "Build Me Up Buttercup," enthusiastically sung by a girl wearing a rhinestone tiara, clutching the microphone to her chest. The door is only open long enough to give Oliver this brief snapshot before it swings shut, the tiara girl and her terrible, terrible voice immediately silenced, safely contained on the other side.

"It's weird," says Oliver. "Most of these people seem truly awful, but at the same time, I want to be just like them."

"We could probably find you a tiara, if it means that much to you."

"That's not what I mean." He leads them down the street, past a particularly rowdy bar called Doc Holliday's, which appears to be filled with Hells Angels.

"I know what you mean," Will says. "At least I think I do. But I was strange even before I got sick. Even if my brain worked right, I don't think I'd have much in common with this mass of humanity. And for what it's worth, you don't seem like you would, either."

"I was never a freak—even after. Althea was the big spectacle. I resented it, then. Maybe she actually did me a favor. I never stopped being the normal one."

"Sounds like a shitty deal for both of you. Look, I'm all up for this adventure, but can we go somewhere less—just less? All this action is making me a little swimmy in the head." Will gestures to the chaos on the street around them.

"Sure. You're being a real champ, by the way."

"What are we doing here, anyway?" asks Will.

"I really don't know."

They head toward a park across the street, the one place the crowd seems to be avoiding, except of course for the homeless, bundled into shapelessness by their many layers of clothing.

"My mom used to live here," Oliver offers.

"In the park?" Will asks.

"On the other side." He nods toward Avenue B. "Somewhere over there."

"With your dad?"

"First with friends, and then yeah, with my dad. She says it was different then. Dangerous. There was a saying my dad made her memorize: 'Avenue A, you're all right, Avenue B, be careful, Avenue C, you're crazy, Avenue D, you're dead.' He used to sing it to me like a nursery rhyme."

"And where exactly are we headed?"

"That was twenty years ago. I don't think you need to worry. It's probably safer than living in a town where everyone is armed."

"We're not all a bunch of toothless hicks, you know. My mom's a dental hygienist. Pop works for the electric company. They read the newspaper. We don't raise our own chickens."

This is exactly what Oliver had been picturing, but he's kind enough to lie. "I was pretty much just imagining the suburbs where I live."

"I'd wager more of your neighbors have guns than you'd care to think about."

This brings to mind an image of a housecoat-clad Mrs. Parker standing on the sidewalk with a loaded rifle, picking off squirrels. Thank Christ Garth collects historical artifacts instead of guns; Althea is one person who should never have access to firearms. In the movies, they always make it look like a girl can't bring herself to actually fire a gun once she's got her hands on it; she might level it at someone for a second, but inevitably she starts to shake and get all teary, and then she's easily disarmed and rendered harmless again. Althea, now; Althea wouldn't hesitate to pull the trigger.

Although, come to think of it, wasn't that what had made her so handy to have around? Suddenly he can't recall why he had been so furious when she'd tackled Jason outside of Lucky's—the clown had keyed her car, after all, and called Oliver a freak, and it was that uninspired dig that finally made her commit to taking him down. No, he can't remember why he'd been angry at all; only the perfect pitch that launched the glinting arc of Jason's keys into the woods and the perverse exhilaration as they peeled out of the parking lot.

"So what does she look like?" Will asks.

"I told you, she's beautiful. Tall, blue eyes. She used to be blonde, and then she dyed her hair black. That I didn't care for so much."

Will stops walking. "Wait. She has black hair? Long black hair, but the roots coming in blonde at the top, like a skunk?"

"Yeah."

"She's tall, right? About your height, but still kind of scrappy-looking? Puffy vest and a real worn-out hoodie with thumbholes, like, chewed into the cuffs? That sound about right?"

"How the fuck do you know that?"

"You were right, man, she is beautiful."

Oliver freezes. "How do you know that?"

"I think she came looking for you. If she'd gotten here, I don't know, half an hour earlier, she would've caught you before you went down. I didn't know who she was—she just looked like some girl who'd gotten lost, wandered into the wrong part of the hospital. I can't believe no one told you."

"Did Stella know?"

"Stella's the one who talked to her."

"Fuck me till I die."

"Are you okay?" Will asks.

"I think I want to sit down somewhere."

There's a pool hall across the street and down a flight of stairs. "Come on," Will says.

It's basically a rec center for grown-ups. In a row of booths by the door, groups of men and women in their twenties are playing all manner of board games: Scrabble, Connect Four, Battleship. Farther back, past the bar, the space widens considerably to accommodate air hockey, several pool tables, and a Ping-Pong area enclosed in white mesh, presumably to keep the players from having to chase the tiny white ball across the filthy floor every time someone scores a point. Underground, without windows, it's stale and close; the heat is cranked up, and it smells like everyone's wet jackets. A row of couches separates the pool tables from a cement clearing where several microphones and a row of instruments, including an organ, are plugged in and ready, waiting for their masters to attend to them.

"You want to shoot a game of eight-ball?" asks Will.

Oliver starts to say no. Just looking at the vacant pool table fills him with dread—not because he's bad at it, but because he's very good. Althea is the one who's useless with a cue, and a sore loser. But wait; he's not here with Althea. "Sure."

After Oliver pays for the game, Will wins the flip for the break and sinks two solids; Oliver chalks up his cue and assesses what's on the table. When Will misses his third shot, Oliver steps up and takes a good look at Will's face, reassuring himself that this guy can handle losing a game of pool.

"What?" says Will.

Oliver smiles. "Don't blink or you'll miss it."

He leans over his stick and lines up the first shot, which sends the thirteen ball trilling neatly into a corner pocket. Examining the new configuration, Oliver circles the table, searching for the best angle to exploit. It's just simple geometry, which he has tried to explain to Althea. He doesn't struggle to block out the sounds—balls rocketing heavily into the pockets, the plastic tapping of the Ping-Pong ball across the room, the steady thrum of enthusiastic, beer-fueled conversation—but as he zeroes in on his task the noise naturally recedes, as if someone has thoughtfully turned down the volume so he can concentrate. It all goes away until it's just him and six stripes, now five, now four. He focuses, and one by one, he clears the rest off the table.

"Eight ball in the side pocket," Oliver says, not daring to look at Will until it's over in case he's judged wrong. If Will is standing there in tears or in a rage, he doesn't want to know, doesn't want this moment spoiled yet, would like at least to finish what he started. The eight ball goes exactly where he wants it, with a precision that feels nearly telekinetic, and Oliver is sorry to see it disappear, because it means the game is over.

I win, Oliver thinks. *I win and it's no big deal.*

Will isn't crying, of course, because he is a normal person, but he doesn't seem astonished by Oliver's performance, either, and this is disappointing. "Nice" is all he says, and starts racking the balls. Oliver wonders if this is how Will is cloaking his irritation with being beaten so handily, by feigning nonchalance. Isn't that what normal people do? There's a name for it, he thinks— passive-aggressive. This is new to him, steeped as he is in so many years of navigating the plain old aggressive.

Oliver rummages through the leather nets lining the table's pockets, retrieving the balls as he finds them and rolling them toward Will. He had forgotten how much he liked their shiny solid weight and the way they gleam under the hooded lamps. Cheers erupt from a smallish crowd over by the microphones. The population of the couches has doubled, and several rows of people are lined up behind them, obscuring Oliver's view of the stage that isn't really a stage. Apparently whomever this audience has been waiting for has just come on.

"Winner breaks," Will says, removing the rack to reveal a perfectly symmetrical triangle.

"Sure," Oliver says. Sliding the cue through his fingers, he thinks about lithium tremors and eye twitches. Two months ago, if a doctor had offered him such a troubled cure, Oliver would have taken it without hesitating, confident that he had nothing else to lose. It seems now that he has more left than he thought.

"What's wrong?" asks Will.

"What would you give to make it stop?"

"What are you talking about?"

"Is there anything you wouldn't give up?"

"My balls," says Will. "And my dick."

"That's it?"

"I don't know. Maybe I could spare one ball." So Oliver repeats what the doctor told him. "That's awesome."

"Didn't you hear the rest of what I said?"

"You know what your problem is?"

"My fucking brain?" Oliver says.

"You're impossible to please," says Will, shaking his head. "Did you think they would just wave a magic wand and make you better? Of course it's not perfect. It's an experiment."

"So you're going to do it?"

"Shit yeah. As soon as we finish this game I'm gonna go back up there, put it all on black, and let them spin the wheel. Maybe they can just write me a script and send me home."

"But it could turn you into a zombie."

"I've been a zombie, believe me. I'm ready to take my chances with the devil I don't know. Now break already, so you can win and we can get out of here."

As Oliver's aiming for the cue ball the organ starts in, and he knows the shot's no good before the balls have even stopped caroming. It's not a foul or a scratch, at least, but he loses his turn to Will, and with it goes whatever advantage Oliver might have had.

He is still processing—*an organ?*—when the music takes shape and a voice that is part James Brown rasp and part Baptist tent revival begins to sing, backed by what sounds like a chorus of three. Oliver's eyes meet Will's over the table.

Gospel? Oliver mouths.

Here? Will mouths back, gesturing around the room.

Oliver tilts his head in the direction of the music. Will nods, and they set down their cues in silent agreement, sidling up to the crowd so they can watch.

It is, in fact, a gospel band, led by a black woman in a white suit and a red beret covered in sequins. She's flanked by her female backup singers, who remind Oliver of three cardinals seated in a row on a telephone line, listening to the best news they've ever heard running through the wire beneath their feet. Poor Will is on his toes, trying to get a better look. Oliver takes his wrist and slips through to the front, where they quickly find a spot on one of the couches. Most of the audience is standing.

The woman in the beret is singing about love, but not the kind Oliver is used to hearing about in songs. There's nothing fleeting about the love she means; she's talking about something that doesn't go away when you're in a fight with your best friend or your dad dies or your mother leaves town to pursue her own nebulous destiny. Oliver supposes she might be singing about Jesus, but she doesn't call him by name, evoking instead the ideas of gratitude, courage, and compassion. Walking up and down the length of the crowd, radiant, she singles people out, turning her performance into a conversation. A thin Indian man wearing a porkpie hat over his shoulder-length, glossy black hair reaches out his hand and she clasps it with her free one, and they look into each other's eyes like there's nobody else around. Oliver assumes she must know him somehow, until she moves on and does the same thing to a tattooed girl with a Mohawk, who is in blissful tears by the end of their encounter.

In Wilmington, the same kids always turned up to see the punk shows, and among that particular clan there was not a whole lot of aesthetic variation; they looked the same because they had to, because that was how you recognized your people. But here there is no common denominator that Oliver can see, nothing that marks this group as a subculture. It's more like a cult that has drawn every kind of person, and the woman with the microphone is their leader. And if the purpose of Minty Fresh's band is cathartic stupefaction, to leave the audience feeling as though their brains have been scooped out of their heads like so many seeds from a pumpkin, then this music is meant to be the opposite. It's meant to fill you up with joy. Behind the audience, people are still playing their games of nine-ball and air hockey. How can they concentrate on anything other than this woman's sublime voice?

The band plays for over an hour. Will has forgotten his rush to get back uptown to the hospital and get busy with the devil he doesn't know. When the woman announces their last song, Oliver can't even bring himself to be disappointed, still reeling as he is from their amazing fortune at having stumbled upon them at all.

As the singer makes one final pass down the length of the crowd, Oliver reaches his hand out and she takes it. Her skin is warm and dry and chapped. For a few seconds, she sings directly to him, and that sense of possibility yawns before him again. *Hopelessness? Is that what that is?* he had asked the doctor, and it's still there, but it's turned transparent and he can see through to the other side, to a time when this will be the origin story he tells, the History of Oliver 101, and this moment was just the beginning. Everything is going to be okay—not now, not yet, but eventually he's going to have some kind of a life again.

And it's going to be awesome.

When the set is over and the band has departed, their listeners in a happy daze, Oliver and Will stumble around looking for their jackets.

"I didn't know I like gospel music," Will says.

"Today has been full of surprises."

On their way out, they pass a couple in a booth huddled over a game of Candy Land. Oliver pauses, watching. He wonders why these adults would be playing such a simple game, one without strategy that requires virtually no thought. All you do is pull a card from the deck and move your piece to wherever it tells you to go, and if you happen to cross the finish line first it's a testament to luck, not skill. But they don't care about who wins; he can tell by their faces. The game is just an excuse to sit together drinking beers and laughing, their feet touching slightly under the table, coats in a heap beside them. Whoever loses is not going to throw a fit, hurl their pint glass to the floor, and stomp out of the bar; there's no drunken confrontation brewing, no uneasy subtext beneath their conversation. They make it look so easy.

"I want to talk to her," Oliver says. "I want to talk to her right now."

"Then do it," says Will.

It's still snowing outside, and the street around the pay phone seems to shimmer. Oliver listens impatiently as the phone rings and rings in Althea's house, and just when he thinks no one is going to pick up, Garth answers in his very sleepiest voice.

"It's me," Oliver says.

"It's a little late to be calling, Oliver."

"Sorry, sir. I didn't mean to wake you."

"It's all right, you didn't really. Are you still in New York?"

"Yeah."

"How's it going up there?" Oliver can hear Garth rearranging himself on the couch in his study, sitting up, taking a sip of his drink, moving a sheaf of papers from one place to another.

"I don't like hospitals and I don't trust doctors."

"Sounds like you're learning all kinds of things about yourself."

"The revelations, they just keep coming. How's the book?"

"Great fun. I'm leaving soon on a research trip to Mexico." Garth sounds strange, unusually loose and jovial.

"You gonna stay at one of those resorts with the cabanas and a swim-up bar?"

"Think ancient temples and dusty manuscripts."

He's drunk, Oliver realizes with astonishment. Garth Carter has been hanging out alone in his study getting lit on his good scotch. Garth always has a drink in his hand, but Oliver has never once seen him intoxicated. "So, more Indiana Jones than winter break?"

"Fortune and glory, kid. Fortune and glory."

Oliver's shock must be showing on his face. Will is gesturing wildly, trying to get Oliver to give him some clue of what's going on. *It's her dad,* Oliver mouths. *I think something's wrong.* "Just don't drink the water," he tells Garth.

"Don't worry, Ol. It's not my first rodeo."

"What's Althea going to do while you're gone?" Oliver looks at Will and shakes his head. He pulls the handset away from his ear a little. Will squeezes into the kiosk, leaning in to listen.

"She's going to go with me. We're leaving after New Year's, as soon as she gets back from New Mexico."

"New Mexico? But she hates Alice."

"There's been some trouble since you left. Althea managed to get herself expelled in a particularly spectacular fashion, and things have been very difficult for her. Trust me. The best thing was for her to leave Wilmington for a little while."

Will covers the receiver with his hand. "Maybe I was wrong," he whispers. "Maybe it wasn't her."

Oliver shakes his head again. "Now I know for sure that it was. She hates her mother." He speaks into the phone. "I want to talk to her. What's Alice's number?"

"Oliver, do you remember the story I told you about Cortés? How he burned the fleet of ships he used to cross to the New World to force the loyalty of his soldiers?" Garth uses a cautionary tone that's hard to take seriously, considering he's slurring his words.

Is he drunk? mouths Will.

Oliver nods, bewildered. "That guy was messed up."

"Just be careful. Loyalty isn't always the virtue we think."

"If it hadn't been for Cortés, those guys would have been stuck in Spain, laying bricks or breeding pigs. Instead they died in battle, their pockets filled with gold. And they gave you something to write about."

"That's one way to look at it."

"Don't forget your fedora." Oliver hangs up. "She didn't go to New Mexico," he tells Will. "She came to New York because I'm here, and I still am, so that means she must be, too."

"Call him back. If you're right, then his kid's missing and he doesn't even know it."

"She's not missing. She's around here somewhere."

"She's not your misplaced fucking sock, Oliver."

"I'll find her. If I find her, then she's not missing, she's with me."

"It's been a month. Where are we supposed to start looking? Should we go back to the park and check under all the benches?" Will says.

"I thought you wanted to get back to the hospital and put it all on black."

"I'm not going alone. What am I supposed to tell them—you heard a little gospel music and now you're off on a mission of mercy? They'll think I killed you and dumped your body in the river. Which I'm considering."

"Thanks."

Will arcs a foot across the sidewalk, making a blurry comma in the snow. "So? Where do we start?"

"What do you mean?"

Will buttons his jacket, adjusts his baseball cap, and rubs his frozen hands together. "If you want to find this girl, then come on. Let's do this. Let's go."

Oliver is trying very hard not to think about his mother. Did she know by now that he was on the lam? Would she still be in North Carolina if she did? Nicky isn't much for sitting by a telephone waiting for news. She's more of a proactive type, although *proactive* in this case might simply mean showing up at the hospital and screaming at the staff. He hopes that prick of a doctor is getting the worst of it.

"You're doing this all wrong," says Will, flagging down the waitress for another cup of coffee. They went into the first diner they saw in order to strategize. "You've got ten years' worth of clues. Imagine you're at home. Where would you look for her in Wilmington?"

"I never have to look for her. She lives down the block."

"Use your imagination. If she wasn't at home, how would you find her?"

"I'd ask her dad."

"You tried that. Think harder. Use your imagination," Will repeats.

Oliver closes his eyes and pictures himself back home. The last time he'd woken up from an episode, he'd gone to Althea's house first, and only one place after that. "Coby's," he says finally, reluctantly. "I would look for her at Coby's."

"Is he a friend of hers?"

"More like a nemesis."

"She has a nemesis?" Will looks impressed.

"He had something to do with her getting expelled."

"Call him."

"He's in North Carolina. What could he possibly know?"

"Nemeses know things."

"This guy is not exactly Keyser Söze."

"Just do it, ace."

Oliver looks around the diner, where the inebriated revelers who struck out tonight are slowly sobering up over waffles and coffee and matzo ball soup. The people outside walking their dogs and buying their newspapers are beginning to outnumber those who have not yet gone to sleep, a sure sign that another night has given way to morning. They pay the check and go outside to find a pay phone. The weak December sun casts a pearly, blue-gray light over Avenue A, and Coby's phone is ringing in North Carolina.

"Yeah?" Coby answers, sleepy and irritated.

"It's Oliver."

"McKinley. What's the good word?" There is a new nasal twang to Coby's voice.

"You sound different. You have a cold or something?"

"More like a deviated septum."

"You broke your nose?"

"Someone broke it for me."

This is welcome and surprising news. "Who?"

"I'll give you three guesses, but you're only gonna need one."

"I think there'd be people lining up to do the job."

"Maybe so, but we only know one with anger management issues."

Oliver laughs. "Althea broke your nose? That explains so much."

"And split my lip, and gave me two black eyes. Why do you think she got expelled? They don't kick you out of school just for cutting a few classes."

"Atta girl. What did you do to make her so mad?"

"I don't think I'm the one who made her mad. You still up there in the Big Apple?"

Oliver winces. *The Big Apple.* "Yeah."

"Then how do you not know all this? She went up there to find you, didn't she? Made some sort of pathetic last-ditch effort to get you to be her boyfriend?"

It stings to learn that Will was right, that loathsome Coby could still be a source of information. "Did she confide that to you before or after she gave you a concussion?"

"She didn't confide shit. But I don't think she went all the way to New York just to learn the fine art of Dumpster diving and serving food to the homeless. Not when she's got two vegan gurus right here at home. She went up there for you. That's the only reason she ever does fucking anything."

"So that's where she is? With Bread and Roses?" For some reason this is the last thing Oliver expected to hear—that Althea had taken shelter with other people somewhere.

"Wait, you don't even know where she is?"

"Did you think I called just to hear your voice? She tried to visit me in the hospital when I was sick. I've been trying to find her since I woke up. Thanks. You've been very helpful."

Coby groans. "Oh, fuck everything. Fuck you, too."

Talking to Coby over the phone, being spared the sight of his smug little face—rearranged though it may be now—makes it possible for Oliver to pity him, sounding all nasal and lovelorn like he does. "If she didn't tell you where she was, how did you know?"

"The Brooklyn Bread and Roses kids called Valerie and asked a bunch of questions. Did she know Al"—*Al? What?* Oliver stops pitying Coby—"why did she leave town. They wanted to know if she was someone they'd want sleeping on their couch. Valerie said she was, but she asked me if I had a different opinion."

"And you said no?"

"I'm not about to get her booted. It sounds like they like her. It sounds like she's making friends. Of course, now you and your dimples are going to walk in and shit all over it, but that's on you."

"I'm sorry you've been so deprived of the pleasure of her company," Oliver says dryly.

Coby snorts. "Yeah, it's been a real fucking pleasure. Do the three of us a favor and let her off the hook once and for all. Set her straight. Minty Fresh told me they stood on your porch when you were leaving and asked for your help and you didn't even care that she was in trouble. Why don't you tell her that when you two have your magical reunion?"

"I was on my way to the airport so I could check myself into the goddamn hospital. I wasn't in the mood to deal with her shit."

"No, fuck you—*fuck you*, McKinley. You strung her along and you broke her heart, and now you're going to swoop in and be her hero and that's fucking tremendous, I'm sure it'll put a real smile on her face, because for five minutes she'll think that it's all finally going to shake out the way she wants. But sooner or later you're going to end up back in the same place because it's never going to shake out the way she wants with you. And you should tell her that before things start to get too cinematic."

Oliver clamps the phone tighter to his face, as if it will help him get his point across. "Don't do that, don't talk about us like you know us. And don't act like if it weren't for me Althea would realize you're the greaser stooge of her dreams, because you are not. You are not some misunderstood Bukowski character, and if she rattled your cage hard enough to get thrown out of school, then it sounds like she's got the right idea about you after all."

"The best things about Althea are the things that you can't stand," Coby barrels on, as if he hasn't heard. "You're like a blank piece of paper, and she can color you any way she wants. You know why you won't just let this thing go? Because you need her to dictate your next move. You need her to push so you know when to pull. I might not be the stooge of her dreams, but when she pushes I push back, and broken nose or not, I'll say this about Althea: She doesn't always need to know what's going to happen next. Sometimes she likes it better when she doesn't. But go ahead, call Val, she's got the address. And when you see Althea, you tell her I said no hard feelings."

All of Oliver's satisfaction and annoyance disappears as he listens to Coby speak about Althea with an authority and intimacy that scares the living shit out of him. Halloween night, after the show at Lucky's, he had seen them off in a corner of the parking lot, smoking cigarettes and talking in a way that would have made them appear, to the uneducated eye, like a couple, and he finally had an idea of how he and Althea must have looked.

Something had happened after that, something that had nothing to do with him, and he's not sure he even wants to know what it was, but he still hates that he doesn't. "Seriously. What did you do to her?"

"Nothing she didn't beg me for," Coby says, and hangs up.

"What did the nemesis say?" Will asks.

"You were right. Nemeses know things."

"We'd better hurry and find her, then." Will's grin fades, and all evidence of gleeful mischief vanishes from his face. He looks at Oliver with a painful seriousness. "I'm starting to get pretty tired."

chapter fourteen.

MATILDA WAKES ALTHEA by snatching back her quilt and throwing open the kitchen curtains. "Rise up, Gemini!" She claps briskly.

"Don't clap at me," Althea mumbles.

"Get up, you foxy fucking bitch." Althea doesn't move. *"Now!"* Matilda yells. "Today is going to be the greatest day of our lives." She says this every morning that she doesn't have a hangover.

Althea fixes herself a cup of coffee and follows Matilda upstairs for their morning cigarette-in-the-bathroom ritual. Ethan is on his way from the shower to his room, wearing only a towel around his waist, dripping all over the floor. He isn't scrawny like Althea thought he would be, although he's so pale, he's practically luminescent. Without asking, he takes Althea's mug and drinks half its contents before returning it.

"Thanks," he says. She watches the muscles in his back as he walks away.

"I know," Matilda says when they're safely in the bathroom with the shower running. "His body is like a hidden treasure.

Once in a while I do his laundry so I can shrink all his T-shirts."

"I wasn't looking at his—"

"Sure you weren't."

Matilda has her back against the tub; Althea's is against the door. Their legs are outstretched, bare feet nearly meeting in the middle. Heat radiates from the moldy baseboards. Matilda points her toes at Althea, who does the same, until the grimy tips touch.

"So today's the day, right? You excited?" Althea asks.

"Yup. Today's the day."

Though New Year's Eve is not until tomorrow, friends of the Warriors are slated to begin arriving sometime that afternoon for their legendary annual New Year's Eve party, the Champagne Derby. The derby starts with a trip to the liquor store and the purchase of every kind of sparkling wine cheaper than eight bucks. It inevitably concludes with profuse vomiting and abject misery, but the time in between is said to be a party so fierce, so robust, like a conveyor belt of laughter and good feeling that delivers fun to every individual faster than fun can be processed by the human brain, that it is worth even the most brutal physical punishment the following day.

Christmas had been quiet, almost nonexistent, the house's residents making grudging pilgrimages back to their respective families. Matilda invited Althea to go with her, back to Queens, but she had demurred, insisting she would be glad to have the house to herself for the first time. Instead, Althea found the place unbearable—eerily quiet and claustrophobic, like the cracked walls and filth were closing in on her, even Mr. Business hiding in a closet somewhere. She called Garth to wish him a merry Christmas, inventing a list of presents she'd received from Alice and a recent trip to the hot springs. She was so lonely she called Alice, but there was no answer in Taos.

After that, she made a command decision: She took the subway into Manhattan by herself for the first time and went to an all-ages show at ABC No Rio, hoping to find relief pressed up against a stage, covered in the sweat of strangers and dodging their fists and elbows, but the show was strangely unsatisfying, too sparsely attended for a decent mosh pit to form, a handful of straight-edge boys with shaved heads menacing other members of the audience.

New Year's, she's been assured, will have a real sense of occasion. "It makes up for Christmas," Gregory had promised her.

"I feel weird," Althea says.

"Why?"

"I'm not going to know anyone."

"Don't be an idiot. You didn't know us a month ago, either."

"Sounds so strange when you say it like that."

"How is it? First New Year's away from home? Away from Oliver?" Matilda asks.

"I don't know."

"I bet we could find you someone to kiss at midnight. If you're interested."

"I'm not." She leans her head back and closes her eyes, listening to the shower pound the dirty tub. "Can we go down to the boardwalk?"

"I wish. I've got to make vegan baked ziti for a dozen people who are going to be here in a few hours."

"You know you love it."

"I do."

"Then why don't you seem more excited?"

Matilda sighs. "New Year's is our holiday. It's like the Christmas you have with your friends, the family you pick. So once a year everyone comes in from out of town and we hang out for days, and that's how it feels, it feels like we're family, like we've all thrown in our lots together and it'll always be like this. Of course, then it's over and the thing I look forward to all year is finished and it's just winter and there's nothing to be excited about until springtime. But for a couple of days, you know, it's pretty great." Matilda brushes the hair from her eyes. "I do hope this weather changes, though. The sunrise on New Year's Day is one harsh fucking mistress. Easier to handle when it's overcast."

Pulling her knees to her chest, Althea balls herself up like a napkin. "Cheer up," she says. "Today is going to be the greatest day of our lives."

In the kitchen, Ethan is paging cautiously through her sketchbook, which Althea thought was safely tucked between the couch and the wall. Pouring herself another cup of coffee, she makes like she doesn't care, eats a fistful of granola over the sink, and watches everyone else building some kind of sculpture out of empty beer cans in the backyard.

"You know I write stories," Ethan says, stating it like a fact, like something she was actually supposed to have known. She waits. "They're not really stories. They're like outlines? For comic books? Or graphic novels? Me and Dennis were supposed to work on one together, but he bailed." Althea stares into the sink. A single soggy carrot peel lingers in the drain. "I had most of the characters worked out, some of the story."

"Aren't you supposed to serve in the park today?" she finally says.

"I am. And you're coming with me."

"I am?"

"Unless you're busy? Or have other plans?"

So Althea layers as best she can, in a T-shirt under a thermal under her filthy, falling-apart sweatshirt under her puffy vest. She puts on two pairs of socks and meets Ethan in the front hallway, where he is wearing one tennis shoe and pawing through the pile for its mate.

"You should tie the laces together when you take them off," she says, holding up her united combat boots. "That way they don't get separated."

"You're not going to be warm enough in that."

"This is what I've got."

Ethan rolls his eyes. "Of course."

"Don't give me your put-upon face, okay? I'm not complaining."

"Come on." He takes her elbow and steers her toward the staircase.

She follows, hesitating in the doorway of the room he shares with Gregory. There are books everywhere, leaning against the walls in unstable-looking towers and stacked up on the dresser and the windowsill. It smells like lemons and clean laundry, not the sweaty boy socks Althea expected, although the can of air freshener on the nightstand implies that this is not achieved naturally. Mr. Business, curled up on the pillow in a small furry comma, meows at the intruders through squinty green eyes. The covers are thrown back on the bed, exposing the imprint of Ethan's body on the sheets. Something about it is uncomfortably intimate, and Althea looks away.

He rummages around in a plastic bin on the closet floor until he finds a green knit hat with earflaps and matching mittens that unsnap to reveal fingerless gloves. The hat and mittens have eyes. He hands them to her. "Is that supposed to be a frog?" Althea asks.

"Matilda gave these to me as a joke." She pulls on the frog ensemble, and Ethan goes back to rooting in the closet. He emerges again, this time with a scuffed black trench coat. "It's not real leather," he says. "It's just some piece of crap I found at a thrift store, but Matilda lined the inside with fleece."

Slipping it on, Althea gets a big whiff of the fake leather, and the scent reminds her so much of the couch in her basement at home that she can't speak for fear of crying. It isn't homesickness or longing so much as it is a painfully tactile reminder that it had all actually happened, she had wrestled with Oliver on that stupid couch and slept on it after he left her and shared meals on it with her father while watching *Jurassic Park* and trying not to contemplate the mess she'd made of everything. All of that had been before. That's what kills her. She had a before, and now she's in the after, and it wrenches her heart inside her chest that such a break has been made and she doesn't even want to go back.

"Are you okay?"

Showing Ethan any weakness would surely be a major tactical error, so she sacks up and breathes through her mouth. "I bet I look ridiculous."

"But in a good way."

The park is empty. They set up their table in the middle of the vast expanse of white as the wind whips hollowly around them. Althea stations herself behind the collard greens, stamping her feet to keep some feeling in her toes. Ethan reads *V for Vendetta* and ignores her.

"No one's coming today," she says after half an hour. "Why don't we just pack up and go home?"

"That's not how it works."

"What's the point of standing here in the cold if no one's going to show up?"

"The point is to be consistent. That's how people know we'll be here when they need us."

Althea sinks into a crouch and starts making a small round pile of snow. "Tell me about this comic book of yours," she says.

"What do you know about diamonds?"

"I know they're all in a vault at De Beers and they're not really worth anything."

"How do you know about that?" he says.

Althea is annoyed by his surprise. "I don't want to shock the hell out of you, but we have books in North Carolina, too."

Ethan opens his mouth to say something nasty, she can tell by his expression, but he changes his mind and starts over. "So I had this idea to do a story about a heist. About a bunch of thieves who boost all the diamonds from De Beers. Not because they want to fence them, but because they want to give them away. Destroy their value, destroy the monopoly."

"How would they do it?"

"It would have to be an inside job."

Without looking up, she agrees. "And you'd need a pretty principled bunch of criminals to steal all those diamonds and just give them away." Unsnapping the tops of her mittens to free her fingers, she molds a set of back legs, then carves away the snow on the sides to make the frog's belly more defined.

"Well, that's the thing," says Ethan. "They would all be tempted. That's the point. They're ordinary people. But eventually they would all realize they had the chance to really do something good, instead of just getting fat and rich."

"When I first heard the story, I didn't think the guy at the top was fat and smug. I imagined"—she pauses, reaching back to that day in the hallway with Valerie—"I imagined him tall. With a pocket watch. And lonely. Sneaking down into the vault at night to look at his diamonds."

Ethan produces a wet sound of derision from the back of his throat. "Please."

"You read too many comic books," she says, rounding out the frog's back and giving more arch to the neck. "The diabolical archvillain, the guy rubbing his hands together, the guy who loves being so evil? That guy doesn't really exist. Nobody ever thinks they're the bad guy. I know that whole Robin Hood thing has a lot of appeal, but it's a little too easy, don't you think?"

"So you think it's a bad idea," Ethan says.

"I just think it shouldn't be so simple. What if the guy at the top was your inside man? What if *he* decided to get rid of all the diamonds? Maybe something happens and he thinks he doesn't deserve them anymore. But he can't just disband the empire. So he has to make it look like a heist."

"A redemption story. Interesting. Is that a frog?"

Carefully fashioning two tiny snowballs for eyes, she affixes them to either side of the head. "It doesn't look right."

"Here." Squatting beside her, Ethan bites the tip of his glove and wriggles his hand free. "He needs toes."

Althea watches the vapor clouds of Ethan's breath as he adds webbed feet to the hind legs. The very tip of his earlobe is exposed below his black knit cap. His pale neck has turned bright red above the place where it disappears into his scarf. She can see the snowy park reflected in the lenses of his glasses, and behind them his blue-gray eyes, which never stray from the ground.

"It's five toes in the back, not three," she says, correcting him. "And four in the front."

"Are you sure?"

"We dissected frogs in biology last year."

"Excuse me?" someone says behind them.

They're interrupted by a man with long hair plaited into two dark shiny braids. He's wearing a Mexican blanket poncho-style. A taxidermied crow sits on his shoulder.

Ethan leaps up. "Sorry about that," he says.

Althea spoons the collard greens onto a plate; Ethan serves the carrots and fake turkey.

"Look out for him," the man says, gesturing to the bird. "He used to be alive."

Surprisingly, Ethan engages him as he eats and allows the

man—Gray Wolf, he calls himself—to deliver a lengthy dissertation on his ex-wife and former career as a studio recording artist. He's about to launch into his history with the Hells Angels—"Once you're a Hells Angel, you're a Hells Angel for life, trust me, you wouldn't want to die by my hands"—when he stops himself. "But that's a conversation for another time," he says, nodding toward Althea. "Not fit for talking about in front of a lady."

"Some other time, then," says Ethan.

Gray Wolf smiles. "You got it."

After he leaves, Ethan turns to Althea. "That's why we stay, even when it's freezing and we think no one's coming."

She nods, chastened.

"Now we can leave." He covers the aluminum trays, carefully sealing all the edges.

Althea detaches the banner from the front of the table. "I could draw it. The diamond story. If you wanted to write it, I could do the drawings."

Ethan dismisses the idea with a quick shake of his head. "I don't think so."

"Why not? You saw my sketchbook. I'm good."

Going around to the other side of the table, he takes one end of the banner and meets her in the middle so it folds smoothly in half. "Do you have any idea how long something like that would take? How involved it would be, working out the story and the panels and doing all the art?"

"It's not exactly like I have a dearth of free time to fill." Angrily snatching the sign away from him, she finishes folding it herself.

"And what about when you leave? What then?"

"Who said anything about leaving? Look, I talked to Matilda. I know you called people back in Wilmington, I know you asked around about me—"

"Tough shit. This isn't witness protection."

"You want me to leave, right? You were pissed from the minute I walked in the door and you can't wait for me to go. Am I cramping your style? Have I inconvenienced you somehow? I'm trying to contribute and be helpful, but you just can't stand having me around."

"I'm saying that you won't stay. That you'll get tired of not having your own room and having to stand here in the park with me—"

"That part I'm getting pretty fucking tired of already."

"It's a matter of time before you get on the phone with your dad and tell him you want to come home. It's happened before. It happens all the time. You'll want things to go back to normal."

Even in the middle of this ridiculous fucking argument, when she would like nothing more than to put her hands around his pasty little neck and squeeze, a warm glow spreads through her stomach and she laughs.

"What's so funny?" he asks, sounding strangely unsure of himself, like he thinks she's laughing at him.

"Nothing," she says. She can't tell him because she knows how bizarre it will sound if she says it out loud.

It just feels so good to have someone to fight with again.

chapter fifteen.

OLIVER'S PLAN STOPS HERE. Standing on this porch, confronted with the house where Althea's been staying, while Will is swaying on his feet, barely able to keep his eyes open.

"We've got to get you back to St. Victor's," says Oliver.

"I'm not leaving until I know you've found her."

"We know she's here. I can take you and then come back."

"We don't know what's waiting for us at the hospital. If you take me in, you might not be able to leave again. You can't just drop me off and say that you have errands to run. For all we know, your mother could be there by now. Go knock on that door. We'll take it from there."

"Goddamnit."

"I told you it wasn't finished with me. It was just waiting until I was finally having a good time."

"I'm sorry."

"I'll live. Now go on."

Oliver takes a tentative step toward the door. Inside the house, someone is haltingly arranging chords on a badly tuned electric guitar.

"'Oh, Mr. Business, if you'll be my baby, I promise, I won't give you scabies,'" the singer proclaims, then stops himself short to call out a question. "Hey, what's the patron saint against scabies?"

"Saint Radegunde," someone answers. "Good luck finding something that rhymes."

Oliver looks back at Will, standing on the snow-covered lawn below him.

"What?" Will asks.

"I just realized I have no idea what I'm going to say to her."

Marching up the steps, Will rings the bell in three short bursts. "Think fast."

Oliver can hear the house take a collective breath—"Is someone at the door?" "Go see who it is." None of the voices sound like Althea. "Maybe this wasn't such a good idea," he says.

"Too late."

A girl answers the door. She's short and blonde and wearing an oversize Replacements shirt as a dress. Oliver pegs her as a handful of years older, and despite her diminutive stature she has an air of authority that reminds him of Nicky. Something in the way she's sizing him up with her sharp green eyes makes him extremely aware that this is her house, and he's standing uninvited on her porch. She doesn't say hello or ask what she can do for him; she just stares and waits for him to speak.

"Hi," he says.

"Hello," she replies. She doesn't even look at Will, keeping her eyes fixed on Oliver.

"I'm looking for Althea."

"I'm sorry, who?"

"Althea Carter."

The girl smiles tightly and shakes her head. "I'm sorry, I think you have the wrong place."

The narrow hallway behind her is filled with piles of shoes and newspapers, and a row of coats and jackets hangs on hooks sunk into the wall. Althea's puffy down vest is among them. "I'm sorry, I don't think I do," he says.

"Look, there's no Althea here," she says, and starts to shut the door.

Oliver braces it open with his hand. Leaning in, he looks down at the girl. "I know she's here. I know because her car is parked across the street and her favorite vest is hanging three feet behind you. I just want to talk to her. And I know she wants to talk to me."

A girl with curly brown hair and bright red lipstick swoops in from the end of the hallway, quickly flanked by two guys and followed by a pissed-off-looking cat. "Matilda, what's going on?" the other girl says, looking at Oliver, wedged in the doorway. "Who the fuck are you?"

"Oliver?"

Oliver turns and there's Althea, standing on the sidewalk with some guy in glasses. She's carrying a folding table like a suitcase, wearing a worn leather coat and a ridiculous green hat, her cheeks bright red with the cold. She looks the same, but completely different.

They stand there, staring at each other. Oliver forgets about their audience, forgets he even had anything to say. He just wants to look at her. She's so beautiful and it's really confusing but she's here and he found her and he's stupidly proud of himself.

"Hey," he says.

"How did you find me?" she asks.

"Remember outside Lucky's at Halloween? When I said I felt like solving a mystery?"

"Yeah."

"I wasn't fucking around."

She takes off the frog hat. All that black hair is gone; she's a blonde again, her angular face laid bare in its surprise at his arrival. She looks wonderful, even if the haircut is shocking. He thinks she's grown an inch or two taller, until he realizes she's just standing up straight. Slowly, her bewilderment fades, and one corner of her mouth turns up in a half-cocked smile. He searches that expression, trying to divine it, determine if she's self-conscious because of all these people or just overcome at the sight of him. Every second that passes with neither Althea nor Oliver crossing the few feet between them serves to call more attention to the fact that they have not yet embraced.

"What happened to your hair?" he asks her.

She makes a face, pretending to be hurt. "What?" she says, fluffing the shorn blonde locks movie-star style. "Don't you like it?"

She's flirting with him. In front of an audience. It's Oliver's turn to be astonished, and that electricity he felt on the street last night returns, that sense of possibility that only happens when you strip away everything familiar. Althea and Oliver are at the center of this spontaneous porch assembly, and it's strangely excellent. These people he doesn't even know are watching this scene unfold like they are actually invested in what happens, and of course that's why Althea and Oliver are paralyzed. Because what happens next matters. So Oliver forfeits and starts to reach for her.

"Jesus jumped-up Christ," says the guy with the glasses, angrily grabbing the table from Althea and making for the door. "Matilda, you're letting all the heat out. And who the shit is that?" he shouts, pointing at the far corner of the porch where, curled in the fetal position and shivering violently, Will is asleep.

Althea gives Oliver a deadpan look that evokes Garth so vividly, Oliver can almost hear the ice rattling in his glass.

"Let me guess," Althea says. "He's with you."

When Oliver imagined getting his wish, to return to his rightful place in the world, to ride shotgun in Althea's car once more, this is not exactly what he had pictured.

"Will! Come on!" he shouts, hanging over the back of his seat and shaking his friend's limp arm. "Wake up!"

"It's too late," Althea says. "His plug's already pulled. Trust me, I can tell."

"He has to stay awake until we get him to the hospital."

"What difference does it make?"

"I can't take him up to the clinic myself. I don't know what's waiting for me up there."

"Then I'll take him in."

"No!" Oliver shouts. "You're supposed to be in New Mexico. Will and I left yesterday without telling anybody. They called our parents. If Nicky flew up, she could be there. And if she sees you—"

"Why did y'all run away from the hospital?"

"Althea, *focus*!"

"Okay, okay, I understand, we have to send him in under the radar." She punches the gas and changes lanes without signaling. The other driver gives her the finger, which she matter-of-factly returns. "So get back there and wake him up."

"Your driving's gotten worse."

"No, it's just that everyone in this city drives the same way," she says, leaning on her horn. "It's actually kind of amazing. Now get back there."

Oliver squeezes himself between the two front seats and hunches on the floor near Will. Slapping his face lightly, he tries to coax him awake. "Hey, Will, wake up. Stella's here and she's naked."

Will groans softly but doesn't open his eyes.

"You're being too gentle," Althea says impatiently.

"You have any suggestions?"

"Try pinching him. That always got your attention."

Oliver reaches up Will's sleeve and pinches the soft, tender skin inside his elbow. Without opening his eyes, Will hauls off and slaps Oliver across the face.

"Fuck!" Oliver cries.

"Stop it!" Will says, and rolls over.

"Ol, are you okay? That sounded bad," Althea says, watching him in the rearview. The car bounces, hard, tossing Oliver around on the floor. "Sorry. Pothole."

"Whatever."

"Keep trying."

"Maybe you're right, maybe it's too late," he says.

"Do you want me to pull over so we can switch? Because I will bet you anything that if I get back there, I can wake him up."

"Everything has to be a competition," Oliver mutters.

"Seriously, I can do it. I did it for you, remember?"

"No, thanks, I don't like the idea of being the only driver on the road who feels invested in getting to his destination safely." Oliver slumps against the door. "Maybe we can just leave him outside the hospital with a note pinned to his chest or something. Or pay some homeless guy ten bucks to take him to the clinic."

He watches Will sleep, envying his oblivion. Althea keeps driving like an eight-year-old behind the wheel of the race car game at the arcade. "You can slow down, you know. It's not like there's any rush," he says. He is no way eager for this ride to end, since when it's over, he'll either be contending with his irate mother or alone in the car with Althea, a prospect he suddenly finds as scary as her driving.

"Maybe *I'm* in a rush," she says.

"To get where?"

"Um, back to the place where I live?"

"Oh, you mean Wilmington, North Carolina?" he says archly.

She's quiet for a minute. Oliver silently cheers, knowing he's scored a point. "You know that's not what I meant," she says softly.

Will's foot twitches in his sleep. Inspired, Oliver unties Will's tennis shoe and pries it off, then removes his sweaty sock.

"Christ on a cross, what is that smell?" Althea says, opening her window.

"Just drive," he says. Holding his breath, Oliver lightly tickles the bottom of Will's foot.

The effect is instantaneous. Will opens his eyes and starts screaming. His limbs jerk wildly, his bare foot catching Oliver directly in the face and slamming him back against the door. Althea nearly loses control of the car, swerving momentarily into the adjacent lane and inciting the significant rage of every other driver on the Brooklyn-Queens Expressway. She hastily rolls up her window again to block out the honking horns and colorful profanities.

Will sits up and clutches his chest. "Oh my God, oh my God."

"What the fuck just happened?" Althea screams. "Is he having a heart attack?"

"Will, are you okay?" Oliver cries. His eyes are filled with water, and Will is too blurry for a visual assessment.

"McKinley, I'm going to fucking kill you," Will says, panting.

"I'm sorry, I needed to wake you up."

As Will's breathing becomes less panicked, he reclines across the backseat again.

"Keep him awake, Ol," Althea says.

Oliver pulls on Will's arm. "Will, listen to me. We're almost there. We're taking you back to the hospital. Just—please. You have to stay awake until we get you there. Please."

"Holy shit," Will says, sitting up gingerly. "We found her."

"We did," Oliver says. "We found her."

"Your nose is bleeding."

Oliver swipes at his nose with the heel of his hand and, sure enough, it comes away red. "Yes, it is."

Will gives Oliver an apologetic look. "Did I do that?"

Oliver pats Will's bare ankle reassuringly. "Don't worry. I'll live."

When they pull up in front of St. Victor's, Will is still conscious, but barely. Oliver opens his door, spilling himself out onto the pavement, silently marveling that they've arrived unscathed. Leaving the engine running and her hazard lights on, Althea leaps out of the car. Two women are smoking cigarettes on the sidewalk. One has pink hair and a nose ring; the other sports a sleek black bob and an IV. They stare openly, curious and amused. Oliver nods at them. "Evening," he says, then turns back to the car. "Come on, Will," he says.

"She put too much relish on my hot dog and now I can't eat it," Will says mournfully.

"He's dreaming," Althea says. "We need to get him on his feet."

Reaching into the backseat, he takes Will gently by the waist. "I know, but it's okay, we're going to get you another hot dog. Just get up."

"Cookies?"

"Hot dogs and cookies, yes. All you can eat."

Together, Althea and Oliver coax Will out of the car, balancing him precariously on his feet. "Will, do you know where you're supposed to go?" Oliver says. "Do you remember how to get back to the clinic?"

"I don't want any sprinkles on mine," Will shouts.

"Put his arm around your shoulder," says Althea. "He's not going to make it on his own."

Oliver shakes his head. "I'm not going up there."

"We can't leave him out here."

"Fine. The elevator, then."

"Leave him in the elevator?"

"We'll put him in the elevator and send him up to eight. It's the best we can do."

The girl with the pink hair finishes her cigarette, grinding the butt under the heel of her combat boot. "Where does he need to end up?" she asks, gesturing to Will.

"The sleep clinic," Oliver says. "Eighth floor."

She looks at her friend and shrugs. "We can get him there."

"Really?"

"Sure. You guys look like you're having a rough night." She runs a finger along her upper lip, and Oliver remembers his is covered in blood.

"Thanks," he says.

Althea and Oliver hand Will over.

"Wait," Will says as the strangers arrange his arms around their shoulders.

Everyone pauses. Will looks at Oliver with eyes that are half-closed but suddenly lucid. "Tell her about the lithium," he says. "See what she has to say."

Althea and Oliver watch as the two women steer him inside the lobby, toward the elevators. Once the strange trio has disappeared, there's nothing left but for the two of them to turn and face each other. Althea awkwardly adjusts her frog hat.

"We'd better get going," she says.

"Yeah," he says. "I guess we'd better."

It's dark by the time they return. To Oliver, the inside of the house looks like someone took Nicky's kitchen and wiped it all over Garth's basement, lit the whole thing on fire, and then threw a party. An elfin guy with dark, spiky hair, wearing a plaid shirt and chewing a cinnamon stick, greets Althea warmly and asks what music she wants to hear; the luscious brunette with the red lipstick asks Althea if she needs a drink. Someone hands Oliver a can of Natural Ice, and he sips it automatically. Althea takes him by the hand and leads him through the filthy kitchen—the whole place smells like curry, wet cat, and burnt coffee—and out back.

The yard is a narrow rectangle, about half the size of Oliver's or Althea's. Old rusty bicycles are propped up against the warped wooden fence, and the remains of a zip line stretch from a second-floor window to a lone tree tucked in the back corner. White Christmas lights are strung all along the fence, although several lengthy sections have gone dark, and in the spots where the snow has melted it's apparent there's no grass to speak of. The centerpiece of the whole thing is an enormous sculpture made of empty Natural Ice cans, currently being admired by Matilda and about thirty of her friends.

"Who are all these people?" Oliver asks. "Do they all live here?"

"Of course not. Some of their friends are in from out of town. They're having a big New Year's party tomorrow."

"So who does live here?"

"The Warriors. Let's see." Althea shivers, and Oliver puts his arm around her. He's a little surprised when she leans into him instead of pushing him away. "You met Matilda. The other girl is Leala; they're, like, best friends from way back."

"Like us?"

Althea laughs. "Not exactly like us, no. Kaleb is the really rambunctious one. At some point tonight he'll probably take his pants off for no reason. He and Leala are together. The guy with the hair and the cat is Gregory. He's sweet, kind of loud some-times, but funny. He really loves that fucking cat."

Oliver nods toward the skinny guy with glasses who was shouting on the porch earlier. "Who's the redhead?"

"That's Ethan. He's okay." She points at a heavily tattooed guy with black plugs in his ears, leaning over Matilda and lighting her cigarette. "That's Dennis; he's a tattoo artist. He's good. I think he has a thing for Matilda. He crashes here a lot. So does the guy in the plaid shirt; he's a drummer, between bands and apartments."

"I'm never going to remember all this."

"It took me a while."

"So who's your favorite?" Oliver asks.

"My favorite?"

"Yeah."

Althea finishes her beer and smiles. "You are. Obviously." She holds up her empty can. "I'm going to give this little guy a home and grab another one."

Oliver watches as she joins the group, looking for a place for her contribution in the ridiculous aluminum structure.

Their ranks widen to make a space for her, then close around her again, absorbing her seamlessly. She stands shoulder to shoulder with Kaleb, surveying his work, talking to him with such ease, an effortlessness she's never had with other people, ever. They like her. He's ashamed of himself for even thinking that—of course they like her. Why wouldn't they like her? If Althea's never really had friends before, besides him, it's only because she's always looked at other people with derision. And the friends she did have were because of him, because he would never go where she was not welcome. It's strange to see her surrounded by people of her own, people who have nothing to do with him. For all of his complaining about her petulance and sudden mood swings, it's always worked to his advantage. He's never had to share her, not with anyone, not really. And something else occurs to him, perhaps the most surprising thing of all: She likes them.

"I'm sorry about before." Matilda has slipped away from her friends and joined him by the back door. "I'm not usually that hostile."

"It's okay. I'm sorry I showed up uninvited like that."

"Is your friend going to be okay?"

"Will? Yeah, we got him back to the hospital. He'll be all right."

"Look, I don't know what your plans are, but I hope you'll at least stay for New Year's. We like to make a big deal of it."

"Althea mentioned you guys have some wild party."

"The Champagne Derby, yeah. I hope you'll stay for it. It's a good time."

Oliver just stands there watching his every frozen breath dissolve from a vapor cloud to nothingness. "Thanks for the invite."

"Anyway. I'm gonna go do my part for the Natural Iceberg. Tell Althea I said you guys should sleep in my room tonight. Everyone's all riled up; you won't get any peace in the kitchen." Matilda leaves him and returns to the group, where she whispers something to Althea, who looks at Oliver like she had almost forgotten about him for a second, then reluctantly separates and comes back to him.

"You look miserable," she says.

"No fucking kidding," he says. "Look, I need to make a phone call."

"Nicky?" she asks.

"I just don't want her to worry."

"Sure. Here." She goes inside and returns with a cordless. "Call collect."

Oliver ducks out the front door onto the porch and makes his call. "Hi, Mom."

"Oliver, I'm going to fucking kill you."

"Please don't." Sitting on the steps, Oliver's entire body sags at the sound of his mother's voice.

"Where the hell are you?" she shouts.

"Stop yelling, okay? I'm in New York, I'm totally fine."

"I'm about to leave for the goddamned airport to try to get a flight up there."

"Don't bother. You don't need to come up here and stomp around the city like Godzilla looking for me. I'm at some punk house in Brooklyn with some friends of Valerie's, and I'm leaving tomorrow." Oliver impresses himself by coming up with this lie on his feet.

"To come home? Or to go back to the hospital?"

"That part I don't know yet."

"And when are you planning to decide?"

"I'm going to flip a coin tomorrow, when the ball drops at midnight."

"Come on, Oliver, don't be smart."

"I mean it, I really don't know. To be totally honest, neither one sounds particularly appealing."

Nicky pauses to light a cigarette; Oliver can hear the Bic's wheel sparking. "Why did you take off like that? You really scared the shit out of me."

"I felt like I was trapped in an elevator that was stuck between floors. I just wanted out. Bad enough I spent Christmas in a coma. If I had to do New Year's with those gorillas, I think I'd open up my wrists." He picks at some peeling rubber on the heel of his tennis shoe. "So do you have a boyfriend or what?"

"What the hell are you talking about?"

"When I was in the hospital, before I went down, you told me you had a date. So how did it go? Is he your boyfriend now?"

Nicky laughs. "Oh, that guy. God, that feels like a million years ago. No, it didn't work out."

"What happened? Didn't he pay for everything? Didn't he pull out your chair at the dinner table?"

"He got all the little stuff right," Nicky says.

A lone deliveryman rides down the street on a bicycle, an

insulated red pizza pouch strapped to his handlebars. "So what was the problem?"

"I don't know, Ol. The effort required at this point doesn't even seem worth it. Sometimes it's easier. To pretend this is the way it always was. Just you and me, the two of us."

"But why—"

"I don't want you to think of me as sad. Okay? I'm not, I'm not the sad mom. But when your dad was—I was—Look, maybe we just never got a chance to grow old and miserable like everybody else. We had a good run. Too good. It spoiled me for anybody else."

"So you're shopping for housecoats?" Oliver asks. "Watching your stories with Mrs. Parker?"

"Listen to me, you ungrateful wretch, if you're not back at that hospital or headed for the airport first thing New Year's Day, I'm going to shake Valerie down for that address, and then I really will be like Godzilla."

Godzilla versus the Natural Iceberg, Oliver thinks, and smiles. "What are you doing for New Year's Eve?"

Nicky snorts. "Are you kidding?"

"I thought you might have plans."

"Actually, Garth invited me to some faculty party. Said he could introduce me to some adjunct history professors."

"You should go."

"New Year's with academics? I don't think so."

"Come on, Mom, shave your legs, pull something shiny out of your closet, and go."

"Can we get back to the topic at hand, please? Are you still making up your mind about the lithium?"

"Do you want to decide? Lithium or not, home or hospital?"

"I don't exactly relish the idea of being to blame for the outcome, should you not be pleased with whatever it is. This one is really up to you."

"It's complicated," he says.

"Yeah, isn't just about fucking everything?"

After he hangs up, Oliver makes no move to return to the backyard and rejoin the party, opting instead to remain on the porch thinking spiteful thoughts. Mostly he wonders how long he'll have to sit here miserably before Althea tears herself away from the revelry and comes looking for him.

Twelve minutes later, she opens the door. "Come on."

She leads him by the hand upstairs to the second floor.

"Nobody leaves!" someone shouts below. Under Oliver's hand, the banister shudders with the force of the house's reply.

Althea closes the door behind them. They sit on the bed, kick off their shoes. The glare from the streetlights turns the window into a hazy mirror; otherwise it's dark.

"You sleep in the kitchen?"

"Usually. How's your nose, by the way? Will really got you good. You're lucky he didn't break it."

"Speaking of broken noses, I talked to Coby today. He says—"

Althea grimaces at the mention of Coby. "Is that what you came here for? To give me a message from Coby?"

"I came to New York to go to the hospital. What did you come here for?"

"It doesn't matter now."

"Of course it matters. Aren't you going to tell your father where you are?"

"I guess I'll have to."

"You've been living here for a month? In this house? With those people?"

"They're my friends, Ol."

This statement hits Oliver like a gutshot. He wants to throttle her. Friends? *Friends?* They don't know the first thing about her—not her savage temper, not her fevered dinosaur dreams. Do they have any idea what she can do with a felt-tip pen and a paper napkin? Have they ever seen her tear down the street on roller skates or leap from a rope swing in the middle of the night? How could she possibly think these people are her friends?

"I know what you're thinking," she says.

"Oh, and what's that?"

"You think I'm like your imaginary friend. You think you're the only one who can see me. You think I'm difficult and spoiled and you can't understand why anybody else would want me around. But you didn't make me up. You didn't invent me. They can see me, too."

"And what about Coby? Does he see you, too? Just how much of you has Coby seen?"

"You know," she says thoughtfully, "when you're sick, it's the only time you and I have anything in common."

"That's not true," he says.

"I'm not talking about history or anecdotes or shared experience. I'm not talking about height and eye color. I'm talking about what I am and what you are. I am nothing like you. But when you're sick, I get it. I see myself in you. That look on the fat mouse's face—you remember it? It was desperation. And then one day you opened your eyes and you were looking at me that way. Like it was me you were desperate for, not a fucking sandwich, for once. But I am sorry, Ol—I'm sorry I couldn't wait until you were really awake and ready to look at me that way. I guess I was scared you never would."

"You think you're more like Coby than you are like me?"

"I don't know. But I know I don't want those to be the only two options. You know? On a scale of one to Oliver, I'm a Coby? I just want to be an Althea."

She's managed to skillfully evade his question about Coby, but he doesn't need her answer anymore. As usual when Althea is concerned, he's well able to draw his own conclusions once presented with a certain amount of information, and it's all starting to fit together now. She had slept with Coby, sure, probably right after Oliver had stood in her driveway and told her she was a terrible person. And afterward she had been sorry, sorrier than Oliver is equipped to understand, and she'd wanted a do-over, she'd wanted to take it back, but she couldn't, so she did the next best thing and broke Coby's nose so he'd understand she'd changed her mind. It made sense, in an Althea sort of way.

"I did come all the way here for you. I came here to apologize and to ask you if you really meant it when you said you didn't even like me very much. And now you're here, so I'll say it again, Oliver—I'm sorry. And if I had my way it would be me who was sick and not you and you know that, so incidentally fuck you for throwing that in my face."

"I didn't mean it, that bullshit about not liking you. You know I didn't mean that."

"You love that I'm like this because it keeps you looking normal in comparison. You acted like you were upset because I took all the attention away from you, but that's exactly what you wanted. You wanted to be the normal one, and thanks to me you still are. On a scale of one to Althea, you get to be Oliver."

"That is so stupid."

"Come on, Oliver, be honest. Which would you rather? Would you rather be the crazy person, or would you rather be the crazy person's best friend? Would you rather be driving the fucked-up bus, or would you rather be the fucked-up passenger? Come on, Ol, don't think about it for too long."

"The driver, okay? I'd rather be the driver."

"Right."

"And you'd rather be the passenger?"

"Oliver, this is what I'm trying to tell you. I don't want to play anymore. I don't want to pick one. I'm opting out. Game over."

"You can't just run away."

"I'm not running away," she says. "I'm walking away."

"You always thought that I could get by without you easier, that you needed me more. You're wrong. I can't make a move without you. You're the instigator, you always have been, and I'm just along for the ride. And after ten years, it turns out that I can be replaced by a bunch of filthy college dropouts and a few cans of Natty Ice."

"Of course they can't replace you—"

"But they get to have you and I get to—what, talk to you on the phone once in a while?" he snaps. "I don't understand. Make me understand. Make me understand how you can do this so easily."

Althea rakes her hands through her hair. "It is not easy. None of this has been easy. I miss you so much, I miss you all the time.

There are days that I remember, totally ordinary days when I was so happy just to be driving around in the car with you, just to have you there, and everything you said was funny and everything I said was clever and every song that came on the radio was exactly the song I wanted to hear. And on days like that I felt so fucking lucky just to have someone to feel that way about, just to feel that way at all, it didn't even matter if you felt the same way. This isn't easy for me. You have no idea how hard it is. That's how I know I'm doing the right thing."

"What if we were together? Would you come back then?"

"*Together* together?"

"Yeah."

"Don't try to play that card with me. I finally stopped fooling myself. Don't start fooling yourself now."

He knows she's right. It's not fair to bribe her with that kind of promise, but God, does he wish he could do it in earnest. Lying down, he pats his chest in invitation. She takes her place, and he wraps his arms around her and strokes what's left of her hair. "It's like we're two sides of the same coin, and I don't know which side I'm on." Althea doesn't say anything. "I remember those days, too," he whispers.

She places her finger gently in the nook at the base of his throat, playing with the few hairs that live there, her palm pressed against his chest. He traces his finger along her spine, first over her shirt, and then under it, and then he kisses her. This time, he thinks, it'll be different. It won't be like she said. When it's over, she won't have any bruises, and he'll remember everything.

There's no jolt of recognition when they undress, even as he waits for some muscle memory to guide him. Whatever it was he did to her before, whatever it was she liked, he doesn't know how to recreate it. He lays his hand over her concave belly, strokes her hipbones. They'd shared a bed so many times, swum the Atlantic together in their bathing suits, the Cape Fear in their underwear; he had seen so much of her, he never realized what a difference that last centimeter of fabric would make. And as she had known two different Olivers, the genuine and the impostor, he understands that what he's seeing now is authentic. Here she is, the real Althea, no cargo pants or combat boots or cigarettes or messenger bag, no scalding cup of coffee, no jumble of black hair, no trace of that oft-practiced scowl, worn to perfection. Naked except for his hands and a shy smile. So what if he's not seeing it for the first time, so long as it feels like he is.

"Althea—"

"Shush."

"Don't shush me," he says.

Even in the darkness, her smile is brilliant. "You love it when I shush you."

He hovers over her, kneeling between her legs, pressing his lips to her neck. "I love it when you shush me." She glows pale blue-white in the headlights of a passing car.

"You don't have to worry," she says. "It's supposed to be fun."

And she's right. She always is.

chapter sixteen.

ALTHEA WAKES UP next to Oliver, but he's still asleep.
The room is cold, but he's warm, as always, like a puppy, his
face smushed against the pillow and a fist tucked under his chin.
She presses her nose into his neck and closes her eyes, but she
can't fall back to sleep. Her cheeks are raw from Oliver's stubble;
her lips positively exfoliated. The house is alive beneath them,
something sizzling in a pan in the kitchen, Matilda collecting
money for a liquor run, someone strumming a guitar and making up a song about Mr. Business. Rolling over, Althea reads the
walls. The phone numbers and grocery lists and song lyrics, the
chaotic index to Matilda's small and precious life.

Management is downstairs in the hallway counting out a pile
of cash, mostly singles, on a waist-high pile of newspapers. Her
blonde hair is loose around her small face, thumbs sticking out
of two holes in the sleeves of her sweatshirt. There's a patch sewn
onto the front pocket that reads PRAY FOR FOOD. Ethan is stumbling around blindly in his boxers.

"I'm sorry I disappeared last night," Althea says.

"We forgive you," Ethan says.

"This halfwit can't find his glasses again." Matilda gestures to Ethan with friendly disdain.

"They're on top of the fridge," Althea reminds him.

Grunting, Ethan blunders toward the kitchen.

Althea follows him. In the living room, their many house-guests are beginning to wake up; she can hear them coughing and lighting cigarettes and muttering to one another about their hangovers. The elastic of Ethan's boxer shorts has carved a thin red line into the small of his back. His face brightens as he slips on his glasses and surveys the kitchen; she looks away as he wraps his brown blanket around himself like a cape.

"And how was *your* night?" Ethan says.

"None of your goddamn business."

"Did you have a nice time?" He leans against the sink, a smarmy expression on his face. "Was it a happy reunion?"

"Stop."

"Does this mean you guys are going to prom together?"

Matilda enters the kitchen with her pile of cash. "Ethan, quit taunting her. Althea, can we take your car to the liquor store so I don't have to carry all this shit home?"

Althea looks instinctively toward the stairs, thinking of Oliver.

"He'll be fine," says Matilda.

"Hang on." Althea runs back up to Matilda's bedroom and finds a piece of chalk on the dresser. Finding a blank spot on the wall, she scrawls a hasty note to Oliver—*Went to buy booze, back soon*—and surrounds it with a heavy border so he can't miss it.

She pulls the blanket up over his bare shoulder. For a second she's tempted to wake him, just to make sure she can, but she thinks better of it and slips silently away.

Oliver wakes up a little while later and waits, naked and cold, for Althea's return. He doesn't know how long she's been gone, but he's afraid to leave the room without her. The edges of the bed are frigid, so he stays huddled in the center, in the space they warmed with their bodies. The minutes tick by and he doesn't hear her voice amid the house's chorus; she doesn't open the door carrying two steaming mugs, wearing a sheepish grin, ready to dive back into bed with him. His head aches and he needs to take a piss, but beyond the relative safety of this room the house is throbbing with strangers slamming doors and shouting at one another in the hallways; already the air is weed-sweet and tobacco-musty, and he can't remember any of their names.

Finally his bladder gets the better of him. His clothes are strewn scattershot across the floor; he gathers them and dresses.

The bathroom door is locked. Pressed into the wall, he waits, still listening for her voice.

The red-haired boy steps out amid a hot cloud of steam, wiping the fog from his glasses with a corner of the faded purple towel around his waist. Water drips from his hair onto his bare shoulders, pooling a little in his collarbone. As he puts on his spectacles, he finally notices Oliver.

"So you're the guy from North Carolina," he says.

"Oliver." He stands up straighter.

"Ethan. I think we met last night. Briefly."

A girl moans in a bedroom down the hall. Distracted, Oliver clears his throat. "I think we did. Do you . . . Is this your house?"

"It's Matilda's house. I just live here. If you're looking for Althea, she went to the liquor store." Ethan glances back toward Matilda's room. "You staying long?"

The girl moans again, louder. Bedsprings rasp beneath her. Oliver's bladder strains against its contents. "I don't think so."

"Is she leaving with you?"

Though Ethan is the one wearing only a towel, Oliver feels bizarrely exposed. Despite his conviction that these people know nothing of Althea, suddenly it seems they may know plenty about him. What would their story sound like from her point of view? Maybe the Warriors all hate him. Although they seemed to be okay with him last night. The fornication down the hall is reaching its crescendo, a guy grunting in time with the shrieks of both girl and bedsprings, the tempo of all three increasing. Oliver wonders with horror if that's what he and Althea sounded like. Was someone waiting for the bathroom then, listening the entire time? And even if no one heard, everyone knew what they were doing in there; if nothing else, this is a house devoid of secrets. Everyone knew. Matilda knew. The couple in the bedroom knew. This Ethan person interrogating Oliver knew. Was he picturing it right now? Was he imagining what Althea looked like naked, or doubting Oliver's abilities? Was Ethan sneering at Oliver because he was certain he could do better? The bedsprings and cries cease abruptly; after a brief moment of quiet, there are soft giggles and whispers. Oliver doesn't understand why they bother keeping their voices down now. "You never know what she might do," he says.

"Yeah, no kidding." Ethan returns to his bedroom, the soles of his feet already filthy again.

The other bedroom door springs open and the couple dashes out, the curly-haired girl wrapped in a white sheet, the boy in his boxers, a soiled tissue tucked in his fist. Still giggling, they chase each other into the bathroom before Oliver can protest, locking the door behind them and starting up the shower. He tries to ignore the sound of running water. He thinks dry thoughts.

Matilda pushes a shopping cart down the aisle of the liquor store. "I was thinking about letting Dennis tattoo me tonight," she says. "He's been wanting to for a while. I don't know. What do you think?"

Althea picks up a dark green bottle of champagne with a fancy-scripted orange label. "I think that boy wants to do a lot more than tattoo you."

"No, no, no, put that back. Are you crazy? That shit costs forty-five bones. The magic number is eight." She keeps going, stopping right before they reach the Boone's Farm. "Here we go. One of everything that's cheap and sparkling." She pauses. "Really? You think so?"

Checking the price stickers now, Althea loads up the cart. "That so hard to believe?"

"Leala's the one they usually go for. She's like a mobile bur- lesque act. Everything she does. When she plays a video game, it's like she might as well just take off all her clothes. But if there's one thing that isn't sexy, it's being Wendy to the Lost Boys of Brooklyn. No one wants to fuck the girl who cleans the toilet." Matilda holds a milky bottle by the neck, squinting at the label. "What is this?" The liquid inside is the color of a runny egg yolk.

"I think it's a premixed mimosa," Althea says, reading over her shoulder.

"I feel sick just holding this in my hand. Can you imagine what would happen if we actually drank it?"

"It's only four dollars."

Placing it in the cart, Matilda shakes her head. "Breakfast, I guess."

"Do you think you'd like to be, you know, tattooed by Dennis?" Althea idly looks over a bottle of blackberry merlot.

"I haven't been tattooed by anyone in a long time. It might be nice. Course, you'll have to change my sheets first."

Althea looks at her shoes.

"Don't be embarrassed. Everyone should get tattooed at New Year's. How was it, anyway?"

At first, she had been waiting for Oliver to turn on her, to turn her over and push her head into the mattress or throw her to the floor. She kept watching his eyes, wondering if they would suddenly go blank and he would be gone. What if it was her touch that did it, brought the fat mouse back? What if she broke him? But Oliver had been there behind his eyes the whole time. "I think it was like it's supposed to be."

Matilda lowers her voice. "Was it, you know, better? Worse?"

"It was better, I guess. I mean, if I had to pick between being with Oliver or not-Oliver, I'll take Oliver. But it doesn't change anything. All it means is that I'm forgiven."

"It doesn't change anything?" Matilda asks, casting a coy, sidelong glance Althea's way. "Nothing at all?"

"Do you know how closely I've watched him over the last couple of years for any sign that he suddenly saw me differently? I would know if something had changed. You know how? He would be relieved. He would be so relieved that he could finally make me happy, that he could stop worrying about disappointing me every goddamn day, and it would be written all over his face. The tattooing was inevitable, but it doesn't change anything."

"So does that mean you're still disappointed?"

Althea runs her fingers over the script on the wine bottle's label. "Of course I'm disappointed. But I used to feel like I would never be satisfied until he came around, like everything depended on me getting the answer that I wanted."

"That sounds miserable."

"Yeah, no kidding. And it's still miserable. But now it seems, you know, conceivable that it won't always be that way."

"It won't." Seeing the bottle in Althea's hand, Matilda sighs. "God, I used to love that stuff. Drank it all the time in college. Come on, let's go."

Matilda leads them to the register, pulling out the stack of bills held together with a thick purple band, the kind normally used to bunch asparagus and broccoli. "All these dollars, and we're just going to puke them up in the morning."

"It's your favorite holiday. Show a little enthusiasm."

"I guess. It's so pathetic; I'm already dreading tomorrow, when everybody leaves."

Althea waits until they're back at her car to respond to this. "Not everybody's leaving tomorrow."

Matilda raises an eyebrow. "Oh no?"

Althea shrugs, trying to be casual. "I mean, I just got the hang of alternate side of the street parking. Seems like it would be a shame to leave now."

Matilda considers this. "Are you sure that's what you want? To keep on sleeping in the kitchen?"

"What I want is for Oliver to wake up today and realize he's in love with me. But that's not going to happen, so yes, I want to keep sleeping in the kitchen. I like sleeping in the kitchen. I like it much better than sleeping in the basement."

"Well, you do make good muffins. And you don't take any of Ethan's shit. I'll have to clear it with everybody else. And you'll have to start coughing up for rent. Have you thought at all about what you're going to do for money?"

"I thought money was for people with money?"

"We can probably figure something out." Matilda looks up at Althea, squinting her green eyes thoughtfully. She laughs.

"What?" Althea asks.

"It's funny. A month ago you were afraid to ask for a place to crash for the night."

"Look at me. I'm growing."

They nestle the bags in the trunk with Althea's ancient beach blankets, crusty with salt and sand.

"Your car smells like summer," says Matilda.

Althea pats the dent in her bumper affectionately. "'North Carolina. First in Flight.' You're lucky I have a car. I don't know how you would have gotten all this home otherwise."

"I told you. I've had good luck ever since that quarter turned up."

By the time Oliver enters the shower, there's no more hot water. It starts out lukewarm and tapers off to cold until he can't stand it anymore, and he gets out before he's even rinsed the shampoo completely from his hair. When he leaves the bathroom, the gray cat is scratching at the door, eager to get in and use the litter box. Is there ever a time in this house when someone isn't waiting for the bathroom?

Downstairs, he works out a cup of coffee. Most of the Warriors and their guests have bundled up and moved to the backyard to further craft the Natural Iceberg. The curly-haired girl wanders in from the living room, wearing a Sex Pistols shirt and socks that come up to her thighs. She refreshes her coffee, watching Oliver watch the others.

"She drove Matilda to the liquor store," she says, joining him by the window. "If you're wondering where she is."

"Thanks. I know where she is."

"It looks like they're going to be out there for a while," she says. "Wanna play Tomb Raider?"

They sit on the living room floor, their backs against the couch, the cords in a tangle at their feet. She hands him a controller, and he's soothed by the atmospheric sound track and the mechanical hand motions that come back to him as he plays. It's been a while. She trounces him repeatedly, with ease, but Althea has trained him to be a good sport about losing by refusing to ever do it herself.

"How long have you lived here?" he asks.

"About six months. I was living with some guy— Well, you don't need to hear the details. Matilda said I could stay here until I sorted out my shit."

"I guess it's taking longer than you thought."

"I got together with Kaleb, so I stayed. But who knows, maybe I would have stayed anyway." She gestures around the room with her controller. "I know it doesn't look like much. It's dirty and crowded. One time the toilet overflowed and there was water pouring from the ceiling, and I swear to God, Matilda just put her head down and cried. Said we were all living in a Superfund site. But there's always someone around to talk to, and if you want to be alone you can go take a walk on the beach. And it's cheap. Beats working for a living."

"You don't have a job?" asks Oliver, surprised.

"Most of us don't. Not real ones. We pick up cash here and there."

"How do y'all get by?"

"Off the fat of the land, that's how," she says, and a key rattles in the door.

Althea's favorite mug is drying in the rack on the kitchen counter, the same mug Matilda handed her the first morning. THERE IS

NOTHING EITHER GOOD OR BAD, BUT THINKING MAKES IT
SO. There's half an inch of burnt coffee at the bottom of the pot;
she takes it, starts a fresh one. The only official rule of the house
may be not to burn it down, but Althea's learned some other
courtesies. Take off your shoes in the front hallway. If you finish
what's in the coffeepot or the rice cooker, replenish it. If the trash
stinks, take it outside, don't wait for Matilda to do it.

She brings her coffee and the cordless phone to the front
steps. Matilda's lucky quarter is still glued to the sidewalk. A
sharp wind blows across the street, hard and cold, stinging the
back of her neck, biting at her fingers as she dials.

"Hey, Dad."

"Althea. How's it going out there? You getting ready to come
home?"

She can almost see him, sitting at the kitchen table, the house
silent except for the ticking of the old grandfather clock, maybe
the heat coming up through the pipes. "You know, it's a lot better
than I thought it would be."

"You're not just saying that?"

Althea can hear everyone in the backyard, throwing snowballs and insulting one another. She takes a swig of her coffee
and then a deep breath. "Dad, I'm not in New Mexico."

"Pardon?"

"I'm not in New Mexico. I never went to New Mexico. I'm in
New York City."

"With Alice?" Garth asks, confused.

"No. Not with Alice. I came here alone."

"Oh. To see Oliver?"

"Yeah." She presses her ear closer to the receiver and plugs the other ear with a finger, trying to block out all the noise in Brooklyn and anticipate his reaction.

Garth pauses, presumably to collect himself. When he speaks, his voice is oddly tight, his words clipped. "Althea, I don't even know what to say. Did it really seem more reasonable for you to concoct an elaborate cover story about going to see your mother than to just tell me you wanted to visit your best friend in the hospital? And you left over a month ago—what have you been doing this whole time? Have you been living in your car, in a shelter somewhere?"

Althea has a harder time staying calm; her words come tumbling out in a rush. "Oliver was already asleep when I got here, but I found a place to stay with these kids in Brooklyn and I sort of, like, fit right in. I made friends with them. It's not a shelter. It's a real house, with a cat, and a kitchen, and a coffeemaker."

His chair scrapes against the floor as he stands up; he's on the move, she can tell, probably pacing across the kitchen. "Althea, I don't give a good goddamn about whether you have access to fresh coffee. I want to know when you're going to get in your car and come home."

She reaches for a lock of hair to gnaw on before she remembers Matilda cut it off. "It's going to be a while, I think."

"What are you talking about?" Exasperation is creeping into his voice. "You've already been there for a month. You can't just stay there, waiting for Oliver to wake up."

"He's already awake. He's here with me now."

"He's not at the hospital? Does Nicky know where he is?"

"He talked to her yesterday."

He pauses, trying to process this. "I don't understand. If you went up there to see Oliver, and you've seen him, then why aren't you coming home?"

"Look, Dad, I know you were probably hoping that I would finish high school and go to college, and I don't know, maybe eventually I will," she says, trying to sound reasonable, like she's thought this all out and it's totally logical. "But right now I just want to stay in the place where I seem to do the least damage. You said I'm almost eighteen and I could decide for myself."

"I was talking about North Carolina or New Mexico," Garth says, not yelling but as close as he's come to it in a long, long time. "Staying in New York City with a bunch of strangers was not an option."

"Alice is more of a stranger to me than anyone," Althea snaps. "She's just DNA and a voice I hear every six months on the other end of the telephone. What has she ever done to make you think I'd be better off with her?"

"So everything you said about snowshoeing and red chiles—"

"I'm sorry, Dad. There was no showshoeing. I'm sorry I had to lie—"

"You didn't have to lie. You *chose* to lie. Over and over again, for a month. What would possess you to—Althea, are you on drugs?"

"Not even a little," she says, trying to be reassuring. "I promise. No drugs. I barely even eat meat anymore."

"So I'm supposed to believe you're living some kind of ascetic existence in New York City?" Garth asks sarcastically. "What, did you meet a boy up there?"

"Why does it have to be about a boy? Give me a little credit."

"What about Oliver?"

"I can't gush blood over him forever, Dad. If I stay here, I have a chance."

"A chance to what?"

"To get over him. If I go back to living four houses down from him, I'll be done for."

"So it *is* about a boy."

She takes a deep breath, because she's still figuring it out herself. "It's not that simple. It's not just because of Oliver. And it's not because of you, if that's what you're worried about, or anything you did. You didn't do anything." The words hang there uncomfortably. In the most literal sense, they're true. Garth *hadn't* done anything, which was part of the problem.

"I know that this hasn't been an easy few months for you," he says. "Maybe this seems like a good idea now—a change of scenery, some new faces. Some kind of adventure. But have you thought about what you're going to do for money? What kind of job you're going to get without even a high school diploma? How well do you know these people you're staying with? You might think you're doing some brave, exciting thing, but there's a difference, you know, between courage and stupidity."

"You said you wanted me out of the basement, remember?"

"You know damn well this isn't what I meant. And don't pretend like this phone call is about asking me for my permission to stay in New York, wherever you are. We both know that's not what you're doing." There's a loud bang on the other end of the phone—a cabinet slamming shut, it sounds like. Garth going for the scotch, no doubt.

"You're right, it's not," she admits. "Are you mad?"

"When have you ever seen me mad?" he asks.

"There was that time with the Jell-O," she reminds him.

Garth pauses for a moment. "I made a grown man cry last week."

"You did what?" Althea asks, confused. She reaches for her mug, but the coffee inside has gone cold.

"I suppose he was more of a man-child," Garth continues. "A senior. I caught him plagiarizing his final paper. He came to see me in my office and I made him cry. I didn't raise my voice. I didn't even fail him. I was disappointed and understanding and I gave him a chance to rewrite the paper for a lower mark. The nicer I was, the harder he cried. By the time I was finished, he felt three times worse than he ever would have if I'd shouted. I don't go in much for all the drama, Althea. I leave it to the Greeks. But what am I supposed to do now? Call the police? Go up there and drag you back by your hair?"

She considers telling him that she cut off all her hair, that there wouldn't be much for him to grab hold of, but it doesn't seem like the right time for jokes.

"I can finish high school here, or get a GED. There're a million art schools in New York."

"You can come home to North Carolina and finish school at Laney. If you want to be in New York so badly, you can be back there by the fall."

Althea takes a stab at speaking Garth's language. "It's the Cortés thing, Dad. When you hit the shore, burn the ships. There's no going back."

"I can't believe you lied to me. For weeks." Despite his protests that he is not mad at all, Althea can hear the anger in his voice. Not just anger; something worse. A painful dejection running underneath his words, threatening to surface. "I was going to take you to the ruins of Tenochtitlán. I made appointments with colleagues down there, planned for two weeks of research. If I cancel now—"

"There's no reason for you to cancel. I want you to go. It'll be better if you go alone, anyway. You'll get more done without me there. Oliver's going home tomorrow. You ask him when he gets there. Ask him if I'm doing okay here, if I'm better than okay, if I'm happier than he's seen me in years. Ask him if I'm safe. Ask him if this is the right place for me. He'll tell you."

"What if we went someplace besides Mexico?" he asks, suddenly quiet and entreating. "I can cancel the trip, and we can go to Crete. Or anywhere. Anywhere you want."

She listens with her eyes closed, concentrating on the soothing timbre of his voice, the Georgia accent that makes her think of white-gloved debutantes and simpler times. Althea sees herself as rebellious, but realizes now how unaccustomed she is to openly defying her father; she's used to doing what she wants because he doesn't pay attention, not because she battles him and wins. She feels like she does after too much coffee on an empty stomach, or a couple of Oliver's pills—sweaty, queasy, weirdly euphoric. Maybe he's right. Maybe it won't work, and she'll go home and get the biggest "I told you so" of her life. But for now, in this moment, there's no room for doubt. "I don't want to go anywhere," she says finally. "I want to stay here and explore the New World."

The softness in his voice disappears. "Cortés was an asshole, you know. The man was not a role model. He was a greedy megalomaniac, and you're a teenage girl coping with her first romantic disappointment. This matter isn't settled, so if I were you, I wouldn't set fire to the Camry just yet. You've bought yourself a couple of weeks, but this conversation isn't over."

Althea considers this. Maybe by the time Garth gets back from Mexico, he'll be so engrossed in his book and the new semester that she can put him off a while longer. She'll be eighteen in June—six months away, but still, if she tries hard enough, maybe she can run out the clock on him. He's a formidable adversary, but she's played enough Risk; she knows how to wage a war of attrition. "Can I take a rain check on Crete?"

"I should have locked you in that basement when I had the chance," he says, and she's pretty sure he means it.

"No matter how miserable I was in Wilmington, I would have never gone to stay with Alice," she says, as if that will bring him any solace. "I'd never switch teams in the final inning like that."

"Am I supposed to find your loyalty touching?" he says. This is the tone he used with the student plagiarist, Althea's sure of it: gentle but icy. It's his confidence that makes him scary, how certain he is that his words will find their mark. "Considering how much you loathe your mother, you've got more in common with her than I ever imagined."

She opens her mouth to respond with something equally cruel, and then stops. They've hurt each other enough for one day, so all she says is, "Happy New Year, Dad."

"Good-bye, Althea."

She disconnects. In the backyard there is a crash, the clatter of hundreds of empty beer cans as the Natural Iceberg collapses, and then a united, devastated shout of grief.

Oliver tries not to stare at Althea while they peel potatoes in the living room. It's her neck in particular that interests him. He never realized how long it was before.

Althea flicks her peeler nimbly, and potato skins fall into the bucket. Oliver can't match her pace. There's a pink scar on her wrist he hasn't seen before; he runs his finger along the puckered line. "That's new," he says.

"It was no big deal." She shrugs, without offering to elaborate. Just last night he finally saw her naked; he had uncovered whatever might remain of her body's secrets. But a new one has sprung up already and he hates it, this little piece of her story that she doesn't want to share.

"Tell me about the lithium," she says.

"The lithium?"

"Right before he went back up to the clinic, Will told you to tell me about the lithium. So go ahead."

He repeats what the doctor said, about how the medication might help and the possible side effects.

"And you don't know what to do?"

"Yeah."

"Flip a coin," Althea says.

He shakes his head. "I'm sorry I told you."

"Let me see if I understand. The doctor told you he could help so you ran away from the hospital. Are you sure you actually want to get better?"

"It's not much help, is it? Right now, I'm not sick. Right now, I'm sitting here peeling potatoes and I feel fine. I'll be fine until I'm not, and then I'll be asleep and I'll be someone else until it's over and I'm me again. But if I try it, I might feel like someone else all the time. I could be the guy with the facial tic hanging out at the 7-Eleven trying to find enough change on the ground to buy myself a Snickers bar. What if I start walking differently? What if I don't talk the same?"

She keeps peeling without meeting his eyes. "You're thinking that maybe the KLS isn't so bad, because at least you know what to expect. Sort of. You're thinking maybe you can just sack up and stick it out. Except you already tried that. You didn't come all the way to New York because it wasn't so bad—you came because it was. You're thinking that you're fine when you're in between like this, but you aren't fine, you're terrified. All the time. You're worried that the medication might change you. Do you think the last year hasn't?"

"You seem a little different yourself. That doesn't mean we should lobotomize *you*."

Her potato slips out of her fingers, landing on the rug in a pile of cat hair. She picks it up and makes an earnest attempt at wiping it off. Oliver confiscates the ruined potato, setting it on the coffee table. "We don't eat things that are covered in fur."

"What are your choices? Just keep white-knuckling it?" Althea says. "Come on, Ol, give yourself a chance. You should go to college. You've got shit to do. You've got a wormhole to find."

They work, falling into one of their comfortable silences, as if they were sprawled out on Oliver's bed doing their homework and not here in this strange house in Brooklyn peeling potatoes filched from a Dumpster. The smoke-stained curtains and unraveling carpet, the dusty painting of Saint Cajetan hanging above the sofa—it's surprising that it doesn't seem more surreal. He's amazed by how quickly he's been able to adjust to this reality after all that fear of the unknown; even Althea's short blonde hair no longer garners a double-take when it appears in his peripheral vision. Her knee is touching his knee. Salsa music plays in the kitchen.

Althea had done it. She wasn't sitting around in the basement waiting for him anymore; she wasn't looking around expectantly for some sign that things were finally going to get back to normal, or change between them the way she wanted, knowing they never could. She had put it all on black and found these people; she had won something, something real. Maybe he could do the same. Maybe it's time he sees what else is out there for him.

"You know," he says, "I really do like your new haircut."

In the kitchen, Kaleb is serving food onto sectioned paper plates, handing them to everyone as they filter in from the backyard and drift toward the living room, where twenty-five people are eating dinner off their laps. Althea and Oliver hover in the doorway, awkwardly holding their plates, but Ethan stands up, vacating his Papasan chair.

"Here," he says. "You guys take it."

Gregory and the cat, the drummer, the dropout, someone from Philly, and someone from Cambridge are all squeezed onto the couch; Matilda and Dennis are on the floor by their feet. Leala sits on Kaleb's lap in the recliner, and everyone else is piled in together like a litter of puppies. Althea and Oliver curl up in their chair, pressed together, watching the room share a year's worth of anecdotes and misadventures.

"Tell them about the scavenger hunt," Dennis says, elbowing Matilda. "Tell them how you went to the bad place when you thought we were going to lose and you acted like a fucking lunatic."

"You guys had a scavenger hunt?" the brunette from Cambridge says. "What a fucking awesome idea."

"It was Althea's idea," Matilda says quickly.

"Who won?" someone else asks.

"We won," says Ethan.

"Because of me," Althea chimes in. "Because I was willing to cut off the finger to save the hand."

"What did you do?" asks Cambridge Brunette. "Tell us the story."

Althea sets her plate on the floor; Mr. Business leaps off the couch, races over, and laps up the carrots like a dog. In the backyard, a trash can full of ice and champagne is waiting; the clock ticks on toward midnight. Oliver, smelling like apples, puts an arm around her shoulder. Something prickles gently inside her. It's not the racing feeling, it's not that. It might be contentment, but she can't be sure.

After dinner, Leala and Matilda whisk her upstairs to get dressed.

"But I'm already dressed," Althea says.

"Not for New Year's, you're not," says Leala.

The two older girls change into slinky black dresses; Althea is too tall for any of Matilda's clothes, but Leala finds something in the back of her own closet, a royal blue number, short and tight.

"There's no way I'm wearing this," says Althea.

"That dress makes your legs look three miles long," Matilda says.

Leala puts on red lipstick in her vanity mirror. "You got great gams, kid. It's a crime not to show them off. I heard this rumor, by the way."

"About Ethan and the syph?" asks Matilda. "I've heard that one, too. It's not true."

"A different rumor." Leala smiles into the mirror, brushing her hair. "I heard a rumor—Oh, fuck it. I don't feel like being all mysterious. Althea, is it true? You gonna stick around for a while longer?"

Althea tugs at her hemline. "If it's okay."

"Shit yeah, it's okay," says Leala. "Finally. Another girl."

"What about Oliver?" asks Matilda. "You're really going to send him home alone?"

"You know what?" Althea says. "I don't want to talk about

Oliver. I'm sick of feeling like all I ever talk about is Oliver."

The girls descend the stairs to a chorus of catcalls. Kaleb passes around the bottles of champagne, one to every person, and the corks pop off one at a time, the sound filling the house like fireworks, foam spilling down everyone's hands. The TV doesn't get any channels so they don't watch the ball drop, counting down with the wall clock to midnight instead. When everybody cheers "Happy New Year!" Oliver pulls Althea in for an earnest kiss. People crowd into the living room and the kitchen for an impromptu dance party led by Leala and Matilda, while a frantic Gregory looks for his misplaced cat, only to find him on top of the refrigerator, his fur vibrating with the hum of the motor.

The colored flashing Christmas lights taped to the ceiling are the only illumination as everyone writhes around in the near dark, and it's not unlike being in the pit at Lucky's. Althea dances with Matilda to the Replacements, feeling strangely exposed without her old mess of black hair flying around her face, but drunk enough not to care, whirling around her new friend—her housemate, now—the living room windows steamed up from the heat of everyone inside. Matilda's blonde hair comes out of its tidy knot while she moves; they circle each other, shouting lyrics and stomping their feet.

Leala comes over with the Polaroid camera and tells them to smile. Matilda puts her arm around Althea's waist and they look into the camera; the flash pops, the picture slides out, and Leala waves it eagerly.

"This one's going on the fridge," she says.

Kaleb walks into the room naked, received by an exasperated chorus of groans.

"Here we go," Leala says. "I don't know why he insists on getting naked at parties."

"Dude! Cover up your junk!" Ethan yells.

"Lick my chicken, motherfucker!" Kaleb shouts, cupping one hand over his crotch.

Althea, afraid of giggling or staring or in some way betraying her age, slips outside onto the front porch to roll a cigarette and get some air. Dennis is already out there with some other people, so she bums a smoke instead and, emboldened by alcohol, tells him that she draws and sketches and paints a lot. They talk for a while about how one actually goes about becoming a tattoo artist, and he tells her about being an apprentice and how having a trade is great because if you're good at it you'll never go hungry. He asks if she has any tattoos yet, and that's how she ends up in the bathroom, sitting on the toilet seat facing the wall while he tattoos the top of her spine with the zodiac symbol for Gemini, Matilda snapping pictures from the bathtub, Kaleb in the doorway wearing boxer shorts now, assuring Althea he will never question her commitment to fun again.

When it gets too hot inside, everyone puts on shoes and takes their champagne into the backyard, maneuvering around the Iceberg detritus. Ethan brings his baseball bat and Kaleb builds a pitcher's mound out of snow. Soon everyone is taking turns swinging at the empty beer cans, hitting them onto the roof of the house. Althea scores three in a row before she hands the bat to Oliver.

"Give it a shot," she says.

Kaleb scoops up another can and winds it up. "You ready, champ?"

"Come on, Ol," Althea says. "Knock it out of the park."

He points the bat at the roof, Babe Ruth–style, and winks at her; Kaleb tosses the can underhand and Oliver takes a swing.

Ethan sidles up to Althea as she watches. "You guys make a cute couple, in a *Flowers in the Attic* sort of way."

Althea finishes the beer she's drinking and crushes the can in her hand. "Kill yourself. Seriously."

Ethan takes off his glasses, folds them, and puts them in the pocket of his coat. He leans in, so close she can see each pore and freckle and the tiny flecks of green around his irises and smell the whiskey on his slightly parted lips. Behind her, she can feel Oliver frozen in place. Everyone's watching and waiting, dozens of people she barely knows elbowing one another and whispering, holding their collective breath, and she can sense the hive mind's confusion and excitement. It's like she's plugged into the electrical current of their thoughts and right now everyone is wondering the same thing: *Is Ethan really going to kiss Althea?*

"Go ahead," he says softly, but still, everyone can hear. "I want you to. Go ahead and hit me. As hard as you can."

"What?"

"Punch me. In the face. As hard as you can."

"No." She's shaking.

"I want you to. Come on. It'll feel so good."

Of this she has no doubt. It would feel tremendous. But she didn't climb all the way to the top of this slide just to enjoy the ride back down. She's a backslider, no doubt about it; there's something built into her that makes her love to lose her shit, and sooner or later it'll probably happen again because Matilda was right, it is exhausting to hold yourself in check all the time, and eventually Althea will get tired and slip up. But not tonight, and not at Ethan's invitation.

"Cut it out, Ethan," she says, dismissing him. "You're making a goddamn fool out of yourself."

"Jesus jumped-up Christ," says Matilda. "It's like watching two twelve-year-olds taunt each other."

To Althea's utter, utter surprise, the intense, determined expression on Ethan's face dissolves and he begins to laugh. Not mean laughter, either. Sincere. Althea steps back, confused by his sudden merriment, until Kaleb comes over and cuffs Ethan on the back of the head.

"Asshole."

And that's it. It's over. Everyone just shakes their heads and shrugs and reaches into the garbage can to grab another Natty Ice. Still smiling, Ethan puts his glasses back on.

"Sorry about that," he says. "Sometimes I get a little carried away."

Eventually all of the beer cans find their way onto the roof, lining the gutter, blown across the cracked and peeling shingles by the wind. The Warriors' guests mill about, disappointed that the game is over. Matilda stares up at the roof, squinting and drunk.

"Is it bad that those are up there?" she asks. "Or is that just where they go now?"

"They make pretty music," Leala says. "Like wind chimes. Sort of."

"We need them back so we can collect the deposit money," says Ethan. "Who feels like climbing out a window?"

"Who's sober enough to climb out a window?" someone else asks.

"No one," says Matilda. "No one in this entire city is sober enough to climb out a window right now."

"I can do it," Oliver says, eager to have maybe a few minutes alone, or away, somewhere a little quiet and removed. The roof sounds perfect.

"Are you sure?" Matilda asks.

"Yeah."

"Be careful. We can't afford any lawsuits."

"I'll go with him," says Althea.

He follows her upstairs, into a bedroom he hasn't yet glimpsed, the one that Kaleb and Leala share. A mangy, taxidermied deer head hangs on the wall over the bed, a thong dangling from one of its antlers. The mattress is bare and stained, the dirty sheets in a pile on the floor beside it. Althea plows right through the mess and heaves open the window, giving Oliver a mischievous smile over her shoulder.

"Is it me, or is there something kind of familiar about this?" she asks, climbing onto the fire escape.

"I guess sometimes the Non-Stop Party Wagon travels in a circle."

They hurl the beer cans down into the backyard. Oliver tries not to aim too many directly at Ethan's head. When they're finished, instead of retreating back inside the house, they sit on the edge of the roof, their feet dangling below them. Althea produces two fresh beers from her coat pockets and hands one to Oliver.

"Where did you get these?" he asks.

"The back of the toilet."

Oliver thinks about it and decides he's too drunk to care. "Remember when I had to drag you to parties like this? Now I can't drag you away."

"I bet you could stay here, too. They'll take in anyone who promises not to burn down the house."

"I'm not sure that's a promise I'm willing to make."

"You don't have to like them—"

"Don't worry, I don't."

"You want to hear something weird?"

"What?"

"I'm going to have a boyfriend someday. I'm going to have a boyfriend someday, and it isn't going to be you." Althea stares up at the sky dreamily.

Oliver drinks his beer. "I bet he'll look like me, though. Not exactly, but just enough to be creepy. He won't be as handsome, of course, sort of like the budget version, but older, with more tattoos, and drug experience. He'll play the guitar, you know, but not very well. He'll have a temper like yours. The kind of guy you end up throwing a lot of plates at."

"You guys are totally going to hate each other. You'll be terse but civil when you meet him. He'll barely be able to conceal his hostility."

"And you're going to love watching us squirm."

"Yes, McKinley, I believe I will. And you'll have some awful perfect girlfriend who plays softball and studies chemistry and has a really high ponytail. The kind of girl you meet at the library. And the four of us will try to go out to dinner together, just once, and it'll be so uncomfortable, you'll end up drinking too much and making a scene at the restaurant."

"I'll make the scene? You're sure?"

"Oh, yeah. You don't even know it, but you're already saving up for that one. It's gonna be a real shitshow."

"Are we going to get thrown out of the restaurant?"

"No, you're going to storm out, and then your stupid girlfriend and I will have one of those awkward moments where it's unclear who should chase you. Then I'll go ahead and do it, and she'll get stuck with the check."

"What about your greasy boyfriend?"

"Are you kidding? That clown never has any money."

"I hope we can do better than that."

"It's not like I'm going to marry the guy."

"That's not what I mean. It all sounds like a bad romantic comedy. I don't want to be that predictable."

"You won't be, Ollie. You're not."

The rest of the party has been driven inside, not by the cold but by the fear that the cold might make them sober. From their perch on the roof, Althea and Oliver survey an empty backyard. The whole block feels silent, and like it's theirs. Any minute one of them will want to go inside and get warm, or pee, or locate more alcohol. Suddenly Oliver feels pressure to manufacture some kind of a moment, to fashion her a memory like a child's crude valentine, something she can look at over and over again after he's gone.

"What will you say that I was to you?" he asks her. "The first time you tell that tattooed barfly a story that's got me in it, and he asks, 'Who's Oliver?' What will you say?"

She opens her mouth to answer, like she thinks it's going to be an easy question, and then she realizes none of the standard answers apply. To simply call him her best friend would omit so much as to be nearly duplicitous. He had never been her boyfriend; v-cards have been cashed in, respectively, but that was just one part of the last ten years. Her forehead creases with the effort of finding the right word, and when she's got it, she nods to herself, like it was so obvious. "I'll say," she finally says, "that you were my favorite."

"Your favorite what?"

"That's it," she says. "Just my favorite."

He takes her hand and together they look up at the cloudy, starless sky. The warped shingles are digging into his back and the cold January wind is taking great big bites out of his neck, but he doesn't want to be the one to say they should go back inside. He doesn't want her to remember it that way.

"And you?" she says. "What will you tell that girl when you get all weird around the holidays because I'm coming home to visit?"

There was a snag somewhere in the last fourteen months, and if he could unravel them like a thrift store sweater he's sure that he would find it. Maybe it had started in his brain or maybe in Althea's—whichever, it doesn't matter anymore. In any case, it happened, and everything that came after had been tainted by it, by some feeling of wrongness that hasn't gone away but is slowly becoming a constant, pervasive sense of the unfamiliar that is—he admits it—maybe a little addictive. A year ago, every day was the same, a variation on a single theme, Althea and Oliver. Now he doesn't even know when he'll see her again. He kisses her, the kind of sloppy, sentimental kiss New Year's was made for, and wonders how many more of them—New Year's, not kisses—it will take before their saga is played out the rest of the way.

"I'll tell the softball player that you were my almost," he says.

Althea sits up and finishes her beer, then casually crushes the can, like she's balling up a failed sketch, and throws it in the trash directly below her feet. "She's really going to love that," she says finally, sliding toward the edge of the roof.

"Tough shit. That's my story," he says, "and I'm sticking to it. You don't want to go back in the window?"

"Windows are for climbing out, not climbing in. Roofs are for jumping off." And she demonstrates.

For the rest of the night, they play. They chase each other up and down the stairs, they arm wrestle, they argue and make out. They keep each other close. Laughter rings and rings through the house, over the sound of glass breaking and the low, deep throb of the bass from the stereo. Matilda and Dennis disappear upstairs for a spell; Althea shares a knowing smile with Leala. Eventually someone turns off the music and the revelers gather in the living room again, passing around the guitar and making use of the old snare drum tucked into the corner. Althea claps until her palms sting. By the time the sun comes up, the sky is so overcast they can barely tell it's daylight. So when someone yells "Let's go to the beach!" it is actually within the realm of possibility for them to venture out, without fear of being turned to dust and ash by the harsh mistress of the New Year's sun, and walk en masse to the boardwalk at Coney Island, most of them still toting half-empty bottles of room-temperature champagne. Althea and Oliver bring up the rear of the unlikely parade as they file through the empty streets of Brooklyn, toward the ocean.

If this were a movie, she thinks, it should end here. With champagne, by the water, while everyone is still celebrating, while she still has everything she needs. Before the sun muscles its way through the clouds, before her hangover springs to life, before her new tattoo starts to scab over and itch and she has to help clean the house. And then she would never have to watch Oliver go, or wake up after he leaves, terrified that she did the wrong thing. It should stop now, before her choice becomes a reality and she has to prove that she's strong enough to live with it; while Oliver is still relishing that he finally has a choice at all, before it paralyzes him to realize that whatever happens next will be all his own doing. She watches Dennis sling Matilda over his shoulder while she screams and kicks her heels. Althea raises her champagne bottle to her lips, banging her teeth with the thick green glass, then she holds it out to Oliver. "Now you drink half."

They pass it back and forth until they're trying to parse a single drop of flat champagne. Oliver really does look gorgeous, standing on the beach drunk in the early hours of the morning with the wind in his messy blond hair. It would be so easy to sleep it off and then get in the car with him and leave. And if

Althea heads back to Wilmington with him, things will go back to the way they were—not exactly, but still. It will be *The Oliver and Althea Show*, airing around the clock. But she recalls her conversation with a forlorn Matilda and what she said about the family you choose. With Oliver, it would always be just Oliver, because she doesn't know how to do it any other way. Matilda and the rest of her warriors are dancing around one another in the sand. Maybe they won't come to mean to Althea what they mean to Matilda; maybe they don't even mean to Matilda what Matilda thinks they mean. But it's too late for Althea. The seed has been planted. There's more out there, more to be had than one person who's known you since you were six. Everything would be different if he loved her the way she loves him; the entire universe would still consist of a single constellation: Castor and Pollux, set together among the stars, fettered only to each other. But he doesn't.

She knows that he doesn't understand, and she wishes she could make him, that she could show him all the things she imagines will happen to her after he leaves. Drawing a comic with Ethan, learning a trade from Dennis, exploring this strange dirty city until she knows it by heart. Learning to cook like Matilda, to sew like her, how to be a good friend like her. And there are flashes in her head of things she can barely grasp—a coffeemaker of her own, in a place that's just hers, a line of potted plants sitting on a fire escape, an easel placed by that window, pictures on the refrigerator of dozens of people she hasn't yet met. There's an Althea-sized place in the world somewhere, waiting to be claimed. She lets the unfinishable bottle fall to the sand.

"I have to go back to the hospital," Oliver says.

"I can drive you."

"It'll be days before you're sober enough to drive again."

"You've had a few yourself, you know."

"Maybe so."

"So you'll do it, then?"

He'll do it. He'll take the fucking pills, and if his hands start to shake, if he can't line up the equations the way he used to, if he can't look up into the sky and find Cassiopeia as effortlessly as he knows he can, then he'll stop. But he'll try. He wants to go home and finish his senior year, see Minty's band play at Lucky's, swim in the Cape Fear, and get one of those fat envelopes from MIT on a spring afternoon; he wants to watch the leaves change in Massachusetts in the fall, see for himself if the foliage is as glorious as it is in the catalogs. He wants to have an annoying roommate, and meet the softball player Althea predicted for him, and send his mother postcards from New England. He wants to know what happens when he isn't the smartest person in the class. He wants to plant his telescope somewhere new. He wants to see what else is out there.

When he'd imagined the end of the universe, the wormhole that would bring them all salvation, he'd pictured the other side as being identical to this one. Even in the face of Armageddon, he'd dreamed of a solution where nothing had to change, where even a parallel dimension would contain no uncertainties, where everyone could cross the threshold with their entire lives intact, emerging on the other side without a hint of vertigo. But the truth is, when the solar system starts to collapse, nobody's going to give a fuck about what's on the other side.

This is it, then: the end of hope. Her hope that he would love her back, his hope that things would return to normal. The things they'd willed so hard to happen have failed to manifest, and their respective efforts have brought them here, to Coney Island of all places, standing on the beach as if they've just landed in a new world, the chances of returning to the old one as surely torched as if they'd set a fleet of ships aflame. There's only one way to go now: forward, into the unknown. Welcome to the jungle.

Down the shore, the Coney Island Polar Bear Club is racing toward the ocean. Althea catches Matilda's eye and smiles, unbuttoning her coat. Matilda does the same, and their jackets drop in unison.

"Come on!" Matilda yells at her friends.

They giddily carry out her order. Althea and Oliver watch as everyone else undresses, unlacing their combat boots, slipping out of their secondhand coats, littering the sand with piles of clothes, unmasking the milky parts of themselves that haven't seen daylight in so long, until they're all standing on the beach in their underwear, and of course Kaleb removes even that. Althea steps out of her shoes.

"Are you crazy?" Oliver says.

"Just drunk," Althea says. "Fuck! It's cold out here! Can you unzip me?"

"It's going to be cold."

"You're already cold."

"It's going to hurt."

"It'll feel good once we're in," she says.

Matilda and the others are running toward the Atlantic. Oliver gives in and takes off his clothes. Althea grabs his hand and pulls him along, her toes going numb before they've even reached the ocean, the wet sand stinging the soles of her feet, the tide sucking at her ankles and drawing them in. When she's in up to her thighs, she lets go of his hand and dives in, flippering her feet behind her. The icy water burns like a million lit matches held to every instant of her skin, but she knows that she can take it. When she surfaces she half expects that Oliver will have run back to the shore, but he's swimming out to meet her, his lips already drained of color. Quickened, she waits. He closes the distance between them by half, and then half again, and when he reaches her, he proves Zeno's paradox of infinite divisibility is exactly that. Eyes shocked wide open, laughing wildly with disbelief that he's doing this at all, he treads water beside her, looking horrified and ecstatic. Sensation displaces thought completely, and it's a relief to see it go. All that's left is this, this astonishingly cold water, the gentle rocking of the waves, that first treasonous break in the clouds. Everyone is thrashing madly in the ocean, screaming through chattering teeth, and Althea yells "Nobody leaves!" and everyone shouts it back, but she hears only Oliver's voice, loud enough to make the Polar Bear Club stare down the beach at the commotion.

Turns out, they're both right—it feels good, and it still hurts.

Acknowledgments.

Thanks to my agents, Michele Rubin and Brianne Johnson, for believing in the kids so completely, and for all the soothing noises; and to Sharyn November, editor of my dreams, for making sure this book would be the best I could do.

I am so grateful to everyone from Brooklyn College who coaxed this manuscript through its nascent stages, especially Michael Cunningham, Ernesto Mestre-Reed, Joshua Henkin, and Francisco Goldman. Special thanks to the Carole and Irwin Lainoff Foundation for their support and generosity, and to the inimitable Jim Shepard for all his kindness. Thanks to Reese Kwon, who asks after the kids by name; Marie-Helene Bertino, who looks after my heart; and Andy Hunter, who knew why Althea was going for the medicine cabinet.

Thanks to my family for their faith and encouragement—sorry about those teen years, Mom and Dad. Thanks to all my friends—there's a piece of each of you somewhere in these pages. Special thanks to Caitlin Meister, who told me about Kleine-Levin Syndrome; Saki Knafo, for his tacos and enduring patience; the Warriors of 30K, who provided much inspiration; particular thanks to Ryan Hanlon, a friend as good for my soul as he is hell on my liver. Love, thanks, and heartlights to Sarah McCarry, beloved jarmate and boon companion—it doesn't matter that I wrote it before I met you; I wrote it for you anyway.

Q&A with Cristina Moracho.

Where did you get the initial idea for *Althea & Oliver*?

A friend of mine came in to work many years ago and told me she had seen something on television about this strange disease called Kleine-Levin Syndrome, which affects mostly teenagers and makes them sleep for weeks or months at a time. I was totally fascinated and spent the day in an Internet K-hole doing research instead of any work. By the time I finished, I already had the spark of an idea for a novel that would explore not only what it was like to have KLS, but also what it would be like to be in love with someone who suffered from it— someone who at any moment could just disappear from your life for an indeterminate amount of time. So the original idea came from KLS, which Oliver has, but it was always meant to be a story about these two characters. In my imagination, they arrived together.

What challenges did you face when writing these characters? Who did you have a harder time writing, Althea or Oliver, and why?

A lot of the challenges I faced writing *Althea & Oliver* were about striking a certain kind of balance. I wanted to create a set of characters who were smart but not unbelievably clever. I wanted them to talk like actual teenagers. I wanted them to have a certain level of self-awareness without being overly sophisticated. I definitely faced a greater challenge writing Oliver—trying to authentically portray someone who is suffering from a rare illness but not defining him by that illness was not easy, especially considering the fact that he's asleep for large chunks of the book. It's comparatively simple to express the unrequited romantic love Althea has for him, but in some ways his feelings for her are more complicated, and so were harder to articulate: he loves her and is attracted to her, but he isn't *in love* with her, even though he often wishes that he were.

Althea & Oliver is your first novel. What has that experience been like?

I love that it seems to have genuinely moved some readers. You can write in a vacuum for so long you almost forget your endgame—to get the book out there so people can actually read it. Althea and Oliver felt like my imaginary friends for so long, so I love that finally other people can see them, too.

There's been a lot of really positive responses from both the teen and adult audiences. A few readers have been disappointed that the book doesn't have a typical happy ending, but mostly I think people have found it refreshing to come across a story that takes its characters on a less traditional path.

Who's your favorite author, living or dead?

Oh god. I never realized how impossible it is to answer this question until now. I guess I'll say Donna Tartt, if for no other reason than that I've reread *The Secret History* more than any other book. But I will say that Megan Abbott, Sara Gran, Cara Hoffman, Sarah McCarry, Lauren Grodstein, and Kelly Braffet all fall in the "favorites" category. So does Stephen King—I read all his new books as soon as they come out, and I reread his old ones on a regular basis as well. (I've also provided a list of my favorite books for this paperback edition.)

If you could spend one year on a deserted island with one character from literature, who would you choose?
Raoul Duke, from Hunter S. Thompson's *Fear and Loathing in Las Vegas*.

Who is your favorite hero or heroine of history?
I tend to gravitate more toward morally questionable historical figures. One of the nice things about making Althea's father a history professor was that it allowed me to work my fascination with Hernando Cortés into a novel about teenagers growing up in North Carolina. Garth refers to Cortés as an "asshole" at one point, which is totally accurate, but there's something about his "hit the shore, burn the ships" mentality that's undeniably compelling. The guy was committed.

If you could teleport anywhere in the known universe right now, where would you go?
Nairobi. I spent a month there last summer staying with friends, and I still miss it, and them, every day.

Where do you write?
There's a cozy little alcove in my apartment where I write, surrounded by my bookshelves. I painted the back wall of this nook with black chalkboard paint, so I can make notes to myself or jot down quotes I find particularly inspiring.

Do you have any writing rituals?
So many. Too many. It's difficult for me to write while listening to music—too distracting—but I also can't write if it's too quiet, so my solution is to write with the television on, the volume down low, and a movie that I've seen a million times playing on repeat. When I was writing *Althea & Oliver*, I alternated between *The Usual Suspects* and

The Royal Tenenbaums, occasionally throwing *Armageddon* into the mix for a little variety.

I also had day jobs in offices for a long time, and writing was something I did after work, at night, and that association is so strong in my subconscious that I still find it difficult to settle in and write if it's light out. On the one hand, I feel like you do whatever you have to do in order to make the writing happen; on the other hand, those little rituals can turn into obstacles if you need all these elements to fall into place so you can work. When I did my first writer's residency, I actually worried about how I would do in a cottage with no television, but I managed.

What is your idea of earthly happiness?

That moment right as the show is about to start, when the lights go down and the band comes onstage. And then the moment after it's over, when you're sweaty and exhausted and your legs are all shaky, and you walk outside with your friends and light a cigarette in a daze. And of course every moment in between.

What do you hope readers will take away and value from *Althea & Oliver*?

The idea that the book is really about beginnings, for both of these characters—the beginning of the rest of their lives.

What are you currently working on?

I'm working on a new novel that's very different from *A&O*; it's darker, and it has a sort of noir/crime feel. I think of it as a YA noir. At the heart is a story about vengeance and justice, where they overlap and where they diverge. One of the quotes on my chalkboard right now is from Confucius: "Before you embark on a journey of revenge, dig two graves."

An *Althea & Oliver* Playlist.

Rocket from the Crypt, "Drop Out"
In the very first scene, when Althea is trying to drive home before Oliver can fall asleep, Rocket from the Crypt is playing on the radio. Would Rocket from the Crypt really have been playing on the radio in Wilmington, North Carolina? I have no idea. But I like to pretend it's possible.

Guns N' Roses, "Welcome to the Jungle"
Oliver sings this classic a number of times as they walk to Waffle House, thoroughly freaking out Althea.

Iggy Pop, "Lust for Life"
This plays at the house party, before Althea locks herself in the bathroom and the cops show up. When I was a teenager in the nineties, this song was on the *Trainspotting* soundtrack and totally ubiquitous for at least a year or two.

Control Machete, "Si Señor"
This song is from the Mexican rap album that plays in Coby's apartment before his unfortunate dalliance with Althea. I don't know Spanish, so I tried running the lyrics through Google Translate, and what I got was completely incoherent. I believe there is, however, at least a passing reference to a flavor and a butterfly.

REO Speedwagon, "Take It on the Run"
This song comes on the classic rock station as Althea and Coby are driving out to the abandoned meat packing plant. I will admit that I have a soft spot for this band and this song in particular.

Bruce Springsteen, "Rosalita"
Althea can hear Bruce Springsteen playing in her mother's house when they talk on the phone. I'm a huge fan of the Boss, and "Rosalita" is kryptonite for any bad mood.

Althea curates the music for her road trip to New York City very carefully. The next few songs are all from her drive up north.
Concrete Blonde, "100 Games of Solitaire"
Team Dresch, "Screwing Yer Courage"
The Gits, "Seaweed"
Sugar, "A Good Idea"
Pixies, "Tame"

Blur, "End of a Century"
When Oliver is in the hospital he listens to Blur's *Parklife* over and over on his Discman.

Tom Waits, "Tom Traubert's Blues" (which most people refer to as "Waltzing Matilda")
Althea really falls in love with the Warriors when they're all cooking one morning and Greg bursts into song, dancing Matilda around the kitchen while singing Tom Waits. It's sort of a turning point for Althea, and anyone who's ever heard the song can probably understand why.

The Foundations, "Build Me Up Buttercup"

When Oliver and Kentucky are wandering around downtown, there's a brief moment where a door opens to a karaoke bar and they get a harrowing glimpse of some drunk girl butchering this song. I have been that girl.

Naomi Shelton & the Gospel Queens, "Heaven Is Mine"

This is the one band that didn't exist in the 1990s at all, but it ended up in *Althea & Oliver* anyway. Seeing them perform shifts everything for Oliver (as "Waltzing Matilda" does for Althea). If you want to experience them for yourself, they perform every Friday night at Fat Cat, a pool hall and music venue in downtown Manhattan.

The Replacements, "Unsatisfied"

I think the epigraph says it all.

As for a turning-point moment of my own . . .

What is the best concert you've ever been to?

An impossible question, but I'll do my best. A few years ago, I saw The Hold Steady perform at this weird recreational center in Westchester called Life: The Place to Be. To this day I have no idea how or why THS ended up performing there; it's the kind of place you rent for your bat mitzvah. My old roommate and I took Metro-North there, got off at the wrong stop along with about a dozen other people, and had no idea how to get to the show. There was literally only one cab in the whole town to shuttle everyone back and forth; the driver had to make all these trips between the station and the venue. In the end we had the best time—we ran around playing video games and skeeball until the show started, we made friends with all these other people who had come up from the city to see the band, and THS played a killer set.

Something about being out of the city made everyone friendlier, and the setting was so bizarre, and the whole night just had this great feeling to it, like we were all on this weird little punk rock adventure that had somehow taken us to the suburbs. My roommate and I took the train home with all our new friends, and for years afterward when I saw THS play in Brooklyn or Manhattan I'd run into people I recognized from that show.

Cristina Moracho:
My Favorite Reads.

BOOKS

Megan Abbott: *Dare Me*

Russell Banks: *Rule of the Bone*

Francesca Lia Block: *Dangerous Angels: The Weetzie Bat Books*

Amanda Boyden: *Pretty Little Dirty*

Kelly Braffet: *Josie and Jack*

Janice Erlbaum: *Girlbomb: A Halfway Homeless Memoir*

Grace Krilanovich: *The Orange Eats Creeps*

Sarah McCarry: *All Our Pretty Songs, Dirty Wings,*
                             and *About a Girl*

Blake Nelson: *Girl*

Jim Shepard: *Project X*

ZINES

During my own adolescence, I read fanzines as much as fiction. It might be hard to track down the original issues, but a few of my favorites have been rounded up into books and collections.

Iggy Scam (Erick Lyle):   *Scam: The First Four Issues*

Al Burian: *Burn Collector: Collected Stories*
                             from One Through Nine

Lisa Darms, editor: *The Riot Grrrl Collection*